7 SOULS

7 SOULS

barnabas miller
&
jordan orlando

Delacorte Press

Copyright © 2010 by Barnabas Miller and Jordan Orlando

All rights reserved. Published in the United States by Delacorte Press, an imprint of Random House Children's Books, a division of Random House, Inc., New York.

Delacorte Press is a registered trademark and the colophon is a trademark of Random House, Inc.

Visit us on the Web! www.randomhouse.com/teens

Educators and librarians, for a variety of teaching tools, visit us at www.randomhouse.com/teachers

Library of Congress Cataloging-in-Publication Data
Miller, Barnabas.
7 souls / Barnabas Miller and Jordan Orlando—1st ed.
p. cm.
Summary: Inexplicable things have been happening to Manhattan socialite Mary since she awoke on her seventeenth birthday, and by the end of the day she has been killed, inhabited the bodies of seven people close to her, and faced some ugly truths about herself.
ISBN 978-0-385-73673-2 (hc : alk. paper)—ISBN 978-0-375-89381-0 (e-book)
ISBN 978-0-385-90625-8 (glb : alk. paper) [1. Interpersonal relations—Fiction.
2. Spirit possession—Fiction. 3. Death—Fiction. 4. Blessing and cursing—Fiction. 5. Sisters—Fiction. 6. New York (N.Y.)—Fiction.]
I. Orlando, Jordan. II. Title. III. Title: Seven souls.
PZ7.M61216Aaf 2010
[Fic]—dc22   2009043530

The text of this book is set in 12-point Goudy.

Book design by Angela Carlino

Printed in the United States of America

10 9 8 7 6 5 4 3 2 1

First Edition

Random House Children's Books supports the First Amendment and celebrates the right to read.

7 SOULS

I Stand in the Center of the Infinite Circle
I Stand in the Sign of Blood and Flame

Around Me Billow the Forces of the Air
Around Me Flow the Forces of Water
Around Me Flare the Forces of Fire
Around Me Rage the Forces of the Earth

I Cast Wide My Arms
The Powers of Death
The Powers of Life
Are Mine

I

THE DAY SHE DIED

1

6:47 A.M.

THERE WAS THE PAIN, first and last, that booming drumbeat of agony in her head—the kind of pain that made her want to curl up and die. It was woefully familiar. She recognized that pounding, that rhythm: her heartbeat, as slow and regular as a muffled bass drum from the worst band in the world, playing their worst song over and over. Vodka-based pain, she'd once called it—a dismal, throbbing ache.

She tried to squint her eyes tighter against the glare—the white glare, like a dentist's lamp—and that made the pain worse. She was curled up in fetal position, coated in slime that she recognized as her own sweat, overheated beneath some kind of impossibly smooth fabric like the metallic surface of an oven mitt, her hair tangled hopelessly around her face, her ears and head ringing with that endless drumbeat.

Hangover, she thought. *I've got a hangover—a really bad one. It's my birthday and I've got the worst hangover in the world.*

Mary fixated on those two facts, holding on to them like floating planks after a shipwreck in a heavy storm, for the simple reason that, beyond those rudimentary ideas, she was stumped. Her name was Mary and she was seventeen—*just* seventeen, today—and her head was suffering the kind of rhythmic, merciless killing blows ordinarily reserved for tennis balls or nailheads. But that was it. Whatever was supposed to be occurring to her, it just wasn't coming.

Happy birthday, she told herself weakly.

Squinting made her head hurt more, but opening her eyes fully was out of the question—it was as bright as the surface of the sun out there. She twisted around in her envelope of sweat and smooth fabric and tangled black hair that smelled of sweat and Neutrogena and tried to figure out what time it was, where she was, and how she had gotten there.

In bed, I'm in bed, she concluded. Ten points for that one. The problem was that she didn't know *which* bed. There were several obvious candidates. Her own bed, that creaky, narrow, loved-and-hated wooden-framed contraption she'd slept in since she was five, which still had pink and orange paint on its headboard from when her father helped her decorate her bedroom? The bed none of her friends had ever seen, because she'd never invited them to brave the Upper West Side and visit her, because she was embarrassed by her family's tiny, run-down apartment?

But it wasn't her bed, because the mattress was just too good—too wide and smooth and firm. Her own bed was bearable, edging into comfortable, but it was nothing like where she was now. *I'm not at home.*

Patrick's bed? That was the next possibility: that wide, deep, soft, platform bed that always had perfectly steam-laundered sheets with the highest thread count available, not that *Patrick* ever made the bed. He didn't have to, with the cleaning girls and the concierge and the entire staff of Trick's five-star hotel waiting on him hand and foot all the time, pretending to ignore the tequila bottles and thumbed-open plastic bags they cleared out of the way as he bounded off to school and they began the hopeless task of cleaning his suite.

Mary wrinkled her nose and decided she wasn't there. *No booze smell,* she noticed groggily. *No Hugo Boss cologne, no Dunhill cigarettes.* None of the expensive continental aromas of the young, wealthy gentleman who's been affecting high-class vices since before he started shaving. The bed-clothes—their smooth, unearthly, sweat-drenched surfaces like some kind of NASA space-program fabric against her naked skin—felt *expensive* enough to be Patrick's, but again, no young-dangerous-man-of-the-world smells.

So I'm at Amy's, Mary thought, through the ongoing drumbeat in her head. That was reassuring, somehow: it made her feel safe. *I'm in a beautiful Upper East Side town house*, she thought hopefully, *on Amy's big quilt-covered chaise longue, the one she's always begging me to sleep in so I don't have to go home in the middle of the night*.

But no.

There just was no way. Mary began to open her eyes, facing a solid horizontal bar of pure diamond brilliance, a blade of white light that nearly made her throw up with renewed pain and queasiness. *I could be anywhere*, she told herself as her headache seemed, incredibly, to get *worse*, that drumbeat increasing like the sound of a tribal ritual, like a group of cannibals who were all through playing around and were about to start their main course of Brunette Girl. *I'm not at home; I'm not at Patrick's; I'm not at Amy's.*

It occurred to her in that moment that she was naked—she'd noticed it before but blocked it out—and, for the first time since that drumbeat from hell had awakened her, she began to feel uneasy, even a little bit afraid. Mary's heart began racing; then she heard the cannibals' drums get faster and louder as adrenaline flooded her bloodstream like an electrical current and she began to feel frightened in earnest.

I have to open my eyes, Mary thought. *I have to open my eyes now.*

Taking a deep, trembling breath, she got her eyes open and winced in stinging pain at the unbelievable brightness, blinking repeatedly to shed the blind spots. Her vision blurred with caked sleep and smeared mascara and then the details of her surroundings began to penetrate through the white blur.

She was in a room as big as a gymnasium. There was another bed only a few feet from hers—a big queen-size bed with a cherrywood frame. The room was *filled* with beds: steel-framed modernist beds; beds with suede headboards and beds with white faux leopardskin headboards; beds with gleaming, ornate brass frames. Beyond the rows of beds were faceted-glass side tables and Asian-influenced end pieces with gold trim and wide black leather couches and oak desks, room-size groups of expensive-looking furniture, all arranged into ensembles like a series of bad soap-opera sets.

Mary turned her head, squinting against blinding sunlight. Her bed was inches from a window that ran all the way from floor to ceiling and wall to wall, its brightness interrupted by regular shadows that she suddenly realized were *words*—huge, backward white letters imprinted across the glass like a movie title seen in a mirror:

CRATE&BARREL

She sat up in bed and her body went rigid. She was frozen, mortified, staring out at the vast, morning sky beyond the enormous letters, trying to convince herself that she was dreaming—but she knew she was awake. This was actually happening—she was sitting bare-naked on a display bed in the second-floor window of Crate and Barrel, the biggest furniture and housewares store in SoHo.

Outside the glass, down below, she could see motionless morning traffic up and down Houston Street, the lines of honking cabs and SUVs and delivery vans stretching out in both directions. A hundred eyes were staring at her—a thick crowd of Manhattan gawkers had formed on the sidewalk, *right below the window*, craning their necks as they stared at the naked girl.

Bike messengers with dirty satchels and baggy rolled-up jeans gazed slack-jawed at her like they'd just found free Internet porn. A gang of preppy businessmen clutched their morning Starbucks and grinned like naughty schoolboys. A frizzy-haired woman in a faux Chanel jacket and white sneakers scowled with disgust. A few joggers gazed half-heartedly as they ran in place, and a group of fanny-packed Euro tourists stared in amazement, thrusting out their camera phones like handguns and relentlessly firing off shot after shot of her nude body.

Dreaming—this is a dream, Mary told herself helplessly, fumbling with the comforter and trying to pull it around her. *I've got to be dreaming—this has to be a nightmare.* That kind of thing happened all the time, didn't it? You *thought* you'd woken up, but you were actually still dreaming, so when—

There was blood on the bed.

What—?

Four razor-thin streaks of drying blood snaked down the mattress. Mary reached awkwardly behind her back and winced from the sudden painful sting. Riding her fingertips along her broken skin, she could trace the tender, rough scratches from her smooth shoulder blades all the way down to her waist.

Oh my God—oh my God.

Mary was paralyzed with shock. She felt tears welling up

in her eyes and chills emanating from the back of her neck, crawling across every inch of her skin. Her head felt like a delicate ice sculpture, a fragile, melting, crystalline jewel about to crack and shatter. Her ears were humming and her throat was dry. She didn't know what time it was—she didn't know how long she'd been lying beneath the comforter, on this bed in a row of beds lined up rank and file like headstones in a graveyard. Before she could completely panic, she lunged to pull the comforter around herself, its metallic fabric hissing against the mattress, and spun away from the window, ducking her head and trying to get herself out of sight.

Her bare feet slapped against the vast floor—cold, hard, grooved linoleum that had been textured to look and feel like wood. Through the glass, she could hear the muffled catcalls and shouts and murmurs of the crowd outside, the random passersby who had chosen the right Friday morning to walk down Houston Street and cast their eyes upward at the naked teenage girl in the display window.

Mary felt desperately sick. Her back itched painfully— a reminder of the unexplained scratches that had left bloody trails. *DNA*, she thought randomly. *I'm leaving my DNA all over Crate and Barrel for the cops to find; they're going to hunt me down and make me pay for what I did to the bed display.*

And I'm naked, she thought helplessly. *I'm naked. What do I do?*

In one convulsive movement, Mary staggered to her feet, trying to pull the comforter after her. It didn't quite work. The comforter got caught on the bed and slid heavily to the floor. The crowd outside cheered. *This can't be happening, this can't be happening,* she thought dazedly.

Bending down to tug at the comforter (and trying as hard as she could not to think about the view she was giving her audience), Mary pulled it off the floor, again, and tried fruitlessly to get its billowing white folds around herself. A loud bang, very close by, made her jump. Frantically staring around, she saw white-painted pipes and recessed sprinklers against the wide ceiling . . . and nothing else. No explanation of what had made that noise.

The light from the big plate-glass windows was becoming brighter. Mary heard her own rasping, hoarse breath as she finally pulled the comforter free, wrapped it around her shoulders, and began walking—shuffling, really—across the wide, empty showroom, toward the steel-framed, backlit EXIT sign over a doorway against the far wall.

Is the store open? Mary wasn't sure. The entire floor seemed empty, but there was no way to tell what time it was. People could be walking in any moment.

Mary's feet squeaked and thumped against the textured fake-wood floor. The comforter dragged behind her, hissing its way around the display beds as she got to the edge of the showroom, beneath the glowing, ruby-red EXIT sign, where a wide, dark metal door faced her, with no handle except a big red steel bar labeled EMERGENCY EXIT and WARNING ALARM WILL SOUND.

"Come on," Mary heard herself murmuring, pleading. "Come on, come on—"

There had to be another way out, didn't there? If an

alarm sounded, she would have to deal with store security, or even worse, the actual cops, the NYPD, New York's Finest, with their slow, patient questions and their cordial dislike of private-school kids' amusing problems. And it would all take so long and it might even get in the *newspaper,* for God's sake . . . and she still didn't have any clothes. She pictured herself in a holding cell (or whatever you called them) like on television, still wrapped in this billowing comforter made of oven mitt, sweaty hair tangled over her face as she tried to answer the leering cops' questions. . . . No.

Staring at the metal sign, the word EMERGENCY swimming in her watery vision, she almost blacked out again. Her head spun and her body collapsed sideways against the wall, her bare shoulder scratching the rough paint as she shuddered. She was going to be sick. . . . Her head was still pounding and her vision was darkening . . . and then the wave passed and she pushed against the wall and stood up again.

What the hell—? How much did I have to drink, anyway? She couldn't remember *ever* feeling so weak and dizzy— except once: her first hangover, the very first one after she and her little sister drank the leftover wine from one of their parents' cocktail parties, back when they had two parents and the young girls would sneak into the living room and approach the coffee table covered in half-empty glasses and sodden paper napkins, and dare each other to drink the sweet-smelling Chablis. She had ended up curled in bed with her mom cleaning vomit from the bathroom floor as her father's rough hands stroked her hot face and he told her that everything would be all right, that the pain would go away.

Bang. Clang. Bang. That same dull metallic noise, from close by now. *Somebody's here—*

"Hello?" Mary called out.

She had turned a corner, past the edge of the store's display panels and was headed toward a doorway she hadn't seen; a metal doorframe with a paper calendar Scotch-taped to its inner surface. In the small room beyond the door, Mary could see nothing but a dented plastic Diet Coke bottle on the linoleum floor and a grimy time clock bolted to the white cinder-block wall. She could hear salsa music, dimly, from somewhere inside.

"Hello? Anybody here?"

The flawless white comforter snaked behind her like a snail's trail as Mary moved forward through the doorway. She nearly jumped when she saw a middle-aged woman in a coverall—a dowdy-looking polyester dress that you'd have to call beige (it didn't really qualify as taupe)—slumped behind a plastic table, reading a Spanish-language newspaper and peering at her. The woman didn't move; she and Mary had locked eyes. An acrid smell of bleach permeated the room.

"Hello?"

"*¿Sí?*"

Great, Mary thought dismally. *A language barrier, just to make this more fun.* "Can you help me? I can't—I lost my clothes. I don't have my clothes."

"*¿Que?*"

"Look." Mary stepped forward, stumbling on the edge of the comforter, reaching for the cleaning lady's arm. "I need *clothes*; I need something to wear and I've got"—the woman flinched as Mary plucked at the rough fabric of her sleeve—"I've got no money; I need to get home."

The woman squinted at Mary. Her eyes were like black flint. She didn't move. Mary could feel rivulets of sweat sliding down her body beneath the comforter, down the curves of her back, across the raw edges of the fresh scratches along her spine. *Come on!* she wanted to shout. *Are you blind? I need help!* Mary was trembling with cold now, the dirty linoleum pressed against her bare feet like a sheet of ice. *Come on, lady—I'll come back here later and pay you what I owe; I'll make Patrick buy you a Prada outfit, I'll do anything. . . .*

The woman rose to her feet, without any change in her expression. She leaned close, so that the veined cracks and wrinkles in her face were visible, around the ragged edge of her brown lipstick; Mary could barely smell some kind of geriatric floral scent.

"Wrong," the woman said with a thick Spanish accent.

"What? What do you—"

"Something wrong," the woman went on, nodding firmly. Mary's forehead was coated in cold, clammy sweat as she stared into the cleaning lady's black eyes. The woman was pointing at her with a bent arthritic finger. "Something wrong with you. You go to church."

"Look." Mary was in no mood for whatever Sunday-school lecture the cleaning woman wanted to give her. "You don't understand. It's not my fault I'm—"

Mary stopped talking because she'd noticed something

incredible, the first recognizable thing she'd seen since waking up. Just past the woman's shoulder, on a bare wooden shelf, was an electrifying, familiar sight.

"You go to church, you say prayers," the woman repeated, turning away toward a green storage locker. "I help you—I give you money. I no have much, but I give you—"

"My *phone*." Mary pointed at the small, gleaming black and maroon BlackBerry she'd spotted, nearly dropping the comforter again. "That's my phone, ma'am. If I could just—"

The cleaning woman seemed to have some kind of special need to move as slowly as humanly possible. She was painstakingly pulling out a coverall identical to the one she was wearing. She slammed the locker shut—Mary winced at the loud bang—laboriously turned to follow Mary's slim arm and saw the phone. The BlackBerry's green light flashed right then—the phone was on.

"Is yours? I find it," the cleaning woman explained, picking up the BlackBerry delicately, like it was a piece of Steuben glass. "On the floor, I find it when I—"

"*Yes*, that's mine," Mary said, stumbling as she reached for it. "Thank you, thank you—"

I dropped it on the way in, she thought. *Whenever that was—whatever I was doing here.*

Whomever I was with.

But she still couldn't remember a thing.

Once the phone was in her hand she felt better. Flipping it open, she saw no messages, no texts, no missed calls—and a nearly dead battery. One bar, flickering.

"Such a pretty young girl; you no need to be in such trouble. You go to confession," the cleaning lady told her.

She was handing over a beautiful new twenty-dollar bill that nearly made Mary salivate because she needed it so badly. The comforter was slipping to the floor as she took the money—and the cleaning woman took her hand and squeezed it. "You confess your sins, you feel better."

"Right." *Confess my sins?* She would have settled for *remembering* her sins.

THE AIR WAS DAMP and cool. The sky was white, as featureless as untrampled snow—it was the kind of windless, overcast day that could make you squint from the glare of the city's low, cold blanket of clouds. The echoes of SoHo traffic ricocheted harshly around her ears, around the cloud of dirty black hair she swept back from her sweaty forehead as she pressed forward, hurrying down the shaded edge of the sidewalk.

Everyone was looking at her, the eyes of passersby widening before they turned quickly away. Mary understood: she saw her fast-moving reflection flow past in the windows of the storefronts along Houston and knew that she looked like a homeless waif, a drug casualty, a hospital escapee or a runaway, her makeup smeared, her hair askew, her body clad in a ridiculous beige coverall that fit her all wrong, with a waistline high up on her rib cage, and a zipper she couldn't reach tugging painfully on a tangle in her hair, making her eyes water with every step. Her feet were clad in oversize white tennis shoes that had seen better days; a blackened wad of gum was smeared over one of the soles.

She hunched her shoulders against the cold March air as

she darted around a pair of skateboarders who grinned wildly, obviously reacting to her crazy Amy Winehouse appearance. Her ankles were aching from the speed at which she'd been moving. The polyester coverall was rubbing against the cuts on her back, rhythmically scratching them like sandpaper.

Mary had to swallow to hold off a sudden need to vomit—and the faint, nauseatingly stale taste of tomato sauce filled her dry throat.

Why am I tasting tomato sauce?

A fleeting image of a dark red tablecloth flickered into her mind. Faint opera music in the background . . . the clatter of silverware and the babble of dozens of voices . . .

Nothing else. She couldn't remember.

I've got to get home, Mary thought. It was a few minutes past seven, according to a big, old-fashioned clock on a bank she was passing. *I've got to get home and get dressed for school—and get ready for my birthday.*

Mary wasn't quite ready to think about that part yet. Here it finally was—the morning of her seventeenth birthday, a day she'd looked forward to for *years*—and it wasn't exactly starting the way she'd imagined. Nobody was bringing her breakfast in bed and handing over brightly wrapped presents. None of her friends had texted her with a morning birthday greeting.

Come on—it's early yet, she told herself. *Everybody's just waking up.*

But were her friends waking up with hangovers too?

Whom was I with? What happened?

Walking into the shadow of a fire escape, Mary realized that the air was thickening with heavy humidity; already the flat white sky was darkening, showing watery gray traces of lower, heavier clouds. Five cabs had cruised past, each with its sign maddeningly unlit. Like all Manhattan residents, Mary knew that the chances of finding an empty taxicab downtown in the morning were about the same as the chances of finding a hundred-dollar bill on the sidewalk.

Eduardo's!

That was it. She suddenly remembered going to Eduardo's—the, well, the "budget" Italian restaurant in her neighborhood—with her sister and her mother, who didn't think of the local one-star spot as a budget restaurant at all, since she almost never ate out (or even left the apartment). *Mom took us to dinner—a pre-birthday dinner,* Mary remembered. The stale, ghostly tomato taste in her mouth made sense now: she could dimly remember the tiny, cramped restaurant and the red tablecloths and the piped-in opera and the plate of fettuccine marinara that Patrick or her friends Amy and Joon would have taken one look at and refused to touch, sending it scornfully back to the kitchen— and then bodily dragged her down to Balthazar or a place more her speed.

Because that was the point of Mary Shayne's birthday; it had been the point since forever. It was always something big, something crazy. In middle school it had been tame stuff: pizza parties at Two Boots, ice-skating parties at Chelsea Piers, frozen hot chocolate at Serendipity. Then it had changed; it had exploded into an underground legend for the private school set—New York's self-described "playas under eighteen." Mary never even *planned* the parties; they just formed out of the ether like darkening storm clouds: last year's ridiculous scene at Nana's, an underage speakeasy by the West Side Highway; two years ago, when they commandeered Inganno on Gansevoort Street and distributed free pancakes to everyone in the restaurant on Mary's friends' dime; a succession of bottle service bills and backstage passes and ragers in parent-free apartments, escalating—everyone knew—to the big One Seven, Mary's last Chadwick blowout, and to whatever was coming tonight.

Which was why Mom had taken them out last night—rather than try to compete with all that—actually leaving their apartment and bringing Mary and Ellen to that red-draped table at Eduardo's. Mary remembered it all now: chewing and swallowing the mediocre fettuccine and drinking the red wine they'd brought, sitting through the awkwardness while Mom watched her proudly across the yellow candlelight and beamed, her little girl already seventeen (or nearly), my God, how time flies. Which was the *last* thing Mary wanted to hear, because she just *knew* what came next: *It's too bad your father's not here to see this . . .* , Mom's cue to get misty about her husband, which Ellen always encouraged. Wanting to be anywhere else; refusing dessert (even while looking around for a waiter with a cupcake and a candle in it, ready to smile and cover her face as the restaurant patrons sang "Happy Birthday," but that never happened); finishing the wine . . . as Mom (her feelings hurt, as usual) made a big self-pitying show of dropping money on the table and leaving early; and after that, Mary and Ellen getting the check and their coats and then . . .

And then *what?*

She had no idea what had happened next.

"Taxi!" Mary yelled, vaulting forward into the street. A lone cab was approaching, its rooftop lights shining. Mary was still so queasy that she was afraid she'd stumble and faint with the effort of running, but she was already in a footrace with a pinstriped Wall Street type who obviously had to get to the trading floor by the first bell and wasn't going to let a crazy-looking teenage cleaning lady take his cab away no matter how high her cheekbones or how luminous her pale blue eyes, glittering through slits of smeared mascara.

"Taxi, taxi!" she called out again, burping up more marinara-flavored stomach gas and sprinting toward the cab.

She won the race—barely—grabbing the cab's chrome door handle and giving Wall Street Man a pleading look (with a slight pout), which seemed to do the trick: he smiled tightly as she heaved the door open and tumbled inside the cab.

"Ninety-fourth and Amsterdam," she told the driver, who obediently hit the gas. Behind them, she caught a dwindling view of Wall Street Man scanning the empty street.

Have I got enough money? she wondered suddenly. SoHo to the Upper West Side—five miles of Manhattan traffic—was going to cost more than twenty dollars. Yet another thing to worry about.

Deal with it later, she told herself. *One problem at a time.*

The back of the taxi was freezing. Mary had her arms wrapped around herself as she huddled against the backrest, still shivering (nonstop since she'd awakened), her dried-sweat-covered skin scratching against the cheap weave of the borrowed coverall (which she was so tired of being grateful for, because she *hated it*), the cuts on her back itching.

Mary's BlackBerry was giving its familiar, hateful LO BATT chime. She peered at the screen again—still no calls, no texts, no e-mails. *It's my birthday and nobody cares*, she thought dismally, before reminding herself that it was only 7:08 A.M. (according to the BlackBerry's display). Scrolling back a day, she saw the indicator for a "To Do" item and thumbed it—and stared at it, suddenly remembering.

THURS EVE TEST PREP SCOTT

That's right, Mary realized, leaning forward as the taxicab banged over steel plates in the street, heading west. *Of course, of course—that's what happened next.*

Or what was *supposed* to have happened next.

The one blight on her day, today, the one flaw in the perfect diamond of her seventeenth birthday, was Mr. Shama and his hateful physics test—something about Bernoulli's Principle, which she had never come close to understanding. Shama's frantic blackboard scribbling—all those symbols and numbers scrawled across the board while the diminutive teacher waved his arms, fluorescent lights gleaming on his bald head—was nonsense to her, pure hieroglyphics. Which was where Scott Sanders came in.

Scott was in the class with her. He was quiet and shy and round-faced, with gold-rimmed eyeglasses like those worn by Mr. Shama, whose every utterance Scott seemed to instantly comprehend in his preternaturally calm way. Scott had gotten early acceptance at Princeton or Stanford—Mary couldn't remember which—and would soon be joining the ranks of pasty-skinned, virginal *Star Trek* and *Battlestar Galactica* fans who handled all the engineering and ran all the computers in the world.

But, more important than any of that, Scott was Mary's "nerd lifeline" (although she'd never say it that way to him). Out of the goodness of his heart and his Borg Collective brain, Scott had agreed to help her with physics (just like he'd helped her with chemistry and geometry last year, and, come to think of it, every hard class they'd shared since he'd arrived at Chadwick in eighth grade). In a school full of snarky pseudo-debutantes and trust-fund jocks, Scott was that wonder of wonders: a legitimately nice person who was willing to help those less endowed with genius than himself. How many times had Scott's homemade flash cards and drill sheets and "private tutorials"—evening hours spent together at Chadwick or at the Midtown branch library—completely saved her? Mary wasn't sure, but the thing that amazed her the most was that Scott never seemed to want anything in return. He was "happy to help"—he was always happy to help, and left it at that.

And that was the next stop, Mary remembered now, her head throbbing as she stared across the Hudson River's pale, gleaming surface at the haze-choked New Jersey buildings that stood far away, beneath the cold white sky. After dinner with Mom and Ellen, she was supposed to meet Scott at the Midtown library. He was going to be there anyway, he had explained, working on some kind of Advanced Placement research paper or whatever he had said—and Mary was welcome to join him and get a quick prep for the Shama test today. *That was the plan—dinner with Mom (groan) and then a cab ride to the library and one of Scott's patented tutorials.*

But what happened next? What *really* happened?

Mary still couldn't remember any of it. Fettuccine, red wine, Mom's proud, watery eyes—and then, nothing.

Her thumb was already scrolling through the Black-Berry's contact list, finding Scott's cell number and dialing it. The phone gave another of its LO BATT chimes, and Mary clenched her teeth in frustration as she raised the handset to her aching head, straining to hear the low hum of Scott's cell phone ringing.

"Hel—hello?"

Scott's voice—thank God for small favors. He sounded groggy; she was pretty sure she'd woken him up.

"Scott!" she began, pressing the phone closer to her ear. "Can you hear me?"

"Wh-what—?"

"It's Mary," she went on, more loudly. The connection wasn't that great—Scott seemed to have dropped out. "You there, Scott? I need your help."

"Mary—wait, *what?*" Scott sounded profoundly confused, like he was still half-asleep. "*You're* Mary. What the— What day is it?"

"It's *Friday,*" Mary said impatiently. This was not going

well. Who would have guessed that the smartest kid in school would be such a basket case when he woke up? Some little nerd-wife was going to have to deal with that, sometime—if Scott ever got married, which was doubtful, since he always seemed more interested in equations than girls. "*Friday*, Scott, the day of the *physics test*—the big killer test. We were supposed to meet last night to power-cram, remember?"

"Physics test," Scott repeated, as if she was speaking a foreign language. "The physics test—of *course*. But—but, holy shit, that's—"

"It's *today*, Scott. Come on—will you *wake up*, damn it? Snap *out* of it! This is *serious*."

"Serious," Scott repeated. It took all of Mary's self-control not to scream into the phone, to insist that he put his brain back in or perform whatever mysterious morning ritual turned him from this confused zombie into the supergenius she knew. "Right, I was—you were supposed to meet me—I forgot that we were— But—"

"*Scott!*" Mary tried again. The phone was dying; there was no getting around that. Mary stared over the cabdriver's shoulder at the West Side buildings. "Scott, I'm trying to remember last night—what *happened* last night, I mean. I'm blacking out on some of it and I can't remember if I met you after dinner or— Hello?"

Nothing. Silence. The call was over; the BlackBerry's glowing display told her the call was ended. LO BATT indeed. As she stared, the phone's screen went dead.

*   *   *

THE TINY FIFTH-FLOOR LANDING of the Shaynes' apartment building was warm and dark, filled with the familiar smells of musty air and Pine-Sol cleanser and that faint garlic aroma that never seemed to go away, barely lit by the dim yellow light from what must have been a five-watt bulb within a cracked glass fixture on the brown-painted wall. The ancient elevator door was rolling shut behind Mary as she approached her family's black front door, enormous borrowed tennis shoes squeaking on the cracked tiles.

What she hoped for, what would have been really ideal, was for Mom to be still asleep and Ellen to be right there, on the other side of the door, loudly moving around as she prepared to leave for school. Pressing her ear against the door, Mary strained to hear, hoping for the familiar sounds of Ellen's quick footsteps creaking on the floorboards.

Nothing. No such luck. Silence.

Taking a deep breath, Mary raised her fist and pounded on the door.

The dizziness wasn't quite as bad now, but it was still there. The cold metal of the door was soothing against her cheek. She pressed the doorbell, and heard its piercing buzzer rattling deep inside the apartment, and then the slow, dull padding of her mother's slipper-covered feet coming closer.

"Just a minute," Mom called out in her perpetually weak woe-is-me soprano. "Who is it?"

"It's me, Mom," Mary said. "Sorry—I don't have my keys."

Or my clothes. Or my bag. Or anything else.

The door's five latches thumped and clattered as Mom

slowly threw them open. Mom did *everything* slowly—Mary and Ellen were used to that. "Just a minute, honey," Mom called out.

Mary felt herself stiffening as the door swung open. She had watched all her friends get yelled at by their parents at one time or another. Even Joon, whose formal, austere mom and dad seemed to believe that she walked on water—Mary had seen Joon return from Sunday lunch-and-mani-pedi with her own mother and had noticed the dim pain in Joon's eyes, the ordeal of getting called out by your parents when you were old enough to realize just how little their opinions really mattered but still young enough to feel it in your gut: that unavoidable shame and fear that made it seem like you were five years old again—the last remnant of childhood that you knew—you hoped—you'd finally grow out of, one day.

But for Mary, it was different. Mom *never* yelled at her. Since Dad died there'd never been a single time when Mary could remember her mother scolding her, even mildly. When the usual argument started, like at dinner last night, Mom made her favorite move: she just left. It was like all of Dawn Shayne's parental instinct—even the occasional desire to play the role of a stern mother—had vanished on that winter day ten years ago when her husband was taken from her.

And honestly, Mary missed it. She hated to admit that—she *loved* to tell her friends about how great it was to have a truly "hands-off" single parent and watch their eyes widen with jealousy at the concept of being *left alone* the way Mary was. But it wasn't really true.

Now, as Mary's eyes adjusted to the darkness and her

25

mother stood in front of her in a pale yellow nightgown, her unbrushed graying hair clouded around her head like a dandelion flower gone to seed, Mary knew she wasn't going to get scolded. No "Where have you been?" No "What happened to you last night?" No nothing.

And, of course, no "Happy birthday"—but you got that last night, remember? Mary told herself. *You got a whole plate of fettuccine from her. Don't push your luck.*

"Hi, Mom." Mary entered the warm apartment, shivering again as the door swung shut. The familiar Mom smells of cigarette smoke and aloe filled Mary's nostrils. "Um—sorry; I didn't have my keys."

"That's okay, angel," Mom told her while she slowly twisted the five latches, not looking at her. Mom hadn't seemed to notice Mary's bizarre attire or her escaped-maniac wild hair and smeared makeup. "I was awake. . . . It's almost time for my meds anyway."

"Is Ellen still here?" Mary asked, following Mom down the apartment's narrow corridor, past the kitchen and the hall closet and the study door, which was tightly closed as usual. Dad's "study"—the apartment's tiny fourth bedroom—hadn't changed in a decade, and both Mary and Mom avoided going in there (although Ellen apparently found it a soothing place to read, which was all she ever liked to do). Even after ten years, the unmistakable aroma of Dad's pipe smoke (Borkum Riff tobacco—Mary still remembered) had barely dissipated; probably nothing short of a fire could remove that distinctive smell from the walls and rugs and furniture in there. The slightest whiff forced a nostalgia trip that Mary was never in the mood for, and she usually found herself holding her breath as she passed the study door. The corridor could have used a paint job—like the rest of the apartment—but nothing like that had happened in a long time. They were living off Dad's life insurance, which was a good thing, because Mom couldn't work. The insurance kept them in groceries and necessities, but nobody was hiring any painters anytime soon. "Mom? Is Ellen—"

"I think so; she didn't say goodbye yet, sweetie." Mom was moving as quickly as she ever did, back toward her bedroom. She didn't like to be away from her own bed for longer than absolutely necessary. "I've got to take my pills now."

"Okay, Mom," Mary said, noticing the line of bright yellow light beneath Ellen's door that meant her sister was in there. "Thanks."

And would it kill you to say happy birthday?

Apparently it would. The bedroom door swung shut, the noise echoing in Mary's still-aching head, and she was alone in the hallway. She turned to Ellen's door, pushed it open without knocking and propelled herself inside.

"MY GOD, GIRL!" ELLEN stared at her in surprise, smiling with her eyes wide. "What the hell happened to *you?*"

"That," Mary said, nodding weakly as she collapsed into Ellen's desk chair, "is *definitely* the million-dollar question."

"But what *happened?*" Ellen was covering her mouth, obviously trying not to laugh. This was Ellen Shayne every single morning before school: facedown on the bed, her feet resting on her pillow, her head at the foot of the bed, thrift-store book in her hands, pinky in her mouth and her second-hand laptop open next to her for intellectual blogging. The laptop had been slowly crumbling to pieces, but she managed to hold it together with gaffer's tape and vintage David Bowie stickers. For some reason, Ellen had recently switched from listening to those unbearable old Kate Bush albums to David Bowie. Even her musical tastes leaned toward ancient history. "Nobody had any *idea* where you were! I had the usual suspects"—Ellen's cute term for Mary's friends—"*all* calling me, *all* evening. Amy *Twersky* called; Joon *Park* called. . . ." Ellen ticked them off on her fingers. *It's almost like they're* her *friends,* Mary thought bemusedly. Ellen was so used to fielding Mary's calls, she'd developed her own rapport with the popular seniors Mary hung out with (even though they absolutely weren't Ellen's type). "Even *Patrick* couldn't find you."

So I wasn't with any of them, Mary realized. *Who was I with?*

"They each called twice, as usual. You should *see* yourself," Ellen went on. "You look like—I don't even know *what* you look like."

"I know, I know. You wouldn't believe it. I was—"

"Where *were* you?"

"At Crate and Barrel—I woke up in one of the damned *display beds* at Crate and Barrel. Listen, can you help me figure out—"

Ellen was laughing uncontrollably. "I'm sorry," she told Mary, shaking her head. "I'm sorry; I don't mean to laugh.

But that's—I mean, that's pretty spectacular even for *you*. A *display bed?* Why are you *dressed* like that?"

"I borrowed this from some cleaning lady. Listen, Elliebelle, this is *serious*—I can't figure out what happened to me. I mean, I can't remember any of—"

"'Borrowed' like you'll return it, or Mary Shayne-borrowed?"

Mary shook her head impatiently—which was a mistake, given the lingering, painful fog inside her skull. "We had dinner with Mom at Eduardo's; I remember that part. But after that"—she spread her hands helplessly—"who knows."

"Poor Mary." Ellen pouted, slapping her laptop shut. When Ellen did that, when she made a face like that, Mary could see the ghost outline of her sister's attractiveness hidden behind her glasses and boring hair. *She's not as pretty as I am*, Mary thought—she tended to dispense with false modesty inside the privacy of her own mind—*but she's definitely got something, if she only let herself realize it.*

Mary really didn't get it. The only crushes her sister ever had were on yellowing history books that she'd found in the dollar bin at the Strand bookstore. The only clothes she ever wore were solid-colored hoodies and cords from the Gap. It was a shame, too, because Ellie could have been pretty if she'd just been willing to try the tiniest bit. She actually looked a little like Mary, but with her dark hair always cut in a shapeless bob (Ellen called it practical), and her refusal to wear makeup (Ellen called it *naturale*), it was hard to see the similarity.

29

It wasn't the first time Mary had thought that, but she'd learned not to bring it up. Ellen didn't react well to discussions of her appearance. She didn't think it was important. She wanted to be judged as who she *was*, damn it, she kept telling Mary, not by what she looked like. The hidden rebuke was hard to miss, but Mary politely ignored it. Ellen wasn't interested in boys or clothes or anything like that, and Mary had stopped trying to change her mind.

The only boy Ellen ever spent time with was Dylan something, a quiet intellectual type she'd met at—big shocker—a book fair near Columbia University. On those few occasions when Mary had seen Scruffy Dylan in the kitchen, he had been so painfully quiet that she'd thought he was an exchange student. Mary had repeatedly explained to Ellen that having a male best friend—even if Scruffy Dylan *was*, technically, an Ivy League freshman—was the absolute kiss of death if she wanted to land a guy, but Ellen didn't care, since she wasn't in the market for a boyfriend.

"Okay, let's be systematic," Ellen began wearily. "You remember Eduardo's—"

"Yeah." Mary's memory focused, now that she was facing Ellie again. "And Mom left *first*, right? She got into one of her—"

"We talked about Dad." Ellen put it matter-of-factly, as she always did, and Mary had to force herself to remember that her sister wasn't upsetting her on purpose—she just didn't seem to realize how uninterested Mary was in that endless, ongoing argument. "You remember? Mom said that she wished he was here to see you turn seventeen, and you couldn't—"

30

"All right, all right." *And can we drop it?* Morton Shayne had been in the ground for ten years, but his absence was always a fresh topic for her mother and sister at precisely the moments that Mary was trying to have a good time. "I didn't say the right solemn thing and Mom got all sad and left. Can we not—"

"Whatever, whatever." Ellen waved a hand impatiently. "Sorry—it is what it is. Anyway we stayed another ten minutes, and then you had somewhere to go."

"*Where?*" Mary tried to concentrate, but she couldn't recall anything about what her motives or whims had been—besides, of course, getting *away*. "Did I say where I was *going*? Did anyone *call* me?"

Ellen shook her head serenely. "You got in a cab and took off. You were in some kind of hurry, but you didn't say anything else."

"Ellie, this is *serious*—I'm freaked that I can't remember what I *did*."

"Oh, you're *fine*—come on," Ellen said dismissively. The lamplight gleamed off her glasses as she checked her watch. "Nothing *happened*—you met some people and killed some brain cells and—"

"*Ellie*—"

"—partied somewhere until you did a face-plant and stumbled home in the morning just like a million other nights. Honestly, get over it."

"Mary . . . ? Ellen . . . ?"

Both sisters' shoulders slumped, in unison.

Even though their mother's voice, muffled by two closed bedroom doors, was barely audible, it still cut through to

Mary's ears like a surgical scalpel. *That voice*, with the double shot of eternal tragedy and helplessness, like she was calling her daughters' names through mosquito netting as she lay dying in a Ugandan leper colony.

"Mary-fairy? Ellie-belle? Can you come here?"

Every morning was exactly the same. Before the girls left for school, rain or shine, Mom had to have her bronchodilating drugs for her emphysema and a glass of diluted orange juice (two parts Tropicana, one part Fiji). She needed it all brought to her in bed, followed by her pack of Virginia Slims from the dresser and her antidepressants and mood stabilizers for the bipolar disorder and her OxyContin and B12 for the chronic fatigue syndrome. It had been the same nearly every day for a decade—for so long that Mary could barely remember what her mother had been like before, when Dad was still alive. It was like she had been a different person altogether.

Ellen and Mary stared at each other, hopelessly.

"Can you take this one?" Mary asked.

Ellen gave her a nasty smile. "What's it worth to you?"

"Come *on*, Elle! *Look* at me! It's *already* like eight o'clock and I've got to take a shower and figure—"

"It's only seven-forty-five."

"—out what to *wear*. I will buy you a pony, I will steal you a new laptop, I will do your dishes for a month. . . ."

And you don't really mind, she added silently. It was true. Ellen obviously got some kind of codependent satisfaction from taking care of Mom. If Ellen ended up doing it more often, Mary had determined, it had to be because, on some

32

level, she *wanted* to; it made up for not having a boyfriend to take care of.

Not that Mary would have ever said that to Ellen.

"Ellie? Mary-fairy?" Mary heard Mom's stricken voice, that patented deathbed voice, calling for them again. "I need you, honey. . . ."

"Please, please, please," Mary chanted, gazing yearningly at her sister. "You're *already dressed!* I've got to *change*, I've got the worst hangover in the history of America, I've got a *Shama test* I haven't even *studied* for—"

"And it's your birthday."

"What?"

Ellen was smiling at her, gently, sweetly, but her eyes were flat and expressionless behind her glasses. "What'd you think—I *forgot?*"

Mary hadn't thought that Ellen had forgotten. But hearing her mention it, Mary felt a familiar wave of anxiety passing over her. *My birthday,* she thought, with a sinking feeling. *All the attention, all the praise . . . all the pressure to be perfect, to give everyone the little bit of me they need.* All the energy it took to play the part—to be *Mary Shayne* for another day—was going to be amped up double, triple, today. *Gorgeous! Bold! Raven-haired!* Stylish without trying, cynical without being too dark, smart without being intimidating, funny without pissing anybody off, sociable but unapproachable . . . all those qualities she had to effortlessly exude, all the responsibilities of being the senior class's very own superstar for another day. And she hadn't even *begun* to figure out what to wear, which was a major struggle in and of itself. It was the kind of thing Ellen would never understand.

"You don't have to do the dishes—that's silly," Ellen said. "But there's one thing you *can* do for me today."

"*Anything,*" Mary pleaded desperately. "*Anything,* I swear."

But the desperation was an act—Mary was already relaxing. Ellen was going to do it; she was going to take care of Mom and let Mary off the hook. Mary could tell.

"What I want you to do"—Ellen had leaned crazily to one side and was reaching down for her canvas book bag, on the book-cluttered floor beside her bed—"is have a wonderful birthday."

Mary stared at Ellen, who held out a small object—something wrapped in a pretty cloud of bright purple tissue paper with a gold ribbon. A birthday present.

"Where are you . . . ?" Mom called plaintively.

"Go ahead," Ellen said. "Take it. I'll totally handle Mom; don't worry about it. I've got three free periods anyway—I was going to skip homeroom and chill. You go ahead and I'll see you at school."

"Oh, Ellen . . ." Mary lunged over and grabbed her sister, pulling her into a bear hug. It should have lasted only a few seconds, but Mary found herself not wanting to let go. "Ellie-belle, you are a *goddess.*"

"*Yuck!*" Ellen's voice was muffled by Mary's crazy, matted hair as she firmly hugged back. "You smell *awful,* girl. Hurry up and take a shower while I do Mom."

"*Thank you,*" Mary whispered, giving Ellen a final squeeze before letting go. "Thank you."

"Here," Ellen said awkwardly, pressing the gift into Mary's hand. "Now, come on—stop wasting time. You're seventeen—go out there and seize the day."

"You're a goddess—truly," Mary repeated, rising to her feet. One part of her mind was already scanning through her wardrobe, facing the terrifying challenge of figuring out what to wear. "You're *sure* you're okay with this?"

Ellen smiled serenely. "Of *course* I am, dear sister. Now get out of here."

2

9:06 A.M.

WALKING SOUTH DOWN PARK Avenue under the
pale white sky, right thumb beneath the faded strap of her
familiar book bag, Mary tried to tell herself that she felt better—that everything was back to normal.

It almost worked.

She definitely *looked* better—but then, that wasn't saying much. She had probably never looked *worse* than the
crazed, polyester-and-tennis-shoes-clad vagrant she'd been
just ninety minutes before, climbing out of the taxicab (and,
as expected, facing a $24.99 fare—before tip—that she had
to pay for with the Crate and Barrel cleaning lady's twenty-

dollar bill and the sweetest, most apologetic smile she could muster). After a three-minute power shower and a few minutes at the mirror, cleansing her poreless vanilla skin and blowing out her shoulder-length jet-black hair and applying Givenchy Illicit Raspberry to her full lips and Shu Uemura Basic around her ice-blue eyes, she'd begun to feel almost human again. The steam had been billowing from the Shaynes' tiny bathroom as Mary riffled through her overstuffed closet full of size zeroes, impatiently hurling useless couture across her hatefully cramped bedroom. The discarded tops and trousers and dresses on their store hangers cascaded loudly against the thin, cracking wall, while behind that wall, Ellen was ministering to Mom—Mary could hear their muted voices and the clinking of glasses as Ellen struggled to get the orange juice mixture just right.

Finding something to wear hadn't been easy. All the clothes were wrong: the silver Badgley Mischka dress from Amy was too much; the floral Nela dress that Joon bought her at the Bendel preview party was too pretty; the Dior shirts from that sample sale were utterly ridiculous and needed to be burned in some sort of voodoo bonfire. Mary tugged down more hangers, scanning each outfit within milliseconds, asking the same embarrassing question over and over—the question she had secretly asked herself every morning and every night out for the past three years: *What would you wear if you were Mary Shayne?*

She never asked it out loud because she knew what Amy and Joon would say if they heard it: "What do you mean, *if* you were Mary Shayne? You *are* Mary Shayne." They just didn't seem to get it. There *was* no Mary Shayne—there was

37

just this skinny, wet-haired girl who happened to have been born pretty, standing in her last pair of clean white panties and a black Victoria's Secret bra that she'd dug out of the middle of the hamper and sifting anxiously through unreturned loaner dresses in her musty closet.

The worst of the hangover seemed to have washed away with the sweat and dried blood that had spun down the shower drain beneath her feet. *You met some people and killed some brain cells and partied somewhere*, Ellen had said, dismissing all her fear, all her confusion about the night before. Mary tried to believe it. Whatever had happened, she was determined not to let it ruin her birthday. The shower felt like it had cleansed her completely, and she vowed not to worry anymore—especially since she had to concern herself with the far more pressing issue of what to wear to school.

The outfit had to be birthday presentable without drawing attention. It couldn't be too dressy or it might convey the promise of a late-night rager to the sex-crazed seniors, but it couldn't be a Strokes T-shirt and some get-away-from-me sweatpants or it might draw a totally different kind of attention. She didn't want anyone asking, "What's wrong with Mary today?" She couldn't have anyone thinking there was anything remotely unusual about this birthday—that was essential. She'd finally settled on a black FCUK tee, True Religion jeans from Patrick, black leather Frye boots and her black Michael Kors trench. Another minute and a half to snag a banana and swap in her spare BlackBerry battery, and she was gone.

For the next hour—as she'd done once a week, without

fail, all senior year—Mary tried to restore her sanity. Her first class on Fridays was a free period, and using that precious hour as her own private time was practically the only thing that got her through the end of the week and into the weekend. She'd seen an old movie called *Breakfast at Tiffany's* once and fallen in love with it (and with Audrey Hepburn as Holly Golightly, the luminous, vulnerable, adorable, perfect main character). The movie's title wasn't hard to figure out, since the opening scene showed Holly standing in front of the perfect limestone facade of Tiffany & Co. on Fifth Avenue (in a perfect black gown she was obviously still wearing from the night before), eating a danish and drinking from a paper cup of delicatessen coffee while looking in the famous jeweler's windows at the diamonds on display. Later in the movie, Holly explained how good those windows made her feel, and Mary understood exactly.

Ever since then—all senior year—Mary had spent her Friday mornings the same way: after getting off the crosstown bus, she would buy a Starbucks cappuccino and wander down Madison Avenue for the next hour, looking at the clothes in the fashionable store windows and making her peace with the universe. She had never tried to explain it to anyone (except once, to Ellen, who, predictably, sympathized without really understanding), but her solitary, peaceful, Friday-morning *Breakfast at Tiffany's* routine actually kept her sane. She even found herself humming "Moon River" under her breath, like in the movie, as she gazed through the plate glass at the tall, skinny, perfect mannequins in their perfect clothes, their lovely, sculpted cheekbones catching the morning light, radiating serenity and self-confidence and perfection that Mary imagined she could soak up like a recharging battery, preparing herself for the hours and days to come.

Now, crossing Ninetieth Street, coolly returning the avid stare of a reasonably cute young businessman who was walking in the other direction, Mary tried to tell herself she felt fine. Men looked at her so constantly, so dependably, that their attention was really only notable when she *wasn't* getting it, or when she was getting the wrong kind, like during that horrible Crate and Barrel moment—a memory she was determined to permanently expunge. She was never going to tell anyone about that.

But what happened last night?

A flock of birds circled silently in the featureless sky. The air was wet and still, with a faint scent of rain to come.

Forget it. Whatever it was, it's over now.

On the corner of Eighty-second Street, she checked her BlackBerry again—still no birthday texts or e-mails—and leaned to inspect her lipstick one last time in the mirrored window of a parked Porsche Cayenne. Then she took a deep breath, tried to clear her head, and turned the corner, ready to face the day.

CHADWICK STUDENTS WERE SPREAD out across the entire block like grazing cattle, smoking cigarettes, making phone calls, leaning against the granite walls of the neighboring apartment buildings and sitting Indian style against the tall iron gates of the school, screaming with laughter and, no doubt, spouting off about Eastern philosophy and the sociopolitical ramifications of Britney's latest comeback.

Mary strode confidently down the sidewalk, approaching the crowd, trying to look completely disinterested while she furtively scanned the faces for her friends. Any minute now they would see her coming—one by one, the heads would turn, as they always did: a chain reaction of avid male eyes and envious female eyes as the one and only Mary Shayne arrived, fashionably late, flawlessly dressed as usual.

And then the birthday greetings will start. She remembered what it had been like, a year before—the nonstop attention of her adoring fans had begun moments after her arrival at school: Melanie Kurzweil ran up and poured a small bag of Hershey's Kisses into her hand; "Giant Brian" Moss had grabbed her from behind and given her a ticklish birthday kiss on the back of the neck; even the eternally depressed Darin Evigan broke his two straight days of black-turtlenecked silence to hum her an emo rendition of "Happy Birthday" (she had pressed her hand to her heart and complimented his "haunting" voice). It started immediately and continued all day long.

But now, as she waded into the thick sidewalk crowd, nobody was looking at her.

Nobody acknowledged her at all. There were a couple of glances from students who blocked her path—they spared her a look as they got out of her way—but basically nothing. All that stress over her clothes, and it didn't seem to make any difference.

The overcast sky shone overhead, cold and white. The front gates of the school—where the usual Zac Efron wannabes and bargain-basement Hayden Panettieres sat with their backs against the wrought iron, trying to look sullen and disaffected—were veiled in dark shadows. Mary caught herself shivering. The expensive fabric of her T-shirt rubbed painfully against the raw scratches on her lower back, making her squirm—she was twisting her body around, reaching beneath her book bag to rub her tender skin when she saw him, and froze.

Trick.

Patrick Dawes, devoted boyfriend, was standing right in front of her. Somehow, she had managed not to see him at all until the last moment. He was wearing a vintage Cambridge University blazer over an A&F hoodie with extra-low-slung jeans, which exposed the slim trail of light blond hairs that ran down from his navel, disappearing behind the taut elastic waistband of his Calvins. He stood squarely on both feet, fingers in his jeans pockets, steel TAG Heuer glinting on his wrist. It was impossible to read his expression: his dark brown eyes gazed coolly at her, as if she wasn't his girlfriend—as if she was a Starbucks barista who'd just asked him how she could help him.

He was still so unbearably beautiful. That's what had made Patrick such a maddening (but exciting) puzzle in her life during the three months they'd been together. Those little blond Greek-god curls, those naturally golden eyebrows, that flawlessly sculpted, lean, sinewy body—his beauty was completely impervious to his C-grade personality. No matter how tiresome he could be, no matter what he'd done to piss her off, she *still* felt that bolt of sugar-sweet electricity run through her chest whenever she saw him.

Something's wrong, Mary thought. She knew it, immediately; there was just no question about it. *Did someone die?*

But it wasn't that. He hadn't been crying; he didn't look stressed at all. He looked fine—rested, even, which was unusual; his telltale reddened eyes usually betrayed his pot-related insomnia and fatigue, marring his classical features in a way that was only visible up close. But not today: he looked like he'd gotten nine hours of sleep and run ten miles. Mary began to feel a tightness in her stomach, as if the day's bleak chill was seeping into her body and making her shiver with nervousness.

"Trick?"

She hadn't wanted to speak first. She had wanted to stand there and smirk prettily as he unveiled a turquoise Tiffany's box with a milky white ribbon, or a pair of Fall Out Boy tickets, or even a single daisy from behind his back; she wanted him to kiss her deep and hard in front of the whole school and whisper happy birthday in her ear. But he just *stood* there, looking at her. His eyes narrowed slightly, but he didn't move.

"Come on." Trick jerked his head, beckoning her down the street. "Let's walk."

"Walk?" Mary had completely lost her composure. The sea of kids around them was still jostling her, talking and texting and wandering from place to place, but their voices seemed to change, to dissolve into a mounting roar like an approaching subway . . . and Mary realized that she was more than nervous: she was frightened. Something was definitely up. "Where do you—"

The scream she heard next, the desperate, distant voice behind her, made Mary flinch as if jumper cables attached to a car battery had suddenly been jammed against her shoulders.

"*Mary!*"

A high male voice—a teenager's voice, calling her name.

"*Mary! Mary!*" it repeated. The fear, the desperation in the voice nearly made her forget to breathe. *Everyone* was looking, craning their necks to peer behind her.

Mary turned and looked. Through the crowd, she could see someone—a small figure—running right toward her, but could only make out thin, sandy blond hair and a dark Windbreaker.

"Mary, *look out!*" the boy screamed. "*Look out, you're in danger!*"

The crowd was moving now, pulling back in shock, eyes and mouths wide. Mary finally saw who was screaming her name.

Scott Sanders.

In another context it would have been funny: short, plump Scott Sanders, her physics buddy, her savior in so many classes and before so many tests, his plain, kind face distorted in wild-eyed, crimson-tinted fear, his gut visibly swinging up and down as he ran clumsily toward her. His glasses tumbled from his face, clattering to the sidewalk as he rushed at her like a bull charging a matador, his unbrushed hair corkscrewed around his head like he'd stumbled out of bed and run all the way to school.

But it wasn't funny at all.

"*Mary, for Christ's sake—*" Scott was no athlete; he couldn't run and scream at the same time without stumbling and panting. His book bag was flying up and down behind him like a red canvas piston. "*Mary, you've got to listen— you're in serious danger—*"

And then they stopped him. It wasn't the whole Chadwick football team, just a few of the linebackers (who, as usual, had been lounging against the fence punching each other in the arms); they moved fast, darting forward with their muscular arms raised, converging on Scott as he propelled himself down the sidewalk like a runaway train headed straight for Mary.

"Hey, assface," Pete Schocken snapped—he had gotten there first, and he moved his tall, thick body directly in Scott's path so that Scott slammed into his raised arms like a thrown garbage bag smashing against a tree. "What the hell, man?"

The crowd was still staring—some at Scott, some at Mary—and for once, she didn't want their eyes on her at all.

"Mary, *please listen, you've got to get out of—*"

The smacking sound of Pete's open hand slapping Scott's face echoed like a gunshot and the crowd of students gasped. The other linebackers had flanked Scott—this was what they *did*, after all; they could intercept downfield rollouts without even thinking—and he was so hopelessly overmatched it was hard to even look. Scott's pudgy, waving hand was visible for one second, silhouetted against the distant sky, before the linebackers converged and he was invisible. "Chill *out*, you goddamned freak," Billy Nelson snapped—and then everyone was talking at once, the crowd converging on the fight, racing across the wide sidewalk.

"Mary, *run!*" Scott screamed. "*Please listen! You've got to— Ow!*"

Mary barely saw Scott go down, through the forest of arms and legs and bodies that blocked her view. She could hear the sliding thump as Scott dropped to the sidewalk, his book bag slipping from his shoulder and tumbling to the ground. She was hyperventilating. She could feel her pulse in her throat, clicking like a metronome. The fear was so intense that she weakened and nearly lost her balance; she might have fallen, but someone banged against her in a rush toward Scott and the linebackers, knocking her back upright.

"Come on." A hand grabbed her shoulder, making her flinch again. It was Trick, pulling her away. "Let's talk."

"But—" Mary turned her head to stare at him, strands of hair flicking against her cheek. Patrick didn't seem concerned about what was happening to Scott, ten feet away. It was like Mary *always* got insane screaming warnings from geeks on the sidewalk—like it was so routine it didn't even bear mentioning. "Patrick, Jesus, look what they're doing to Scott! Why did he—"

"Come on," Patrick repeated gravely. His hand was still on her shoulder; his face was set in a tight, impenetrable mask. "We've got to have a conversation."

"Let *go* of me," Mary said, squirming and pulling out of his grip. Her headache was coming back and the queasy feeling in her stomach was making her tremble. So much adrenaline had flowed into her bloodstream so quickly that she felt like she was drunk. "Patrick, Jesus, what the hell is your problem?"

"*Mary, run!*" Scott called out one last time.

Trick didn't seem to care, or even notice. He was already walking east, smoothly extracting a Dunhill from his scratched gold cigarette case, drawing it out with his sexy lips while he whipped out his engraved silver lighter with his other hand—a practiced movement that she had probably see him do a thousand times. A cloud of exotic smoke billowed from his nose as he exhaled, still walking away from the school's gates, as if expecting her to follow.

Mary had *never* seen Trick act like this. Usually, he was pleasantly chatty in the morning, in his low-key, medium-cool way, telling stories about some pathetic coked-up lawyer he'd met at an after-hours bar or some cheesy peach-fuzzed entrepreneur who wanted him to invest in an oxygen nightclub for teens. Now it was like he'd joined the Secret Service.

"Trick?" Mary asked, struggling to keep up with his long-legged strides. "Trick? What the hell—why are you being so weird?"

He looked at her. "Weird how?"

Mary, run! Scott's shriek was still ringing in her ears.

"Weird, like—like *this*," Mary said helplessly. "Come on, Patrick, seriously—what's the joke?"

"No joke."

It's a conspiracy, she thought suddenly. *Sure—it's a birthday thing.*

That had to be it. Everyone had conspiracy theories on their birthdays. It was natural; it was routine—you spent the whole day waiting for somebody to surprise you.

But she didn't believe it. Not really; not for one second. The way Scott had *screamed* . . . it wasn't a game; it couldn't have been.

"All right," Trick muttered, slowing as they got past the last stragglers, away from the Chadwick crowd and toward a flock of baby strollers steered by sinewy yoga moms or Jamaican nannies. "Here's as good a place as any."

"As good a place—" Mary didn't know what he was talking about, but she didn't like it one bit. She still felt dizzy. A cloud of Dunhill smoke blew across her face, straight from Trick's nostrils. Usually, Trick was very careful to blow smoke away from her, but now he was letting the wind decide. "Trick, seriously, you're freaking me out. What the hell is *wrong* with you? Are you high? Are you high *right now*? Because that would be—"

"Not high." Patrick smiled humorlessly down at her. "In fact, I think I'm seeing things more clearly than I ever did before in my life."

"What—"

"That's why I want to talk to you."

This wasn't just a hangover. It was different, somehow. She had been trying to ignore how she felt, but there was no getting around it anymore. Something was wrong.

I've got the flu, she thought dismally. *I've got some kind of* bug—something you get from sleeping naked in a climate-controlled furniture store.

(*Mary, you've got to listen—you're in serious danger—*)

Whatever it was, Mary was beginning to realize it wasn't getting better. It was getting *worse*, more noticeable. The noises and scents of her surroundings seemed unusually strong, unusually acute. Her heart was still racing, she realized—and a soft, quiet dread was beginning to grow inside her.

This is the moment, Mary told herself. *He's going to suddenly smile and then pull out some plane tickets—he's going to laugh at my reaction and hug me and kiss me, and then, later, when we're all jammed in around a club table sharing bottle service, he'll keep telling Joon and Amy how scared I looked.*

But Patrick didn't do anything like that.

"It's time to wake up," Trick told her. "It's time to face facts."

"What—?" Mary gazed into his brown eyes. That cold feeling in her stomach wouldn't go away. "What the hell—Okay, *what's* wrong? Just tell me now so we can have a normal day."

"A normal day?" Patrick smiled again, slightly, with one side of his mouth. "You think this is a 'normal day'? Is that really what you think?"

I think it's my birthday, Mary thought angrily. *What the hell do you think it is?*

"I think you're on *another fucking planet* and you'd better return to earth this instant, or—"

"Or what?" Trick's face wasn't registering any emotion. His eyes were blank. "Or you'll do what? What are you going to do to me, exactly?"

"*Excuse* me?" Mary's eyes widened. "Patrick, anytime you want to snap out of this . . . this *thing* you're doing and tell me why I should—"

"You're boring." Patrick looked deep into her eyes. "You're so fucking boring, it's starting to hurt my head. Don't talk unless you have something interesting to say, okay?"

She couldn't believe it. *How dare he talk to me this way? On my birthday?* She still couldn't believe this was actually happening—that this avalanche had landed on her so quickly. And there was something else—she was suddenly *picturing* something. A dark image, murky and unrecognizable, floated into her head right at that moment.

"Don't act offended," Patrick went on, still maddeningly calm. "Seriously, I've seen that show before."

"You are such an *asshole*!" she snapped uncontrollably. She could feel tears welling. "You're such a fucked-up asshole! What is the *matter* with you?"

"Oh, *hell*, yes!" Trick pumped his fists as he raised his voice. The effect was not funny in the least. "Thank you! Thank you for calling me by my *actual* name! 'Asshole'! Hey, here's a question for you. If I'm such an asshole, then *why* are you going out with me?"

"Wh-what?"

Mary couldn't believe her ears. The owner of the corner candy store had come outside to watch the pretty teenagers' drama unfold—he was probably one of those forty-something pervos who liked to watch *Gossip Girl*. All he needed was a remote control and some microwave popcorn for the show.

The image in her head wasn't going away. Mary could see a darkening evening sky, with bands of fading light streaked across the horizon. A vast nighttime sky and the sharp edges of a shape in front of her, across a pale white clearing—a shape like a building, a barn, maybe—tall and wide, looming over her.

"You heard me just fine," Patrick said, looking away as he dropped his half-smoked Dunhill and stamped it out. "Why would you want to go out with me?"

He wanted to talk, she remembered. The dread in her stomach had spread to her throat. *He led me down here because he wanted to have a conversation in private.*

Are you really doing what I think you're doing, Patrick?

She stared into Patrick's eyes and suddenly wanted him to grab her and kiss her like he'd always done, cupping her slim face in one hand and sliding the other hand up the small of her back, beneath her T-shirt, fingers probing her bare skin, then grabbing the elastic of her panties just below the waistband of her jeans.

Are you breaking up with me?

It was insane, unthinkable.

"Can't think of any reasons, can you?" Patrick said quietly. "Because I really can't either."

Mary felt her hot eyes itching, her vision blurring as she stared back at Patrick. *Is this the same boy?* she wondered. *Is this the boy I fell for?* She remembered how they'd started, like it was yesterday: that December night at Rockefeller Center, where the gang always had their traditional pre-Christmas skate, going back years. Everyone was there, even

Patrick, although he and Joon were all but broken up by then. Mary remembered the terrible cold she'd had, her determination to push through the evening for old times' sake. She'd kept mounds of snotty Kleenex buried in the pockets of her white parka, hoping no one would notice her slow, unsightly death by phlegm. But Patrick noticed—he'd seen her sneezing like an actor in an antihistamine commercial, and after another huge fight with Joon, he'd appeared as Mary was leaving the rink, rising from the sunroof of a stretch limo and whisking her to Katz's Deli for emergency chicken soup and noodle pudding. They spent the whole night there, trying to figure out how to patch up his relationship with Joonie.

And now here we are, she thought dismally, *just three months later.* She'd been no fool, of course: she'd known exactly what she was getting into, beforehand. She'd known he was arrogant (everyone did); she'd known he could be a spoiled elitist baby (everyone did). But dating him was different. By the third month, she'd realized that Trick's shortcomings were deeper, more profound than the mere ego problems everyone could see: something basic was missing. Under that golden blond, rock-hard shell was a soft, weak center—a basic indifference that made her want to shake him violently and force him to give a shit about *something.* It was right around then that she'd discovered the delightful trait that tied all his other delightful traits together: the unavoidable fact that he was a drug addict.

"You're going to do it like this?" Mary said quietly. She tried to sound hard, tried to sound tough as nails—but she could hear the dread in her own voice as the full force of what was happening sank in. "Right here, right now?"

Patrick squinted disdainfully. "Not dramatic enough? You want to wait until later? You want to make a show of it, back at school? Big opera scene in the lunchroom?"

"No," she said weakly. She could feel herself slumping; the wide white sky was blinding her and the tears were close. "Here and now. Fine, done."

"Beautiful! Can I go to class now?"

Mary searched his eyes for even an ounce of the old sweetness, a glimmer of that adorable boy who'd watched her sneezing at the Rockefeller Center ice rink, but there was no sign of him.

"I can't *believe* you did this," she whispered. Patrick was already reaching for another Dunhill. "I can't believe you did this *today*."

"Believe it."

In her mind she saw the dark sky and the black shape. It wasn't a barn, she realized—it was a house. And she could sense something else—something bad. Some reason to leave, to get away.

(*Mary, run!*)

"*Why*, Patrick? Why?"

There was no expression on Patrick's face at all—until he smiled, a gentle, calm smile that didn't spread to his beautiful brown eyes.

"You know why."

Then he turned away and walked toward Chadwick while she stood there shivering, watching him go.

*   *   *

THE ROOF OF THE CHADWICK School was officially off-limits to students, for all kinds of good reasons having to do with insurance and panicky parents' groups and the perennial danger of an accident.

But the rules didn't really stop determined kids from going up there. There were dozens of crazy stories Mary had heard over the years about Chadwickites who'd done various illegal or immoral things outside the easy-to-jimmy steel door at the very top of the school's ten-story stairwell.

Mary didn't really know where she was going; she was just climbing the stairs, around and around each linoleum-covered landing, her legs burning like a cyclist's, her eyes blinded by tears. Chadwickites were passing her in both directions, thundering between floors, between classes, and Mary kept climbing, just wanting to get away from everyone. *If I have a heart attack, so be it,* she thought—and then realized that she was following an old impulse that occurred every time she wanted to be alone at school: she was headed for the roof.

Patrick dumped me!

She still couldn't believe it had actually happened. Maybe she'd seen it coming—maybe, in her heart of hearts, she'd had *some* idea that all was not well, that there was trouble in paradise. She kept remembering the snowy night in December when it all had started: sitting in Katz's Deli and listening to Trick's laments about Joon while sneaking glances at his delicately modeled lips and high cheekbones when she was sure he wasn't looking. Trick went on and on about how he couldn't see eye to eye with Joonie anymore,

54

about all the ways their relationship was "dying on the vine." All those sentences that began "I know she's your best friend, but . . ." Mary had sympathized and held his hand and understood what he meant. Maybe she'd thought about what Joon was going through—how Joon must have *known* what was going on, must have *known* that she was about to lose her boyfriend—but that wasn't something Mary could change, was it? Besides, she was *helping*, wasn't she?

But now it was happening to *her*. And it was very different, she realized.

She got to the top landing, leaning on the banister to keep from stumbling with fatigue. Her legs were aching and her heartbeat was thwacking in her ears. *That's today's workout*, she thought dazedly. There was nobody around; the landing was deserted. A blinding thread of overcast light framed the windowless metal door to the roof, which somebody had wedged open with a shim. Mary lunged forward, forearms bashing against the door, pushing it open.

A cool wind tossed her hair around her face as she stepped forward onto the tar paper, letting the door clang shut. Other East Side buildings shone through the haze beyond the chain-link fence perimeter. Mary wasn't alone—two student-shaped silhouettes loomed in her tear-blurred gaze, facing each other from very close, haloed by the blinding sky. *Too bad*, she thought—the last thing she wanted was to deal with anyone else. That was the whole point of coming to the—

"Oh, thank God!" Mary yelled. Her eyes had cleared, adjusting to the sunlight, and she recognized one of the shimmering figures—Ellen. She was dressed in the same tangerine Gap hoodie and gray sweatpants she'd been wearing in her bedroom two hours earlier—no pre-school makeover for her. "I can't believe you're up here—" Mary ran forward and wrapped her arms tightly around her sister.

"What the hell—" Ellen hugged back automatically, but her grip felt awkward and clumsy. "Mary, what's the matter with you?"

"Sorry—I'm sorry," Mary said, pulling away, throat burning as she finally gave in to the tears. "I'm sorry, but—Trick dumped me!"

"Really?" Ellen squinted oddly, as if surprise was blending with another emotion that Mary couldn't recognize. She wasn't looking at Mary—she was looking *past* her, at the third person on the roof.

Mary turned around. A male figure—a boy—stood facing them, returning Ellen's gaze. Mary had no idea who he was. He wasn't a Chadwick student—she was sure of that. After ten years at the same school, Mary could probably pick any of the seven-hundred-or-so students out of a police lineup—even the ones she'd never met.

And yet, there was something familiar about him. He was tall, and wiry like a swimmer. It was hard to make out the details of his face—his unkempt, wild dark brown hair, which rode a fine line between an actual style and a bad case of bed-head, cast his eyes and cheeks in shadow. A layer of dark stubble coated his angular jaw. He wore an untucked, unironed (but clean) white oxford shirt and a loosened gray tie, worn-out jeans and scuffed Puma running shoes.

"Um—" the boy said.

Mary looked at him, hot tears running down her face,

still squeezing Ellen's shoulder with one hand. *Go away!* she felt like yelling. *Get out of here and let me cry on my sister's shoulder.* But suddenly she was sure she'd seen him before.

"Mary, you remember Dylan?" Ellen said. "My friend Dylan, from—"

"Scruffy Dylan!" The words popped out before Mary had a chance to think. "Of course!" Just like that, she had recognized him: Ellen's bookish friend, whom she'd passed in the Shayne kitchen more than once without either of them ever saying hello.

"Yeah," Dylan said, nodding and smiling. He didn't sound offended. "I guess. Scruffy Dylan."

"I'm sorry," Mary said quickly. "I'm sorry. I just—"

"No, no—please." Dylan stared down at his weathered Pumas and scratched the back of his neck. "Don't worry about it. It's accurate."

There were lots of these scruffy boys in the Shaynes' neighborhood; they were all Columbia students (which, she now vaguely remembered, Dylan was too). She'd grown up seeing them hunched over outdoor café tables up by 114th Street, each with three open textbooks, three empty espresso cups, tons of sugar packets everywhere, and chewed-up pens in their mouths, trying to solve a world health crisis or translate some ancient Greek. Mary had never even considered talking to Dylan, those times he'd been at her apartment, given the chances of her feeling like an idiot halfway through the conversation. If he was smart enough to be friends with Ellen, she reasoned, then he was *way* too smart to be friends with her.

"Wait—*what's* this about Patrick?" Ellen reached up to her shoulder, protectively covering Mary's hand with hers. "What happened?"

"He dumped me," Mary repeated. Sobs were knifing through her now, catching in her throat. "He just *dumped* me, out of the b-blue—"

"Wow." Ellen still wore the same startled look—she was staring past Mary at Dylan. "Just wow. Did he—did anything prompt this? I mean, were you fighting, or—"

"No, nothing!" Mary still couldn't believe it.

(*You know why.*)

"Poor girl!" Ellen pulled Mary close to hug her again. "Poor Mary. Don't cry. . . ."

"But it hurts," Mary whispered, Ellen's flat, nonconditioned hair pressed against her face. "It hurts so much."

"Now *you're* crying," Ellen murmured. "Funny how things change."

"What?" Mary pulled away, wiping her nose. "What did you—"

"I'm sorry," Ellen said, the wind whipping strands of hair around her face. Her glasses reflected the bright sky. "I'm sorry, it's just—you just reminded me of last night, when Mom was, you know, when Mom got sad. I didn't mean to—"

"When *Mom* got sad?"

You've got to be kidding, Mary thought. She always had to remind herself, over and over, of how emotionally immature her sister was. It was the result of not having a social life, of never having a boyfriend, she supposed. But here Mary was, facing the devastation of losing her boyfriend—her *boyfriend,* for Christ's sake—and Ellen's first thought was that this was somehow comparable to middle-aged Dawn Shayne, displaying all the emotional stability of a petulant five-year-old as she let her daughter's birthday and her long-dead husband's absence move her to tears.

"Come on, Ellie, you really think this is—"

"I'm just trying to make a point," Ellen went on, pleasantly enough. "Just twelve hours ago, *Mom* was crying, asking you about Dad, and you couldn't even—"

"I don't remember." Mary was conscious of Dylan standing patiently behind her, waiting for the Shayne sisters to finish their emotional scene. *Serves me right,* she thought bitterly. *I turn to a family member for help and get pulled right into a family argument.* "I don't remember, Ellen, but can't we just—"

"Last night at dinner," Ellen went on, still maddeningly calm. "The waiter had taken the plates away and Mom was crying, talking about your birthday and asking you about Dad's last—"

"I mean I *don't remember,*" Mary snapped. She was in absolutely no mood for this. "I remember last night, but I don't remember the fucking story Mom keeps referring to, when Dad, you know, when he died, because I was *fucking seven years old!* Why can't you and Mom both just—"

"All right," Ellen said quickly. "All right, sorry. We'll get into it later."

"Do you want me to leave?" Dylan said. He'd picked up a rumpled messenger bag from the tar paper—a folded jacket was draped over it. "If you're having some private thing, I can—"

Yes! Mary thought furiously. The emotional rawness, in

59

front of a total stranger, was making her feel even worse. *Leave! Get out of here!*

"No, that's okay," Ellen said, more loudly. "Forget it—I'm sorry, Mary. It's hardly the appropriate time. Wow," she marveled, shaking her head. "Patrick actually— Wow."

"Excuse us, Dylan," Mary told him, trying to muster a smile and barely managing. "It's just, you know, sister stuff. Listen"—she looked back and forth between Dylan and her sister, affecting a scandalous tone, trying to cover the embarrassment she felt—"what are you two doing up here, anyway? What's going on between you guys?"

"What? Nothing. We're just, um—" Dylan gestured. "Having a conversation."

"Something intellectual, right?" Mary smiled. "Talking about an old book or something."

"Yeah." Ellen had picked up the jovial tone, clearly trying to smooth over the awkward moment. "You could say that, sure. An old book. I'm consulting my resident language expert."

" 'Expert'—right." Dylan rolled his eyes and slid his bag over his shoulder. "Ellen, you've got class."

"Don't roll your eyes, Dyl!" Ellen smiled as she pushed her glasses up the bridge of her nose. "That's a very kind thing to say! If you're going to compliment somebody, mention their erudition, or their—"

"*Class*—you've got class," Dylan repeated, looking at his watch. "Right? History or whatever, at nine-forty. You're going to be late."

"Oh, *shit*—he's right," Ellen said, reaching for her own

overstuffed book bag. "Mary, I'm sorry—I've got to get down there. Really, I'm sorry."

"That's okay." Mary accepted Ellen's quick, strong hug, but she'd already written Ellen off. *She's not going to help,* Mary thought. *She can't do it, no matter how well intentioned she is—she just doesn't have the emotional vocabulary.* "We'll talk later."

"Nice to meet you," Dylan said, prying open the door in the brick shed that covered the stairwell's top landing, and holding it for them both. "Sorry you're having a bad day."

"Thanks," Mary said, sniffing. *And mind your own business.*

AT TWO-FORTY-FIVE in the afternoon Mary realized, dully, that she hadn't gone to a single class. She'd moved up and down the Chadwick staircase with the other students at one-hour intervals, buffeted by the crowd, whenever the way-too-loud class bell rang out from (it seemed) a corner of every ceiling, up and down the ten floors of the school. Around noon, she'd wandered into the cafeteria, seen none of her friends, and wandered right back out. But she hadn't been able to bring herself to actually go into a classroom. The thought of sitting in a metal and Formica chair under fluorescent lights and staring at a blackboard seemed absolutely out of the question.

I'm going to get in trouble, she thought, over and over. *I'm going to be in serious trouble for this.* By her count, she'd already cut three classes and was about to cut a fourth; the consequences (even for a second-semester senior) were pretty dire.

But she couldn't make herself care.

Nobody had wished her a happy birthday. Nobody was looking at her; their eyes brushed against her and then moved away, quickly, as if she was wearing that scarlet letter in that book she'd had to read for English class last year. It was beyond "Worst Birthday Ever," and every time she saw her reflection in the glass panes of the school's classroom doors, she saw her carefully assembled birthday outfit and felt even worse. It was like her own clothes were making fun of her.

It took five minutes for everyone to gallop madly from class to class . . . pausing to slam their lockers open and grab their books and shout and flirt and make jokes while their shoes squeaked on the linoleum . . . and then everyone was rushing back into the classrooms and the doors were closing and that prison-yard bell rang again, and Mary was alone, in the center of the corridor, shivering and trembling with her arms wrapped around herself.

I'm missing Shama, she thought absently. *I'm missing that test.*

Again, she just couldn't make herself care.

And something else was happening, too—something she couldn't ignore any longer.

It had started while she was with Patrick; she had been looking at him but seeing something else—a house silhouetted against a dark sky—that made her nervous, somehow. More than nervous—she was actually frightened, but she had no idea why. It had happened twice more: that same strange *sliding* feeling, like the world was slipping away. Mary had tried to ignore it. *Hangover,* she'd told herself.

An hour later, it happened again.

It was like someone had changed television channels. All the clamor around her was *gone*. Just like that, the school was gone, the warm recycled air with its unmistakable scents of gym clothes and perfume and chalk dust was gone, and she was cold, outdoors in the dark.

A freezing wind blew across her face as she gazed up at the vast sky and the pale bloodred glow beyond the flat, distant horizon. Snow fell like ash; she was *standing* in snow— deep, fresh powder that had seeped through her boots and frozen her feet numb—staring forward at the black shape of the house.

And this time, shivering in the cold, she saw movement, close to her: a darkness in the white ground; a hole in the snow that swirled like a drain. Peering through the dimness between the dancing snowflakes, Mary realized that something was in the hole: a dark shape—something alive, reaching for her and calling to her.

A chill passed through her, making her shiver, and then she was in the Chadwick corridor, alone in the middle of the fourth floor, missing the physics test. The cold wind was gone, replaced by the stale Chadwick air and the muffled sounds of teachers' droning voices from behind the classroom doors lined up on either side of her.

I'm sick, she thought miserably. *I've got to be sick; something's wrong with me.* The morning hangover had distracted her from how bad she *really* felt. Now the hangover was gone, but her head was still swimming; there was a strange, disconnected sensation in her brain that she couldn't place or understand.

And I'm seeing things.

Mary had no idea what to do. She heard herself whimpering, which alarmed her, and tried to *stop,* to *get a grip.* Moving to the wall, she collapsed against the lockers and slid to the floor, wrapping her arms around her knees and rocking back and forth. She only realized that she'd lost track of time when the bell clanged again, hammering her eardrums, and then the same deafening ballet started all over again, the classroom doors banging open and the students leaping out like racehorses obeying a starting gun. Mary didn't move until someone—Jenny Mullen, a junior she barely knew—tripped over her knees and nearly went sprawling across the floor, her book bag spilling its contents.

"*Damn* it!" Jenny yelled, glaring at Mary balefully. "Like, get out of the *road,* yo! You're totally in the way."

"Sorry," Mary said, rising dutifully to her feet.

I'm totally in the way.

Despair was flooding over her like quicksand. This was supposed to be the day she was the center of attention. Everybody has a day like that, once a year—it's as basic as breathing—and this was supposed to be *hers.* Instead, she was "totally in the way." It wasn't fair at all.

"Hey, snap out of it!"

The voice was very familiar and very close. Mary was thinking about the black house in the field of snow—the place she was *absolutely sure* she didn't remember, didn't recognize. It took her a moment to focus and realize that somebody was standing right in front of her, speaking to her—somebody she knew.

"Mary? What the hell—you look awful."

Amy Twersky, Mary's best friend (her *other* best friend, she corrected herself), was looking at her intently. Mary felt a wave of relief at the sight of Amy's familiar, beloved face. She'd somehow managed to miss all her friends so far that day—it was the first time she'd seen Amy since arriving at school.

Amy was pretty—pale, like a figure in a Renaissance portrait, freckle-faced, with long, flowing orange-red locks—but Mary saw she was downplaying her looks, as usual. Amy was the most self-conscious person Mary had ever met. She looked adorable today: she was wearing a cute Gaultier bubble dress with studded Balenciaga gladiator sandals. But she'd hidden the entire top half of the dress with a smocklike J.Crew cardigan.

Amy had no self-esteem. That had been true for as long as Mary could remember: back to the second grade, when they "officially" became best friends—there was an actual Best Friend Contract buried somewhere in Mary's bedroom closet, scrawled out in marker and sprinkled with purple sparkles, notarized by Hello Kitty and signed with thick red Crayolas.

"Hi, Amy," she said weakly. She couldn't muster anything else. The rush-hour crowd of yelling students and the slamming of lockers meant they had to raise their voices, but Mary didn't want to make the effort. It didn't seem worth it.

"I'm sorry," Amy said quickly. "You don't look awful— I can't believe I said that. You look beautiful, totally beautiful. You look hot."

There was no way to stop Amy from apologizing for everything, Mary knew; she had tried many times, over and over. Finally she'd given up.

"That's okay," she said automatically. "I *do* look bad. I'm—I'm having a bad day."

Amy nodded sympathetically.

That's it? Mary found herself wondering. *You're just going to nod? No "Sorry to hear that"? No "Happy birthday"?*

But that was asking for the moon, she thought bitterly. For some reason, nobody was going to say it (except Ellen, at home this morning, she amended). She believed she would get through the entire day without a single birthday greeting. She'd stopped minding—honestly.

Everyone's against me today. The whole world's against me.

Rather than fishing for it, rather than playing word games and hoping Amy would come to her senses and say happy birthday (and apologize and turn red), Mary just reached for her friend and pulled her close, hugging her. She couldn't help it; she just felt so helpless and alone.

Amy stiffened. She *always* stiffened when Mary hugged her; Mary wasn't sure why. Amy's arms came up slowly and hugged back, her thumbs tracing the curves of Mary's shoulder blades.

"I'm having such a bad day," Mary said into Amy's cloud of Renaissance hair, a lump forming in her throat that she forced herself to ignore. "Patrick dumped me."

"*What?*" Amy pulled away, her eyes wide. "He did *what?*"

"Broke up with me. This morning."

"What? *What?*" Amy stared at her. "Wait a second. You're not messing with me?"

Mary shook her head. "Not messing with you."

"Is he *insane*?" Amy wondered. "He broke up with *you*? That's like . . ." Amy pushed her hair back from her face, groping for words. "That's like, I don't know, winning the lottery and then throwing the ticket away."

"Thanks," Mary said hollowly. It was a nice thing to say, but somehow it didn't help. "Look, Amy, can you just—can you just make sure you've got my back today? I don't know what's wrong with—"

"Of *course*." Amy squeezed her shoulder, her eyebrows climbing, yearningly. "I'll do anything for you. You know that."

"Everything except miss your next class," Mary said. She was starting to feel better—and she realized that the corridor's population was thinning out. Amy had a couple of minutes to get to wherever she was going. "Thanks, Ame. Really."

"What about *your* next class?" Amy was checking her watch. "Didn't you just have some big test or someth—"

"I'm going to the nurse," Mary told her. She'd made up her mind, just like that. "I'm not— There's something wrong. I can't explain; I just . . . I just don't feel right."

"Well, you *look* great," Amy said again, her eyes roving appreciatively up and down Mary's figure. "You've got that going for you. Why do you always look so pretty, damn it? I'm such a cow."

Mary had stopped listening because she saw Scott Sanders at the other end of the corridor. Scott was walking briskly, hurrying to his next class, his overstuffed red book-bag bouncing behind him, his thick legs jiggling within his pleated khakis. "Hey!" she yelled, making Amy flinch and then turn to see whom she was yelling at. "Hey, *Scott!*"

"Mary?" Scott squinted quizzically at her. "What in the Sam Hill is the matter with you, woman?"

"What—" Mary couldn't figure out what Scott meant. Scott always used corny phrases like *What in the Sam Hill* and *How in blue blazes.* "What do you mean, what's the matter with *me*? I was about to ask you the same—"

"I'm sorry," Amy interrupted, squeezing Mary's shoulder. "I've got to get to Art History—I'll catch up with you."

Amy leaned to kiss Mary on the cheek and then sprinted away. Mary was barely listening—all her attention was on Scott.

"You just *skipped* the test," Scott marveled. "Brilliant; innovative. Did you actually think that would *work*? Shama even asked us where you were, since your name's not on the absent list. Do you *realize* what kind of bloody hell is going to descend upon you?"

"Never mind that," Mary said impatiently. She was peering at Scott's plump, pleasant face, looking for some sign of the blind panic she'd seen there mere hours before. "What *happened* this morning? What were you—what were you *warning* me about?"

(*Look out, you're in danger!*)

"What?" Scott's blue eyes looked baffled. "What are you talking about? 'Warning' you? The only thing I'd warn you about is Mr. Shama, because you'll have to—"

"*Scott!*" Mary had grabbed both his shoulders. They

were the only people in the corridor now—everyone else had vanished into classrooms and all the doors had shut. "Scott, this morning, in front of the school you, like, *ran toward me*, screaming that I was in danger."

Scott was shaking his head. He looked completely baffled. "Mary, what are you *talking* about? Are you, like, zonked out on drugs or something?"

"They beat the shit out of you!" Mary yelled. Scott flinched—Mary actually saw a droplet of her own spit land on his gold-framed glasses. She realized she was shaking him. "Pete Schocken and Silly Billy and the rest of the damn team—they surrounded you and took you down!"

"Mary, what's wrong? What's wrong with you?"

She let go of his arms. *I'm raving,* she realized fearfully. *I'm raving like one of those homeless people that everyone pretends they can't see.*

What's happening to me?

"Scott," she asked hopelessly, "don't you remember this morning? Don't you remember running down the street and screaming at me?"

"This is the first time I've seen you all day." Scott was looking past her, around her, trying to figure out if anyone else was lurking nearby—exhibiting the healthy paranoia of the geek who never knows when he's going to get persecuted. "Listen, is this some kind of senior prank or something? Because I don't think it's very funny."

He doesn't remember, Mary thought, amazed. She was sure of it—she could see it in his eyes. *He really doesn't remember.*

There was another possibility, one she didn't want to consider.

Or it didn't happen.

Patrick hadn't noticed or reacted, she remembered. He'd guided her down the street like nothing unusual was happening at all.

"Listen, I've got AP calculus," Scott said nervously, checking his antique wristwatch. "I'm sorry, but the big joke's going to have to wait."

I'm losing it, Mary thought. *I'm going crazy; I'm remembering stuff that didn't happen.*

She let go of Scott's shoulders and let him pull away, not watching as he sprinted down the hallway.

A black house with no lights, standing alone beneath a dark sky.

"Something's wrong with me," Mary said out loud. She was alone now; her voice echoed strangely in her ears. *Something's wrong with my brain. I have to see the nurse.* She started moving, walking toward the stairwell, trying to ignore the cold fear that was spreading through her like winter frost.

BY THREE IN THE afternoon Mary was outside the school, leaning on the black wrought-iron bars of the Chadwick gates, hands in pockets, book bag on the ground between her feet. She was staring at the lines in the sidewalk, which were actually kind of peaceful and soothing to look at. The school day was ending soon and she could hear the clashing of the school's doors behind her as kids came out, just a few this early, the beginning of the tide that would engulf the sidewalk with a deafening clamor of voices and ringing cell phones and pounding feet; the repeat of the scene that had started the day.

Why am I still here?

Mary wasn't sure. There was no reason not to leave and go home. Nobody was talking to her. Nobody cared about her. She stared at the sidewalk and saw passing shoes and trouser cuffs and the occasional skateboard or Razor scooter, but she refused to look up. *I won't look up until somebody talks to me,* she thought. *But that means I'll still be standing here when the sun goes down.*

The nurse had been useless. Mary had waited behind a couple of seventh graders who had cut themselves doing some kind of experiment in science class and needed disinfectant and gauze bandages and wouldn't stop *crying,* as if their small wounds were the most extreme pain they'd ever experienced. *Shut up!* Mary wanted to shout at them as she sat and fidgeted in the chair on the other side of the nurses' station's white curtains. *You think that's pain? You don't know what pain is.*

I know what pain is, she thought. It wasn't something that happened to you on the surface; it was something that hit you far, far deeper inside. She could feel the hurt floating in her stomach, beneath the outfit she'd worked so hard at putting together but that nobody had cared about. *This is the definition of pain—the worst day of my life, and there's not a scratch on me.*

Except that wasn't true, was it?

The scratches on Mary's lower back seemed to have

71

closed up and started to heal, but the skin was still tender. She still had no idea where she'd gotten them, or what had happened the night before.

I hope I had fun, she thought bitterly, *because I'm sure not having any today.*

"There's something wrong with my brain," she'd told the nurse helplessly, when the two desperately wounded seventh graders had left and it was her turn. The nurse, a stocky Eastern European woman with a solid helmet of hair pulled back into a bun that looked like a steel soap pad, dutifully took her vitals and made her look at some flashing lights and asked her some simple questions, never really hiding her own skepticism. Mary couldn't blame her—how many privileged young hypochondriacs did this woman have to deal with every day?—but she became more and more uneasy at the thought that *nothing* was wrong with her; that she was being a princess, a crybaby, a little girl starved for attention and not getting it and feeling sick because of it.

Or maybe there's something really *wrong with me*, she'd thought as the nurse rose briskly to her feet and impatiently waved Mary away. *Maybe this is one of those brain tumors or ski accident things where nobody notices anything wrong until it's too late.* She even had tried to ask the nurse about that, but the woman just shook her head impatiently, ordered Mary to go back to class and turned to the sophomore football player (Kip something) with the sprained knee who was waiting his turn.

The wind was picking up, out in front of the school, an hour later. The sky had not cleared. Mary drew her trench coat more tightly around her and continued staring at the grooves in the dirty sidewalk, realizing she'd memorized them. She knew she should go home. She'd long since given up on getting a "Happy birthday"—that was the impossible dream—but she'd settle for a simple "Hey, Mary" from somebody she knew, or even somebody she didn't.

Oh, who are you kidding? Go home. Nobody cares; not Patrick, not anyone else. How much clearer can they make it? All she was doing was making it worse for herself. She could just go home and take a bath and go to bed and sleep late tomorrow morning and watch Saturday cartoons and then maybe throw herself off the Brooklyn Bridge. The only reason she was staying at Chadwick—the only reason she hadn't left, after cutting all her classes—was because home meant her own dismal little room and Mom calling out for her cigarettes and blended orange juice. Maybe watching some MTV or even soaps on the damn Daewoo television, which sucked . . . and that was just too pathetic a way to spend her seventeenth birthday. She drew the line at sitting at home watching television—she would rather stand here leaning against this metal gate and be ignored and wait for—

"Hey."

A male voice—one she didn't know—coming from right in front of her. She could see a pair of scuffed Puma running shoes and the cuffs of some worn-out jeans without moving her eyes. *Somebody telling me to move,* Mary thought dully. *I'm in somebody's way, again. Somebody has to unlock their bike or something.*

"Mary? Hey. You all right?"

I won't look up, Mary thought. *It's not worth it. I don't even know who's talking to me, and I don't care. I refuse to find out.*

The Pumas didn't move. Whoever this person was, he wasn't going anywhere.

"I'm fine," she said.

"You sure?" Mary realized that she had been wrong: there *was* something familiar about the voice. "You don't look fine."

Slowly Mary raised her head.

It was Dylan. Ellen's friend Dylan, from the roof.

"Are you looking for Ellen?"

Dylan shook his head, brushing his hair back from his forehead and giving her a clear look at his face—which wasn't bad, surprisingly. She hadn't seen what he looked like up close: it was the effect of his olive complexion, his thick stubble, and his messed-up hair. He looked like an Indie Rock version of one of those French poets on the covers of Ellen's old books.

"No, I'm not looking for Ellen. I'm actually looking for you."

What?

Mary pushed herself away from the gate and stood upright, bringing herself closer to Scruffy Dylan, who, apparently, was looking for her. At this point in the day, she figured she was ready for whatever dismal surprises were still to come. *After a birthday like this, what else could go wrong?* She didn't know, but she had a hunch she was about to find out.

"Why are you—why are you looking for me?"

"Yeah . . . well . . ." Dylan rocked on his feet, staring down at the ground, his hands jammed in his jeans pockets. As she waited he took a deep breath, then slowly exhaled. "Okay, no more beating around the bush. It's like this: how'd you like to have dinner with me tonight?"

Mary had thought she'd had some idea what to expect— but she had *not* been prepared for this. She was so startled, so surprised, that she couldn't speak; she just stared at him, waiting while he slowly raised his eyes to meet hers.

"Okay, bad idea," Dylan said quickly. "Bad—bad idea; I get it. Never mind; forget I asked. It was stupid of me to—"

"No, wait," Mary said, shaking her head. "Wait, I'm just surprised, that's all. You want . . . you're asking me out to dinner?"

"Yeah." Dylan nodded calmly. "I'm asking you out to dinner. I thought"—he paused, looking at her, tilting his head while he fumbled for words—"you're obviously having a bad day and I've been wanting to ask you out, so here I am." He smiled in a way that seemed to say, *My fate is in your hands.* "Don't be too mean—before you cut me down to size, let me just, um, diffidently point out that it takes a little bit of courage to do this."

"But—" Mary was at sea. "You mean tonight? This evening? You want to go to dinner tonight."

"That's right. Do you have other plans?"

He's got to be kidding, Mary thought. *Right? This is a joke.*

But she could see that he wasn't kidding. It was obvious, looking at his face.

"No," she said finally. "I guess I don't. Have any other plans, I mean."

"Okay." Dylan nodded. His eyes were uncommonly green, she noticed. "Look, please—go ahead and shoot me down quickly, because the longer that takes, the less pleasant it will be."

"But you don't even know me."

"Not entirely accurate," Dylan said. "Ellen never shuts up about you, and she's, like, my sister."

"Which makes us related," Mary told him, smiling. Behind her, the school doors had begun banging open more often as the school day came to a close. "I'm not sure that's—"

"Right, right; forget I said that." Dylan shook his head and his hair flipped back and forth across his deep-set eyes. "She's not my sister and neither are you; we're not related and I don't know you. So will you go out with me?"

She knew how to deal with these situations, of course. She *had* to. Mary Shayne was a brilliant rejectrix—a master of the graceful exit strategy. She had a whole arsenal of prepared rejections for everyone: budding filmmakers, men over thirty, stunt-jumping skater teens, drunken hipsters who smelled like Belgian beer. She even had one for the rich freaks on the Upper East Side in their blue blazers and white turtlenecks and professionally shortened jeans.

"Look, Dylan, I—"

He got the message that fast. "Okay," he interrupted, sighing heavily. "Okay, that's— At least I tried."

Dylan turned to begin walking away, and when he did, Mary had an unobstructed view across Eighty-second Street.

She had no idea how long Patrick had been sitting on

the brownstone's steps. She'd been staring at the ground so long, feeling sorry for herself and posing like a pity magnet, that she must have missed him. But there he was, forearms on knees, smoking a Dunhill and watching her.

Watching *them*.

As fast as she could, Mary flicked her gaze away, desperately hoping that Trick hadn't seen her looking at him. It was impossible to tell—he was too far away. She fixed her eyes on Dylan's face and forced herself not to sneak any more glances at Patrick.

Six hours, Trick. It only took me six hours to move on.

"Yes."

It took Dylan a moment to react; it was like she'd said something so incomprehensible that he was struggling to interpret it. "Wait—really?" he blurted out, and his grin was so natural, so unmannered, that it lit up his face like a little boy's. " 'Yes' like 'yes'? Like you really want to do it?"

Why not? After a day like this, damn it, why not?

Mary smiled. "Yes," she said.

"Wow." Dylan was visibly flustered; he tried to disentangle his jacket from his messenger bag and nearly dropped them both. "Wow. That's—that's just great."

Mary smiled—a full-power, hundred-watt Mary Shayne smile. It had the predictable effect. Dylan was clearly forgetting to breathe.

"What time?" She had to ask it twice. "Dylan? What time?"

"What? Oh—any time. How about eight, at, um, Aquagrill? You know where I mean? On Spring Street, next to—"

"I know where you mean," Mary said warmly. "That's perfect. Aquagrill at eight; I'll meet you there."

"All right," Dylan said, looking dazed. "All right."

Watch this, Patrick, she thought, leaning forward to give Dylan a quick kiss on the cheek, letting her hand linger on his shoulder. *Did you like that? There's more to come.*

3

6:52 P.M.

"NOW, SEE," AMY SAID, pointing at Mary with the well-manicured pinky finger of her wineglass-holding hand, "*that's* what it's supposed to look like!" Her voice was a little too loud and her pale, freckled face had become flushed—it was her second glass of wine, or maybe her third. "What do you think, Joonie?"

"Yeah," Joon said flatly. She was on Mary's other side, straddling a turned-around designer chair, her chin on her smooth forearms, absently twirling her own balloon-like wineglass. She was dressed in a white tank top and designer running pants. "Cool."

Mary was standing in Amy's dressing room—not her bedroom, but her dressing room, a completely separate room, as Mary always marveled—wearing a gorgeous green bustier dress, her feet bare. Her wineglass was on the smoothly polished floorboards next to the mattress-size mirror she was facing. Jason Mraz was blasting from about sixteen speakers downstairs—they'd left the system running when they'd finally stopped wasting time and come up here to get to the business of the hour: preparing Mary for her date.

What a day, Mary marveled, bewildered. *It started in a furniture store—and it went downhill from there.* It was definitely not like any birthday she'd ever had—it was like the *opposite* of a birthday. Now she wanted to put the whole thing out of her head—just drink some wine and dress up and go on a date and forget about Chadwick and Patrick and Mr. Shama's physics test and the nurse's tongue depressor and the awful, disoriented feeling she'd had since she woke up.

Incredibly, her two best friends—flanking her right now—had not said *a word* about her birthday. She had decided not to say anything either, preferring to wait for one of them to remember. It had started out as a test, a game—a way to deal with her hurt feelings—and had progressed through stages of incredulity and astonishment until finally she'd just given up. *They forgot, that's all,* she thought, still not quite believing it. *They forgot, and you can't draw attention to it without sounding like a pouty bitch, so just let it go.*

"'Yeah'? 'Cool'? That's all you've got to say?" Amy was incredulous. "It's *awesome*. *Look* at her!"

Staring at herself in the mirror, feeling the warm effects of the red wine, Mary had to agree. She remembered the first time Amy had shown her the Nina Ricci bustier dress. She'd been afraid to even touch it. She never told Amy, but she had actually checked online to see what it cost, and when she saw the $2,300 price tag, she literally ran away from her laptop.

"That's what it looked like in the store," Amy continued, unperturbed. "That is so *not* what it looked like on me. Thank God I gave it to you. Come on, Joonie, you've *got* to agree with me."

The dress was so simple, and so elegant—nothing but gorgeous dark green silk with ruched paneling and an impeccably tailored bustier top. It fit every contour of her body just the way she liked; it also showed plenty of leg, highlighted her clavicles and smooth shoulders and revealed just the right amount of back.

"I agree, I agree," Joon said wearily. "This is all taking so long. Let's get to the makeup, shall we?"

Amy Tovah Twersky was known to many as the Sturgeon Princess of Fifth Avenue. Of course, she loathed her title (bestowed upon her by a bitchy Chadwick girl on Facebook), but she did have to admit that her family had been providing high-quality sturgeon to the greater New York area for nearly a hundred years. They had grown into a gourmet food dynasty, second only to Zabar's in the city's heated Smoked Salmon Wars. As Amy often explained to Mary, the Twerskys had been feeding people for a century, and that was where she'd gotten her insane generosity.

But Amy's compulsive giving extended way past the mere provision of foodstuffs. Mary couldn't even count the number of times she had crashed at Amy's Seventy-first Street town house, where they would disappear to the third-floor library and indulge in their guilty pleasure: late-night Wii golf on the sixty-five-inch plasma. Amy would bring up Bellinis, beluga, and toast points from the industrial-size kitchen for a two A.M. snack. She was simply generous to a fault. Nearly two-thirds of Mary's designer outfits were gifts from Amy—handpicked from her shopping surplus and expertly tailored by her crack team of seamstresses to fit Mary's petite frame.

"I love it," Mary said conclusively. She turned left and right, admiring the view. She was feeling a nice buzz from the wine she'd already drunk, and the more she drank, the less she had to think about her Day from Hell and the lack of birthday wishes (or birthday presents, or birthday *anything*). "I love it, Amy—totally. I think we have a winner."

"About time." Joon yawned. "Seriously, Mary, it's divine. Now can we advance to the next level, already?"

"Meaning more wine, of course," Amy said, glaring comically at Joon. "Here—open this." Amy picked up the second bottle she'd brought upstairs from the wine cellar and tossed it to Joon, who caught it easily, diving toward the floor to snag the corkscrew with her other hand.

Joon Park, Patrick's ex—*Patrick's* other *ex*, Mary thought, still getting used to it—had inherited those perfect reflexes from her golf-obsessed father, along with glowing skin and a Mercedes Roadster convertible and a $2.3 million, tax-exempt trust fund (her dad was some kind of partner or something at the Bank of Korea). From her mother (also a Korean banker) she'd inherited perfectly straight hair, cute little puckered lips, a tiny nose and a lust for couture—not to mention the perfect body to wear it.

"Be careful," Amy yelled, laughing. "That's, like, a ten-year-old bottle of Romanée-Conti. Special occasions only. I think it cost like a thousand dollars or something."

"Ain't gonna drop it," Joon muttered, getting busy with the corkscrew, her white-socked feet tapping to the music. "Shayne! It's refill time—looks like you're ready."

"Cleanse your palette first," Amy warned.

"Fuck that," Joon said, reaching with her long, sinewy arms to pour the most expensive glass of wine Mary had ever held in her life. She poured in the proper Korean fashion, as usual, stiffly holding her left hand beneath her right elbow. "Here, Mary—*l'chaim.*"

"*I'm* supposed to say that," Amy complained.

I could spill all the wine on the dress, Mary thought dazedly. *How much money would I be wasting if I did that?*

But the wine was exactly what she needed. When Amy had found her at the Chadwick gate an hour before, as the sky was darkening and the last of the students were scattering, and Mary had reported that Dylan had asked her out, *tonight*, Amy was astonished. She quickly added that it was

the best thing ever—a fantastic way to get back at Trick—
and had insisted that Mary come over to get ready for the
date. Mary agreed immediately, not just because Amy had
included Joon but because she really, really wanted to have
a glass of wine beforehand.

I'm having the worst birthday ever, she thought, *and I cut
all my classes and my boyfriend dumped me and I just don't care
anymore.*

Mary could never decide what she envied most about
the Twerskys' town house. Some days it was the stately limestone facade, with its early twentieth-century balconies and
polished brass trim. Some days it was the expansive foyer,
with its white and gray marble floor. She loved the way the
setting sun poured in through the domed copper skylight,
casting its webbed, ethereal glow down all five flights of the
spiral staircase.

Some days it was those rare moments of Manhattan
serenity in the courtyard's bamboo garden, or the feeling of
pure love emanating from the professional kitchen in the
basement stacked to the gills with aromatic Italian coffees,
teas from East Asia, and every conceivable kind of cookie,
from Oreos to the finest hazelnut biscotti. Obviously, she
loved the plasma TV in the library—the Hall of Wii Golf
Champions—and she salivated over Amy's four-poster bed
and wood-burning fireplace on the fourth floor, not to mention Mrs. Twersky's Roy Lichtenstein prints, which surrounded the cylindrical second-floor hall.

But once the sun set, without question the most envi-
able feature of the 1903 town house was its well-stocked

wine cellar. Isaac Twersky had excavated the basement in 1968 to reclaim the original wine grotto and make room for his vast collection—and when it came to wine, his legendary generosity didn't waver.

"Does it taste expensive?" Joon asked, smiling nastily. "But then, you wouldn't know, would you, Mary?"

"Hey! Leave my best friend alone, Joonie," Amy scolded, taking Mary by the wrists and leading her toward the makeup table. "Sit down, Mary—let's get to work."

"Yeah, it's getting late," Mary noticed. "Can we get things *moving*?"

"She doesn't want to keep the Mystery Man waiting," Joon said, refilling Amy's glass. "Who *is* this guy, anyway? I've never heard of him."

"Ellen's friend," Amy told her, pulling open drawers and scattering mascara tubes and compacts across the surface of the makeup table. "You never listen to what she tells you."

"Oh, whatever with the 'protect delicate little Mary' routine," Joon complained, finally sipping the thousand-dollar wine herself. "Anyway, she may be *your* best friend, but *I'm* Mary's best friend. This is good."

"You are not!" Amy was appalled. "Mary, I'm your best friend, like, since forever, aren't I? It's in writing!"

"That's true," Mary allowed. She was riffling through the lipsticks, trying to find something she liked. "But Joon's my *other* best friend. You're *both* my best friend."

Even though neither of you remembered my birthday.

"That's ridiculous," Joon scoffed. She had put down the

85

glass and come over to help pick through the lipsticks. "We can't *both* be your best friend; it doesn't make any sense."

"Too bad," Mary said, sipping some more of the wine. She tried to appreciate the thousand dollars' worth of taste, and for a moment, as the rich, dry aroma filled her nostrils and the smooth wine slid down her throat like velvet, she imagined that she actually could. "Because that's the truth."

"Suppose you *had* to choose?" Joon wanted to know. "If you could only save one of us from, like, a burning building, which one would it be?"

The Mraz had ended downstairs and something else had come on—whatever Amy's genius playlist had selected for them. Mary thought she recognized the Decemberists. "I'm not going to go near that one," she said, beginning to brush her hair away from her face in preparation for making herself up. "What kind of question is that?"

That's really what I want to think about right now—burning buildings.

What's come over them? Why is everything so damn weird today?

"It's a *good* question! Here, let me," Amy said, leaning in to push Mary's hands away and start applying mascara herself. "Which one would you save? Bearing in mind, of course, that I'm *actually* your best friend."

How am I supposed to answer?

Mary had no idea. Up close, she could smell the wine on Amy's breath, and realized that her own breath probably smelled the same. She made a mental note to brush her teeth before she left to meet Dylan.

"She'd save me," Joon said, "because she'd be standing

there overwhelmed with indecision and then I'd be all, 'Save *me*, bitch,' and she'd do it."

"What*ever*," Amy countered scornfully. "You know as well as I do she'd make straight for me."

"Can we *not?*" Mary said. Her speech was hampered by the fact that Amy was using a powder on her face. "It's a stupid question! You're *both* my best friend, okay?"

Joon was pouring herself another glass. The wine's price tag obviously didn't faze her. "One of us," she said, "is *actually* your best friend. It's just not always the same person. It depends."

Depends on what? Mary was getting irritated. *What kind of conversation is this, anyway? Can't I just get drunk and have a rebound date and then go home and cry myself to sleep like a normal birthday girl?*

"Look at *that*," Amy said, delicately grasping Mary's chin and turning her face so that she could see herself in the magnifying mirror. "What do you think, Mary-fairy?"

"Good," Mary said. The moment she'd spoken, she knew it wasn't enough—Amy's need for compliments was insatiable. "I mean, *really* good, Amy—great job."

"I don't know what it would be like to be that pretty," Amy remarked.

"Oh, get *over* it," Joon said disgustedly, rising from her chair and reaching for the bottle yet again. "Here, Mary— let's finish this, and then you'd better get going."

"Here's to best friends," Mary said, raising her glass. "And to *not* dating Patrick Dawes."

"Amen, amen, amen," Joon said, laughing. "Oh, *hells* yes—I'll drink to that."

THE RESTAURANT STARTED FILLING up just after they were seated. Dylan faced her across a small table with an avocado-colored cloth and a candle in a glass globe with a fishnet around it. Dylan had ordered a Dewar's, neat, which, she had to admit, impressed her a little bit just because it was so simple—an adult drink, really. Her vodka martini looked enormous by contrast, like a top-heavy glass monument. She was tipsy enough that she was afraid to touch it the first time, afraid she'd spill it. The dining room was elegant, and loud.

"You look very pretty," Dylan told her. "But then, you don't need me to tell you that."

"What do you mean?" Mary was afraid she'd slurred, but she was pretty sure she'd gotten the words out all right. Dylan had changed into a charcoal-gray suit, which he wore with another white oxford—ironed this time—and no tie. It wasn't a bad look for him, she conceded. His hair, on the other hand, was awful; he'd clearly taken the Scruffy Dylan remarks to heart and had tried to tame it with gel, or just with water. At least she could see his face clearly now. High cheekbones and a strong nose and jaw. He had shaved; that made a difference too. "What do you mean, 'You don't need me to tell you that'?"

"I mean," Dylan said, leaning forward, toying with his glass of scotch, "that you're fully aware of how pretty you are."

"Oh, hardly," Mary muttered, shaking her head.

Dylan's eyes widened.

"What? What's wrong?" Mary was afraid she'd slurred her words. Why was she so nervous? *He* was the one who was supposed to be nervous.

"You can't be serious," Dylan objected. "Half the people in this restaurant are looking at you like you're either famous or you're about to be. I bet it took you two minutes to get ready for this date."

"Not exactly." She recalled the two hours she'd spent with Joon and Amy, meticulously creating tonight's Mary Shayne from the ground up. "Don't let your eyes fool you."

"On the subject of beauty, I trust my eyes."

Mary had nothing to say to that. Dylan had stumped her, that fast—she hadn't even seen it coming. It was like he'd anticipated the whole game of complimenting a girl's looks and decided to skip it, to just get past it. *I'm supposed to object,* she thought. *To argue the point; to get him to compliment me some more.*

Or was it that she *needed* him to compliment her?

"If you spent more than two minutes," Dylan went on, "then I wonder about your priorities or your sanity. I mean, wouldn't you rather move on to more interesting topics? I'll bet you get tired of everything being about how you look."

Leaning forward, she moved her lips to the enormous martini glass, trying to take the first precarious sip without spilling the drink or making an audible slurping noise. The vodka was smooth and fiery; the lime peel was barely there, like a gossamer wisp of citrus against a sky of pure, clean alcohol. On top of all the wine she'd drunk at Amy's, it hit her like a hammer.

"Well—well, yes and no."

But I'm lying.

"Yes." She changed her answer. "Yes, I'm tired of it. *Really* tired of it."

Her head wasn't exactly spinning, but she noticed that she was speaking carefully, making sure not to slur her words. *It's been the same thing all day,* she thought resignedly. *It's that same mystery hangover from last night—it never went away. It just laid low. But now it's back.*

"Is the drink all right?" Dylan seemed concerned. "Do you want something else?"

"No, the drink is—the drink's fine," Mary said quickly.

What's the matter with me? I've done this before.

This wasn't even close to being Mary's first date, or her first martini, or her first conversation. But, somehow, sitting at Aquagrill facing Dylan Summer, the boy who, before today, she'd never spoken one word to, it was like the first time for all those things. She wasn't sure why—and the tipsiness wasn't helping—but she felt like she had lost whatever conversational skills she'd ever had to begin with.

He's not a kid, Mary realized. *That's what's different.*

Which was ridiculous, because he *was* a kid; he couldn't be more than a year older than she was, if that. Nevertheless, he seemed . . . older. He'd found a way out. He wasn't *trapped* in his life, like she was. It wasn't just that he'd already had his high school graduation and had turned himself into one of the intense intellectuals she saw on the rare occasions when she walked north of 100th Street up in

Morningside Heights. *He got out,* she thought. *He found a way out of the trap.*

Mary wasn't sure what she meant by that.

"You're right," she said suddenly, pointing at Dylan (and *just* missing knocking over her drink, which would have been very bad). "You're, like, *exactly* right. It's *not interesting.*"

" 'The true mystery of the world,' " Dylan said, " 'is the visible, not the invisible.' "

"What?"

"Nothing; it's Oscar Wilde." Dylan looked embarrassed. "Sorry. I told myself I wouldn't start pulling out quotations. That I wouldn't ask what's going on between you and Ellen. But I guess I just did. Sorry."

"No, that's okay," Mary said, taking another sip of her martini—the level had gone down enough that her panicked fear of spilling vodka and vermouth all over herself was abating. "It's nothing. Mom's got this thing—you heard us talking on the roof, right?—she's got this thing about our dad. He died, like, ten years ago, and she never really got over it. She always brings up the day he died, which I guess was traumatic or something."

"Well, that's understandable, isn't it?"

"Yeah, but"—Mary took another sip of her martini— "she wants *me* to talk about it, and, you know, I'd love to oblige her, but I just don't remember it."

"Sometimes people block out difficult memories so they can't—"

Mary shook her head firmly. "I don't remember it. I was

seven years old and it's just a total blank. I don't have a good memory *anyway*, you know, but Mom just won't accept that. She thinks I'm doing it on purpose. And Ellen takes her side. Always reminds me that she was *six* and hasn't forgotten." Mary finished, swallowing the fiery vodka and shaking her head. "That's it. End of family drama."

She was seeing the house in the field again, just like that—the restaurant and Dylan and the big martini glass and the avocado-colored tablecloth and the piped-in piano jazz were gone. Her feet were freezing in the deep snow and the house was facing her like a black wedge, its eaves sharp like a knife's edge against the deep indigo sky. A forest was nearby, bare winter trees whose branches clutched at the sky like skeletal hands. The wind howled and screamed and the snow fell and the hole was open now, the deep, collapsing hole in the snow, like a drain, like a doorway to the underworld, from which that unearthly moan wafted toward her through the wind, and the black hands reached out toward her, fingers groping like skeletal tree branches stripped bare by the frost.

And then it changed. For the first time all day, the vision (or whatever it was) changed and Mary felt the cold air engulf her like arctic ice as she cowered in the snow, surrounded by nothing but moonlight and barren winter, heart nearly stopping in terror because she wasn't alone. A giant figure, limned by moonlight, loomed over her, leaning down like a toppling granite statue—reaching for her.

Mary tried to pull away, tried to run, but she couldn't move. The huge man-shaped silhouette drew closer, its arm reaching forward, and she realized that its extended hand was holding something toward her—a thin rectangle that glowed in the moonlight. A piece of paper—a note. There was writing on the note, which Mary couldn't read in the dark, but it was like all the forces of the universe converged on that single page.

"Mary?" Dylan was looking at her, frowning in concern. "I'm sorry; I didn't mean to—I didn't mean to offend you."

Just like that, it was gone.

Something wrong with my brain, she'd told the Chadwick nurse.

(*Nothing* happened—*you met some people and killed some brain cells.*)

"What? No—you didn't offend me at all. I'm sorry you had to see—" Just then her BlackBerry rang, its warbled chime muffled by her purse. "Just a second," she told Dylan, raising a finger. She reached into her bag and extracted the phone, looking at its display.

DAWES, PATRICK

"Oh, give me a break." Mary sighed heavily. The number was Trick's cell phone; no way to tell where he was or what he was doing.

Don't answer it, Mary thought. *Don't even think about it.*

But she had to—that was the thing. She had to because she was on a date; he was interrupting her date and she just couldn't pass up the opportunity to tell Trick that she was out with a college boy, and so sorry, Trick, whatever you want, it will have to wait.

"I'm sorry," Mary told Dylan. "Do you mind? This will just take a second."

Dylan was sipping his scotch. He seemed totally uncon-cerned. He raised his eyebrows, swallowed. "No, that's fine. Go right ahead."

The BlackBerry was making another of its incredibly loud rumbling chimes as she hit the Talk button and lifted it to her ear.

"Hello?"

"Come get your stuff."

Whatever semblance of a good mood Mary had been in collapsed like a house of cards. *You've got to be kidding*, she thought. *Trick, you asshole, you* know *you're interrupting my date, don't you?*

And behind that, another, infinitely sadder thought: *It's over. It's really over.*

"Patrick, this really isn't a good time," Mary said quietly. Dylan didn't seem to be listening; he'd taken another sip of scotch and was leaning back in his chair, gazing serenely across the restaurant. "I'm actually in the middle of someth—"

"Come get your stuff," Patrick repeated. "Right now, or I'm throwing it in the street."

"Are you serious?" Mary couldn't believe her ears. The half-drunk martini was swimming inside of her, and for a moment she was afraid she was about to vomit it back up. "Right now?"

"*Right* now," Patrick confirmed.

And hung up.

Well, how about that, Mary thought dully. *A perfect end to a perfect day.*

So what do I do?

But she knew the answer to that. She had to go up there.

She knew Trick well enough to know he wasn't kidding. If he said he'd throw her stuff in the street, he meant it.

"Dylan," Mary said, "listen. This is really awful. But I've—I've got to go."

"What?" Dylan looked surprised, and maybe irritated—but only for a moment. Then he just looked concerned. "Is everything all right?"

"Oh—" Mary waved a hand dismissively. "Yeah. Everything's *fine*. It's—it's my ex. He's, like, throwing a little emo tantrum, I guess. I have to go get my stuff. He wants me to do it now."

"Get your stuff—I don't understand. You *live* with this guy?"

"No, I just"—she stammered awkwardly—"I've left a lot of stuff at his—his hotel suite. He lives in a hotel suite."

"Nice work if you can get it," Dylan remarked. He was folding his napkin and gesturing for a waiter. "Look, let me come with you."

"Oh, that's not necessary," Mary said.

And it could be a really bad idea.

But then, she realized, it could be a *good* idea, too.

She was gazing across the table at Dylan, at his suit and manner and freshly shaved face, imagining how he'd look to Patrick's jealous eyes. *Maybe I've got that wrong; maybe it's a really good idea.*

"I'm really sorry," Mary said. "Like, I'm *really* sorry, Dylan. If I'd known he was going to—"

Dylan shook his head. "You're sorry; I get it. Finish your drink and let's get out of here. We'll get dinner somewhere else."

"With all my stuff," Mary added, smiling and reaching for her glass.

"Sure." Dylan smiled. "We can find a place that's BYOL—bring your own laundry."

"Well—come on," Mary said, slurring. "Let's get this over with."

AS DYLAN STOOD PATIENTLY beside her in the hotel elevator, Mary noticed that he didn't seem to mind what was going on. He didn't seem to have much of an opinion about it at all beyond mild bemusement.

When they'd arrived in front of the Peninsula on Fifth Avenue, he'd insisted on paying for the cab. Ordinarily, she would have taken things like that for granted—of *course* the boy pays for the cab—but for some reason it seemed different when Dylan did it, like he was going out of his way to do something nice rather than just performing his accepted role. She had thanked him, making lingering eye contact to emphasize that she meant it, but he'd just smiled that absent smile and shaken his head, wordlessly dismissing his own chivalry as the cab sped away.

A few moments later, as Mary led them beneath the billowing flags and between the entryway's massive, over-carved columns, guided by three months' worth of habit, Dylan continued to be unmoved by his surroundings, sparing the gilded, ornate lobby a curious glance, and not commenting. It was so different from Patrick's behavior—from the way *all* the boys that she knew acted—that she was disoriented and didn't know how to react. Dylan wasn't behaving in a disaffected way. He wasn't "behaving" any way at all. Right now, standing next to her in the elevator, hands in his trouser pockets, his hair resuming its natural crazy shape after his misguided attempts to comb it, he seemed so calm and centered that he was actually calming *her* down. She caught herself glancing at his profile, his strong nose and chin, wondering how he could be so serene.

It really was new to her.

The elevator chimed and the gold door slid open. Mary led Dylan onto the bloodred carpeting of the seventeenth-floor corridor, her throat and chest tightening again. *This is the last time I'll be here*, she thought. *The last time ever—I'll walk out with garbage bags full of clothes, with the concierges watching me like I'm a homeless wastrel being ejected from the premises, and then I'll never come back.*

"This way," she told Dylan, pointing down the dim corridor at Patrick's suite. She took a deep, shaky breath—*Let's get this over with*—and strode purposefully forward, toward whatever ugly confrontation awaited.

And then she stopped, so quickly that Dylan nearly ran into her. "Look," she said, turning to face him. "Look, I told you before, you don't have to do this; you don't have to come."

"You're right," Dylan said agreeably. "You told me before."

"But—"

"If I didn't want to be here, I wouldn't have come."

Mary looked at him, trying to find any sarcasm or snark on his face that would betray his easy tone. But his eyes were clear. There was something profound about that, Mary thought. He made it sound so simple. How often could she say the same thing? How many times every week, every *day*, did she find herself somewhere she didn't want to be, doing something she hated? It was like Dylan had casually revealed some secret code, some magic spell that made him immune to all that.

"Don't worry," Dylan said, putting his hand awkwardly on her shoulder. "Everything's going to be fine."

That's not true, Mary thought automatically. *It's never true—and it's looking especially wrong today.*

"Come on." The heat of Dylan's hand on her shoulder made her nervous, somehow; she pulled away and continued down the wide corridor, heels sinking into the thick, expensive carpet with the green and gold threads.

This day is all wrong, she told herself again. *Everything's all wrong; it's like a waking dream, the kind where the whole world's against you.*

Mary raised her fist, hesitated before knocking.

How bad is this going to be?

Dylan reached past her and knocked boldly on the door, three times.

Silence. Nothing.

It's a trick, she thought wearily. *He's not going to—*

The locks snapped over loudly and the door swung open. Mary squinted in the sudden bright light. Patrick's vestibule—how many times had she stood here, opening the door for room service, fishing in Patrick's wallet for a tip?—was brilliantly lit as usual, the gleaming, ice-white walls reflecting the recessed quartz track lights and the tastefully shaded table lamps. Patrick stood with his hand on the gold doorknob, smirking at her. It was the same maddening smirk he'd worn the last time she'd been this close to him, when he'd dumped her.

Patrick's expression changed—slightly—as he looked past her at Dylan. Mary got some satisfaction from that. *Not everything goes the way you want it to*, she thought grimly. *I'm not as helpless without you as you think, Trick.*

But she didn't feel any better, because Patrick didn't look startled, or jealous, or anything that would *make* her feel better. He was smirking knowingly and nodding, as if to say, *You think I'm impressed? You think I care that you found another sucker to pick up where I left off, following you around and doing what you say?*

"Hi," Dylan said casually. "I'm Dylan."

"Patrick Dawes." Trick was stepping aside, making an exaggerated, sarcastic show of welcoming them. His tone implied that he couldn't care less who Dylan was—that it wasn't even worth his time to learn Dylan's name. "Come on—let's get this over with."

"Good idea," Mary agreed. It came out wrong—she had wanted to sound snide and bored, like she didn't care one way or the other, but, hearing her own voice, she realized she sounded like a scared little girl following orders.

I won't cry, Mary insisted to herself as she rushed past Trick into the suite's big living room (with the gold and green couches and the vast picture-window view of the Fifth Avenue lights. She didn't want Patrick to see her face. She

99

didn't want him to see what it was doing to her, being here again, looking around at the place she'd spent so many lazy afternoons and torrid nights and Sunday room-service brunches, realizing that it was all over, that she'd never see it again.

She was trying to figure out a way to brush the tears from her face without Patrick seeing her do it, when she got the biggest shock of the day—or, as she realized much later, the biggest shock *so far*. What happened next was so insane, so unexpected and so *loud* that she nearly screamed.

"*Surprise!*"

They had appeared with incredible speed—from behind the couches, from the kitchenette and the bedroom, even from the *closets*—all her friends and dozens more people; what looked like the entire Chadwick senior class, all dressed up in their sickest party outfits, all grinning at her madly. At that moment somebody triggered a playlist somewhere and Panic! at the Disco started blasting at top volume from Patrick's hidden Bose speakers while the entire crowd flocked toward her. *Surprise*—the word was still echoing in her ears like a thunderclap.

"*Happy birthday!*"

The scream was unanimous, deafening.

A *surprise party*, Mary thought incredulously. *You've got to be kidding—a fucking surprise party.* There was no way to describe the feeling that flowed over her; it was like she'd already pounded four Jägermeister shots.

"*Punk'd!*" Patrick yelled triumphantly, his eyes nearly mad with glee. "Oh, you are so *punk'd!*"

"Look at her little tears!" Joon was right in front of her, playfully wiping at Mary's face, sparkling from head to toe in a shiny zigzag headband, a crystal-covered Elie Saab minidress, and Christian Louboutin heels. "Oh, look at my tragic little Mary-fairy—"

"You *so* bought it," Patrick rasped in her ear, having grabbed her from behind and squeezed her with his powerful arms. He kissed her neck. "You thought I'd *dumped* you! You actually *bought* it—"

Mary was crying—sobbing with relief and shock. *Ruining the Shu Uemura mascara,* she thought randomly. *So what.*

"*Aww,*" Joon said, hugging her. "*Look* at her—look at our gullible little Mary. . . ."

"Someone needs a drink," Amy observed, materializing on Mary's other side and stroking her shoulder possessively. The crowd surrounded them, pressing in like paparazzi flanking a starlet.

"Happy birthday!" Pete Schocken said, leaning in to hug her. He had changed into a nice shirt and pants—it was strange to see him out of the gym clothes he was always wearing. His face was transformed by his warm smile.

Was he really *beating up Scott Sanders this morning?* Mary wondered, hugging Pete back. *Did that really happen? Did I dream it?*

If Scott had been at the party, she would have interrogated him again—but, of course, he wasn't there. Scott's evenings were a mystery that nobody particularly wanted to solve; he was probably off having his own brand of fun, seeing *Iron Man 2* in IMAX for the twentieth time or something.

"Mary, Mary, Mary," Joon said, placing her hands on both sides of Mary's face, staring into her eyes from up close. Mary could see the lamplight glinting in Joon's green eyes as she smiled a nasty smile. "Have a drink and chill. I *promise* you—it's going to be one crazy night."

4

9:12 P.M.

THE PULSE WAS ALL around her, vibrating under her feet, sending tremors through the pale white lamp shades and the black wooden picture frames on the white walls. Pounding drums and shredding guitar and voices upon voices upon yet more voices, a screaming soprano section chiming in over the pounding bass like a sky full of cackling seagulls, warning of a storm still too far off the coast to see.

Mary was slamming a Patrón Silver shot that Patrick had just handed her. Her eyes watered from the explosive force of the tequila. Patrick had his arm around her bare shoulders. The sensation was disorienting, even though it shouldn't have been. The room was packed, filled with Chadwick students and dozens of other people she didn't recognize. The deafening kick drum was pounding its way through a mashup of 50 Cent's "In Da Club" and the Bee Gees' "Stayin' Alive." At the edge of the big living room, a circle of well-coiffed older boys in V-necks and jeans and flip-flops stood at the doorway like a greeting committee gone wrong, barking out lyrics to each other and sharing long, meaningful man-hugs. She had never seen so many straight men hugging in her life—someone was already passing out the Ecstasy.

"So who's that *guy*, anyway?" Patrick grinned down at her. He pointed at Dylan, who was across the room at one of the bottle-covered side tables (*credenzas*, she corrected herself) pouring scotch into a plastic cup. Joon was next to Mary, dancing in place while gazing around regally, like a Korean Alicia Keys.

"Just a boy," Mary said. "A friend of Ellen's."

"A friend of Ellen's," Trick repeated, frowning.

"My *sister*—?"

"Right, right—duh." Patrick was barely listening; she noticed that he was scanning the crowd. "*Mase!*"

Mary flinched as Patrick bellowed, practically screaming in her ear. Following his gaze, she was dismayed to see Trick's ubiquitous dealer friend, Mason, a shirtless, gel-shellacked skeev whose last name Mary had never learned. Mason was gyrating on the makeshift dance floor, waving his huge steroid-enhanced biceps. His gangsta jeans barely clung to his white Calvin Klein briefs. Mason's face was frozen in a pursed-lips, intense squint as he danced, grinding up against a skinny little tweaker girl in a hoochie dress who was shaking her nonexistent junk like she was auditioning for *Flavor of Love*. He apparently hadn't heard Patrick's shout, which was fine with Mary.

"Patrick, don't—" Mary flinched, getting ready to hide from view.

"*Mason!* Get over here!" Patrick shouted, waving. "My *man*—"

Mason did a cartoonlike double take, peering around with his fists in the air before seeing Patrick (*His meal ticket,* Mary thought sourly) and beaming with exaggerated delight. "Mr. *Dawes*," he bellowed, immediately losing interest in the tweaker girl and propelling himself toward them. He was talking to Trick but staring at Mary the way he always did—the way a starving dog stares at a steak.

"Yum, yum," Joon said lasciviously, gazing at Mason's perfect torso, a black-and-white underwear billboard come to life. "Work it, Mase! That's what I'm talking about."

"Solid, man, solid," Mason intoned, arriving in a cloud of Axe body spray and loudly clasping hands with Patrick. "*This* is the shiznit!"

His eyes are dead, Mary noticed as Mason predictably sized her up, scanning her body up and down, before leaning in for a kiss. *He's got to be completely methed out.* The tweaker girl stood to one side, forgotten. "*There's* my girl—'sup, Mary? I got a birthday present if you want it."

"I'm not your girl," Mary said. It was incredible that Mason would hit on her with Trick's arm around her, but he

105

did it every time. She forced herself not to look at his pecs and washboard stomach as she stared back. "Touch me and I'll slap you."

"*Whoa!* I been *told*—" Mason recoiled comically. "'Sup, Joon?"

"Hello, darling," Joon murmured, accepting Mason's cheek kiss, brushing her fingers across his oversize upper arm. "Mmm—*that's* what a boy's shaped like."

"Mase, are you heavy?" Patrick was frowning—Mary noticed something protruding from the back of Mason's low-slung jeans. "That's not cool—"

"*Of course*, man—you want to see it?" Mason's eyes lit up like glossy cue balls. "Check this shit out, man—"

"*No*—Jesus, Mase—"

Before Patrick could stop him, Mason had reached back and pulled an automatic handgun from his pants. The gun gleamed in the amber lamplight as he held it out in his palm—Mary felt a cold wave of dread as she stared at its flawless brushed-satin finish. "Safety's on," Mason assured them as both girls gasped. "It's all good."

"Wow," Joon said, her eyes bulging as she stared. "Can I hold it?"

"You can hold my gun *anytime*," Mason agreed, handing the firearm to Joon. It sagged in her slim hand and she nearly dropped it. "You want to come shooting, baby? I'll totally take you down to the range—"

"This is so—*wow*," Joon murmured, awkwardly turning the gun around, her eyes wide. Mary was terrified—she could barely stop herself from dropping to the floor in a blind panic. "Check this out, Mary! It's so *heavy*, but it fits in your hand like—"

"*No guns!*" Patrick was looking around nervously, but the crowd was too thick for anyone to have seen. "Come on, man—*no guns!* Put it *away*, Mase!"

"No, no, no!" Mary insisted, but it was too late—before she knew what was happening Joon was pushing the gun into her palm. The black steel was like heavy ice against her fingers. "I don't *want* to hold it!"

"Chill, Dawes, chill. . . ." Mason smoothly retrieved the weapon, stuffing it back into his jeans. "I wouldn't have whipped it out, but you had to ask if I—"

"*Are you fucking crazy?*" Mary shouted in Mason's face. The feel of the gun lingered on her fingers. "Get the hell out of my party *right now,* you fucking—"

"You are *so* fine, Mary—*especially* when you get mad," Mason intoned, moving his pelvis toward her suggestively. Mary recoiled, disgusted. Mason did this every time—hit on her with all the nuance and subtlety of a dog humping a person's leg—and there didn't seem to be any way to stop him from doing it, more intensely each time.

"No, it's cool," Patrick said smoothly, taking Mary's empty shot glass and producing another, as if by magic. "He's cool; he's cool. Have another shot, Mary."

She did, and the warm fire of the smooth tequila flowed through her like spreading wings. Mason—adaptable as always—had turned his attention completely to Joon. He made exaggerated hip-hop gestures as he leaned to talk in her ear. Around them, the party seemed to be thickening.

Sweaty, tatted, shirtless white boys, their Sean John jeans hanging off their Hilfiger boxers, were grinding up against a mix of Eighth Street skanks and young Park Avenue fashionistas, as Philippe, the Peninsula bellboy, pushed a hand truck stocked with wine and champagne. Mary's blood pressure returned to normal as the smooth vibe of the party calmed her nerves. She was floating on a beautiful wave of bliss; the first good feeling she'd had since the day began. The feeling was intoxicating. It was hitting her at least as hard as the alcohol.

"Listen," Patrick said, "I hope that wasn't too lame, this morning."

"What do you mean, 'lame'?" Mary wrinkled her nose, looking up at him. Her eyes were watering from the force of the tequila shot. "It was *awful*. It was, like, *totally devastating*." She pouted. "You do a *mean* breakup, Trick!"

"Time to dance," Joon announced abruptly, curling her arm around Mason's bare abdomen and pulling him toward the gyrating couples behind her. "Come on, sexy—let's go find the groove."

"Should we come with you?" Mary asked. Mason made her nervous, no matter what Trick said.

"You stay with Captain Crack Pipe," Joon shouted back over the squeaking Bee Gees. "I'll come find you later."

"She'll be fine," Patrick said, wrapping his arms around her, kissing her forehead. "Don't worry—enjoy your party."

The feel of Patrick's body against hers was more comforting than she'd ever known it could be. *I've got him back—what a relief*, she admitted to herself. *My God, what a relief. Because that was no fun at all.*

It was strange to have all her conspiracy theories con-firmed, in such a *nice* way, but Mary wasn't complaining. It was *flattering*—all the trouble they'd gone to just to fool her—the warm sensation of being liked, being *needed*, flowed through her like a rising tide. That feeling had been missing all day, and she welcomed it back.

Everything makes sense now.

Patrick had taken his hands from her shoulders, snag-ging himself another shot from a tray and bumping fists with someone she didn't recognize. He put his arm around her waist—and his forearm brushed against the scratches on her lower back.

Except everything doesn't *make sense. And you know it.*

Mary pushed the thought away. *Stop that—just relax and have fun*, she told herself angrily. It was clear that something was missing—the pieces didn't all fit together—but she re-fused to think about it anymore. Instead, she gazed over at Joon, who had begun dancing with Mason.

I was being tactless, Mary realized as she watched her friend. *I shouldn't have said that about the 'totally devastating' breakup—that wasn't very nice.*

Because Joon had been on the receiving end of a Patrick Dawes "devastating" breakup—except it had been real.

As soon as I said that, she left. I should have kept my mouth shut.

It was an odd realization. The pounding bass was shak-ing her body like a leaf fluttering in a strong wind as she gazed through the crowd, trying to think clearly despite the cloud of alcohol in her brain.

I was being mean to Joon. Just now, without knowing it.

Who else am I being mean to?

There was an obvious answer to that. Mary disengaged from Patrick's possessive grip on her waist and began moving purposefully through the crowd.

She finally managed to propel herself across the room—everyone she passed stopped her to say happy birthday, some hugging, some kissing, some high-fiving—and came up behind Dylan, reaching for his wool-sheathed shoulder. He didn't seem to know anyone else at the party, and being the only guy in the room wearing a suit made him look even more out of place. He turned around, saw her and raised his drink.

"Hey," Dylan said, affably enough. "So, it turns out you're not single after all."

"Yeah," Mary said, nodding. "Awkward, huh? I'm sorry."

Dylan frowned as he shook his head. "It wasn't your fault. I don't mind."

"Really?"

"Sure." Dylan seemed profoundly unconcerned—but then, she thought, he could be faking it, just to be polite. "Look, if anyone's to blame, it's *me*. I should have realized it wasn't plausible that you'd been dumped." He looked embarrassed. "I mean—anyway, I called Ellen just now, and she couldn't figure out what I was *doing* here. When I explained that I'd asked you out, she was like, 'You idiot.' And she's right—I mean, if I'd taken a second and *checked with her* first, you know, I would have known better. She made me feel really stupid."

Mary felt ashamed, suddenly. She knew the booze was intensifying the feeling, but she couldn't help it. Her face was turning red—she could feel the flush through the tequila—and she turned away from Dylan, looking back across the crowd to where Mason and Joon were dancing. His enormous upper arms contrasted pleasantly with his narrow waist and ripped abdomen—Joon moved closer to him, leveling a regal glance his way. The girl who'd *been* dancing with Mason before—the one Joon had effortlessly brushed aside—was a few feet away, Mary saw; she was pretending to talk to a pair of girlfriends, but she looked upset.

"Happy birthday!"

A younger girl, yelling right in Mary's face: Ally Kleiger, a junior she barely knew. Ally's friend Chloe something (Chloe *Dennis*, she remembered) smiled nervously beside her. Both girls wore what looked like New Jersey prom dresses; the effect was all wrong, but, Mary thought, they'd have another year to get these things right. "We *love* you," Chloe yelled earnestly. "We totally love you."

"Even though you never call us back," Ally added. Everyone was yelling over the music.

"We don't mind!" Chloe said generously. Both juniors were completely plastered. "You don't *have* to call us back!"

"Listen, I'm going to go," Dylan interrupted. He put his cup down, a little too firmly, on the coffee table behind him. "Thanks for inviting me along."

" 'Thanks'?" Mary raised her eyebrows and poked Dylan in the lapel. Her movements were too broad, too overdramatic, but she couldn't help it. It was the tequila, on top of the martini and wine. "Come on—you *volunteered* to come with me and I told you *not* to." That hadn't come out right. "What I mean is, I didn't know I was inviting you to a party."

"Maybe you wouldn't have," Dylan said easily. He was gazing levelly across the party, and Mary realized that he was looking at Patrick. "All things considered."

"That's not what I meant either," Mary said.

"Well, I'm still going to take off."

"Stick around! Have another drink."

"Thanks anyway," Dylan said, beginning to turn away toward the door.

"We never had dinner," she blurted out. "Maybe we can have dinner another time."

"The next time your boyfriend pretends to break up with you? No, that's okay. Happy birthday, Mary."

"I'm sorry," she called out. The music was so loud that it wasn't clear if he'd heard her or not. "I'm really sorry."

"That's all right." Dylan smiled, leaning in so she could hear him. "I should have known better, that's all. I learned my lesson."

He waved and moved away and the crowd closed around him. Mary could just make out the back of his shaggy head as he got to the suite's wide front door and pulled it open against the tide of partiers. Then he was gone.

He learned his lesson, Mary thought, turning away and groping for a champagne glass. *He should have known better than to ask me out.*

A murmur went through the crowd right then—a gasp that spread like pond ripples—and Mary was nearly knocked over by the elbows and backs of the partiers behind her. Turning around, she saw a commotion at the center of the dancing crowd.

What the hell—?

"*What* was that, bitch?" a young man was yelling over the pounding music. Mary didn't recognize the voice—she pushed between bodies, trying to get closer. "*What* was that?"

"Back off, man," came the low, threatening reply. The voice was familiar. Mary could see clearly now; she'd gotten close enough to spot Mason, in the middle of a ring of dancers who'd stopped moving and turned to watch him face off against another skeevy boy—a tall, stoop-shouldered teenager in a Giants jersey and a backwards baseball cap. The kid's head was shaved, and he was so skinny that sinews and veins protruded from his smooth arms like wax dripping down the side of a candle. "Back off—you don't want to do this, man," Mason told him, the track lights gleaming off his sweat-oiled muscles.

"*Fight! Fight!*" Some of the football team at the back of the crowd began chanting. Joon was still dancing, apparently unconcerned, but the rest of the crowd had drawn back, making a clearing around the two combatants. Mary saw the faces of the other dancers, eyes widened in shock or surprise, but she couldn't see anything else. All around, people were talking, leaning to whisper in each other's ears, but there was no way to tell what had happened, how the confrontation had begun.

"You want to *go*, bitch?" The skinny kid lunged forward, shoving Mason in the shoulders. "You want to fucking mess with me?"

The crowd went *ahhh*—Mary could hear it clearly over

113

the music. Joon stopped dancing, stumbling backward as Mason and the kid in the baseball cap scuffled, and then there was a blur of motion and a tumbling, thumping noise.

Bang! A deafening blast filled the room; Mary felt her ears pop. It sounded like something had exploded, like one of Patrick's glass coffee tables (one of the *hotel's* glass coffee tables) had cracked and shattered. The crowd gasped again, pulling away like scattering pigeons from the gleaming black object on the carpeted floor. A girl screamed.

Mason's gun, Mary realized incredulously. *Oh my God, his gun went off—*

"*Break it up!*"

Trick's voice had lost all its languid cadences; suddenly he was right there, pushing the skinny kid backward as Mason stooped to retrieve his gun and Joon stood motionless, pinned in place with her hands pressed against her mouth. "You fucking asshole, you want to get me kicked out of here? *Both of you*"—Patrick's chiseled face was bright red; Mary had never seen him so angry—"*both of you* take it outside."

The crowd was pushing backward, everyone trying to get as far away from the fight and the weapon as they could. Five or six people tumbled into Mary and she nearly lost her balance. *I'm drunk,* she thought dazedly as she spun her arms, trying to stay upright. The kid in the baseball cap made for the suite's front door and the crowd cheered. Then Patrick was handing Mason a crumpled T-shirt (the one he arrived in, Mary assumed) and pushing him toward the door. "I can't have it, man," Trick was telling Mason, shaking his head; Mary could barely hear over the endlessly pounding

114

drumbeats, but the crowd seemed to be laughing again, like everything was all right. When she tried to locate Joon, she couldn't find her; she was wondering what to do about that when somebody pressed a fresh glass of champagne into her hand and she gratefully gulped it down.

MARY WASN'T SURE WHAT time it was—she didn't wear a watch—but it could have been at least an hour later. Nas was pummeling her eardrums. Jake Lebaux had spilled his Bud Light Lime all over the dining table—he'd brought half of the football team with him, and they were all high on God knows what, laughing hysterically as they dug their fingers into the ravaged remains of the Twersky-brand caviar and hummus. The party was overwhelmingly filled with people she didn't know.

Mary was at the edge of the room, standing by the big picture window, gazing through her own reflection at the darkness of the city and the wide vista of the gilded Fifth Avenue towers. A light rain was falling, the drops spattering the plate glass; she could barely hear the howling wind that battered the hotel's stone facade.

Amy was in Patrick's bedroom with a crowd of newcomers, and Trick was at the door, dealing with a bellboy who'd probably been sent there by the concierge to deliver noise complaints. Not that it mattered; Trick could pretty much do whatever he wanted at the Peninsula and get away with it. Nobody wanted to kill the golden goose—the enormous bills always got paid, and everyone got a big tip, and that was that.

"Mary-fairy." A familiar voice spoke in her ear, making

her jump. She turned and was completely delighted to see Ellen Shayne. Ellen looked adorable in a simple black dress—it made Mary realize how infrequently she saw her sister dressed up, or at a party or doing *anything* except reading in her room.

"*Ellie!*" Mary grabbed her sister in a bear hug, squeezing her happily. "Oh my God, Ellie, when did you *get* here? You missed all the excitement. I love you so much—"

"You're drunk!" Ellen laughed, returning the hug and then pulling away. "Wow. How many have you had? That's a gorgeous dress, by the way."

"I've had a few," Mary admitted. Her head was spinning, she realized, but just a bit—she could totally handle it. "But it's *true*—I totally love you."

"Okay, Drama Queen," Ellie said. "So, were you surprised?"

"Of *course* I was surprised, Ellie-belle!" Mary returned Ellen's mischievous smile. "You knew, didn't you? Were you, like, behind the whole thing?"

Mary's BlackBerry vibrated. She almost didn't feel it, but her purse was pressed against her hip by the radiator beneath the picture window—the radiator that was covered in empty glasses and sodden cocktail napkins and full ashtrays.

"Hang on," Mary told Ellen, snapping open her purse and pulling out the phone. "Somebody's calling—"

But it wasn't a phone call—it was a text. Mary realized her eyes were blurring with drunkenness as she leaned to peer at the tiny screen. The message was from Joon, and it read:

Mary stared at the digital characters. The music seemed to fade away.

"What is it?" Ellen frowned. "What's wrong?"

"Look," Mary said, turning the BlackBerry so Ellen could see it. "Oh my God, what—"

"She just sent this," Ellen said, checking her wristwatch against the time stamp on the text message. "Like, two minutes ago."

"When did she *leave?*" Mary complained. "How long ago? I can't remember—"

"Wait—is she kidding?" Ellen asked. "Is this some kind of a joke?"

"Of *course* not!" Mary held up the phone again, so its pale glow reflected on Ellen's makeup-free cheeks. "*Look at this*. Of course it's not a joke. Where *is* she?" Mary was looking around at the crowd, beginning to feel panic creeping over her. "Oh my God, she left with that fucking meth head—"

"All right, don't panic," Ellen said sternly, gripping Mary's arm. "Come on, let's find out."

Why did I let you go, Joon? Mary could feel a cold weight in her solar plexus as she remembered the track lights gleaming on the smooth surface of Mason's handgun. *I was standing right there—why did I let you leave with that creep?*

Ellen had her by the hand and was leading her through the crowd, toward the dancers in the middle of the room. Mary could see Patrick, off to one side, chugging beers with

117

Silly Billy and some of the other football players—she tried to attract his attention, waving with her free hand, while Ellen got Stephen Ambrosio's attention, standing on tiptoes to yell in his ear.

"Trick!" Mary yelled, waving her arm fruitlessly. "Trick! Get over here!"

"She left with a guy," Ellen screamed in Mary's ear, against the pounding of the music and Christina Aguilera's caterwauling. "Steve says they took off a while ago—some guy with no shirt; maybe you saw—"

"I know who you mean," Mary yelled back impatiently. She felt a sinking sensation, like she was trapped in a dropping elevator, as she stared around at the crowd—everyone was pressed in, like a rush-hour subway crowd that had suddenly decided to start dancing. "We've got to find the girl he was with—maybe she knows where they went. He was with this tweaked-out— *There!*"

Mary pointed, picking out the girl—the tweaker girl in the hoochie dress, Mary had mentally dubbed her—who was sharing a joint with two other skanky-looking girls. Mary pushed Darin Evigan (the obvious source of the weed) to one side and got close to the unfamiliar tweaker girl.

"*Happy birthday!*" Tweaker Girl sang out. Her voice was very high. Up close, Mary could see her nostril studs and the multiple piercings in her tiny ears.

"The guy you came with." Mary leaned in to scream to the girl, whose breath stank of scotch. "Mason, the ripped guy—do you know where he went?"

Right then the music changed, mercifully, segueing into a White Stripes ballad that they didn't have to scream over.

"Like, don't even mention that dirtball," Tweaker Girl sniped contemptuously. Around them, couples were falling against each other for slow dances while others abandoned the dance area, fleeing for more drinks.

"He told us he had a great party for us. And he was going to score some X, but he, like, totally ditched us for some Chinese bitch."

Mary ignored that. The wave of dread spreading over her was making her feel cold again. "Do you know where they went?"

"What's going on?" Patrick's voice, right behind her— Mary reached for his hand and squeezed. Patrick was peering at Tweaker Girl like he'd never seen her before. "What's the big deal? Who are you?"

"She wants to know where Mason took that girl," Tweaker Girl enunciated, as if Patrick was too stupid to follow the discussion. "He's got, like, a crib?" Tweaker Girl went on. "A real house—a place outside of the city."

Outside the city? Mary's despair kept growing.

"I know where it is," Patrick said, putting an arm around Mary's shoulder protectively. "You drive north, like, for twenty minutes, and it's easy to find. I was there one time."

Drive—? Mary didn't like the sound of that at all. "Trick, we've *got to go*," she yelled. "He's got Joon and she just texted for help. You said you know where it is, right? You've got to get your car out of the garage and— What?"

Patrick was shaking his head emphatically. "There's *no way* I'm leaving," he said firmly. "Are you fucking kidding? With all these people here? And I'm in *no* condition to drive. Neither are you."

"But—" Mary was wondering where her learner's permit was; she was reasonably sure it was back at home. "But what do we—"

"*Amy* can drive," Ellen said firmly, holding out her hand, palm up, toward Patrick. "She's sober—I just saw her. Hand over the keys."

Hurry up, Mary thought. *Hurry up—we've got to move. We've got to save her.*

"I'll give you directions," Patrick told Mary, fishing in his pocket for a thick, heavy key chain. "You'd better get a pen."

5

10:19 P.M.

MARY FIXED HER EYES on the murky view of the Saw Mill River Parkway shining in the bright headlights of Patrick's brand-new Mercedes-Benz SLK300—a "pre-graduation" present, Mary remembered. It was the first time she'd ridden in this admittedly very sexy roadster, with its gray and chrome flanks and its German steel-panther design, but right now she wished that Trick's parents had given him a *safe* car.

They were zipping forward as fast as Amy could drive, but the Friday-night leaving-the-city traffic was still fairly heavy and they kept getting caught behind a series of nearly identical gray SUVs ferrying families to the Berkshires. A light rain was falling, spattering the windshield, and Mary's seemingly permanent dull headache was magnified by the drone and thump of the miniature wipers and the low-pitched whine of the car's powerful engine.

"I can't believe I agreed to this," Amy repeated. "Why didn't we call the police? Why didn't we call the police, like, the *minute* that girl told—"

"Because *the room was full of drugs and booze,*" Mary told her doggedly for the second or maybe the third time. Amy's scatterbrained questions kept making Mary's stark terror even more unbearable. "Let somebody else deal with all that. Meanwhile, we're on our way there."

"Yeah, but—"

We already had the argument—please can we not?

"You can't go any faster?" Mary complained. The scrap of paper in her hand was suffering from being folded and re-folded—she had tried to force her hands to stay still and stop fidgeting, but it was impossible. Her nerves were firing like a sputtering cable in a manhole, the kind that makes Con Ed show up with hard hats and sirens and cordon off the entire street as an electrical hazard.

"I can't," Amy said regretfully. "Stop asking me that. You see the traffic."

"Sorry."

Mary could hear the fear in Amy's voice, and she realized that she must have sounded the same way. They were both frightened; that was no excuse to bother Amy. She *was* driving, after all—Mary was just a passenger in a borrowed dress.

"What's that number again?" Amy was leaning forward, peering through the rain that splashed against the clean, brand-new windshield. The dealer's stickers were still in the back window of the car; it was that new. "The turnoff? The exit?"

"Forty-nine," Mary repeated, staring at the directions again. "Almost there, I think."

Ahead of them, the darkened road seemed to narrow. The slow-as-molasses black Volvo SUV in front of them— the car that was causing all the trouble, since there were at least five cars stacked up behind them—flashed its turn signal and Mary rejoiced silently as another Manhattan family and their damn bicycle rack and Dartmouth bumper stickers exited. Now the road was clear, and Amy stamped on the gas—the engine roared like an amplified chain saw as they surged forward.

"What do you think *happened* to her?" Amy repeated. She'd asked the question five times already. Amy didn't deal well with stress. Mary had noticed this time and time again, watching her friend panic before math tests (she'd apparently never managed to corral Scott into helping her cram, the way Mary had). Amy's hands would shake and her voice would tremble and she would freeze up. Not the person you'd necessarily pick when you wanted help responding to a friend's distress call.

But she's got her license—and she's sober, Mary told herself. *And, anyway, we're all friends.*

Best friends.

"Exit forty-nine," Mary called out, pointing through the blurred windshield. "Right there, Amy!"

123

"I see it," Amy said, fumbling with the gearshift—the transmission grated and the car shook as her foot slipped on the clutch. *It's not her car*, Mary remembered in exasperation. *She's not familiar with it. I hope we don't crash into a tree.*

"Now, pay attention, because it's, like, *right* after the turnoff. We have to—"

"You told me," Amy snapped.

Even as frightened as Mary was, that startled her. Had Amy *ever* snapped at her? She didn't think so, not as long as they'd been friends. Amy had to be more frightened than Mary had ever seen before—and Mary had seen her so scared (like when they were caught shoplifting in eighth grade) that she'd been literally unable to move.

They were almost there. The car slowed, its engine moaning and humming like a powerboat motor as Amy got them off the Parkway, following the scrawled instructions. Mary almost reminded Amy of the directions and then firmly clamped her mouth shut. Amy was nervous enough.

There was no sign of life or activity anywhere. Twenty-five minutes north of the city, they might as well have been in the middle of an Appalachian forest. The road was as flat and glossy as a satin ribbon, and flanked by trees that flowed past the car like the black ink that a deep-sea squid sprays into the icy ocean water right before it comes after you and kills you. The sky was invisible; the rain had picked up. The Mercedes' weak headlights were the only illumination for miles in every direction.

HELP HELP COME HELP ME, the text had said. Mary had called it up again and again on her BlackBerry screen, its shaky yellow glow filling the car like a miner's lantern each time, but there was absolutely nothing else she could learn from it.

What's happening? What the hell is happening?

The car slowed and Amy waited at an intersection, looking both ways as patiently and carefully as they had been taught in Drivers Ed. *There's nobody around!* Mary wanted to scream. *Run the damn stop sign!*

"Left turn," Mary reminded Amy.

"I know."

"Sorry."

She was trying not to talk, but she couldn't help it—the shock and noise of that gunshot was still echoing in her head, forcing her to speculate about what could be happening to Joon at whatever meth lab or underage brothel or *whatever* bad, bad place she'd been taken. Mary had never realized how quickly you could become absolutely terrified, how the feeling came over you like a big ocean wave with a riptide that knocked you off your feet, plunging you into the cold surf.

"Okay," Amy said, peering at the odometer, brushing her red hair back from her smooth forehead. "I think we're there."

She slowed the car and turned into a muddy, rain-drenched driveway, the tires crunching on gravel and twigs as the engine whined. The windshield wipers whipped back and forth as the driveway tilted upward. They splashed through puddles that sprayed brown water like molten chocolate that gleamed in the headlights and then they coasted downhill and Mary looked out the window and stopped breathing.

No, no, no—

Before them lay an empty field—a broad clearing that was just barely visible beneath the wide, flat sky. The light from a nearby town glowed weakly in the distance, silhouetting the faraway trees.

Standing on the near edge of the field, looming over them like a gravestone, was an enormous, sharp-edged black mass. Not a barn—a house. A deserted country house.

The place she'd been seeing—that she'd been dreaming, hallucinating, *whatever* she had been doing—over and over all day: it was real. They were here, and it was real.

It was like seeing a famous European building or monument for the first time, after spending years looking at postcards. The view out of the Mercedes windshield *exactly* matched the vision she'd been having. The only difference was the season and the weather—the snow was replaced by damp, trampled dead grass that shone in the headlights, and that awful bloodred evening sky was replaced by the luminous overcast glow beyond the rearview mirror.

But it was the same place.

It's not possible, she thought weakly. Her pulse pounded in her ears. She felt a sharp pain in her palm and realized she was clenching her fist around the BlackBerry so tightly that her fingernails were cutting into her palm.

"Um—okay," Amy whispered, her hands still clamped around the steering wheel. She sounded terrified—and Mary, for her own reasons, couldn't blame her. "Wh-what do we do now?"

"I don't know."

Yes you do, a maddening voice in her head insisted.

You've got to go in there. You've got to get out of the car and go in there.

But how could they do that? The house was like a black wedge in front of them; it seemed to absorb the headlights' glow without reflecting any of it. There didn't seem to be anyone else around—there wasn't the slightest sign of human activity.

"You're sure you got the directions right?" Amy whispered. "Because I don't see anything."

"This is the place," Mary said firmly.

"Are you sure?"

I've been seeing it all day, Mary thought. *Of course I'm sure.*

But there was no way to say that to Amy without sounding like she'd lost her mind. Which, Mary realized, wasn't too far outside the realm of possibility.

"I'm sure. Cut the engine."

"No." Amy hadn't moved; her hands were trembling, white-knuckled. "No way."

"You can leave the headlights on," Mary said gently. "Come on, Amy—we've *got* to."

Amy took a deep breath and shuddered as she let it out and then killed the engine. The silence made Mary aware that her ears were still ringing from the deafening music at the party. As her hearing adjusted, she realized that the nighttime country around them wasn't *completely* silent—she could just make out the gentle patter of the scant raindrops on the untended lawn.

And she could hear something else—something that made her want to curl into a ball on the floor of the car and put her thumb in her mouth and whimper like a baby. She could barely hear the faint murmur of running water. It sounded like a natural stream or brook, not that far away. Just like she'd been imagining all day long.

"What the hell is this?" Amy was nearly hysterical. "There's nobody *here!* Where's that guy? Where's Joon?"

"I don't know."

"But it doesn't make any *sense*," Amy went on, her voice climbing in pitch. "Where's Joonie? What happened to her, Mary?"

I want this to stop, Mary thought weakly. *I want this day to end—I want to go home.*

It took all Mary's courage to open the passenger door—letting in a blade of cold, wet wind that blew the dress away from her bare legs—and step outside. Her heels sank into the gravel and mud, and the dress was instantly drenched.

"Come on."

"I don't want to," Amy whined from behind the wheel. "Don't make me—I don't want to."

"We *have* to."

The rain was falling delicately around them, drumming against the car's steel roof. Mary could see steam rising from the rain-beaded hood. Amy opened her door and climbed out of the car, and Mary led them forward, toward the dark, deserted house.

THE CLOSER THEY GOT to the house, the harder it became to take each step—and not just because of the rocks and gravel that interfered with their high heels. Amy and Mary both stumbled more than once, swaying against each other and barely managing to keep from toppling into the mud.

Mary's eyes were adjusting to the darkness; she could see the house's flanks now. Sagging, cracked wide beams spanned its facade. A small, rudimentary porch had fallen away from the house and sunk into the weeds; protruding nails gleamed in the weak glow of the Mercedes's headlights. Razor strokes of rain kept falling, spattering against Mary's cheeks and bare shoulders. She was freezing and her hair was drenched, but she could barely feel any of that.

The windows were cracked and missing panes. The front door was standing just slightly ajar.

"We don't have a flashlight," Amy whispered.

Too bad, Mary thought. *Too bad, because we've got to walk up and go through that door. Because this is where Joon is.*

Mary led them through the wet grass and weeds, up to the front door. They had to step over the collapsed porch and directly up onto the landing. Mary had taken Amy's hand, and she felt her pulling back, pulling away. She gave her hand a squeeze and, squinting in the wet gloom, pushed on the front door.

The door slowly pivoted inward, its ancient hinges creaking and squealing. Inside was nothing but darkness.

This is the part where the audience is screaming at me to run away, Mary thought miserably. It was totally true: how many times had she sat in a warm, comfortable room nursing a Stella Artois and watching a television screen where some idiot girl was doing *exactly this*—opening a door just like this one? And everyone laughed and threw popcorn at the screen and yelled at the stupid girl to *turn around*; what kind of idiot was she? *How could anyone be so stupid*, they would all scornfully yell, and the girls would cower under their boyfriends' arms and hide their faces and squeal in anticipation of what was coming next. *Why* would that doomed girl in the bad movie keep walking forward? Why would *anyone* do that?

And yet here I am, Mary thought, *doing it*.

She made a mental note never to make fun of those horror-movie girls again.

The door creaked all the way open and Mary stepped into the house. It was pitch black, and cool. The smell hit her immediately: a damp, musty, ripe aroma of earth and dead leaves and mold.

Nobody's been here in years, Mary thought dismally. *This is some kind of trick; I don't care what fucking "visions" I've been—*

Amy grabbed her bare arm from behind in a sudden, viselike grip that nearly made Mary leap a foot in the air. She could *feel* her heart racing like a stuttering lawn-mower engine: she had heard it too.

A female voice—moaning in the distance.

Oh my God, Mary thought weakly. She felt light-headed and bit her lower lip because it seemed like the only way to keep herself from fainting. Turning her head sideways, she couldn't see anything of Amy but a murky shadow. Amy's grip on her arm got painfully tight, and she could tell that Amy was within an eyelash of succumbing to pure animal terror and running from the house.

She'll panic and get in the car and drive away, Mary thought crazily. *And I'll be here all alone with the moaning girl*.

The whimpering penetrated the silence again, and Mary realized that the sound was coming from *outside* the house—from directly ahead, where she could now make out another door.

"Come on," she whispered to Amy, pulling her forward. They nearly collided with a huge black shape—an overturned wooden table. Mary got them around that by feel and then advanced toward the back door. Amy was leaning against her like an invalid, she was so frightened.

Another moan in the distance—and Mary recognized the voice.

Joon.

The back door was wide open; she could see it clearly now, a pale gray rectangle framed in splintered wood. Beyond it, more weeds and a ruined lawn stretched away into the blackness. Mary's eyes had adjusted enough that the glow of the car's headlights, shining past the house, let her see clearly—and now it was *her* turn to get weak in the knees, swaying sideways against the door's warped, cracked frame.

In the darkness, just past the edge of the tangled, wet, black forest beyond the lawn, a figure was suspended in the air—a human figure, just barely visible, hanging from some kind of rope or chain, twirling slightly in the wind.

As Mary and Amy edged just beyond the doorway, the shadowy hanging figure moved. The moans intensified to high-pitched, frantic whimpering that so frightened Mary she couldn't think at all for more than ten seconds.

It was Joon—Joon had been tied up and gagged with silver gaffer's tape and suspended from a rope, out there in the

131

woods behind the house. She could see them—her hanging figure bucked and twisted spastically, the rope creaking, as she squealed and kicked and shook in panic. The rope led upward from her bound wrists, disappearing into the shadows of the thick branches overhead. Mary could clearly see Joon's black hair tossing and swinging as she moaned and whimpered more and more frantically.

"Oh my God," Amy whispered. She was crying. "Oh my God—"

"Come on," Mary said, pulling Amy forward. "Come on, Amy—"

"I can't." Amy grabbed Mary's arm painfully. "I can't, I *can't* go out there."

"Amy—"

"*I can't*," Amy nearly screamed. "Oh Jesus, don't make me go out there—"

"Okay," Mary whispered. She hadn't taken her eyes from Joon's shadowy figure. "Okay. But I'm going."

"*No*—"

A staccato blast of lightning, a row of flashbulbs igniting, shone through the trees like silent fire.

"Amy, I've *got* to," Mary hissed desperately. Her entire body was wet and shivering now—she could only imagine what Joon was going through or how long she'd been hanging there in the cold rain, all alone just within the wild edges of that black forest. "I've got to."

Thunder rumbled, giant boulders smashing in the sky.

"Don't leave me here," Amy pleaded, crying. "Don't leave me here alone."

Then come with me! Mary wanted to scream. But that was impossible. Mary could tell from Amy's voice, there was just no way she was going to take another step forward. It was like asking her to walk off a cliff.

"Listen to me," Mary said, taking Amy's head in her hands. "Listen—I'll be *right back*. You just stay *right here—don't move*—and I'll be back. Okay?"

Amy nodded. She wiped tears from her face.

Mary gently disengaged her arm from Amy's death grip, took a deep breath and then stepped down the porch stairs and out into the cold night air. Mary could see Joon's face now, behind the tape that gagged her. Joon saw her coming and started whimpering and moaning again. The sound was horrible: it was obvious that Joon was completely beside herself with terror and was trying to scream at the top of her lungs, but the gag made that impossible.

The rush of water was easier to hear now.

"I'm coming!" Mary called out, stumbling forward through the mud. The weeds were waist high, thwacking against her bare thighs as she walked, and both of her heels snapped, the left and then the right. Mary left the shoes in the mud and continued barefoot, shivering as her feet plunged into the cold jelly of mud. "I'm coming, Joon!"

She didn't see the worst part until she got halfway there—the light was just too feeble, and her view into the forest was murky, obscured by rain. But when she got close enough to see, she gasped and another wave of fear swept over her like a spray from a firehose.

The ground beneath Joon fell away. Where she was

hanging, the ground was *gone*—she was suspended in the air past the edge of what looked like some kind of embankment.

And down below the cliff—*far* down below, judging by the sound—was the roar of a stream.

Jesus, Mary thought weakly. *How am I supposed to get to her?* She kept moving forward, but it was slow going—each step meant pulling a foot from the mud's suction.

"I'm coming, Joon!" Mary yelled. "I'm coming! I'll be right there!"

Joon was bucking and shaking even more wildly, making the rope she hung from whicker and twang like a plucked guitar string. Her wet hair tossed wildly from side to side. She was frantically shaking her head.

"*Mary!*"

Amy's voice behind her—*screaming.*

The scream went through her like a javelin. It was so loud, so piercing, that it made her ears hurt.

"Mary, *help! Help! Hel*—"

And then, suddenly, silence.

Mary pivoted, peering backward through the gloom.

She couldn't see anything. All she heard was the whisper of the rain and the moan of the wind in the trees.

Running back toward the house, she took a bad step and fell flat on her face in the mud, tearing the Nina Ricci dress. A tree root slammed against her shoulder hard enough to make her eyes water. Panting, she rolled sideways and got her numb, cold hands beneath herself to get her body upright.

"Amy!" Mary screamed, sobbing as she stumbled up the stairs and rushed through the splintered, empty doorframe. "Amy!"

Nothing.

This isn't happening, some part of Mary's mind was repeating over and over. *No, no, no, no—*

"Amy!" Mary screamed at the top of her lungs. "Amy, *where are you?*"

Nothing. No answer. Nothing but the rain.

Amy had vanished.

Where did she go? Oh, sweet Lord Jesus, what happened to her?

Mary retraced her steps out the back door. *She followed me outside,* Mary thought desperately. *I've got to go after her—*

But she knew better. Amy had been *inside the house* when she'd screamed and then the scream had been cut off with the terrifying finality of a plug being pulled.

Mary waded through the mud and weeds toward Joon's dangling body.

"I can't find Amy!" Mary sobbed, her hoarse throat burning with the strain of screaming. "Joon, hang on—"

Joon was violently shaking her head as Mary moved toward her. Ten feet, fifteen feet—and now she was finally close enough to see the whites of Joon's wide, panicked eyes. Joon's squeals and moans had become so frantic that she sounded like an animal caught in a trap. The sound was unbearable.

Amy, Mary thought desperately. *What happened to you, Amy?*

Mary took one more step and heard a thunderous wet crack and then suddenly the world was spinning . . . She had half a second to realize that the ground had given out beneath her and that she was falling painfully through sharp twigs and brambles and dead leaves, the edge of the earth slamming painfully into her forearms as she dropped.

"*Aaah!*" Mary yelled, winded. She'd plunged through a jagged, gaping hole and was caught in the ground up to her chest. Her upper arms were on fire; the pain was overwhelming. Her feet had collided with something deep underground—rocks or tree roots—and her left ankle sang with agony.

She couldn't move. She was completely, utterly trapped.

Above her, just ahead, she could see Joon wriggling again, moaning through her gag as she stared at her.

"Joon!" Mary screamed. "I'm trapped—I can't move!"

She whimpered as she strained her body, trying to free herself. It was impossible. She was cemented in the ground as firmly as if a gardener had planted her there.

Joon kept wriggling—and as she did, Mary heard something new—the most horrifying sound she'd heard yet.

The rope was breaking.

Joon's panicked movements were straining its fibers, and, before Mary saw it start to unravel, she heard the low, wet tearing sound of its filaments splitting and coming apart.

Joon heard it too. She arched her back, straining against her bonds, twisting her head to look upward. Then she started wriggling even more frantically.

"Don't move, Joon!" Mary screamed. "Jesus, don't—"

The rope cracked and snapped and tore apart all at once and Mary screamed *No*, practically breaking her spine trying to wrest herself free from the hole she'd fallen into, and then the rope came apart and Joon fell and there was a fleeting instant—frozen like a photograph—of Joon's horrified, wide-eyed face blurred beneath her hair, which stood on end as she dropped out of view.

Mary was still screaming, but like in the movies, it was a silent scream—drowned out by the sound of the rain.

And then, after a long, long delay, the most horrifying sound of all—a distant, thunderous splash.

That's where the stream is, Mary remembered. *Way, way down there.*

"Joon!" she called out desperately. *"Joon, can you hear me?"*

Nothing. No answer at all. She was alone, trapped in the wet earth like an animal, freezing, shivering, moaning. Amy was gone, and now Joon was, too.

THERE WAS NO WAY to tell how much time had passed, but the rain had finally stopped. Mary hadn't blacked out; she'd just stopped thinking. It was easier to stay half-buried in the cold ground and not think and just wait to die. Now she was slowly coming out of it, waking up from whatever shocked stupor she'd drifted into after the rope had broken and Joon had dropped out of sight like somebody tumbling down an elevator shaft.

She could still be down there, Mary thought. *Legs broken, bleeding, dying—*

But Mary didn't believe it. No matter how hard she strained, she couldn't *hear* anything—nothing after that horrifying cannonball splash that had sounded so distant, so far down below. Mary realized she was crying again, sobbing gently in a way that made her throat hitch painfully. In that moment, Mary wished she was dead.

And then, suddenly, she heard something.

A car was approaching. Somebody was coming.

I'm going to get my wish, she thought. She was sure of it; the dull hum of an engine was getting louder, and, a moment later, she could just make out the dim sweep of headlights through the vast trees around her. There was no question about it: a car was approaching the house.

They're coming for me, Mary thought. *Whoever did this— whoever brought Joon here; whoever took Amy away—they're coming for me now.*

There was nothing she could do. She couldn't move. Her face stung with dried tears. She was all screamed out; she had nothing left.

The engine got even louder and the headlights swept over the far side of the house, casting crazy shadows against the trees. Then the engine cut and a car door slammed—a loud, metallic bang that made her flinch—and footsteps crunched in the wet gravel, coming toward her, around the house.

Make it quick, Mary found herself praying. *Please, God, make it fast—whatever's about to happen, whatever's about to happen to me, make it fast.*

Heavy footsteps were approaching through the long grass and the weeds. She could only see a tall, thin silhouette, haloed in the damp air.

It's him, Mary thought. She was numb with terror,

remembering her vision—the dark shape that loomed over her, coming closer, like a falling statue. *It's him—the giant man.*

Mary heard herself whimpering in fear and was powerless to stop. The figure approached, getting closer and closer, growing taller and taller, looming over her like the sharp, jagged silhouette of a bare tree in the coldest depths of winter, and she found herself praying again: *Don't hurt me—kill me if you're going to kill me, whoever you are, but don't hurt me. Don't make it hurt.*

The giant figure stopped right in front of her, a tall, featureless shape like an angel of death, or a giant in a fairy tale, the kind of giant who strides through the dark primeval forest and snatches small children, who are never seen again.

"Please," Mary whispered, gazing helplessly up at the black silhouette. "Please don't hurt me—"

The figure leaned forward, reaching out a hand and, suddenly, she saw who it was. It wasn't a giant at all.

"Come on," Dylan Summer whispered urgently. "Grab my hand—we've got to get out of here *right now.*"

6

11:21 P.M.

"DYLAN?" MARY TRIED TO blink the rain and tears and strands of wet hair from her eyes. "Dylan? Is that you?"

"Grab my *hand*," Dylan repeated. He was crouching, his arms outstretched. His own sodden hair flicked back and forth as he whipped his head around in near panic like a trapped animal. "Come on—*do it!*"

Mary reached up and fumbled with Dylan's hands, grabbing his wrists with her freezing fingers as he did the same to hers. The rain was picking up again; big drops spattered on her shoulders and face as Dylan leaned backward and heaved, pulling her upward. She nearly screamed as her bare ankle scraped against rough tree roots and stones. Dylan was grimacing, his eyes clenched tight, his face crimson with the effort.

I can't get out, Mary thought, biting her lip at the pain as the roots scraped against her rib cage, tearing the green fabric that Amy Twersky had paid so much for—the fabric you were warned not to dry-clean too often, since it was so delicate. *He's not going to be able to do it; he's not strong enough.*

But he was. With a sudden, scraping sound like the screech of a nail being pulled from a piece of wood, Mary catapulted upward, muddy water flowing into the hole as she collapsed onto Dylan, knocking him into the tall weeds. Dylan grunted as her weight drove all the air from his lungs.

But he was trying to get out from under her, wincing with the strain as he clamped his fingers around her shoulder and pushed her aside. She rolled sideways into the mud and he wheezed as he got his legs under himself and awkwardly rose to his feet.

"Ow, ow, ow," Dylan muttered as he clamped his hands around his shin—she realized he'd banged it against something. Beneath his thick, lined overcoat, he was still dressed in the charcoal suit she'd seen him in back when everything was at least *close* to being sane, before she'd dropped the rest of the way off the edge of the world and into this nightmare.

"*Joon!*" Mary screamed as soon as she could breathe. Dylan was pulling her to her feet, hunching over and looking back and forth, like a fugitive escaped from a chain gang. "*Amy . . . Joon . . . Oh my G—*"

Dylan clamped his hand over her mouth, nearly making her gag.

141

"*Quiet*," Dylan hissed. She could hear the fear in his voice. "For God's sake, don't make so much noise."

"*Mmm—mmm—*" Mary was shaking her head, trying to pull away. Her body was so wet and freezing that she suspected she might be in the early stages of hypothermia. It was still nearly impossible to see; the black, primeval forest hissed and swayed in the cold wind. Mary tried to push Dylan's hand away from her mouth.

"Will you be quiet!" Dylan snapped. She stopped struggling and nodded and he took his hand away.

"They're *gone*," Mary sobbed, grabbing Dylan's neck and pulling him toward her. She nearly toppled into the mud and then managed to regain her footing, but it was difficult, because her scratched feet were numb. "Oh my God, Dylan—we have to go down there—"

"We have to *leave*," Dylan whispered grimly, pushing his sodden hair back from his face and pulling her toward the house. "Mary, Jesus, *come on*."

"But—"

"There's *no time*," Dylan insisted, grabbing her by the shoulders and shaking her. "Don't you understand? We're going to be next if we don't leave."

"But I have to save Joon," Mary sobbed, pointing behind them at the frayed end of the rope that still hung from the tree. She was struggling frantically, trying to pull away from Dylan's slippery yet firm grip. "She fell down into that stream and—"

"*You can't save anyone!*" Dylan raged in her face. "It's too late! Now, for Christ's sake, *come on!*"

It's too late, Mary thought. She stopped struggling and slumped against Dylan, shaking as she sobbed, letting the tears come in earnest. Her blurred final view of Joon's gagged face, her hair standing straight up above her head as she fell— the sickening finality of Amy's last scream—everything was repeating over and over in her mind like an evil slide show that she couldn't stop watching. She wanted to turn back the clock, to start over from the beginning of the day.

"We've—we've got to get away," Dylan whispered as he pulled her along, around the side of the farmhouse, skirting the edge of the wide field she'd seen visions of all day. "Hurry up—my car's over here."

"But what's—what's happening, Dylan?" Mary was limping slightly from her ankle wound, but the pain wasn't too bad and she could just manage to keep up with him. "What the hell is happening?"

"I can't—I can't explain now." Dylan had let go of her waist and arms and was fishing in his pocket for his car keys. As they rounded the sagging edge of the deserted house, Mary squinted in the sudden glare. A battered Ford Taurus was parked next to Patrick's car, its headlights gleaming through the rain, making wild coronas in her wet eyes. Dylan had left the driver's door open. He pushed Mary roughly toward the car and she stumbled and collapsed against its fender—she could feel the engine's heat throbbing beneath the metal.

"Get in," Dylan ordered, pointing. He continued to look around, his head pivoting like a bird's. In the glare of the four headlights, she could see his mud-streaked face clearly;

she could see the barely contained panic in his eyes. "Door's open. We've got to get away *right now.*"

Mary limped her way around the side of the Taurus and pulled the passenger door open. A chime started bonging as she collapsed on the seat, the thin, wet fabric of the ruined dress pressing against her thighs, freezing them. She pulled her scratched legs inside and yanked the door shut. Dylan had climbed in beside her and slammed his own door, fumbling with the keys as he turned them in the ignition. The headlights dimmed as the engine turned over, nearly stalling and then roaring to life. The instrument panel flared, casting an eerie green glow on Dylan's hands and face. The wheels ground loudly against the gravel and the engine whined as Dylan twisted his head around, clenching his teeth with the effort of peering through the fogged windows, swerving the car as he propelled them backward, trying not to smash into any of the overhanging trees.

Mary's teeth were chattering. She had her arms wrapped tightly around her body, but it was no use—she was frozen to the bone. Her breathing hitched with dry sobs.

Staring straight ahead, through the windshield, Mary watched the deserted house recede into the darkness and disappear. She got one final glance of Trick's empty Mercedes, its long low doors spread wide open like gull wings, its sapphire headlights illuminating the emerald leaves, its windshield wipers flicking back and forth, back and forth.

HE DROVE FAST. THEY were on the Saw Mill River Parkway, speeding south, heading back toward the city. The rain was pounding now, scattering from the highway in front of them in a fine spray that danced in the headlights. Dylan had punched a dashboard button that got the heat going full blast, and the car's interior was warming up. The windshield wipers hummed as they worked.

"There's a blanket," Dylan muttered, flicking his head backward, keeping his eyes on the road. "Back there."

Mary didn't want to move. She wanted to sit in the uncomfortable seat and stare at the converging white lines and the passing aluminum guardrail and stop thinking, stop remembering Amy's screams and Joon's desperate struggle at the end of that fraying rope. She couldn't make herself numb. It was impossible. Eventually, she twisted around and groped in the darkness of the backseat—her fingers brushed against a wool blanket and she pulled it forward, sending a stack of battered paperbacks toppling from the seat to the floor of the car.

"Thanks," Mary managed to whisper.

"Yeah."

Dylan was driving eighty-five miles an hour, she saw. There was almost no traffic—a few sedans whipped past, headed in the other direction, headlights dazzling her as they went by, but the southbound lane was nearly empty.

"How did you—" Mary coughed explosively, her hoarse throat aching with the strain. She pulled the thick blanket around herself, basking in the warmth. "How did you know? How did— What's—"

"Don't try to talk." Dylan sounded as bad as she did. Turning her head against the seat, she could see his profile. He was checking the rearview mirror, over and over. "Please just let me drive."

"Okay." Mary was in no mood to argue. The sodden fabric of the ruined dress pressed against her skin like cold ropes. She was still shivering.

Headlights were coming up behind them.

Dylan noticed it too—he glanced in the rearview mirror again. Mary could feel her breathing quickening. A slow, steady wave of dread was beginning to creep over her, one more time.

It's nothing, Mary told herself. *Just traffic.*

Dylan didn't seem fazed. His driving was steady. Rain beat down on the car's windows. Mary heard a low rumble of thunder, far in the distance.

"Where are we going?" she asked.

"Back to the city."

"Yeah, but *where?*"

"What?"

Dylan sounded confused by the question. Glancing over at his profile, Mary saw an odd look on his face—a strange, puzzled cast to his eyes. The car behind them had caught up, and bands of bright light came sliding across the Taurus's ceiling.

"Dylan," she repeated, deliberately. There was something about his manner that she didn't like—she couldn't put her finger on it, but something seemed odd, out of place. "Where are you taking me?"

"I don't—"

The car was slowing down, Mary was sure of it; she could hear the drone of the engine decreasing in pitch. She glanced over and saw the illuminated speedometer needle twirling backward, like a clock hand sweeping in reverse.

"Dylan, what's wrong?" Mary didn't like this at all. What had come over him? His hands were twitching the wheel oddly and the car was bucking and weaving. The car behind them was nearly tailgating—the Taurus's interior was brilliantly headlit. "What's—what's happening to you?"

"I don't—" Dylan shook his head quickly, as if he was trying to shake off his disorientation. His wet hair flopped over his forehead. Mary sat upright and peered behind them, squinting in the glare of the headlights of the car following them. She couldn't see any details—just the lights, getting closer. "I can't—I can't remember what—"

The car behind them honked. The blast of its horn was deafeningly loud; Mary flinched, shivering as she stole another glance backward at the headlights that were *right there*, mere feet away.

"Dylan!" Mary yelled. She slapped her hands against the dashboard, bracing herself as their car drifted, nearly skidding. The car behind them gave another series of horn blasts. "Dylan, snap out of it! We're going to have an accident—"

Dylan was blinking fast. Something was definitely wrong with him; his hands were slackening on the wheel and the car was drifting to the right, propelling itself toward the blur of trees along the parkway's edge. Mary's body was flooded with adrenaline. The other car swerved and weaved, its headlamps flashing like disco lights as its horn blasted again.

"Jesus Christ!" Dylan yelled.

Mary saw his hands tighten on the wheel. She was pitched against the passenger door, her bare shoulder banging against the window, as Dylan regained control of the

Taurus and pulled back into the passing lane. A band of reflected headlight caught his eyes as he looked in the rearview mirror and punched the gas, propelling them forward—the speedometer showed them approaching sixty, seventy, eighty miles per hour.

The car behind them matched their speed.

"Dylan, what the hell is going on?" Mary shouted. The blanket had fallen to the floor and she leaned to gather it up as Dylan pulled the car to ninety. "What happened to you?"

"Fasten your seat belt," Dylan told her. He sounded frightened. "Jesus, they're right behind us—"

"*Who's* behind us?" Mary was fumbling with the shoulder belt, trying to yank it across herself while the car lurched forward. Thunder sounded, not that far off, as she snapped the seat-belt buckle home. The car was moving so erratically, she was absolutely convinced Dylan was about to flip it over. The pursuers' headlights were falling behind. *"Who the hell is doing this to—"*

The brakes screeched and Mary was flung forward against her seat belt as Dylan spun the wheel, throwing them into a corkscrew spin, aiming the car at an exit ramp. Mary screamed as Dylan hit the gas—she could almost feel the fillings ripping loose from her teeth as the Taurus banged over the curb of the embankment and sped forward along the narrow off-ramp.

The pursuing car roared past, missing the exit. Through the pounding rain, Mary heard a distant squeal. The other car's brake lights flashed, bright red coals through the charcoal darkness, and then it was gone. Mary fell back against her seat, feeling like she was going to vomit—the feeling passed, just barely, and then she was hyperventilating. Dylan slowed down, breathing heavily himself, his hands shaking on the wheel. They drove beneath a yellow streetlight and onto a narrow Riverdale boulevard. Mary realized where they were—less than a mile north of Manhattan—as a flash of lightning lit up the deserted suburban street. The street was flanked by trees and lined with two-story homes.

"*Okay*," Dylan rasped. He was still shaking. Mary could see his whitened knuckles gripping the steering wheel. "Okay, okay. We lost them. I think we really lost them."

"Who *were* they?"

"If I told you," Dylan said, rubbing perspiration from his forehead with a shaky hand, "you'd never believe me."

"But—"

"Just give me a minute," Dylan muttered. He was looking around them, peering through the rain-streaked windows, apparently trying to find road signs, landmarks. "Okay? Please—just let me drive. I've got to figure out how to get us where we're going."

IT HIT HER AGAIN, as she climbed the steep stairs of Dylan's tiny apartment building. She was trying to remain numb, not to think about anything but her freezing, battered body and the effort of taking each barefoot step up the filthy worn tiles of the brownstone. Dylan wordlessly fumbled with his keys, looking over his shoulder again and again, the dread obvious on his chiseled face.

Don't think. Just walk. You can do that, can't you?

She couldn't. In her mind, she saw the rope break, saw Joon's body drop like a stone; she heard Amy's blood-curdling scream before something cut it off like scissors snipping a ribbon; and she was sobbing again, practically collapsing against the painted iron banister.

"Come on," Dylan whispered, behind her, awkwardly putting his hands on her shoulders, over the blanket covering the shreds of her ruined dress (*Amy's* ruined dress, she corrected herself miserably). "Come on, Mary. Climb the stairs. Just climb the stairs."

She nodded. Her eyes were red and raw; her tangled hair hung in her face. She couldn't speak. She could only nod. And keep climbing.

They were on 125th Street, just off Morningside Avenue, near Columbia University. The street was narrow and deserted, flanked by rows of hundred-year-old brownstones with ornate, soot-stained facades and elaborate stone staircases lined up like the teeth of a comb. Mary rarely came up to this neighborhood—she tried to avoid the Upper West Side and anything that brought her close to her own home—but she knew that all these buildings were probably filled with college students and graduate TAs and the scruffy intellectuals you always find around a big school.

Ellen's been here, Mary had thought as she'd climbed out of the car. *She knows this neighborhood—this is where she goes all the time. This is where she is whenever I can't find her.*

Dylan had double-parked down the block from his apartment, as far from the halos of the streetlights as possible. He'd hurried out of the car and come around to open

Mary's door, gently lifting her onto the sidewalk while she cried and held on to his coat for support.

My *friends are gone*, she kept thinking, over and over—she wouldn't let herself think any other word, like "dead," but she knew she was just playing word games. She had *heard* Joon's body hit the water. Joon's arms had been tied, her mouth covered, her ankles bound. The water was far, far below—it had taken a *long* time before Mary had heard the splash. The water must have been freezing.

She was dead. No way around it.

They'd climbed three flights of stairs and Dylan was fumbling with his keys, opening four separate locks on his apartment door and then helping Mary inside. She wandered forward while he snapped the lights on, revealing a tiny, cluttered apartment—framed posters, blond floorboards covered with tall stacks of books, a faded couch draped in macramé quilts—but it was hard for her to keep moving. There didn't seem to be any point.

Poor Amy . . . poor Joon . . .

All she wanted to do was close her eyes and never open them again.

"Um, sit down," Dylan offered, lunging to clear several big piles of papers from the lumpy couch. "Sit down for a second and I'll see if I can find you some clothes."

Mary did what she was told.

I couldn't save either of them. I couldn't do anything.

It's all my fault.

At some point in any nightmare you give up—you accept your fate and hope the dream doesn't hurt too much, that you'll wake up before you die. But this wasn't a dream—it was really happening.

"I've got a full tank of gas," Dylan muttered while moving around his small living room. He kicked over stacks of paperbacks as he pulled open drawers, gathering things—Mary saw him collect a flashlight, grab a heavy winter coat from a cluttered closet, riffle through a desk drawer to collect a crumpled roll of twenty-dollar bills. "Gas, money, car keys . . ." He was still muttering, ticking off items on his fingers as he darted back and forth.

"What are you doing?" Mary asked. She hadn't moved; she was sitting hunched over on the couch, curled around herself in the blanket she'd brought from the car. Outside, thunder crashed, rumbling through the building's thick walls. "Dylan? What are you—"

"We've got to *run*," Dylan told her. He had turned to face her, holding what looked like a passport case. His wet hair was sticking out in wild directions. In the yellow lamplight, she could see that his suit was ruined—his trousers were soaking wet from the thighs down, obviously from wading through the weeds at the farmhouse. "We've got to get out of here and run away, as fast as we can, before they find out where we—"

"*Who?* Before *who* finds out?" Mary was still shaking, and she realized it wasn't from the cold—it was from fear. "Who's chasing us? Is it the same people who tied up Joon and—"

"Not now!" Dylan yelled. He winced, pressed his fingers to his temples. "I'm sorry. Not now, Mary—let me just finish getting—"

"*Now! Tell me now!*" Mary felt her eyes filling with hot tears again as she wrenched herself to her feet, stumbling as the blanket tangled around her legs. "If you know something I don't, then *tell me right now!* You said you—" Mary felt light-headed suddenly—black spots were blooming in front of her eyes and she swayed back and forth, fighting off the urge to faint. "You said you knew who was following us."

"I'm not—I'm not sure." Dylan kept rubbing his eyes. "I think I might remember, but it's so confusing, like—"

"Like *what?*" Mary was crying again. "It's the worst day of my life; it's *sucked* since the moment I woke up. *Everyone's* been out to get me, all day!"

"You sound paranoid," Dylan said. He was shaking his head, looking more confused with each passing second. "There can't be—"

"*I'm not paranoid!*" Mary yelled. Her throat ached with the strain. "What do you mean, paranoid? *You're* the one acting like we've got to flee the fucking country!"

"I know. I'm sorry." Dylan's face was strained; he looked down at the passport case in his hand, as if he'd just noticed it. "Jesus, this can't be happening. . . ."

My friends are dead, Mary thought again. It was like a soul-crushing blow that kept hitting her over and over. *Both dead.*

"Dylan," Mary whispered, sniffing and wiping snot from her upper lip as she cried, "do you know what's going on or don't you?"

He raised his head and looked at her, his brown eyes focusing like a laser. She could *see* him trying to collect his thoughts, trying to be rational, not to give in to fear.

153

"I know part of it," he said finally. "I know that the people chasing us are going to figure out where we are. Look, please, *please* just trust me for a little while longer, okay? Let me get you something to wear and then we can get *out* of here. Once we're moving, I'll try to explain what I know."

She stared into his eyes and he returned the stare, not blinking, not moving. She couldn't see anything in his face but honest concern—and fear.

"Okay," she said, sniffing and wiping her eyes. "Okay."

"Why don't you get yourself a glass of water"—Dylan pointed toward a darkened doorway she hadn't noticed before that led to a kitchenette—"and I'll get you some clothes."

She did need a glass of water. Her throat was killing her, her head was pounding and she was feeling the beginning of the brutal hangover that was going to result from all the drinks she'd had: the wine at Amy's, which seemed like an entire lifetime ago, back before the world tilted sideways and she'd slid into this twilight realm of madness; the vodka martini Dylan had bought her; the tequila shots and champagne at her surprise birthday party. It was all catching up to her, she realized; that was most of why she felt so light-headed.

"Yeah, okay," she said weakly, gathering the blanket and walking toward the kitchen. Dylan nodded and headed in the other direction, toward a closed door. Mary winced as her bare feet collided with the splintered floorboards and kicked more of the ubiquitous paperbacks out of the way.

Reaching through the dark kitchen doorway, she found a light switch and flipped it. After a moment, a weak fluorescent bulb sputtered to life. The kitchen was tiny—

a sink full of dirty dishes, a small fridge, a row of battered metal cabinets, a calendar with a Cézanne print. The cold linoleum pressed against her feet as she headed for the sink. She picked through the dish drainer, trying to find a clean glass.

Rain was pounding against the kitchen window, behind its metal security grate. Mary filled a glass with tap water and gulped it down, gazing at the blackness beyond the windowpanes.

Lightning flashed.

Mary jumped, dropping the glass. It shattered on the floor. She nearly screamed in shock at what she saw.

Joon was outside the window.

Mary had been staring in that direction at exactly the right moment, purely by chance—the flash of lightning had illuminated Joon like a paparazzi flashbulb. Joon, just a foot away, staring right back at her—apparently suspended in midair, three floors off the ground. She was dressed exactly the same as she'd been at the farmhouse—the same Elie Saab dress and shiny headband.

The lightning flickered and flared again, like a dying lightbulb, and Mary felt a scream building in her throat as she stared into Joon's eyes. Joon was moving—raising her hand to her face—as the lightning flashed.

Putting her finger to her lips.

Then it was dark again.

Mary's heart was pounding in her ears, her pulse clicking in her throat like a drumbeat. Thunder boomed, a multi-stage staccato explosion, and Mary flinched, staring at the window in disbelief.

Did I really see that?

Mary didn't believe in ghosts—of *course* she didn't believe in ghosts. The whole concept was ridiculous.

But did I really see that?

Dylan seemed to be moving around his bedroom; she could hear the muffled creaking of the floorboards. No doubt, changing his own clothes before finding things for her to wear.

Mary walked toward the window, wincing as her feet crunched on the broken glass littering the floor. Her skin was crawling with goose bumps; her entire body felt as cold and numb as if she'd been standing in a refrigerator for hours. She got close to the window, panting as she gathered her nerve and then cupped her hands around her eyes, peering through the glass.

Someone was out there.

There was no question about it. She could see a black silhouette against the murky glow of another kitchen window, across the air shaft. The shape was moving, coming closer.

Mary fumbled with the window, her fingers straining as they twisted the soot-covered latches. The window screeched as she began lifting it, emitting a blast of cold, wet wind that blew against her body and made the blanket billow behind her.

As she struggled to lift the heavy window, she stiffened in amazement. Fingers curled around the sash—a pair of strong, slim hands, helping her get the window open.

Mary dropped to her knees, pressing her face to the opening. It was Joon—she was right there, her rain-soaked face inches away.

"Is that—" Mary cleared her throat and tried again. "Is that really you?"

"*Shhh,*" Joon whispered. Mary could see small bands of blackened adhesive around her cheeks and chin, from where the gag had been taped. Joon reached through the opening they'd made and clutched Mary's hand. Mary squeezed back. The feel of Joon's warm skin was making her cry all over again. "Be quiet—he'll hear you."

"But how—"

"Don't trust him," Joon whispered urgently. She kept squeezing Mary's hand through the five-inch gap they'd pried open, but Mary could see red welts around Joon's wrists. *From the ropes,* she realized. *When she was tied up.* "Please—you've got to get out of there."

"But—"

"Just *listen,*" Joon hissed. She was peering past Mary's shoulder, trying to see into Dylan's living room. Mary realized that Joon wasn't floating in midair at all—she was crouching on the cast-iron fire escape. She must have climbed up, from the alleyway below. "Do you have anything else to wear?"

"What? No—"

Joon and Amy had helped her get dressed, hours before, she remembered—it seemed like another lifetime. "He's getting—Dylan said he'd get me something to wear."

"Good. Take the clothes. Get dressed," Joon whispered urgently, "and then get out of that apartment and down the stairs. I'll come around and meet you."

"But how did you—" There were millions of questions she wanted to ask. She heard Dylan's bedroom door swing open and his footsteps on the floorboards. He was coming back into the living room.

Joon raised her finger to her lips again.

Mary nodded. She squeezed Joon's hand—Joon squeezed back and then receded into the dark rain.

"Did I hear something break?"

Dylan's voice, behind her.

She rose to her feet just as he came into the kitchen. "Sorry," she told him—he was staring at the broken glass all over the floor. His eyes moved to the open window, where a thin ribbon of cold air was blowing inside. "I dropped the glass. I started to feel faint and I—I needed some air, so I—"

"Are you all right?" Dylan was looking at the streaks of blood she'd left on the floor. "Do you want a bandage or—"

"Let's just get out of here," Mary said. Walking wasn't as difficult as she was afraid it might be; luckily, she didn't seem to have any glass shards embedded in the soles of her feet. "Did you find anything for me to wear?"

(*Don't trust him.*)

"I put it in the bathroom. Just some old stuff—it probably won't fit you."

Dylan frowned. He looked down at the broken glass and then over at the window again. Obviously, he felt like he was missing something—she could see it in his face.

He's smart, she thought. *He's really smart—remember that, if you're going to try to fake him out.*

"Thanks," Mary said. She got past him as fast as she could, nearly tripping on the blanket—again—as she hurried through the living room and furtively grabbed her BlackBerry from the couch. The bathroom was right next to

Dylan's front door; she could see a pair of jeans and a T-shirt folded on the closed toilet seat, with a pair of sneakers placed on top of them. "Just give me a minute," she called out, getting in the bathroom as fast as she could and swinging the door shut.

MARY UNLATCHED THE BATHROOM door as quietly as she could, gently pulled it open and peered out. She had stripped off her ruined clothes, dropping her underwear and the sodden green rags that had once been a $2,300 dress onto the cold tiles, and pulled on the jeans and T-shirt, bareback, no underwear. Nothing fit, at all—she'd had to roll up the cuffs and cinch the jeans around her small waist with the belt Dylan had provided. Finally, she pulled the shapeless, lumpy-looking sweater over herself and slipped her feet into the sneakers. Her BlackBerry and keys slid easily into the oversize jeans pocket. She had given herself just twenty seconds to splash water on her face and pull her hair back, tying it in a rough knot, before opening the door.

Peering through the crack, she could see Dylan's back as he stooped over his coffee table zipping up an overnight bag. He'd put on his big winter coat—another one was draped on the couch, obviously intended for her.

Now or never.

Mary pulled the bathroom door all the way open, wincing at the creaking hinges. She walked as gently as she could, not breathing as she approached the front door. She could hear Dylan packing behind her as she gently twisted the brass knobs on the locks, trying to keep them from snapping. Incredibly, he hadn't noticed—he was moving back toward the kitchen as she threw the final lock and pulled on the door.

It wouldn't move.

Come on, come on, Mary thought frantically as she strained against whatever maddening force—warped wood or sticky old paint—was holding the door closed. Finally the door gave with a loud pop and a low-pitched creak as she pulled it open. Her heart racing, she slipped her body sideways and, with the latches catching on Dylan's sweater, she pulled herself out into the stairwell and eased the door shut.

Mary actually thought she was going to make it. It was ten or twelve feet along the filthy metal railing to the top of the stairs. *Then three flights down*, if she remembered right. But she didn't get far at all.

The sneakers weren't laced and didn't fit right. She stumbled and fell forward against the stairwell railing, nearly bashing her face against the banister. Dylan's door burst open and he ran out after her. She wailed in fear, her soles slipping on the tiled floor as she desperately tried to pull herself upright.

Too late; no use. Dylan was right there—he reached down and grabbed her, snagging his arm around her waist.

"No!" Mary panted. Black spots began to fill her vision. "No, no, no—"

"Where are you going?" Dylan was fighting to keep his grip on her. She bucked and twisted. Everything was growing dim. "Why are you running away?"

No, no, no—

She was fainting—there was no question about it. The world was fading, turning black, like the end of a movie. She kept struggling, but her arms and legs would barely move; she was getting weaker and weaker.

"Mary?"

Dylan's voice, from miles and miles away. The darkness was washing over her like tar, drowning her in oblivion.

Stay awake . . . stay awake . . .

It was hopeless. She tried to rally her strength, but there wasn't anything left. Mary felt her eyelids fluttering and then—

7

2:05 A.M.

SHE BLINKED, STARING UP at the ceiling. She was stretched out on her own narrow bed, along the west wall of her bedroom, the wall her father had painted pink and gold when she was five years old and that had never been repainted. The overhead light was on, an ancient fixture with three bare sixty-watt bulbs that burned her eyes, making her squint at the glare as they always did. The same bedroom ceiling she'd stared at hatefully for years, with the long crack down the south edge and the triangular patch of cracked plaster that had crumbled and fallen, revealing the lathing underneath.

What—

Waking up from a dream was always like this, particularly when it was a frightening dream—the cold sweat coated you and the final scenes of the dream flashed in your mind like lightning, fierce and brilliant but fading, vanishing into the mist as the cold light of the real world entered your waking eyes.

I was dreaming. I was dreaming—a horrible, horrible dream. And here I am in my own bed.

Mary's bedroom—right next to Ellen's along the narrow corridor—had a tiny window with a dim view of the building's air shaft. She barely got any natural light; their apartment was too far down from the air shaft's apex. That was why the overhead light was usually on—in fact, she tended to fall asleep with it on, particularly when she came home tipsy. Mary couldn't count how many times she'd stumbled in here with her ears ringing, the room spinning, and kicked off her high heels and collapsed onto the bed, passing out in her clothes with the lights on. She'd always wake up early in the morning, around dawn, dehydrated, her head aching painfully, with the same pitch-black view out the window, long before the first dim indigo traces of morning light fell down the air shaft into her tiny room.

What a crazy dream, Mary thought. She stared at the familiar ceiling, at the cracks and the exposed lathing and the triad of lightbulbs emitting their harsh glow, trying to remember the details.

My birthday, Mary remembered. *My birthday, and nobody cared; Patrick broke up with me and . . . somebody . . . asked me out, and then it got worse and worse, running and driving and a haunted house, Amy screaming and Joon dying and coming back as a ghost who wasn't a ghost. . . .*

Mary had never had a nightmare like that before. It had been so real, so terrifying, so filled with vivid sensations: the freezing cold and the night wind and the blasting sound track of blaring songs and grinding gears as the car she was in pitched and swerved, brakes squealing as it spun through the rain and lurched ahead, on the run, speeding out of danger, or into danger. More than any other dream she'd ever had, there was the terrifying way that it had all lingered on the edge of sense; how everything that happened *almost* fit together into normal daylight logic but just missed somehow, veering instead into the surreal landscape of fever dreams and fantasies.

But I'm awake now, Mary thought, arching her back and stretching luxuriously. *In my own bed, and I'm safe.* She couldn't quite remember how she'd gotten here, what had happened the night before, but that was hardly new to her. *I was partying somewhere, out with my friends.*

It'll occur to me soon. It'll all come back.

Mary propped herself up on her elbows, grunting with the effort, and looked around at the room—and then stopped moving.

What the hell?

She stared down at herself, at her clothes.

Why am I dressed like this?

The clothes were completely unfamiliar. A gigantic pair of men's Levi's, cinched comically around her waist with a battered black leather belt fastened on its tightest hole. No socks. White tennis sneakers so large that the heels extended back an inch and a half from her ankles. A thread-bare cotton T-shirt beneath an oversize, lumpy wool sweater.

Mary looked around the room. Same old shambles—the bulletin board with the tacked-up *Vogue* clippings of ensembles she liked; the clutter of schoolbooks and old CDs and club invitations and perfume bottles and gift bags covering her desk; the framed Monet print her father had given her long ago.

Mary frowned, rising to sit on the edge of the bed. The floor was littered with clothes—tops and dresses and pants—still on their hangers.

In the center of the floor, casting triple shadows beneath the harsh overhead lights, a crumpled beige coverall, like a cleaning woman would wear.

Oh.

Looking behind herself, Mary saw her clock radio. Its digital readout said 2:06.

It's dark out, she confirmed, looking at the blackness beyond her window's narrow frame. *It's two in the morning.*

It was coming back all at once, like a blurred image coming into focus, bringing a familiar feeling of dread and fatigue and sadness and pain and confusion.

I wasn't dreaming.

But the alternative didn't make any sense. These were Dylan's clothes; she had clasped hands with Joon through his open kitchen window and followed her advice, taking Dylan's clothes and sneaking out the front door, trying to get away.

But she hadn't made it.

165

Dylan had caught her, literally.

And that was where it had ended.

And now here she was, in her bedroom.

The same night? It has to be the same night, doesn't it?

But what happened *to me? Why can't I remember?*

She could hear something—a muffled human sound, faint and obscure, coming through the closed bedroom door.

Crying. Somebody was crying out there.

Quietly, Mary got to her feet, advancing toward her door, trying to keep the big sneakers from squeaking on her worn-out floorboards, kicking clothes out of the way. She cocked her head to one side, straining to hear. The crying voice was *male*, she realized, feeling a sudden flood of adrenaline. Somebody was out there, in the corridor or the living room, crying.

"Mommy," the voice cried. "Mommy, Mommy . . ."

Mary didn't recognize the voice at all. Her anxiety was growing. She struggled with the doorknob, rattling the door against its warped frame, the brass knob slipping maddeningly in her fingers, refusing to turn.

Who locked me in here? How did I end up locked in my bedroom?

And then she realized what the problem was. Below the knob, the thumbscrew of the door's latch was flipped sideways.

The door was locked from the *inside*.

I locked it, she thought. *Why? What was out there?*

Fear and dread spread through her; her skin broke out in goose bumps as she stared at the door's latch, trying to recall how she'd gotten here; what had happened in that missing hour she couldn't remember.

"Mommy . . . Mommy . . ."

That same sobbing voice.

Mary mustered her nerve and took a deep breath and snapped the latch and pulled the door open. She pivoted out into the corridor, staring past Ellen's bedroom door and the door to Dad's old study, out into the front vestibule.

Mary screamed.

She couldn't help it. The scream burst out of her uncontrollably. She gasped for breath, raising her fists to her mouth, trembling in terror at what she saw.

Dylan Summer was lying on the floor, flat on his back.

A bright red lake of blood was spreading from his body.

Mary had never seen so much blood—she nearly screamed again, watching the pool spread like melting snow from boots you'd just taken off.

Dylan's face was scarlet, wrenched in a grimace of agony, tears running sideways down his stubbled cheeks. He was still dressed in his ruined charcoal gray suit (*from our date*, she remembered dazedly) and the thick overcoat he'd grabbed at his apartment an hour or so earlier in this endless dark drama of an evening.

Mary's mother was crouched over Dylan, dressed in her customary nightgown and dressing gown, stroking Dylan's sweat-soaked forehead. The hems of Mom's clothes were stained red with blood.

"Mommy . . . ," Dylan moaned in agony. "Mommy, help me. . . ."

He's delirious, Mary realized, stumbling toward them, willing herself not to scream again. *He's dying; he's delirious.*

"The ambulance is coming," Mrs. Shayne told Dylan soothingly. Mary noticed that Mom was holding the handset of their cordless phone—the same one Mary had always monopolized, that Ellen used to complain she was always using to call her friends, back before they had cell phones. "I've called nine-one-one; I told them gunshot—they're on their way."

Gunshot?

The word hit Mary like a battering ram. She remembered Mason, the shirtless meth head Joon had left the party with hours before—the hot boy with the perfect torso and the automatic pistol that had dropped to the floor and gone off like a firecracker—and the crib upstate, the deserted farmhouse. Mary finally managed to break out of her paralysis and stumble down the corridor toward them. The pool of blood seemed to grow with each passing second.

"It's Ellen's friend Dylan," Mom told her, in the same flat tone she used all the time. She had raised her head and was looking at Mary calmly, as if her being there made all the sense in the world. "He's been shot—a burglar or something like that. I always knew this would happen, living in this neighborhood. . . ."

"But what *happened?*" Mary fought the urge to vomit as she came closer, trying not to stare at the blood. The metallic smell was hitting her nostrils now, making her eyes water. Dylan was staring at the ceiling, whimpering, his eyes unfocused, as Mom stroked his forehead. "What's he *doing* here, Mom?"

"I was asleep," Mom answered. "I heard the shot and came out here and saw him, so I called the cops. That's all I know."

Some distant part of Mary's brain was impressed with her mother's behavior. She'd never seen her in a crisis—a *real* crisis—and she'd always assumed that Mom would fall apart, running or hiding in blind panic.

But you know better than that, Mary corrected herself. *She wasn't always like that*. Before Dad died, Mom had been *exactly* the person you'd want near you when something went wrong.

"Ow, ow, ow . . . ," Dylan moaned. "Mommy, I'm dying; I'm really dying. . . ."

Oh, Jesus, Dylan, Mary thought, staring at his clenched jaw muscles, watching his hands tremble in agony. She realized that she was probably very close to going into shock, so she forced her eyes away from the bloody view.

In her pocket—the loose pocket of Dylan's jeans—her BlackBerry vibrated.

Mary had no idea who was calling her *now*, at two in the morning. But when she pulled out the phone and looked at its display, she nearly fainted with relief:

SHAYNE, ELLEN

Mary took a deep breath and hit the Talk button. "Hello?"

"*Mary?*" Ellen's voice was hard to hear; there was some kind of interference on the line. "Is that you? Is that really you? Thank God—"

"It's me," Mary whispered. "Where are you?"

"Still at the party," Ellen told her. The alarm and fear in her voice was unmistakable, even through the bad connection. "It's still going. Listen, what happened? I haven't been able to reach you or Amy for, like, *hours*. Did you find Joon?"

I sure did, Mary thought miserably. *I found her and I couldn't save her.* Mary stared at Dylan's body and the blood, like bright red poster paint, on her mother's nightclothes. Dylan's chest was moving up and down rapidly as his breathing hitched.

"Mary?" Ellen sounded even more worried. "Are you there?"

I've got to tell her, Mary thought. *There's no way around it.*

"I don't—" Mary was crying. "Listen, I can't— Amy's gone. Amy's gone and Joon's gone—"

"What? What do you mean, gone? What *happened* to them? Did you find that place up—"

"Dylan's been shot," Mary blurted out. The tears were flowing freely down her cheeks and dripping onto the borrowed sweater. "He's here, in our apartment—he's been shot. There's an ambulance coming, but I don't—"

"What?" Ellen's whisper was barely audible. "Shot like with a gun?"

"He's still alive," Mary yelled. *"Ellen, listen—he's still alive.* Mom called an ambulance."

"What happened?" Ellen screamed. "What did you— what happened? What did you get him into?"

"I don't know," Mary whispered.

"What the hell do you mean, you don't know?" Both sisters were sobbing. "Oh my God, no—"

"I don't know who did it," Mary went on. "I didn't see it; I didn't hear it—Mom didn't see it either. Ellen, listen; he's still alive. There's totally still a chance—"

"I'm coming home," Ellen whimpered. "I'll get a cab—I'll be there in—"

"*No!*" Mary shouted, alarmed. That was absolutely the last thing she wanted Ellen to do. "Ellen, no! You've got to promise me you'll stay *right where you are!*"

"But Dylan—"

"*Stay there!*" Mary was terrified that Ellen wouldn't listen; that she'd leave the safety of the Peninsula Hotel. "Stay right where you are and I'll be there as *soon* as I can get a cab. *Promise* me, Ellen!"

"But—"

"Promise me!" Mary wiped tears from her cheeks with her wrist. *He's not going to make it,* she thought hopelessly, staring at Dylan, who was shivering on the floor. *He's not going to live.* "*Please,* Ellen. I love you."

But Ellen hadn't heard that last part. The line was dead.

"No," Dylan whispered, grabbing her ankle as she tried to move past him. "No, don't—don't go . . ."

"I have to," she told him. "I *have* to."

THE TAXICAB SPED EAST along Central Park South, lurching painfully to a halt at each red light that burned through the windshield like a demon's eye and then speeding forward as the light changed. Mary had told the driver to *hurry,* to move as fast as he could—that it was life and death—and he had taken her seriously, racing down Broadway at nearly sixty miles an hour. Mary curled up on the

171

torn vinyl of the backseat, staring at the passing buildings and overlit closed stores and random, middle-of-the-night passersby. The rain had stopped. The streets were shining beneath the streetlights, soaked in rain that reminded her of the blood pool beneath Dylan's shaking, trembling body.

The ambulance still hadn't arrived when Mary grabbed three twenties out of Mom's top dresser drawer (not the first time she'd done this) and galloped down the stairs and out of the building, screaming for a taxi. She'd tried to call Ellen back, but hadn't gotten through—she'd heard the beginning of Ellen's impossibly chipper outgoing voice-mail message four or five times, like a communiqué from another world, one without guns and ropes and screams and blood and death.

"You wanted the Peninsula, right?" the driver called out. "The Fifth Avenue entrance? I have to circle around."

"Fine," Mary responded hopelessly. *Just get me there—get me to Ellen, because she's the only one left.*

Who was she kidding? There was no way to avoid the real story of the day, was there? It was a chain of disaster . . . a chain that started and ended with her, the one and only birthday girl, Mary Shayne.

Amy was gone, missing; vanished after she'd selflessly agreed to drive Mary out of the city on her ill-fated, desperate attempt to save Joon.

Joon was gone. *Because that* couldn't *have been her, outside Dylan's window,* Mary had to conclude. *I was dreaming— I was seeing things. It's the only explanation that makes sense.*

Especially since I fainted just a few minutes later.

So Joon had taken that wrong turn that every New York girl dreads taking. She'd left with the wrong guy, and he'd taken her on a one-way trip to the dark side.

Dylan, asking her out; getting punk'd along with her; taking it like a man, then showing up out of the blue and trying to save her; rescuing her like an action hero in the movies and taking a bullet in the chest for his trouble.

Amy, Joon, Dylan . . . all gone. And it's all my fault, isn't it?

"Peninsula Hotel," the driver announced, slowing the cab as it approached the gigantic limestone columns of the hotel's vast, ornate facade, which was lit up like an inferno with blinding yellow floodlights.

Mary tossed two twenties at the driver and slammed the taxicab door. She stared up at the looming hotel, the cold night wind blasting through Dylan's sweater and freezing her arms and chest.

I'm in hell, Mary thought, pushing her way through the thick brass-framed doors and crossing the carpeted lobby, heading for the elevators. *I might as well be dead, because I'm already in hell—I've been in hell since I woke up today.*

The concierge recognized her, as always, tipping his cap and waving her by. The elevator doors slid shut and the chimes bonged as the elevator rose, and Mary remembered the last time she'd ridden this elevator upward, with Dylan beside her—Dylan, who'd volunteered to come with her to get her stuff from Patrick's suite, who'd shown up out of nowhere to help her, who was now dying on her bare wooden floor.

All for me, she thought miserably as her ears popped and

the elevator arrived and the doors slid open. *Everyone, all of them—all loving me, helping me, doing everything they can for me, all through the seventeen years of my life.*

And what had she ever done for them?

For a second time that night, Mary wished she was dead. It was a calm, measured feeling, and she welcomed it like you'd welcome getting kicked out of a class you were failing, or getting ejected from the big game—the way she'd seen happen with her jock friends—when you weren't playing well, when you were jeopardizing the team.

WALKING DOWN THE CORRIDOR toward Patrick's suite, Mary sensed that something was wrong. There weren't any party noises—although, she realized, she hadn't heard any sounds behind Ellen's voice, either. It was late; the guests had probably scattered to find ragers somewhere else.

But that wasn't it.

The door to Patrick's suite was half open—and inside, everything was dark.

Mary put her fingers on the glossy surface of the door and pushed. The suite was pitch black and deserted. The only light came from the wide picture window—the blazing golden fire of Fifth Avenue, shining through the glass like a dream city.

The room was trashed. Broken champagne bottles, splintered furniture, discarded cups and plates, cigarette butts and overturned ashtrays littered the floor. The room stank of alcohol and tobacco and pot smoke.

Mary gasped in shock, raising her hands to her mouth. A

word was spray-painted on the wall, its huge, jagged black letters spreading across the silk wallpaper.

GOODBYE

It took all of Mary's courage to step into the hotel suite—to keep herself from running blindly in the other direction.

"Hello . . . ?" she called out. Her voice echoed in the empty room. "Ellen . . . ?"

Nothing.

Mary's eyes slowly adjusted to the darkness, and she saw something familiar on the ruined carpet in the center of the room.

Ellen's cell phone. Open and upside down, resting on the carpet. Its tiny screen was glowing.

"Ellen?" she called out again, starting to cry. Still nothing.

And then Mary realized that she could see something else. A thin band of light, along the floor, off to the far right—along the bottom of Patrick's bedroom door.

Someone's in there.

A strange sensation was coursing over her—a feeling she couldn't name—and she realized that she wasn't frightened anymore. Not really. The feeling was like a cold, calm certainty, a sense of inevitability.

I'm not going to run. I'm going to go through that door.

Apparently, her feet had already decided. She was crossing the trash-strewn carpet.

She pushed the door open.

Patrick's bedroom was empty. The bed had been stripped; all of Patrick's belongings were gone. No Ellen, no Patrick.

The last two, Mary thought, still swimming in the unfamiliar sensation of certainty, the strange deliberate calm that washed through her and made all the fear drain away. She had reached her limit; she simply couldn't run anymore, couldn't be afraid anymore. *Now the last two are gone.*

The ceiling spotlights were on. The wide, deep room—where she'd spent so many lazy weekend mornings devouring eggs Benedict that Patrick had gotten her from room service or lying back on the soft bed as Patrick leaned to kiss her—was empty, bare, deserted.

In the center of the bed, on top of the bare mattress, lay a polished wooden box. Mary walked toward it, her feet moving with the same strange, calm feeling of inevitability.

She watched her feet cross the soft carpet; she watched her hands reach for the box and pull it forward, the expensive wood scratching the mattress as she slid it close and opened the lid.

The inside of the box was lined in bright red velvet. A single square sheet of thick yellow paper lay just under the lid. When she picked that up, she saw what was underneath—the spotlights gleamed on the smooth metal like summer sunlight caressing a car's chrome.

A gun.

A beautifully polished handgun.

Mary watched her hand pull the gun from the box, her wrist straining at the surprising heft, the sheer weight of the weapon. She watched her other hand extract the paper and unfold it.

And she recognized it. The giant man in her vision had held out a gleaming square of paper—and now she had it, in real life. It was the same piece of paper; she was sure of it. An unrecognizable symbol was drawn in red ink at the top of the page—a stylized, asymmetrical line drawing of an almond-shaped eye. Staring at the eye, Mary felt a strange sensation, almost like she was dreaming or sleepwalking.

It's just a drawing; it's not moving, she told herself dazedly, but she found that hard to believe as she stared at the red ink. The eye looked like it was moving—or, rather, it *felt* like it was moving, if that was possible; like it was staring back at her, returning her gaze, filling her with a strange, otherworldly calm. There was writing on the page below the eye—three lines of handwritten block text in the same clean red ink—and Mary tore her gaze away from the mesmerizing, calming gaze of the almond-shaped eye and read the words that had been scrawled below.

WHOM DO YOU HATE THE MOST?
WHAT WOULD YOU DO ABOUT IT IF YOU COULD?
TODAY IS THE DAY.

Mary read the lines over and over, absolutely fascinated. It seemed to her in that moment that she'd never read anything in her life that made as much sense as these three lines. Finally, after all her troubles, after everything that had happened since she'd awakened, here was an answer. Finally, she knew what to do.

A blast of ear-splittingly loud music filled the air right then; somehow, it didn't surprise her as snarling fuzz guitar blasted from the room's hidden speakers—the ones she and Patrick had always been politely asked to lower by the hotel staff when Patrick was smoking his glass bong and turning up the Nickelback. The words seemed to fill her vision, expanding like commandments on a stone tablet, removing all responsibility, taking away all the pain, the need to think and react, the need to do anything but obey. The strange calm spread over her as she lifted the gun—SMITH & WESSON, she read the words engraved on its thick barrel—and pulled back the slide, just like she'd seen in the movies so many times.

GOODBYE, the jagged writing on the wall had said; Mary felt tears tickling her cheeks as she turned the gun around, staring down its barrel like it was a tunnel to oblivion. All she had to do was pull the trigger and it would all be over—the pain and blood and fear and death and tears and agony would be over.

The deafening music was still blasting.

Mary's fingers trembled as she raised the gun to her head.

Goodbye, she thought.

She couldn't do it.

She couldn't make herself pull the trigger. *Come on*, she thought desperately, the heavy gun trembling in her hand. But somehow, she thought of Ellen right then—the pain in Ellen's voice when she'd told her Dylan was shot. Ellen mourning Dylan; Ellen and Mary and their mother mourning their father.

No.

Mary cried out as she forced her arm to drop, forced her fingers to open. The gun thumped to the carpet at her feet. *I can't do it,* she thought wildly as the tears flowed freely down her face.

She stood there staring at the empty box on the bare mattress and the note in her hand, when a tremendous blow knocked into her from behind.

Mary gasped in pain as she was driven forward onto the bed, her face pressed against the mattress. Somebody had tackled her and was now lying on top of her, a heavy weight that she couldn't possibly escape. She felt cold metal pressed against the back of her head and she knew what it was; she had something like one second—the final second of her life—to feel and recognize the pressure of the gun barrel against the back of her skull before a blinding explosion filled the world with silent light and she was dead.

II

7 SOULS

1

SCOTT

IN THE BEGINNING THERE was darkness. Mary was alone, at peace, at rest—all those things they said about you right before they put you in the ground. *Finally at peace*. The thought didn't seem to bring her any grief, or rage, or any feeling at all. She felt nothing, and it was good. The pain throughout her body was gone. The blinding spotlights and the deafening music before the bullet shattered her skull were all gone; everything was gone.

Whatever had happened to her, it had come fast and hard, like the storm that had drenched the city. She had not been ready for its full force, she realized: the rain had fallen, wild and powerful, and there was no getting out of its way. The darkness had shrouded her all day; she had seen it outside the windows, in the gray sky above the city—the rain had lashed down, spattering across her as she lay planted in the cold ground at the empty house, like a girl half-buried by a grave digger, already half dead. Her friends had vanished. She had tried to run, but the storm raged and the bullets came, first for Dylan and then for her—they paid the ultimate price, as those *Daily News* crime stories always put it. The victim paid the ultimate price—and here she was, paying it.

Because I'm dead.

The strange calmness that followed the realization—the way it was no more shocking than *I have a cold* or *I'm late for school*—convinced her. *I can't feel anything,* she confirmed to herself, and it didn't make her afraid. *I can't feel anything because I'm dead.*

But she did feel something: she felt regret. Regret that she had failed to escape whoever had it in for her; regret that she was too slow, too stupid, and now it was too late to do anything about it. Regret that she would never see any of them again, never be able to explain.

And she felt something else. *Physically,* she felt something—which was impossible, an illusion. But, concentrating, she was sure of it: a sensation was penetrating the void, barely there but growing, like the drone of an approaching plane. Something was pressed against her back. There was no getting around it. She wanted to move; she had to move.

I'm sleeping, Mary thought dazedly. *I'm dreaming. I'm waking up.*

That had to be it. *I dreamed all that. I had a nightmare, a paranoid nightmare.*

And why not? An *anxiety dream*—waking up naked with a skull-pounding headache, and a scornful crowd pointing and laughing. Isn't that the standard paranoid fantasy? A slow ride into panic, where everybody's trying to get you, trying to kill you; you try to run but you can't move, you can't get away. And then you wake up.

And it was all a dream.

Right?

Isn't that it? Isn't that what happens next? Mary realized she could hear her own breathing. She'd been ignoring it, pretending it wasn't there. But she was breathing fast; not exactly panting in terror but not exactly calm, either. *I hear my breathing, because I'm alive. It's later and my headache's gone and I'm waking up alone.*

I'm alive.

That made sense, didn't it?

"Wake up."

She heard a female voice, youthful and distorted, blasted with static as if coming in on a radio station. Mary's eyes snapped open. Her heart was pounding. The voice was *right there*, just inches from her head. Her eyes were watering and she reached to wipe at them with hands that felt sluggish and swollen; her fingers felt oddly thickened as they bumped against her eyelids and the bridge of her nose. *Am I bruised?* she wondered dazedly. *Did my face swell up?*

It seemed as though her ears were ringing from the

gunshot to the back of her head. But no. There was no ring-ing at all. *No gunshots*, she told herself. *No rainstorm, no end-less, baffling chase that turns into Death Race 2010 before you're blown to kingdom come.* Just silence, and the low hum, which sounded like it was coming from a fan—an ordinary elec-tric fan.

She could move, she realized. The numbness was slip-ping away, like the rough bedsheets that slid from her body as she flinched and sat up, squinting against the blinding, blazing white sunlight that bathed her face.

"Wake up."

The same robotic voice. *Alarm clock*, Mary realized. Her heart was still thwacking in her ears like a snare drum as she tried to wipe her eyes clear with fingers that were too short and fat. *That's an alarm clock, a novelty alarm clock that talks.*

Taking her hands from her face, Mary could see the alarm clock with the robot voice right next to her. It was a porcelain statue of a slender, buxom young woman holding a sword. The woman wore a colorful costume and a mask that tied around her long blond hair. The base of the statue was a block of stone that had a digital clock face set into it; the bright burgundy numbers said 7:01 A.M.

It was difficult to see anything else; the light was too bright. And her body was *heavy* and bloated. She had to strain to lift her own weight, just to sit up. The effort made her head feel light, and when she moved her shoulders and brought her thick new hands to her face she instantly real-ized her hair was gone.

Someone cut off my hair. All the familiar touches of her

hair—the flicking of the smooth ends against her shoulders, the softer waves that always cascaded down over her eyebrows and cheekbones until she swept them back—were gone. Somebody had taken a razor, a big electric clipper, and cut all of it off during the night.

Oh, Jesus, someone cut off my hair—

She could still hear the fan—*a computer fan*, she realized, looking around as her eyes continued to clear. The room she was in—a cluttered, wide bedroom with a bright triangle of sunlight spearing across its walls—had a big desk, covered in stacks of books and disks and boxes, and a pair of computers, their fans humming, with glowing neon lights, orange and green.

Where the hell am I?

A loud noise drew Mary's gaze to the far wall, and the door in the shadows, back beyond the dim outlines of other furniture she couldn't quite see.

Someone's outside the door. Footsteps were definitely approaching; Mary could clearly hear the repeated thump and squeak of rubber-soled shoes advancing.

"Scottie?"

A female voice, getting closer. Middle-aged, friendly. And *familiar*—Mary wasn't sure why, but she was absolutely convinced that she'd heard it before.

"Scottie? Are you up?"

Mary noticed a sweet, candied aroma. *Industrial blueberries,* she thought: the kind of mass-produced processed food Joon always scorned (while scarfing down one of her macrobiotic box lunches). Those rubber-soled footsteps kept getting louder; it sounded like a basketball player was approaching across a newly waxed court.

Mary looked around wildly, like a cornered animal, trying to find a way out. She blinked but couldn't quite clear her eyes; everything in the distance, beyond the bed, was hard to see clearly. There was a bathroom—with a hexagonal grid of gleaming white tiles stretching off into the blurry blackness beyond—but nothing else. Mary was trapped and the bedroom door was opening—she'd forgotten that door completely, because now she was looking full-on into the mirror on the wall that showed Scott Sanders, soft cheeks reddened by the sheets, short hair askew, brown eyes squinting in the glare of the morning light. Even out of focus, there was no question about it: Scott Sanders was staring back at her with a shocked, comical expression.

"Scottie! Wake up, sleepyhead!" The voice was huge, deafening as the door swung open and the woman with the loud sneakers was there, framed in the doorway. *That's Mrs. Sanders*, Mary realized dazedly; she recognized her voice.

But Mary couldn't tear her eyes from the mirror. She was still staring at Scott's reflection, matching him blink for blink.

"Scottie?" Mrs. Sanders repeated. "Are you feeling all right? I thought you hit the sack early."

"Wh-what?" Mary croaked. She tried not to jump as her voice rang out, reverberating inside her skull exactly as if it were her own, but it was *Scott's voice*, a teenage-male tenor that buzzed and vibrated in her throat—Scott's throat—as she spoke. "What—" she tried again.

"Feeling all right?" Scott's mother repeated. She came forward, recognizable to Mary from years and years of school plays and home games and parent-teacher days. For Mary, the strangest part was seeing her *in her sweats*. "I asked if you were— Scottie, sweetie, what's wrong? I've brought you breakfast."

The blueberry smell was overpowering, wondrous. Mary could feel her mouth watering as she fixed her eyes on the plate moving toward her, and she realized that the weakness and dizziness she felt was hunger. *Scott's mother wakes him up with Pop-Tarts*, Mary realized. She wasn't sure why, in the middle of the hallucination, the dream, the delusion, whatever it was, she found herself thinking about that, about Scott's mother. *She brings him breakfast and asks if he's feeling all right.* But she was fascinated, because it was so utterly strange.

"Go ahead," Mrs. Sanders urged. Mary reached out with Scott's pale, soft arm and took a Pop-Tart. Her eyes were beginning to water along with her mouth. She was *hungry*; she was taking a bite before she even realized it, her teeth squeezing through the hot pastry as if she'd never eaten anything before.

"Take the plate," Mrs. Sanders scolded, mock sternly. "I'm not standing here waiting on you."

Mary was chewing and swallowing. She bit the side of her mouth and winced; even her *teeth* felt strange, irregular and misaligned, and she had to chew carefully not to bite her own—Scott's—tongue. Pop-Tart crumbs flew from her mouth and hit Mrs. Sanders, bouncing off her sweatpants. Mary reached to take the plate, the Pop-Tarts on it rattling and sliding. The sensation of tasting the food was incredible; she was barely done swallowing each bite before she wanted more.

"Look at my hungry little man," Mrs. Sanders murmured as Mary finished the Pop-Tart—it had taken her three bites. She was so close that Mary could smell her scent and identify it—Clinique's Happy—before she turned away. "Come on, champ—better get moving. It's five past. And don't you have a test today?" She was walking away, legs hissing beneath blue terry cloth, shoes squeaking on the polished floor. "That means *no gaming*—and be sure to leave time for a shower."

I want to wake up, Mary thought as the door slammed, feeling a sugar rush kicking in. *I want to wake up now; I've had enough of this dream.* She was breathing heavily again, out of fear; she could see Scott's chest rising and falling beneath his yellow Grand Theft Auto T-shirt—she could barely read the blurred logo, backward, in the mirror.

A phone rang, suddenly. It was so loud that Mary flinched and nearly dropped the plate. The jangling, piercing chime—a cell-phone ringtone—was coming from Scott's cluttered desk. Rising off the bed, Mary came to her feet, holding on to a bedpost as she weaved, unable to support herself and almost losing her balance. The ringtone was still blaring and Mary actually recognized the song it was playing: "Femme Fatale." She stumbled to the desk, the plate clanking loudly as she dropped it there, the Pop-Tarts sliding onto a graph-paper notebook. Mary felt a cold wave pass over her when she saw Scott's blue LG phone—the one that always looked so grimy—with its amber light blinking and its bright screen displaying the incoming caller ID:

SHAYNE, MARY

It was all so real—that was the thing about it—not like a dream at all. The phone's display (four bars; full battery), the seven digital numerals of the world's most familiar phone number . . . every detail was perfectly realistic, even through the maddening blur that she suddenly understood, staring down at the desk.

Glasses—Scott's glasses!

There they were, on the desk beside the phone: Scott's familiar, gold-framed antique glasses. As Mary fumbled them onto her face, the surrounding room snapped into exquisitely sharp focus. Looking in the mirror was unsettling; now she could see the red veins in Scott's eyes and the millions of tiny white hairs on his smooth skin. A few yellowed, sticky grains of sleep were gummed to his eyelashes, and his lips were slightly chapped.

She reached down and touched the cool plastic of the phone, feeling its vibration along her arm as she picked it up, flipped it open and brought it up to her ear. Her thumb brushed against her—Scott's—hair as she pressed the green Talk button.

"Hel—hello?" She jumped again at the sensation of hearing Scott's voice coming from her own throat.

"Scott!"

A young female voice, garbled and distorted by the cell phone's tiny speaker. "Can you hear me?"

"Wh-what—?" she heard herself responding—again, in Scott's familiar tenor.

"It's Mary. You there, Scott? I need your help."

"Mary—wait, *what?*"

That's me, she thought. *That's me. Oh my God.*

"*You're* Mary," she managed to rasp out. "What the—What day is it?"

"It's *Friday,*" her own voice blared in her ear through the erratic connection. "*Friday,* Scott, the day of the *physics test*—the big killer test. We were supposed to meet last night to power-cram, remember?"

"Physics test." There was something familiar about those words—something she couldn't put her finger on.

I said that, Mary suddenly remembered. *That's me, this morning. I called Scott at seven, from the taxicab—on the way home from Crate and Barrel.*

Before it all started.

"The physics test—of *course.* But—but, holy shit, that's—"

"It's *today,* Scott. Come on—will you *wake up,* damn it? Snap *out* of it! This is *serious.*"

"Serious," Mary repeated, as the memory came into focus. Her mouth tasted like blueberry Pop-Tart. "Right, I was—you were supposed to meet me—I forgot that we were— But—"

She was gazing around Scott's bedroom, squinting through the dust motes at the East Side morning sky beyond the plate glass. She had never been here, of course. Probably, *no* girl had been here, *ever.* Posters around the room showed fantasy girls, all pretty and skinny with big chests, all drawn or painted or digitally rendered, pubescent dreams frozen and reproduced in rows across Scott's walls.

"*Scott!*" On the phone, her voice louder—her impatience was growing. To Mary, it was the voice of the happiest, most carefree girl in the world. "Scott, I'm trying to remember last night—what *happened* last night, I mean. I'm blacking out on some of it and I can't remember if I met you after dinner or— Hello?"

Mary could hear the world's squeakiest sneakers beyond the bedroom door. Mrs. Sanders was moving around. Mary really didn't want to deal with her again.

I have to get out of here, she thought. The cell phone was warm in her hand, its amber light blinking. *I have to get out of here right now.* It was nearly an animal impulse; her spinal column felt electrified and her breathing was getting faster. Her bare feet were cold from the parquet floor.

Mary slapped the phone shut. A flush was coming over her face and her vision was darkening; she clenched the edge of the desk with Scott's fat fingers and tried to clear her head. Frantically looking around at the mess strewn around the floor, she saw a pair of nearly new Adidas along with a tangle of T-shirts and the pleated pants that Scott always wore. Mary had managed to get her balance, but she was still stumbling since Scott's arms and legs were so different from hers—she banged her elbow against the desk's edge and felt a dull pain spread through her arm.

I've got to get out of here. She was close to panic as she picked Scott's loose khaki pants up from the floor and began pulling them on, reeling back against the bed, getting the pants on over the loose gray sweatpants and reaching for Scott's familiar-looking near-virgin Adidas running shoes. *Why does he even wear these?* she thought distractedly as she fumbled with the laces, impatiently tangling Scott's sweaty fingers around them. *He never runs, anywhere.*

But she had to. It was like the times that Mary would end up collapsed somewhere, at the end of a party, on a sofa or along the edge of a well-made bed, the room reeling drunkenly around her, and she would think, *time to rally*— she would understand that Joon was gone and Amy was gone and she was going to have to make it out of there, wherever she was, alone. She would picture the obstacle course: getting to her feet, finding her coat, putting on her coat, checking if she had both earrings, then propelling herself down an unfamiliar corridor to a big front door, past whatever drunken people were still there, and outside. Then an elevator and a lobby and a sidewalk and a taxicab and she would be home, her ears ringing, the party sounds fading behind her.

Time to rally—she was doing it now, stone-cold sober, in the bright morning light, and it was exactly the same: stumbling out into a strange corridor, trying to find her way to the front door. The apartment was huge—Mary glimpsed a concert grand piano through one doorway and a kitchen table with a pitcher of grapefruit juice and an unfolded *New York Times* through another. *Got to get out of here, got to get out of here*, she was thinking over and over, her heartbeat clicking in her ears again as she propelled Scott's heavy body toward the giant front door.

"Wait! Don't leave!" Scott's mother called out, from somewhere in the vastness of the apartment. Mary froze, cringing. She could hear the basketball-court sounds of Mrs. Sanders approaching. Frantically, she started fiddling with the brass knob on the front door. "Scottie, wait!"

Mary finally got the door open as Mrs. Sanders appeared behind her. "Aren't you forgetting something?" she said, holding out Scott's red backpack—Mary noticed its familiar Harry Potter and Dandy Warhols stickers. "You're not going anywhere without this."

Mary tried to speak, but couldn't quite get herself to make any coherent sound. She reached out and took Scott's book bag—it felt much heavier than she'd expected—and catapulted herself out of the Sanders apartment, pulling the heavy door closed behind her as fast as she could.

LEANING AGAINST THE SMOOTH mahogany walls of the descending elevator, ears popping as chimes indicated the floors, Mary wondered if she had lost her mind. All her thoughts were going in tight little circles, faster and faster, as the elevator dropped toward the ground. It was obvious that she wasn't dead; she had already figured that out, but she was beginning to accept that she had gone crazy somewhere along the way. *Somebody help me*, she thought, pressing her sweat-covered forehead against the glossy wood wall. It was all so real: she could smell the lemon in the polish that somebody had used not that long ago to bring out the expensive mahogany glow, which right now showed Scott's fat, reddened face, reflected back at her from inches away. *Help me, help me; I want to wake up.*

The elevator suddenly stopped and a quivering jolt shook her bones. Another chime rang out as the big wooden door rolled open. If she was dreaming, the dream was amazingly realistic—*impossibly* realistic.

195

"All right, my man Scott," a loud male voice called out—Mary saw what looked like a United States Marine in a crisp uniform and cap but was actually just a sallow-faced Manhattan doorman. Stumbling out of the elevator, she noticed a red shaving nick on his pale chin, above the starched white broadcloth collar. "What's the matter—tough day ahead?"

(*Tough day*)

What was it about that phrase? It reminded Mary of something. The memory seemed very recent; it flashed into her head all at once, vividly: she could feel a pain in her shoulder and fatigue through her body—she remembered standing in a cold, brightly lit reception room talking to a woman with a headset, a woman she knew.

(*Tough day*)

"TOUGH DAY?"

"You have *no idea*," Scott agreed.

Two weeks ago, Scott was coated in dried sweat (not an unusual sensation for Scott, unfortunately and lamentably), facing Sheila, the receptionist at McDougall Sanders Construction's worldwide headquarters on the fourty-fourth floor of the Blakeman building on Sixth Avenue. Expensive air-conditioning chilled the sweat in his hair and on his arms and back.

"What are you *carrying?*" Sheila asked, squinting critically at him while reaching for the phone headset. It must have been easy to see why Scott was covered in sweat: his book bag was stuffed. As it happened, he was carrying *two complete loads* of books—his own and somebody else's. The book bag's straps were cutting into his shoulders like knives. The pain was exquisite; Sheila could see it in his face.

"Don't ask," Scott had told her. Sheila laughed politely.

Because I can't explain, he had finished, privately. He never could explain, ever. It was the curse of his divided life. His experiences were unique.

To Scott's friends (using the word lightly; Scott thought of them as "the math guys" or "the sci-fi guys" or "the comic-book guys," manfully weathering the inevitable *Simpsons* reference), Scott was a good gamer, a fair comic collector and a way-cool Star Wars fan (not to mention the builder and owner of an airplane fleet to fill a modeler's heart with lust), but he had done something heroic, something amazing, something they all worshipped him for.

He'd become friends with Mary Shayne.

Scott Sanders had actually managed to score a *friendship* with the most jaw-droppingly, smokingly, sickeningly, desperately hot girl at school; the one who you *tried* not to stare at . . . honestly, how hard you tried . . . but it was impossible. She was Megan Fox. She was Aeon Flux. She was Angelina Jolie (back when Angelina was young and wild). She was Wonder Woman. She was all of them at once, and she was *real*, right in front of you during physics class, every day; you could talk to her (if you dared); she breathed the same air as you. It was insane, unbelievable; there was just no way to handle it. She was the heroine in whatever book you were reading in English, when the teacher was droning on about the Romantic Age in literature and reciting Shelley or Keats.

She's just normal, Scott would tell his friends, to their

constant frustration. *It's just like talking to anyone else. And no. I certainly won't introduce you, like, ever, so stop asking.*

And that was why nobody understood. Spending those fleeting moments with Mary was bliss, was ecstasy, not because she behaved like a "babe"—whatever that meant—but because she was a normal person. The eye candy was unbelievable, nearly religious, to be sure; but, in the end, they were *friends*.

What Scott wanted more than anything else was to be real friends with Mary—to be part of that crowd, that living, breathing Abercrombie & Fitch ad that surrounded her like drone planes around an aircraft carrier. He knew he didn't fit in; he didn't have the look you needed in order to become part of that particular club, the one everyone at Chadwick hated and disdained and desperately wanted to be part of. Scott didn't care about clothes or gossip or sports or any of that, but he still thought his friendship with Mary might be the entry ticket he needed. If he kept getting closer to her, then he figured he would start being accepted by her crowd.

Dude, you do her fucking homework, Brian Anderson had sniped, when Scott had shyly admitted his ambitions. *Don't kid yourself—you're part of her pit crew, nothing more than that. In three months you'll never see her again.* But Brian was just jealous; that was obvious. Mary was a good friend.

Mary's personality wasn't bad either, was the thing. It wasn't *spectacular*; she was no Rachel Maddow, that was for sure. And she obviously had no patience at all; everything had to be done for her. But she was funny. She could be clever. And she said interesting things, sometimes, when she wasn't so busy playing the starring role in her opera. (Scott figured that Mary's life was too grand for soap opera—he'd long ago decided that she was the epicenter of a full-on opera, with expensive sopranos and tenors and the kind of thousand-dollar ticket that his dad gave his mom for Christmas.) It was exactly like what happened with movie stars: if you knew who they were, then you knew whom they dated, who broke up with them, whom they'd gone home with, accepted, toyed with, refused, pined after, dumped. You knew it all. You couldn't help it; even if you didn't *want* to follow the story, you had to, because they did it all in front of you. The more attractive and popular the kids were, the more they played out their biggest scenes in plain sight, right in front of you when you were at your locker or trying to get by. It was the world as a stage.

But Scott couldn't blame Mary for that, either. So she was the star of the show. Who wouldn't want to be the star? It's always the best role: you get to laugh and cry and fight and kiss and everyone's on your side; they've all got your back.

And Mary was a *great* star. She played it to the hilt. She didn't solve her problems—she experienced them; she *re-acted* to them, grandly. If life was a Broadway show, Mary would get all the big numbers—the Tony-winning songs people wanted played at their weddings. Mary's problems were epic. They became global projects everyone was encouraged to participate in.

Which was why Scott was carrying a two-ton book bag that day.

Scott had agreed to come down here, to West Fifty-second Street, walking the whole way, because it was part of the deal to keep Dad happy. He had to walk because his father wanted him to "observe" the buildings that flanked the wide avenues on his way down, noticing their facades, their "footprints," their "zoning envelopes"—all the perfectly boring details of the Manhattan real estate market that his father insisted he pay attention to. He'd tried to get out of it, once or twice taking the subway rather than walking, but he'd never gotten away with it. His dad would always quiz him about the buildings he'd observed on the way, and he just couldn't bring himself to fake it. Today, even with a two-ton book bag, he'd walked the full thirty-six blocks— and here he was, dutifully pushing the heavy glass door that opened into the enormous mahogany-faced conference room where Dad was about to present to a client. Scott had agreed to assist, but he wished he could be *anywhere else*. And, of course, "anywhere else" just meant one place—the real destination he was headed, after this meeting—Mary Shayne's Upper West Side apartment.

Mary had been absent from school that day. Scott had noticed immediately; he caught himself strolling down the fifth-floor hallway where Mary's homeroom was, casually glancing at the crowd flocking out of the room as the bell rang, and not seeing her. When Scott's cell phone blasted "Femme Fatale" that noon, he rejoiced, forcing himself to be cool and to nonchalantly answer on the second ring. Mary had sounded awful—the hoarseness of her voice created an alarmingly sexy effect that he almost complimented her on, before getting a grip on himself. Mary outlined her request— she needed him to get several of her books out of her locker

(Scott wrote down their titles and her locker combination number, straining to hear over the crowds in the Chadwick corridor) and bring them to her house after school. Could he do that?

Scott could. And finally, two hours after the meeting with his dad, here he was, feet aching, heart pounding, shoulders screaming in pain as he entered the Shaynes' apartment building.

I'm here again, Scott thought excitedly as the elevator rose to the fifth floor. It didn't matter that the fake wood paneling was peeling off the elevator walls: this was Mary Shayne's building, and that made it a palace. When he alighted from the elevator and rang the Shaynes' doorbell, he felt like he was walking on a cloud. *Maybe she's feverish,* he thought, standing nervously in front of the scuffed metal door and trying to compose his features into the correct expression. *Maybe she's weak and feverish and lying in bed in a gauzy nightgown, and she'll need me to bring a glass of water to her lips.*

Then the door latch snapped over and the door swung open and Scott realized that he wasn't going to be bringing any glasses of water to anyone's lips.

Mary was holding her phone with one hand, pressing it against her ear, while she pulled the door open with her other hand. She was smiling, dazzlingly. She wasn't even remotely sick—Scott had never seen a healthier girl in his life.

"No, Trick's not coming until seven; if we get carded we'll just go somewhere else. Hang on—someone's here," Mary said into the phone. "I'll call you back." Scott was trying not to stare at Mary's flat bare stomach as she beamed at

201

him, raising her lovely eyebrows. She was obviously dressed to go out: she wore tight leather pants and a scanty sequined top that covered her chest and shoulders while exposing her midriff. He could smell some kind of seductive perfume wafting from her. "Scottie!" Mary sang out happily, beaming at him. "You gorgeous guy, you—thanks so much for coming!"

"Um—" Scott couldn't think of anything to say. Mary looked so beautiful that he could barely breathe. It was like she had stepped off the cover of a magazine and into this dingy Upper West Side apartment, right in front of him. "I brought all your books."

Aching at the effort, Scott swung his book bag around and dropped it between them on the floor. Mary stood waiting as he fumbled with the straps, extracting her books. *She's not sick,* Scott marveled. *She's going out—she's about to go out.* He wasn't angry—not exactly. He just couldn't find the anger inside himself, not while Mary was standing there, arms crossed, the perfect pale skin of her abdomen visibly expanding and contracting as she breathed.

"That's the lot," Scott said, rising to his feet—he had produced a big stack of schoolbooks. "You're all set."

Mary looked delighted. It was a good look for her. "Scottie—*thank you,*" she sighed, staring yearningly at him. She leaned toward him, her soft black hair brushing against his cheek as she gave him a kiss that almost touched his lips. Scott trembled; it felt like he'd just brushed against an electrical cable. "Thank you *so much.* Listen, I'd say come in, but I'm actually about to go somewhere."

"Go somewhere?" Scott repeated weakly. His cheek was

still tingling from Mary's kiss. *She's not going to invite me along. Of course she's not.*

"Alas." Mary raised her eyebrows prettily—and Scott realized that that was his cue. "Thanks again, Scottie. I really don't know what I'd do without you."

You'd find someone else to deliver your books, he thought bitterly. *You'd find another sucker.*

"Please—it's nothing," Scott said magnanimously, shouldering his book bag, now a much more manageable weight. "I'm happy to be of service."

Mary smiled again and then swung the door shut, and Scott turned away, toward the elevator. He could hear Mary resuming the conversation he'd interrupted.

So much for my Tour of Midtown Manhattan and Points West, Scott thought. He was trying to be cavalier, whistling as he exited Mary's building. But by the time he was collapsed exhausted, defeated, in the rearmost seat of a crosstown bus (while Mary, no doubt, was zooming downtown in a taxicab), he was starting to feel sick—sick like he wanted to get into bed and hide under the covers and not move until he finally fell asleep. Then the morning would come and his mother would bring him Pop-Tarts and he wouldn't feel so bad; he'd go back to Chadwick, and count the minutes until he saw her again.

Tough day.

"—HEAR ME? I ASKED if you've got a tough day coming, Scottie."

Mary stood there, blinking, confused. *What the hell?*

An entire, detailed memory had come into her head

right then, just as the doorman had used that phrase. She'd been reminded of something that happened and suddenly the entire experience was recalled to her, all at once.

But that was Scott's memory.

The sensation was bizarre, almost hallucinogenic: a piece of Scott's past had just dropped into her brain, as easily and seamlessly as if it were her own. *It's because I'm Scott,* she realized with growing wonder. *I'm not just in his body— I'm experiencing his memories, too.*

No time had passed at all. Mary was still standing in the same spot, facing Scott's doorman. *That whole thing just occurred in a millisecond.* Just like in real life (as opposed to this insane dream or hallucination or whatever it was), memories didn't take up any time; they just *appeared* in your mind when prompted—even when they were somebody else's memories.

The doorman was still right behind her, gold buttons gleaming, watching her stand there like a chess piece waiting to be moved. What should she do? Go back upstairs? Stay here? The fear made it difficult to think.

She remembered the phone call—the one she'd been on both ends of, without realizing it. She remembered the beginning of the day, making the call and hearing herself—

Hearing what I just *said,* she realized. *What I said just now.*

Maybe I can stop it, she thought suddenly. *Maybe I can change what happened.*

I've got to get there—I've got to get to school.

Pulling up the slipping strap of Scott's book bag, Mary blundered outside, the seven A.M. overcast light gleaming in her eyes as her feet hit the sidewalk. The building's awning had a round convex mirror bolted beneath it, and Mary saw her own reflection moving—saw a fish-eye view of Scott Sanders in an unusually rumpled sweatshirt, blinking comically.

Where the hell am I?

Mary gazed up at the white morning sky. She didn't remember where Scott lived. It was embarrassing to realize: she knew Scott had told her, more than once, but she was drawing a blank. In the distance, the MetLife Building gleamed in the morning haze. *East Side—somewhere in the fifties*, she realized. That seemed correct: she vaguely remembered that Scott took the Lexington Avenue subway to school.

Don't think—just move, Mary told herself doggedly. It was starting to feel like she would genuinely lose her mind if she kept thinking. *Even if you're dreaming, just follow the dream—follow it wherever it goes.*

Like she had a choice. Mary pulled the slipping straps of Scott's JanSport book bag up higher on her—his—soft, sloping shoulders. Walking north—still trying not to lose her footing as she propelled herself on Scott's short, overweight legs—she crossed East Fifty-eighth Street (nearly getting sideswiped by a loudly honking taxicab whose driver cursed at her furiously in a Middle Eastern language) and ran away from the grinning doorman and the fun-house mirror, hurrying toward the Chadwick School.

IT WAS ALL SO real, but it moved like a dream. She was not herself—*literally* not herself—painfully biting her cheeks with Scott's large teeth, stumbling over the cuffs of

205

his rumpled sweatpants, feeling his soft, doughy stomach quivering as she walked, rather than her own tight abdomen (and the narrow band of skin she made sure was occasionally visible), or the cold air on the bare back of her neck rather than the cascade of jet-black hair that was supposed to be there. It was like wearing a heavy Halloween costume, but vastly stranger.

There was something else, too: there was something wrong with the pedestrians around her. She'd been noticing it since she stepped onto the street. She couldn't put her finger on it; it was like one of those body snatcher or zombie movies where the ordinary people in the crowd were not what they seemed. But, crossing Sixtieth Street, she suddenly figured it out.

Nobody's looking at me.

It was true. The difference was subtle, but she noticed it. Businessmen and kids and mothers and random passersby: nobody was looking. What did it mean? *Am I a ghost?* But that was ridiculous; Mrs. Sanders and Scott's doorman had seen her, reacted to her.

But nobody's looking.

It wasn't just that nobody was checking her out— nobody was noticing her *at all*.

It made her feel invisible; it was somehow more unreal and unsettling than being transported back to the beginning of the day. No girls were whispering about her as she went past, furtively scoping the brand names on her clothes; no men were trying to sneak a look at her chest or her ass while she went by. Nobody cared.

Because I'm Scott.

Mary had *never* experienced anything like that. She was used to *avoiding* people's glances, never returning the leers and stares of men she passed in the street—even if you *wanted* to look, you couldn't, in case they got the wrong idea. She was so used to that rule, she obeyed it without thinking. Now she found herself *trying* to make eye contact, but it was impossible. It reminded her of the memory she'd just experienced—Scott's memory. *Is that really what happened?* she thought. She remembered that night, of course; she'd faked being sick and made plans to go clubbing with Amy and Trick—and she remembered how sweet Scott was for bringing her books over.

But she'd never thought about what it had been like for Scott. She'd never considered the effort he'd put into helping her, or the sacrifices he'd had to make just to bring her the books she was too lazy (or too much of a truant) to get herself.

And there's more to it, isn't there? Mary had to face the fact that there was.

Have I been taking advantage of Scott?

It was a brand-new thought. She'd always assumed that Scott did what he did—helped her—out of kindness, because he was, well, such a sweet guy. It never occurred to her that Scott might have ulterior motives. Like, say, an enormous crush on her. She'd never dreamed that she was asking a lovesick boy to perform menial tasks and leveraging his crush to get what she wanted.

But that's not really true, is it?

Mary had to admit that it wasn't.

Because who was she kidding? Of *course* she knew Scott

had a crush on her. She'd seen his eyes skate over her body many times (not just that night two weeks ago when he'd appeared at her apartment door with her books). If she wasn't aware of Scott's attraction, then why did she flirt with him? Why did she play it up the way she did, getting close to him, calling him sweetie and honey, touching his shoulder, kissing his cheek? (The memory of how that had felt for Scott—that desperate, mournful cocktail of fear and desire and frustration and loneliness—was completely vivid.) She'd been taking advantage of Scott for a *long* time; really, as long as she'd known him.

How often have I done that? Just demand that the people around her help her? As far as Scott was concerned, she had to admit that she couldn't remember a time when she wasn't leaning on him. *Didn't I introduce myself just to get the notes for a math quiz?* she thought uncomfortably. *I did, didn't I?*

It was even worse than that. Scott *knew* it. He could see it in her eyes. Mary thought she was fooling Scott, but she wasn't.

And yet he does it all anyway, she marveled. *He knows what I'm doing—he knows the score—and yet he doesn't stop; he still does what I ask.*

Mary was fascinated, engrossed with what she'd realized. She kept propelling Scott's soft body forward, her mind overwhelmed by these new revelations. *I take advantage of Scott,* she admitted. *I totally take advantage of him—and he suffers, because of me.* She thought about Scott's memory of hauling her books all over Manhattan and nearly felt sick. *I'm sorry, Scott. I'm so sorry.*

*　　*　　*

THE FIFTY-NINTH STREET subway station was much more confusing than Mary had realized—she hurried onto a departing train, jamming Scott's thick body in among a harried crowd of late-morning commuters, only to realize, four stops later, that she was going in the wrong direction. She pushed through the irritated crowd, escaping, only to realize that she'd disembarked at a local station and would have to climb to the street to catch the train headed back the other direction.

By the time she got to Chadwick, Mary's body—Scott's body—was covered in sweat, and she was panting hoarsely as her heartbeat thumped dangerously. *Heart attack; Jesus Christ, I'm going to have a heart attack*, she thought dazedly as she collapsed against the cast-iron mailbox on the corner of Eighty-second Street. Her lungs were on fire; she felt like she'd smoked an entire pack of Trick's Dunhills in one night. She gasped, burping slightly (and tasting blueberry), and had a single, horrifying moment when her vision darkened and she was sure, *absolutely positive*, that she was about to vomit, but she waited, the taste of blueberry Pop-Tarts replaying through her mouth as she coughed up spit, and then she felt all right; she could see and breathe again.

This morning, she thought again, incredulously. It was beyond real—the overcast sky, the crowds of students in front of the school, the cell-phone calls and blaring headphones and endless screeching of the younger children; Mary took it all in, through the haze of pain.

Scott Sanders was not in shape—that much was obvious to anyone—but Mary had never stopped to realize how much *it hurt* when he tried to exert himself. Back in eighth grade when Scott had just barely missed the school bus that was leaving for Chadwick's famous year-end day trip, all the students had laughed, pointing out the windows at his diminishing figure as he tried, and failed, to catch up. Mary had laughed just as loudly as the rest of them. She remembered it vividly, staring through the bus's safety glass window at Super-Dork Scott running pathetically after them, finally collapsing against a parked SUV and—for the grand comic finale that Scott always managed to orchestrate back then—setting off its car alarm, which made the entire eighth-grade Chadwick class applaud in unison. The bus drove away and left Scott on the sidewalk, his anguished red face vanishing into the streetscape behind them. Mary had thought it was hilarious.

Now, with her lungs burning like twin blowtorches, she didn't see what was so funny.

Trick . . . ?

Her own voice, in the back of her head. Unusually vivid; it didn't sound like a memory at all. Mary didn't know what had made Trick's name pop into her head, but—

"Come on."

Trick's voice, Mary realized instantly. It was hard to hear; difficult to pick out in the crowd. "Let's walk."

"Walk?"

Mary's own voice again—also distant.

I'm not remembering, she realized suddenly. *I'm hearing that.*

That's really me.

Mary craned her—Scott's—neck, squinting as she

strained to see. It wasn't easy. Scott's short body was getting battered around by the thickening crowd of Chadwick students as Mary pressed forward, trying to catch a glimpse of herself. She'd seen Trick's golden curls, just for a second, but then her view was blocked again.

She hadn't intended to scream—not at first. But the moment she saw herself—saw freshly showered Mary Shayne in her darling little FCUK T-shirt and her billowing trench coat and her blown-out hair—she was overcome with a frenzied need to protect herself from everything that was coming.

"*Mary!*" she screamed.

A clump of first graders in front of her turned toward her, their mouths and eyes wide open, like alarmed cartoon characters. As soon as she got her breath back, she screamed again. "*Mary! Mary!*"

The crowd was moving now, surging closer. Somebody's hand slapped Mary in the face as another student pinwheeled around, startled. The view through the crowd on the sidewalk was wide and deep, flickering with movement. She realized she was moving again, feeling Scott's muffin-top fat rolling up and down as she stumbled forward. She couldn't see Patrick or herself through the rest of the crowd, when—

There. Eye contact—Mary Shayne's bright blue eyes, looking right at her.

"Mary, *look out!*" she screamed. "*Look out, you're in danger!*"

Scott's glasses tumbled from his face, dropping to the pavement—she heard their gold frames clattering and scraping against the cement. Blinded, she kept running through the blur.

But that's me! she thought desperately. *It's still morning— I don't have to do* any *of it! I've got time to get away.*

"Mary, for Christ's sake—" she screamed again. Her voice—Scott's voice—was rasping so painfully that she had to start over. "*Mary, you've got to listen—you're in serious danger—*"

It was like slamming into a tollbooth gate at high speed. The pain was incredible as Mary's chest—Scott's chest— slammed into some kind of horizontal immovable object, like a padded bar of cement.

"Hey, assface!"

Pete Schocken's voice, from right up close. Mary couldn't see a thing, but she suddenly smelled spearmint gum.

"What the hell, man?"

Definitely Pete. Mary was astonished. For years, Mary had thought of Pete as a buzz risk—a boy not to be around when he'd had a couple too many trips to the keg, because a drunk Pete Schocken would always manage to make the World's Most Inept Pass at one of the girls (okay, at her) be- fore the evening was over. He was basically harmless and he never remembered any of it by Monday morning, but push- ing his hands away while trying not to spill a plastic cup of Belvedere vodka onto someone's kitchen floor was not how Mary liked to spend her time when she went out.

But Pete's so nice, she marveled. He had never seemed to have a mean bone in his body, as far back as she could remember. He was a teddy bear, a sweetheart, a boy who would always buy you another drink or call you a cab. Hearing him call anyone an assface—let alone her—was as shocking as hearing a nun say it.

"Mary, *please listen*," she tried again, panting as she shouted some more and her throat burned. The football players were surrounding her, pressing in, and she couldn't see a thing. She had to assume that Real Mary was still within earshot. *"You've got to get out of—"*

It was like getting struck by lightning—her vision flashed white and her ears popped as she was smacked, powerfully, in the face. Her eyes were stinging; she was now truly blind—the pain spread across the skin of her cheeks like flame through paper.

"Chill *out,* you goddamned freak!"

That's Silly Billy, she recognized distantly. Billy Nelson—another boy she'd never imagine raising a hand to hurt anybody—calling Scott Sanders a "goddamned freak," his voice booming down like God yelling the Ten Commandments.

"Mary, *run!*" Mary screamed again. *"Please listen—you've got to— Ow!"*

A fist collided with her collarbone, hard. She'd never stopped to think about how *hard* a boy could hit you if he was really trying, if there was nothing to hold him back. She lost her balance, tipping over backward as she kicked with Scott's short legs and felt her feet slip. Real Mary still hadn't responded—she seemed to be getting further away. Scott's book bag slipped from her rounded shoulders and thumped to the ground, its contents spilling out. She landed against somebody's crumpling legs, and the sidewalk was pressed against her cheek, rough and cold. Between somebody's running socks, she could just make out the diminishing figures of Patrick and Real Mary, walking farther down Eighty-second Street.

"*Mary, run!*" she screamed one final time. Real Mary didn't pay any attention at all—she just kept walking away.

No, no, Mary thought weakly as she rolled painfully up from the ground, trying to pick out individual voices from the yelling and laughing all around her. *Please, no more . . . I can't take anymore.*

Her face was swimming in a sea of red—*Scott's book bag,* she realized, wiping tears and dirt from her eyes and face, staring at the red fabric as she gasped for breath. They had stopped hitting her; that was the important part. It meant she could—

Mary froze in place, on all fours on the crowded sidewalk, staring down at the contents of Scott's bag, which had corkscrewed out along the sidewalk. Shama's physics test, and an iPod, and a stack of notebooks—

—and a roll of silver gaffer's tape.

The spool of tape rolled lazily across the cement, circling like a dropped coin. Mary stared at it, mesmerized—in her memory, Joon squealed and twisted and panicked in the slashing, freezing rain, the silver tape over her anguished mouth, blocking her screams.

Inside the book bag, Mary finally saw what she'd been carrying, why the bag had felt so heavy. Coils of thick white nylon rope—yards and yards of it—were stuffed inside, nearly filling the bag.

It was Scott, Mary thought dazedly. *Oh my God—it was Scott!*

Was that even possible? Could Scott have killed her?

The stampede of students had somehow missed what had happened; they kept moving, legs and hands colliding with her as she stared into the bag. There was something else in there, something she didn't recognize at all—a folded sheet of silver cloth. She had no idea what it was, or why Scott had it.

Was sweet little Scott Sanders a *murderer?*

Another, even stranger possibility occurred to her right then—a new thought that made her feel a deep, arctic chill.

Have I come back as my own killer?

Was there some cult or religion in which that happened? The murder victim comes back as her own murderer? Mary didn't know anything about cults or religions. It sounded more like *The Twilight Zone* than any kind of—what did you call it?—theology.

But I'm here, she told herself, staring at the tape. She was still sitting on the sidewalk. *I'm here, and I'm Scott—and it looks like he killed me.*

The woozy feeling was coming over her in earnest. Bright lights, bright sky—it was all very bright. *Scott killed me*, she thought again, but somehow the idea seemed harmless, meaningless—she was drifting, she realized, losing her bearings, returning to whatever strange white void she'd first encountered ninety minutes ago, when she woke up in Scott's bedroom.

"You okay, Sanders?" A distant voice—she couldn't recognize it. It was a voice from another planet, coming from far, far away.

Is this it? Mary wondered as the brightness from the chrome reflections and flecks of mica and the dazzling sky grew brighter and brighter. The whiteness engulfed her like the whitecaps of a coastal tide flooding a beach, like snow engulfing a landscape, covering all detail, blotting out all shapes and colors, washing the world away into an endlessly bright field of white.

2

JOON

BLINDING WHITENESS, A FLASH of lightning, silent and bright, like platinum fire; the roar of heavy rain and the freezing sting of cold water on her face. Mary blinked at the pain of the bright light, the afterimages fading as she shook the water from her eyes.

Oh my God, it hurts—

She had been lying on the sidewalk, nursing the pain of her—Scott's—bruised backside and thighs, and then, with all the smoothness of a particularly good DJ mix, she was somewhere else, with incredible pain running through her arms.

It was difficult to breathe; something was covering her face. She didn't know what it was.

What the hell—? Where am I?

Her eyes finally cleared and she looked around, gritting her teeth at the incredible agony in her arms. She was suspended, she finally realized; her arms were pulled straight upward, with the entire weight of her body hanging straight down. She struggled, wriggling in place, and felt herself swinging like a pendulum, which made the pain in her arms even worse.

Lightning flared again, a silent fire like a photographer's flashgun, and Mary saw where she was.

She was outdoors, at night, in the middle of a rainstorm, surrounded by primeval forest, suspended from high above by ropes that cut into her wrists like barbed wire. Straining to tilt her head upward, black hair falling in her eyes, Mary saw the thick ropes stretching far overhead, converging in the blackness above.

Tipping her head downward, she felt a horrifying wave of vertigo and nausea come over her. She was high up in the air, suspended over a vast drop.

Far below, a wide, rushing stream was raging like a river, casting foaming spray around jagged rocks, running down a steep incline toward a tremendous black culvert beneath a spillway of moss-covered boulders. She got all that in one flash of lightning—just the bare outlines, lit up like an X-ray—but it was enough. The vertigo was overpowering; it reminded her of the feeling she'd gotten once, years ago, when she made the mistake of leaning as far as she could over the edge of the Brooklyn Bridge guardrail.

Straight ahead, she could just discern a pale haze of yellow light, and in front of it, a wide black mass.

Mary tried to scream—and couldn't. Her mouth was sealed shut.

She heard herself making a desperate, high-pitched wail, like the crying of a wounded, trapped animal.

And suddenly, Mary realized where she was.

It's changed, she realized. *I'm somewhere else—I'm someone else.*

She had spent an hour—if that—as Scott Sanders at the beginning of that same Friday, the day she died. Just long enough to get to Chadwick and try to warn herself to *run* from all the horrible events to come.

But it hadn't worked.

And, just as she'd discovered what Scott had in his book bag—something that barely began to explain the mystery of what had happened to her—she'd gone somewhere else. She'd become someone else.

And she knew where she was, of course. The slipping headband and the glitter of the sequined dress she was wearing only confirmed it.

I'm Joon, she thought, incredulously. *I'm Joon, hanging from the tree. I'm about to die—I'm about to fall to my death.*

The black mass in front of her—the enormous shape looming like the evil witch's gingerbread house in the fairy tale—was the deserted house; the farmhouse she'd driven to, with Amy, after panicking that Joon had been abducted at her surprise birthday party.

The glow behind the house was coming from the

headlights of Patrick's Mercedes. *Amy never turned the lights off*, Mary remembered.

She barely managed to avoid vomiting, realizing it would be fatal—there was nowhere for the vomit to *go*, with the wide piece of gaffer's tape that was plastered over her mouth—as she felt the ropes vibrate and shake, and, a few feet above her, begin to fray and snap.

No, no, no—

Mary remembered vividly what had happened to Joon.

The raging stream far below was bubbling and roaring, miniature white-water rapids splashing the jagged, mossy rocks that were scattered between its banks.

I don't understand, Mary thought miserably. Her suffering seemed to go on endlessly, without any rhyme or reason. She moaned again and struggled with the ropes, and her move‑ment made her begin to pivot in place, to twirl like a yo-yo on a string, to spin in circles—

(*spinning in circles*)

And, again, something jogged her memory; a sudden wave of déjà vu tickled against the extreme edge of her per‑ception, maddeningly out of sight.

(*spinning in circles*)

JOON WAS SPINNING IN circles—slow, dizzying and painful. She was twisting in the wind like a creaky weather vane, pirouetting clumsily on her ice skates in the middle of the Rockefeller Center ice rink. This was what it had come to: dangling herself out there for him like a shiny red orna‑ment hanging off the eighty-foot Christmas tree.

It was her last resort, really: the scratch spin—the only

skating move she'd ever done halfway decently despite six years of lessons forced on her by her father in the hopes that she'd become Korea's answer to Kristi Yamaguchi. Her form was an absolute wreck, but she didn't care. She didn't even care if all the spinning made her puke, just as long as it got Trick's attention away from Mary.

Her old, neglected skates were cutting off the circulation in her ankles. Sleet was pricking her nose and eyelids and soaking her red Prada coat, which she'd only worn to look Christmas-perfect for him. Her shivers were coming in thick, crashing waves now, but her skating coach had taught her to put on a stiff, sparkling smile no matter how cold, no matter how much it hurt. She could ignore it all—the ice on her eyelashes and the sharp pains in her feet. None of it mattered if Trick was watching her twirl like he'd promised.

But as she fell awkwardly out of the spin, she couldn't find his face anywhere in the crowd. He had disappeared from the railing.

"Patrick?" she called out, sliding involuntarily forward. The next thing she knew, she'd fallen flat on her ass like a slapstick tramp in a choppy silent movie.

Hundreds of tourists watched her splatter on the ice in a pool of Prada, and they laughed with Christmas glee. It wasn't even derisive laughter; watching people's pratfalls was one of the joys of Rockefeller Center. Joon knew they were all laughing with her, but she couldn't find the humor in anything right now. There was nothing funny about the massive group of guffawing middle-schoolers pointing at her as they waited for their turn to skate, or the pairs of giggling lovers in flowing white scarves and wool hats, gliding past her in the silver shimmer of the rink's bright spotlights. Even the gilded statue of Prometheus that watched over the rink seemed to be laughing at her with his fiery Grecian eyes. *You're humiliating yourself, Joon*, he seemed to be saying. *Just let the guy go. You've already lost him.*

But a deeper instinct took over: some strange little piece of Joon's heart that apparently had no shame. She climbed back onto her skates, dusted the ice shavings off her black tights, sped off the ice and clomped her way onto the hard rubber of the waiting area, making a beeline for the locker room, every wobbly step on her three-inch stilts stinging her ankles. She knocked a tall hot chocolate onto a beefy frat boy's yellow ski jacket as she elbowed her way through.

"Patrick? Trick? Are you in here?"

She stumbled past rows of benches and lockers, and scads of barefoot Chadwickites who'd just arrived for the traditional Christmas skate. It wasn't even nine o'clock yet, so there was no way Trick had already abandoned her for another party (something he'd been doing more and more in the past few weeks). She peered over as many heads as she could manage, searching for his golden curls, and she finally spotted him, sitting on one of the benches, putting on his pristine Timberland work boots.

"Hey," she called.

Trick flinched ever so slightly when he heard her voice. No one else would have noticed it, but Joon knew every one of his gestures almost as well as she knew her own. She knew what his tiny half-smile meant (he wants to fool around), and what his devastating grin meant (he hates your guts), and what that slight flinch in his shoulders meant. She'd seen it when she found him using in the bathroom of Chez Bernard after he'd promised to stay straight for their six-month anniversary dinner. He only flinched when he'd been caught.

"Hey," he said, standing up and brushing the specks of snow off his tailored coat and hoodie.

"Where are you going?" Joon asked, trying not to sound like a lost, orphaned child.

"I feel like crap," he said. "All that going around in circles—it's just not something you do with a hangover." He quickly pulled his BlackBerry and TAG Heuer out of the locker and snapped the watch on—the BlackBerry gave a notification beep, and he glanced at it before dropping it in his coat pocket. "I think I'm going to head home and sleep it off."

Joon's eyes followed the BlackBerry into his pocket, and then she watched him avoid her eyes as he slammed the locker shut.

"You're lying," she said.

"What?" He laughed. "What are you talking about?"

"You're lying," she repeated. "Where are you really going?"

"Oh, Joonie, not again. Please." He gave her that pitiful *Girl, Interrupted* look, like she belonged in a mental ward with Angelina and Winona. "I thought we were past this shit."

"What shit?"

"The paranoia shit. You promised you'd stop."

"I'm *not* being paranoid," she snapped. She knew it only made her sound crazier, but she couldn't help it. She couldn't.

Patrick threw up his hands like he was being mugged by a raving psychopath. "O-*kay*. Jesus. You're not being paranoid. Cool. I just need to get home and get some sleep, okay? I've got a car outside, so I'm going to run, all right?"

"Let me see your phone."

Trick raised his eyebrows. "Excuse me?"

"Your phone. You just got a text. Who texted you?"

"My *driver*. I just told you, he's waiting for me outside. Jesus, Joonie, just call your shrink, all right? Seriously, I'm begging you." He squeezed her shoulders and gave her a peck on the forehead. *"Bye."*

"Where's Mary, Trick?"

His shoulders flinched again. She was absolutely sure of it. "Mary who?" he said. "Mary Shayne?"

Joon shook her head, disgusted by his ridiculous answer. "Yes." She laughed bitterly. "Mary *Shayne*. My *good friend* Mary Shayne. The one you've been tending to every *fifteen* minutes tonight to make sure she doesn't die of the *adorable sniffles*! *That* Mary Shayne!"

"Stop." Trick brought his voice down to a whisper as tourists began to stare. "What the hell is the matter with you? I was trying to be nice to your friend. She's got a cold, and I was trying to be nice."

"Nice is *one time*, Trick! 'Hey, you look a little under the weather, Mary. You feeling okay?' *That's* nice. You were *waiting* on her hand and foot! Every time you were supposed to be skating with me, you were buying her another freaking hot chocolate!"

"I gave her the *rest* of my hot chocolate. *Half* of one *already-purchased* hot chocolate. She looked like she was dying from the freaking cold."

"Well, what if *I* was dying from the cold, Trick? What if *I* was dying out there too? Which one of us would you save? Who would you rescue with your precious half a hot chocolate?"

"God, will you stop with that ridiculous game already? I'd save you, Joon, okay? You get the hot chocolate, one hundred percent."

"You're such a goddamned *liar!* You're a *liar* and you know it!"

The locker room went silent. Trick looked altogether mortified, and Joon didn't care in the least.

"Joonie," he said quietly. "You just need to take your meds, all right? Just take your meds."

He gave her one last kiss on the cheek and then rushed toward the exit. She called out to him again.

"Patrick—!"

"What?" He stopped briefly at the doorway.

"Did you even see my scratch spin?"

"Your what?"

"My spin . . . on the ice . . . you said you'd watch. Did you even see it?"

"Of course I did," he said. "It was perfect, Joonie. Really. Nine point five from the German judges."

He raised his hand for a pathetic wave goodbye, and

then he disappeared into the crowd like he was running from a ticking time bomb. Joon fell back against the lockers, staring down helplessly at the gray sludge on the floor. She suddenly felt exhausted. Her head was throbbing and so were her ankles.

Only a few seconds passed before Amy came clomping into the locker room, towering awkwardly on her rented white skates and panting desperately.

"Have you seen Mary?" she asked, trying in vain to catch her breath. Her eyes darted around the room.

"No," Joon said. "Isn't she out there skating?"

"I *thought* she was," Amy heaved. She slapped her hands on her sides. "*Damn* it. She promised she'd skate with me. She *promised*. Jen Morris said she just saw her leave."

"What?" Joon felt the acid in her stomach rising up to her throat.

"Mary told Jen she was feeling sick," Amy said, "so she left. Just now. Can you believe that? She just walked out. Why did she tell Jen, why didn't she tell *me*? She didn't even tell you, did she? God, do you think she bothered to tell *anyone* else she was leaving?"

Joon's mouth went dry. Her heart began to race uncomfortably like a scampering bug in her chest. She was sure Mary had told someone else she was leaving. And she knew exactly who that person was.

"Ugh, that *bitch* . . ." All of Joon's muscles contracted at once as she violently clutched her Dolce winter hat in her fists. "That *bitch*."

"What?" Amy looked a little shocked by Joon's reaction. "Who? What's wrong?"

But Joon was already elbowing her way back through the crowd, laboring skate by skate, making her way to the stone and marble steps that led out of Rockefeller Center and down to Fifth Avenue. Now she understood. Now she knew why he'd left in such a rush. Because she knew Mary. She knew how she operated. All Mary had to do was drop the hint to him that she was leaving. That was all Mary had to do, and she knew it. She knew he would follow.

Joon only got as far as the top of the icy steps—just in time to see Mary standing alone in a swirl of snow and sleet on the corner of Fiftieth and Fifth. She had one arm crossed over her immaculate white parka for warmth, and the other barely raised in the air, half heartedly trying to hail a cab when she knew there wasn't an available taxi for miles. She was still holding Patrick's hot chocolate in her hand.

A gleaming black limo drove up through the heavy traffic, sloshing through the gray water, past a Salvation Army Santa cheerfully ringing his brass bell. It pulled up next to Mary, and Patrick emerged from the sunroof like the world's most beautiful jack-in-the-box—like Mary's knight in snowy armor. He said something to Mary, and she threw her head back and laughed in that particular singsong way that made all the boys her slaves. It was the laugh that made them feel like she'd already had sex with them at least twice, even if she'd never touched them.

At that moment Joon shut her eyes tightly, and she actually made a wish. A cold, hard wish, like a desperate little girl wishing on a star.

Mary, please don't get into the limo. Please, just this once, don't take a boy away from me. I'll forgive you for all the others, if you'll just leave me Trick. Just once, show me our friendship means something to you. Show me that you haven't conveniently forgotten I exist again. Please. I'm begging you. Don't get in. . . .

But of course Mary got in. Of course she did. Giggling and innocent, and completely heartless.

Joon raised her skate off the ground and stomped the blade down into the icy stone with all her might. It sent a bolt of exquisite pain through her shin, a pain she almost welcomed, because it was physical, unlike the pain in her heart, which she knew wouldn't fade, which would grow and spread and hang over every day to come.

(*pain*)

MARY'S TEETH WERE CHATTERING as she clenched her jaw against the pain in her arms. *Joon's right*, she thought miserably, still reeling from the overwhelming force of her memory—*Joon's* memory—the entire sordid night that had come into her head all at once. The pain in her arms was nothing compared to *that* feeling: that dull, anticipatory ache of losing something, losing someone you care about, of seeing it all beforehand and not knowing how bad it will get but knowing it won't stop at unbearable, it will go *right past* unbearable and just stay there, forever, morning to night, every day from now on.

Mary was crying, Joon's exquisitely applied mascara running down her cheeks. Patrick had dumped her that morning—the memory (the *real* memory) was still vivid.

At least Patrick had done it fast and hard—it only took five minutes, from the trepidation she'd felt when she'd first seen him standing on the sidewalk waiting for her, to the final shock as he did the deed and walked away.

Fast and merciful, she thought, *just like one of those movies where somebody prays for a quick death.*

Not at all like what Joon had gone through.

Gone through because of me, Mary added miserably.

And he hadn't even meant it! The breakup pain had lasted—what? Maybe twelve hours? Twelve hours of indulging her pain like a little girl. *Twelve hours without Patrick and I couldn't even function.* How could she have possibly endured what Joon had gone through that December night, and all the time since? Watching her and Patrick parade their relationship like models in a sexy jeans ad, taking every opportunity to rub Joon's nose in it? Endlessly talking to Joon about Trick, and, at the end of every day, going back to the Peninsula and settling onto one of the plush hotel couches while Joon went home alone?

The savagery of Joon's memory—the depth of the pain Mary had caused her best friend—was amazingly strong, like being kicked in the stomach and having to smile and ask for more.

And then she'd gotten him back—and forgotten all about it.

But it was even worse than that, Mary realized bitterly, swaying in the darkness on the fraying rope that burned her wrists like hot metal shackles. She'd actually *made jokes* about Joon and Patrick's breakup, right to Joon's face, as if Joon had nothing better to do than laugh at the merry whimsy of her life. *And it wasn't the first time,* Mary realized miserably. *Going back through the years, how many boys did I—*

She stopped thinking about it, because something was moving.

She could barely see it, straight ahead—but she was sure of it. The memory hadn't taken any time, she realized; exactly like when she'd been Scott, the whole thing was *there,* just as with any vivid memory.

In the center of the black shape of the house, a pale rectangle of light appeared, widening slowly, revealing a silhouetted figure.

That's me.

Of course it was. As soon as Mary had realized where she was, and had identified the glow of the Mercedes's headlights, she understood what was about to happen. Once again, she was looking at herself, earlier in the day, watching herself do exactly what she remembered doing.

Behind Mary, framed in the dim doorway, another shadowed figure appeared.

It's Amy. The silhouettes of the two girls were immediately, completely recognizable. Mary would have known Amy anywhere. It was clearly her.

Straining to listen, Mary could just make out their distant voices through the whipping wind and the rain.

"I can't," Amy was yelling—her voice drifted through the wind, barely reaching Mary where she hung from the fraying rope. "Oh, Jesus, don't make me go out there—"

Go with her! Mary pleaded mentally. She remembered what had happened to Amy . . . what had happened to both of them.

In the distance, barely visible in the farmhouse's door-way, Real Mary said something inaudible, and Amy's voice got more anguished. "Don't . . . me here," Amy's thin, high voice carried over the wind. "Don't leave me here alone."

If I can hear them, they can hear me, Mary realized, breathing painfully through her nose and trying to scream again. The bandage over her mouth made it impossible, but she squealed and moaned desperately, kicking her legs and wriggling to get their attention.

Real Mary was already moving, wading forward into the dark rain, moving closer to the hole she couldn't see. *"I'm coming!"* she called out—Mary could hear her voice clearly, now. *"I'm coming, Joon!"*

No, no, no, Mary thought desperately, watching herself start wading into the tall weeds. *Stay there, idiot! You're going to fall into the hole—you're going to get trapped!*

The rain kept falling, freezing her to the bone like an endless cold shower. Tipping her head back again, Mary stared upward, following the ropes as they climbed above her, impossibly high, converging like high-tension cables flanking a desert highway, vanishing into the blackness of the trees, far above. *Can't climb,* she thought desperately. *No way up—no way down.* As she stared upward, trying again to scream—and hearing her own muffled moaning, recogniz-ing Joon's voice—the ropes twanged like guitar strings, vi-brating like a rush-hour subway platform.

"I'm coming, Joon!" Real Mary was bellowing, straight ahead, back at the farmhouse's back door. *"I'm coming! I'll be right there!"*

Lightning flashed brilliantly then—a long, extended

multiple flash like a fireworks display—and suddenly, Mary got a clear view of something she hadn't seen before. Another big surprise.

Below the edge of the embankment—the steep, ragged cliff where the tall weeds ended and the ground dropped away. There was a flat shelf of rock, like a recessed butte set into the earth well below the cliff's edge. The shelf was wide and relatively dry; it was sheltered from the rain, she realized, by the overhanging curved wall of earth, clogged with tree roots and rocks. The stone shelf wasn't that far down— just about five feet below the tips of her dangling feet.

Someone was *down* there, Mary saw.

The lightning was like a Times Square movie-premiere klieg light. It was so bright that, for a half second, she had an unobstructed view of the figure that stood back against the edge of the embankment, completely out of sight of the farmhouse.

A boy in an oversized bright yellow Patagonia raincoat. Scott Sanders.

Mary's eyes—*Joon's* eyes—widened as she stared incredulously. Scott was standing *right there*, just a few feet away, gazing critically up at her, frowning in concentration. A coil of rope lay on the wet rock ledge next to him, along with a giant flashlight and his ever-present red book bag.

Scott again, Mary thought. *Jesus, did he tie me—Joon—up?*

Scott was holding something in his hand—a small device—but she didn't recognize it. Beside him, on the rock face, was what looked like steel netting from a construction site, holding a thick pile of cinder blocks.

"Amy!" Real Mary was screaming. "Amy, *where are you?*"

She tried again to scream, but, again, all she could do was moan and squeal. The bandage on her mouth made it impossible to speak.

Mary remembered watching Joon squirm and buck and moan, from right over there—from exactly where Real Mary's shadowy figure was moving forward. *It's just like Scott, in front of school,* she realized, astonished. *The exact same thing. This is* me, *warning myself.*

"I can't find Amy!" Real Mary sobbed. "Joon, hang on—"

No, no, no—Mary shook her head frantically, trying to signal Real Mary to *stay put;* she was about to drop into the—

Crack! Even hanging from the rope above the stream, Mary could hear the force of the impact as Real Mary dropped into the hole in the ground.

Below her, Mary could just make out the dim yellow of Scott's oversize raincoat as he moved, reacting.

"Joon!" Real Mary screamed. "I'm trapped—I can't move!"

Below, out of Real Mary's view, Scott was moving again. Mary barely heard an electronic click just as she saw a red light flashing on the device in Scott's hand.

Another click sounded, far above her—tilting her head back again, Mary saw a tiny flash as sparks detonated on the rope above her, and the rope started to come apart.

Some kind of trick, Mary thought. *He put something up there, on the rope, so he could just press a button—some kind of clever Scott gizmo.*

It was incredible, amazing. *This was a setup. It was done on* purpose. *Scott was deliberately faking me out—making it look like the rope was breaking.*

"Don't move, Joon!" Real Mary screamed, from her spot planted halfway in the ground. "Jesus, don't—"

Scott fumbled with whatever he was holding and another tiny light flashed and the rope broke.

This is it, she thought, squeezing her eyes shut. *I'm dead—*

Mary felt the sickening nausea of sudden free fall as she dropped straight down—and then something grabbed her, roughly pulling her, and she felt a blast of pain as she tumbled forward, Scott's arms around her waist as he pulled her on top of himself. She rolled, banging her kneecaps against the wet stone as she and Scott tumbled backward.

She was safe. She was on solid ground, her knees and scraped shoulder blades screaming in agony, raising her head, her hands still bound to the rope that now draped across the stone like a limp snake.

Up above, out of view, back toward the farmhouse, Real Mary was screaming.

Scott stood up, letting go of her, and then he lunged to one side and pushed against the steel netting, propelling the pile of cinder blocks so they toppled over the edge of the narrow embankment. After a moment, the entire cluster of steel and cement dropped into the stream, making a very loud splash.

That's what I heard, Mary marveled. *I can't believe it. He completely fooled me.*

But why?

Scott had returned to her side. She stared up at his shadowed face, hidden behind the hood of his ridiculous yellow raincoat. Scott was kneeling on the wet stone, mud smeared on his khaki trousers, fishing in his red book bag. He pulled out the soft silver cloth Mary had seen before (*When I was him*, she remembered) and, as he unfolded it, Mary suddenly recognized it as a space blanket—the kind that marathon runners draped around themselves after a race.

He was prepared for this, Mary realized, as Scott sidled over to her, producing a gleaming Swiss Army knife. He flicked on a flashlight (looking around critically first, to make sure the light wasn't visible from up by the house), then leaned to cut the ropes, freeing Mary's ankles.

"You okay, Joon?" Scott whispered.

Mary nodded.

"Good. I think I pulled my back out." Scott was helping her to her feet, draping the metallic blanket around her. Mary was too astonished to react—she just shivered, staring at Scott as he stooped to gather all his belongings, including the flashlight and the knife and what she now saw was a plastic controller from a child's remote control toy.

I don't believe it, Mary thought weakly. *Like a fucking movie stunt.*

"I warned you it would be touch and go," Scott told her, collapsing the antenna on his toy remote and coiling the rope. "I'm sorry, Joon—I thought I'd do a slightly better job of catching you."

Mary couldn't believe her ears.

They did it together—Joon was totally in on this.

But that was nothing compared with what she saw next.

In the near distance, behind where Scott was briskly packing up his belongings, a silhouetted figure was coming toward them, slowly edging along the narrow shelf of rock. Mary had been fumbling with the wet ropes on her wrists, trying to get herself free, but when Scott's flashlight beam flickered in the right direction and Mary saw who was joining them, she froze in complete, mute shock.

Amy.

"That worked *great!*" Amy whispered, brushing her wet hair from her face as she joined them, leaning to help Scott latch his bag. Amy grinned at Mary, her eyes glittering in the reflected glare of the flashlight. "Joonie, did you *see* me? Did you *hear* me? I deserve a fucking Oscar for that!"

You sure do, Mary thought, totally bewildered.

She couldn't believe her ears.

It wasn't just Amy and Scott. It was Joon, too.

"You okay, Joon?" Amy had walked closer, carefully picking her way across the mud-streaked embankment and reaching to pull the silver blanket more snugly around her—Joon's—shoulders. "You totally had the hard part—I can't believe you agreed to just, like, *hang* there."

The rain kept falling around them. Real Mary was still sobbing—her voice penetrated through the howling wind.

What the hell are you all doing? Mary wanted to scream at them. But her mouth was still taped shut, just like her raw wrists were still bound with loops of rope—there was nothing she could do but move along the narrow rock shelf with them.

"You took your bloody time getting here," Scott complained in a harsh whisper, looking at his watch. "Listen, we've got to get moving. Dylan'll be here in just twenty minutes."

Jesus, Mary thought weakly. She'd raised her bound hands to her face and was trying to find the edge of the adhesive, to pull the bandage from her—Joon's—face.

Him too?

They all ganged up on me! She still couldn't believe it. Her head was reeling.

That doesn't make sense. She was trying to remember everything that had happened next—after Joon's fall—and how it fit together with what she'd just learned.

Like any of this makes sense.

"Do that later, Joonie," Amy told her impatiently, pulling Mary forward. She was referring to the bandage. "Where's your car, Scott?"

"On the other side of the parkway."

They brought another car, Mary thought weakly. She remembered Amy sitting next to her in the Mercedes, driving intently—fooling her completely, playing her like a violin. She still couldn't believe it.

Scott was checking his watch again as he led them along the embankment, back the way Amy had come. The rain kept falling as they followed the narrow rock ledge's path as it sloped upward. They passed the edge of the farmhouse, far off through the trees, and suddenly the Mercedes' headlights were shining right in her eyes.

"Patrick's going to have a dead battery," Scott whispered to Amy. "The headlights are going to be on all night."

Their voices seemed to be fading away into the roar of the rain and the wind—Mary caught herself staring sideways through the weeds at the distant glare of the headlights, glowing like phosphorescent moons.

"Yeah." Amy used a nasty tone that Mary had never heard before. Her voice was barely audible now—the whole world was fading to white. "But did you hear the bitch *scream*? It's totally worth it."

3

AMY

A DEEP BASS ROAR—a blast of noise—accompanied the blinding white light, making Mary's eyes water, growing louder and brighter until, just like that, the noise and light were gone. Mary was warm and dry, and her body didn't ache, for the first time in what seemed like forever. She was in the backseat of a car, being driven at night, and the heat was up way too far. The roar of white noise had been a car whipping past in the other direction.

"High beams!" Scott Sanders muttered, from directly in front of her. Scott was driving fairly fast—Mary felt the car lurch back and forth as Scott flinched at the blinding head-lights that had just dazzled her. "Imbecile," Scott added.

It happened again, Mary realized.

This was the third time—she'd come back from the dead (the phrase stuck in her head like some kind of crazy comic-book tale, something out of a kid's campfire story or a horror movie) as Scott, and then as Joon, and now—

Amy, she realized, looking down at herself, seeing her soaked party clothes and her conspicuously protruding chest. *I'm Amy now.*

Joon was in the passenger seat, still wrapped in her synthetic sheath. She was using a hand towel to dry her hair. Mary didn't recognize the car they were in; it was some kind of enormous Japanese luxury sedan with rich leather seats and a new-car smell. Scott drove it confidently; Mary assumed it belonged to his parents.

The glowing green numerals on the dashboard clock said 11:34 P.M.

A little bit later, Mary realized, thinking it through. She wasn't quite as panicked or freaked out by what was happening as she'd been the previous two times. She still had no idea *why*, but it was obvious that she was moving through time, re-cycling the events of the fatal day, her last day on earth.

Am I really dead? Mary wondered again. The car's interior was uncomfortably hot; Mary could feel her skin—Amy's skin—breaking a sweat.

The car was racing down the Saw Mill River Parkway. Mary could see the same dark masses of foliage whipping by outside the rain-streaked windows, just like the last time she was here, driving south with Dylan.

Dylan, Mary thought, feeling a lump in her throat. She pictured him lying in the pool of his own blood on her living room floor, crying hysterically while Mary's mother crouched over him.

But that hasn't happened yet, she realized. *Not for . . . three hours.*

Which meant that she might be able to prevent it.

Mary wanted to say something—to talk to Scott and Joon, to ask them what the hell they were doing, what this insane conspiracy was all about. But she couldn't even start talking. She was too dazed, too baffled.

"There they are," Joon said, pointing. "You want to get a little closer, Scott?"

"Right," Scott confirmed. The muted whine of the Japanese engine cranked up as the car cruised forward. Mary was still too stunned to say anything, but she gazed intently through the windshield.

Ahead of them, Mary saw a familiar Ford Taurus.

She could just make out two people inside, in the front: a man, driving, and a woman in the passenger seat.

Of course.

It all made sense. *That's us—me and Dylan—up there.*

Mary remembered their frantic drive—Dylan's insane rush to get back to the city as fast as possible.

The car behind them, the car that had chased them all the way to Manhattan, was *this* car—Scott's car.

Mary remembered asking Dylan who was following them. *If I told you, you'd never believe me*, he'd answered.

Mary realized he'd been right—she couldn't believe it.

Sitting there in the backseat, furtively gazing forward at

Scott and Joon, Mary felt sick. She was seeing her friends in a completely different light now that she'd learned what they thought of her—what they *really* thought of her.

They hate me.

Amy—darling Ame, who'd signed a Best Friend Contract with her more than a decade ago—whose body she was now inhabiting, had just called her a bitch. And had *laughed* as she said it. The sound of sweet Amy *laughing* as she relished hearing Mary Shayne screaming in agony and grief was so painful that Mary could barely endure thinking about it.

And Scott, whom she'd mercilessly exploited for years, evidently harbored a grudge so deep that he'd planned (or helped plan) this elaborate revenge scheme.

"That's right, Dylan . . . that's right," Joon was muttering grimly, gazing ahead at the Taurus as it sped down the rain-slicked Parkway. "Keep moving fast—keep Little Miss Shayne nice and scared."

"Are you warm enough?" Scott asked Joon. For Mary, it was strange just to see the two of them talking at all. She'd never thought that Joon would give a second of her time to a supergeek like Scott.

Obviously, she'd been wrong about that. Mary was learning that she really didn't know her friends as well as she thought she did.

"I'm fine," Joon said.

"Are you sure you're okay?" Scott reached down to shift gears. The Taurus had sped up, and Scott had to work to keep his position behind them. "You were hanging there a long time; I'm sorry I fumbled when I caught you."

Mary didn't dare interrupt. She wanted to hear every word.

"I feel really weird—I must be stunned or something." Joon was frowning quizzically at Scott. "What do you mean, fumbled? What happened?"

"When the charge blew," Scott explained, "and the rope came apart, I just barely managed to catch you. You almost fell into the creek."

"I almost *what?*" Joon was still frowning at Scott, looking confused. "When you caught me? I don't—"

"What's the matter with you?" Scott returned Joon's gaze before flicking his eyes back to the road. "Don't you remember?"

"*No,*" Joon muttered. "No, I *don't* remember. What the hell—"

"You must be stunned." Scott sounded worried. "If you really can't—"

"I remember *hanging* there, I remember all the planning, all the setup. I remember getting the bitch ready for her date; I remember everything we did today," Joon went on. "But then—it's actually a blank. The strangest thing—I actually can't remember anything until, um, until we were done—until afterward. You said you caught me wrong?"

"Your knee banged the ground."

"No *wonder,*" Joon said. "I couldn't figure out why it *hurts* so much."

"The same thing happened to me!" Scott said suddenly. "All day long, I've been—" He took a breath and started over. "I mean, I remember being at school; I remember something about dropping all my stuff on the sidewalk. But

I can't—I can't remember how the day started. I can't remember waking up. It's been driving me batty."

Suddenly, Mary understood.

That's when they were me.

From the moment he'd woken up in the morning to the moment the linebackers had tackled him on the sidewalk in front of the school, Scott had been *her*—had been Mary Shayne. That was why he couldn't remember, she realized; he hadn't *been* there. His soul had been temporarily replaced by hers—by dead Mary Shayne's.

Possessed by the dead girl, before *she died.*

It was definitely like something out of a *Twilight Zone* episode.

And the same thing had happened with Joon, she realized, thinking about it some more. The exact period of time Joon had described—hanging from the rope; falling and being caught (badly) by Scott; banging her knee against the stones; walking back, along the ledge that flanked the abandoned farmhouse's property—was when Joon wasn't Joon at all, but was actually Mary.

They don't remember what happened, Mary thought, *because I was them.*

Amy won't remember this car ride, she realized. *She'll have a blank in her memory.*

It was impossible, of course—but here she was, inside Amy's body, not dreaming.

I'm coming back as each of my friends, she thought.

Mary realized she was covered in sweat. It wasn't *her* sweat, of course; it was Amy's. Amy Twersky and her cardigans and layers of extra clothes; always covering herself up,

244

always so modest. She reached to brush her wavy red hair away from her perspiring forehead, and her hands came away damp. Scott had the heat cranked up all the way— obviously because Joon was freezing cold; in danger, probably, of catching pneumonia. Mary's body—Amy's body— was overheating beneath the cardigan.

And there's something else, Mary thought right then— something that had happened during the course of her day, her last day alive, that now made sense, that fit together like pieces of a jigsaw puzzle suddenly matching up. Something about time, and remembering—something about *missing* time.

But she couldn't quite figure out what it was—as soon as the idea had come into her head, she'd lost it.

(*overheating*)

Mary had something like half a second to realize it was happening again; she was about to experience another hijacked memory that wasn't hers.

(*overheating*)

SHE WAS OVERHEATING. MARY'S arms were wrapped tightly around Amy's waist as she tumbled through Amy's front door at 2:36 in the morning. Her skin was warm against Amy's cheek—hot, even—and it was moist. Amy wasn't sure if Mary had been crying or dancing or just sweating at one of those underground clubs with no ventilation she always went to. She smelled like alcohol, but she also smelled like cigarettes and violets and freesia, and something else . . . cinnamon, maybe? One of the spaghetti straps on her lemon-yellow cocktail dress was falling off her shoulder. Mary was the only girl in the world who could pull off a lemon-yellow cocktail dress without looking like some sort of Texas prom queen.

"I'm staying over," Mary said, barely opening her mouth.

"I know." Amy laughed gently. "You told me when you called."

"I did? See, I don't even remember calling." Mary ended with a giggle. She was too out of it to lift her head, so every word was breathed directly into Amy's ear—warm, wet lips against skin. Amy tried to keep her breathing regular.

Mary let her tiny handbag drop to the marble floor of the foyer and leaned more heavily on Amy. Amy would have normally stiffened up, but she was barely awake herself. There had only been a two-minute delay between Mary calling and Mary tapping at her town house door. Amy had just had time to climb out of bed and throw on a thin silk robe over her pajamas. She wished she had gotten a chance to at least put on some lipstick.

"I don't wanna go home tonight, Ame," Mary mumbled into her ear. "It's so frikkin' depressing there. I want to live here. You have a giant fridge and ten million different cookies. And *you're* here," she added.

Amy's cheeks turned warm. The flush in her face and the heat from Mary's body made her underarms suddenly begin to sweat. She was used to having her thick black cardigan as a buffer between them when they hugged, but tonight she could feel every contour of Mary's chest and stomach and hips pressed against her own through her tissue-thin silk pajamas.

Just breathe, she told herself. *Breathe through it. Don't move your hands too much. Don't pull her closer. Don't claw at her back no matter how good she feels.*

"Do you want some cookies?" Amy asked, hearing a breathless catch in her throat.

"Bed," Mary said. "I want bed."

"Right, come on. . . ."

Usually Mary gave Amy more warning before she showed up drunk and exhausted to crash at her town house. That way, Amy had more time to get dressed, put on some makeup and some Secret and make up the chaise longue in her bedroom. But, from this point on, Amy had the routine down: pull off Mary's heels so she didn't fall on the marble floor; scoop up whatever she'd dropped when she stumbled in; wrap Mary's arm around her shoulder (Mary preferred the left arm) and walk her step by painfully slow step up the spiral staircase, just to be sure she wouldn't get dizzy or vomitocious (as Mary called it). They walked even slower tonight, because Amy had forgotten to flip on the staircase's track lighting. The half-moon showed through the domed copper skylight at the top of the stairs, casting a blue shadow across the Lichtenstein prints on the wall as the two girls traveled down the third-floor hallway to Amy's bedroom.

Once they finally got there, Amy began to walk Mary inside, but then she glimpsed her open closet door.

Her heart nearly stopped. The screaming voice inside her head caught up with her feet just in time, and threw on the brakes.

Stop. You forgot to lock the closet door. Stop.

Just the slightest turn of her eyes, and Mary would have seen it. She would have seen the entire closet mirror. Now the trickles of sweat fell from Amy's underarms, riding down the flush of panic goose bumps on her chest.

"Wait," she said, tugging Mary back a step.

"What? What's wrong?"

"My room is disgusting. I wasn't ready for you. You have to give me a second to clean it up."

Mary clutched Amy's silk robe. "You've *got* to be kidding me," she slurred. "Who cares? You're my best friend—I don't care about mess. I want bed."

"Just *one* second," Amy insisted. "Just wait here."

"What if I fall?" Mary whined. She was definitely wobbling as Amy let go of her.

"Just think happy thoughts and you won't fall."

Amy slammed the door behind her and darted to her second closet. The inside mirror was smothered in the glued-on pictures she'd been collecting over the years. All those adorable, heart-stoppingly sexy pictures: Mary frolicking in her Mizrahi bikini at the beach in East Hampton; Mary in her white parka, lying on her back, making a snow angel in Central Park; Mary in a bulky robe and cucumber face cream, trying to swat away the camera; Mary in her purple lace bra and panties, raising her arms triumphantly after winning a late-night Wii golf tiebreaker; Mary's perfectly perfect, inhumanly perfect body stretched out and naked on Amy's antique velvet chaise after she'd kicked off the covers in her sleep.

Amy slammed the closet door shut and locked it, just as

she always did when Mary came over. Once she was sure it was secure, she darted to her chaise, swiped it clean and laid one of her pillows and a billowy white quilt on top for Mary. Then she ran back to her door and opened it.

"All clear," she laughed nervously.

"Whatever," Mary murmured, stumbling past the Italian marble fireplace.

"Here, I made up the chaise," Amy said.

"I want the bed." Mary took two giant leaps and threw herself into Amy's canopy bed, landing with a thud. She rolled around in the sea of light blue Ralph Lauren accent pillows and let out a string of snort-laughs. Mary always snorted her laughs when she was drunk and, of course, hearing her own snorts only made her laugh more, which only made her snort more, and so on. . . .

Amy took the chaise longue, instead. She plopped down on the quilt, crossed her arms over her embarrassingly bra-less chest and chewed on her pinky nail, still recovering from the spike in her heartbeat when Mary almost saw the Mary Closet.

"Amy," Mary said, laughing. "You don't have to sleep on the chaise, you can come on the bed. It's your bed."

The suggestion launched another uncomfortable spike in Amy's pulse. "No, you can take the bed tonight."

Mary propped herself up on her elbows and rolled her eyes. She took a long, unexpectedly penetrating look at Amy. "Ame. Take that ridiculous robe off and get in here."

Something about that look sent a burning sensation through Amy's chest. It wasn't pain exactly, or panic, it was just . . . something. Something like excited, something like thrilled, something like longing, but mostly just confusion. "Are you sure?"

"That chaise thing is like sleeping on cement," Mary mumbled. "Come on." She coaxed Amy over with a pat on the bed, like she was coaxing a distrustful puppy. Then she turned her back to Amy, flipping onto her side, and bunching up the pillow in her hands. Amy waited in the ticking silence of her antique grandfather clock until Mary reached her hand back and patted the bed again.

Finally, Amy swallowed hard and stood from the chaise. She stepped gingerly over to the bed and dropped her robe to the floor, feeling absolutely buck naked despite the fact that she was wearing pajamas and Mary's back was turned. She quickly climbed into her bed and lay flat on her back like a stiff corpse. She pulled the sheet up to her shoulders and shuffled herself to the very edge, trying to keep an appropriate distance from Mary.

But Mary erased the distance when she took hold of Amy's arm and pulled it around her waist, spooning them together like a mother and child.

"G'night, Mamy," she whispered. Then she snorted out another laugh. "I mean, Amy," she giggled into her pillow. "Mamy. That's a good name for you. Mamy . . ."

Mary's breaths grew lighter. Bordering on sleep, Amy thought. Amy's arm was still wrapped around Mary's taut stomach, but it felt completely detached from the rest of her body. It was like her arm wasn't allowed to hold Mary like this and be attached to her body at the same time. She was straining her neck awkwardly to keep from letting her chin rest next to Mary's long tendrils of hair on the pillow. She was startled out of her skin when Mary spoke again.

"Mamy," she said, half asleep. "Is it just me, or am I only awake like a third of the time?" She laughed.

"Yeah," Amy said. "I think you only pay attention to about a third of what's going on."

"Yeah," Mary whispered. "Don't want to pay attention. Just want to sleep." She pulled Amy's arm more tightly around her waist.

Amy studied the contour of Mary's bare shoulder where the other lemon-yellow spaghetti strap had now fallen down. "Do you need anything?" she asked. It was all she could think to say.

"Just you," Mary said, cuddling closer. She smiled with her eyes shut. "You're a good person, Mamy." She snorted another little laugh to herself, pressing Amy's hand flat against her stomach.

Something happened to Amy in that moment. Something she couldn't understand and didn't really want to—something about Mary's relaxed laughter, or the darkness in the room, or the smell of cinnamon and violets. Maybe it was the way Mary's stomach quivered against Amy's outstretched fingers as she laughed. Maybe it was the way they were spooning when Amy had been fast asleep only minutes before. Whatever it was, Amy felt something give—the fear and caution and tension in her entire body that she held so constantly in Mary's presence. She only noticed all that tension now that it was gone. Even if it was only for a moment, something in Amy finally let go.

"Mary?" she said.

"Hmm?"

"Can I kiss you goodnight?"

Mostly asleep, Mary turned her head back toward Amy and puckered up her lips like a four-year-old who'd been trained to kiss her grandmother goodnight. Amy leaned down and gave Mary a peck. Mary turned her head back to sleep.

"Mary," Amy whispered.

"Hmm?"

"Can I kiss you again?"

Mary brought her head back again and puckered up. "Quick one," she said with her eyes still shut, now speaking purely in a baby voice.

Amy leaned down more slowly this time, feeling everything in her give over to this seemingly unreal moment. She slid her hand carefully under Mary's neck and cradled her fragile body in her arms. She felt just like she was Burt Lancaster cradling Deborah Kerr on the beach in *From Here to Eternity*. They were wrapped up together in every perfect love scene from every classic 1940s movie, floating on the blue sea of throw pillows in her bed. But, as surreal as it was, Amy had actually never felt so real in her life. This, she realized, was what real felt like.

She pressed her lips against Mary's and let her tongue graze Mary's perfect lips.

"*Ewww!*" Mary shoved Amy's face back with a snap and rolled away. "Watch it there, L Word! *Puh, puh.* . . ." Mary swiped at her lips like a little kid who'd just accidentally eaten dirt. "Ugh, gross!"

Amy felt her entire body go numb. "I was just *kidding*," she insisted. "God! It was a *joke*."

The room suddenly felt so cold. Everything felt cold and ugly and awful.

"Bluch. Euch. . . ." Mary swiped at her lips a few more times. "Grossest joke ever. G*od*."

Amy catapulted herself from the bed and snagged her robe. She tied the sash so tight that the knot cut into her stomach. "It was a joke," she said again. She didn't know what to look at. She crawled back onto the chaise and rolled herself up in the quilt, fixing her eyes on the cream-colored wall. "God . . . you really can't take a joke, can you."

"Yeah, right," Mary muttered. She settled back into her pillow, then flipped over onto her stomach. Amy could tell she had decided to fall back asleep on purpose. "Whatever," Mary added. "You know you're totally in love with me."

Amy couldn't speak.

"Gay Amy," Mary muttered. "Gamy." She snorted out another laugh.

"What?" Amy felt a hole growing in her chest. A dark black hole. "What did you just say?"

"I know, Joon says it's mean, but I'm just kidding around, Ame. You can't help it if you're—"

"Just go to *sleep*, Mary," Amy snapped. "Go to sleep. Just pretend I'm not here. You're good at that."

"Okay," Mary said easily. "G'night, Gamy." She snorted again at her own joke. "Come on, it sounds funny."

Amy could only pretend to sleep now, her eyes tensely

shut. That was all she could think of to make it out of this night and to never think of it again.

"Amy . . . ?" Mary's voice drifted over from the bed. "Ame . . . ? Don't worry, okay? I probably won't even remember this in the morning."

"Yes you will," Amy said, staring at the wall. "You'll remember. But you'll act like you don't."

COLLAPSED IN THE BACKSEAT of Scott's luxury sedan, trapped inside Amy's tall, buxom body, Mary found herself trembling uncontrollably. Outside the car, the rain pounded down and thunder blasted again, crashing hammers on a heavenly scale, like warfare of the gods.

I was drunk, Mary insisted weakly. *I was drunk and I didn't say or do any of that as a conscious, sober girl because* I don't remember.

But again, was that really true?

The tingle on her lips; the odd sensation of reacting and not reacting; something familiar becoming strange and vice versa . . .

No! I don't remember!

But she did. Amy had been right about pretending. Mary knew—she knew it all.

It was just like what she'd learned from Scott's and Joon's memories—the same miserable pattern of rationalization and denial.

I've been using everybody, she thought dismally. *This is no different from what I've been doing to Scott.*

But it *was* different. It hit closer to home; it made her feel something deep inside herself that felt wrong, almost

254

criminal. Her love of Amy was so strong; it was one of the fundamental pillars of her life. Their Crayola-rendered Best Friend Contract was a precious artifact, planted deep in her bedroom closet like a secret relic, a symbol of everything and everyone on earth she could completely trust.

And she called me a bitch, Mary remembered, feeling her eyes—Amy's eyes—beginning to sting. *She enjoyed hearing me scream.*

Somehow, every one of her friends had snapped at once—they'd all come together into a single juggernaut, a tightly planned conspiracy to ruin her life.

What made them all snap? Why today? Why now?

"How much farther?" Joon was asking. Mary could hear a strange eagerness in her voice that chilled her to the bone despite the humid air inside the car. She still felt powerless, unable to move or speak. "He's taking her straight to Trick's, right? And then it's revenge city."

"That's right," Scott said. He sounded eager, too—like they were driving to Disneyland. "Then—" Scott held his hand up to his head and mimed a gun firing.

"Where's my bag?" Joon asked suddenly, looking around at the front seat and the floor. "What happened to my b—"

"In the trunk," Scott told her. "I put all your stuff in the trunk, when I picked you up."

"Good." Joon exhaled in relief. "I was afraid I'd lost the gun."

(*WHOM DO YOU HATE THE MOST?*)

They're going to kill me. This was just the warm-up; later they'll kill me. They'll try to get me to do it myself, and when I don't go through with it they'll shoot me dead.

255

That was all it took—her paralysis snapped and she lunged forward between the front seats, slamming her left hand against the steering wheel. Honking the horn.

"What in the Sam Hill—" The blast of the horn was huge, deafening; Scott swerved the car, trying to keep them moving straight. "Are you insane?"

Joon was reacting, turning in her leather seat and grabbing Amy's—Mary's—arms, trying to pull them away from the horn. They struggled and the car swerved, speeding forward as Scott inadvertently stamped on the gas while trying to elbow Mary's arms aside.

"What the hell are you doing?" Joon shouted, while Mary kept the pressure on the horn—a series of blasts that echoed across the Parkway like the screams of a wild animal.

In front of them, the Taurus picked up speed.

Joon finally managed to push her back. Joon's eyes were blazing with fury—in all the years they'd known each other, Mary had never seen such *hatred* in her eyes.

"What are you *doing?*" Scott asked, staring in disbelief at her in the rearview mirror. "Have you lost your *mind*, Amy? Are you trying to blow the entire plan?"

"I'm not—" Mary coughed. She realized that Joon's flailing fists had hit her in the throat; it was painful to speak. "No, I'm not—"

But it doesn't matter, she told herself bleakly.

Who was she kidding? She couldn't warn Real Mary in the next car about what was going to happen. She'd tried three times now to change the day, to somehow make Real Mary aware of what was coming. And it hadn't made any difference. Obviously, it *couldn't* make any difference.

Whatever she did, it had already happened, already been done. Scott had yelled at her on the street that morning in front of Chadwick—and she'd ignored it. Joon had tried desperately to keep her from falling into the treacherous hole in the ground—but the bandage on her mouth had kept Mary from understanding her. Now Amy had honked the car horn, but, she remembered dismally, that hadn't made any difference either.

No, she told herself firmly. *I won't accept that. I won't give up.*

Lunging forward, her hair dangling on Scott's shoulder, she slammed the car horn again—a series of frantic blasts.

Look out, Mary! she thought desperately.

This time Joon *hit* her—struck her so hard in the face that her vision flared, a series of bright stars that exploded across her view of the rain-drenched windshield. A blast of pain spread across her temple and forehead and cheek; it felt like she'd been clocked with a lead pipe. Her hand slipped from the steering wheel and she fell back against the rear seat, whimpering.

"Nobody chickens out, Amy," Joon told her severely. "Nobody turns back. We're all in this all the way—that was the deal."

"Oh, *not good*—" Scott yelled, slamming on the brakes.

In front of them, the Taurus suddenly slowed and pinwheeled. Mary could hear its tires squealing and skidding on the wet road. Scott somehow managed to avoid a head-on collision; all three of them were tossed back and forth like dice as the Japanese car's antilock brakes absorbed the momentum. A high-pitched, metallic screaming came from the left side of the car as Scott sideswiped the steel divider that separated them from the oncoming traffic.

Mary knew what had happened, without looking. She remembered perfectly.

Dylan's Taurus had corkscrewed on the road, suddenly making for one of the Riverdale exits.

"*Goddamn it!*" Joon shouted at the top of her lungs. She was pounding her slim fists against the dashboard, beside herself with rage. "*God-fucking-damn it, Mary Shayne*—"

"What *happened?*" Scott was in shock, it seemed—his chubby hands were trembling on the steering wheel. "What the hell happened?"

"He changed his fucking mind!" Joon raged. "God-damned Dylan what's-his-name, he changed his mind! Just like every goddamned man who gets anywhere near that *bitch*! She batted her eyes at him and he melted and now he's going to save her!"

"Jesus—" Scott barked, downshifting as he pulled back out into the passing lane. "What do we do? What the hell do we do?"

"Turn around!" Joon snapped. "Go back and get them!"

In the backseat, Mary was trembling, nursing the bruise on her face. She was so frightened she didn't dare move or speak. Both Scott and Joon seemed nearly insane with fury.

"I can't!" Scott yelled. His face was crimson. "I'd have to get off the Parkway; by the time I got back there, they could have *gone anywhere!*"

Joon slammed her fists against the dashboard again. "You're right," she muttered. She was flipping open the glove compartment—its tiny lamp illuminated her fingers as she extracted a cell phone. "You're right. Okay—okay."

"Are you getting instructions?" Scott asked. His nerves seemed to have settled down. "Are you calling in?"

"I *have* to," Joon muttered, dialing rapidly, her thumbs hammering the illuminated buttons. Mary craned her neck, trying to read the number, but there was no way. The pain in her—Amy's—temple was spreading like a coffee stain.

Who the hell is she calling?

"Hello? It's Joon," Joon said. They were passing a sign for the bridge to Manhattan. "We've got a problem—Dylan flaked. He took her somewhere."

With the thumping windshield wipers and the drone of the engine, it was impossible for Mary to make out the sound of the voice on the phone.

Who's she talking to? Mary wondered again.

Is somebody in charge? Somebody else?

It seemed like somebody *was*—somebody to whom her friends were reporting all of their movements. Mary was feeling an entire new level of fear now.

"Are you sure?" Joon was straining to listen. "Where?"

"What do I do?" Scott asked. Joon waved a hand at him impatiently.

"Okay, I'll handle it," Joon said confidently. "I'll get her back—don't worry. You can count on me."

Joon snapped the phone shut. Scott looked at her, his chubby hands twitching the wheel.

Who the hell was *that?* Mary wondered. She couldn't even begin to think of the answer. *Who's giving them orders?*

"We're going to the Upper West Side," Joon told Scott. "Take the Morningside exit—I'll tell you where to go."

Mary was trying to figure out what to say—how to ask Joon who she'd been talking to—but before she could, the roar of the highway expanded like the dull sound of a seashell held to the ear and the pain in her temple grew unbearable, like a white flood; the whiteness and noise overwhelmed her again.

No! Not yet!

But it was too late—her time as Amy was over. Once again, Mary was lost in an infinite sea of white noise.

4

MARY

HER EYELIDS FLUTTERED IN the glare.

The bare overhead bulb shone blindingly in her eyes as she struggled with the much stronger shadowy figure who held her arms.

I'm dreaming; I'm not dreaming—

She was struggling with Dylan, who, in his ridiculous winter coat, was pulling on her arms and trying to get her back into his apartment. Dylan, who had *not been shot—* who was still hours away from that horrible fate.

"Mary? What's the matter with you?" Dylan's grip relaxed on her wrists as she slackened them. "Mary?"

Hello.

The balance of her body; the feel of her hair against her forehead; all of it was back to sweet normality. *I'm me. I'm me again—I'm Mary Shayne.*

I'm awake.

That has to be it, she thought conclusively. *I just kept dreaming, imagining that I was each of my friends. Didn't Sigmund Freud write about that? How your dreams are a story; you're exploring your subconscious mind?*

"Mary, can you hear me? What's—" Dylan was obviously considering releasing her hands, but he didn't seem sure that he could trust her—that she wasn't about to stumble down the stairs and run away the moment his back was turned. "Are you going to come back inside?"

We just got back to Manhattan, Mary reminded herself. *He wants me to run away with him—to drive out of New York and keep going all night, all day, whatever it takes until we're safe.*

That sounded like a good idea. Mary was relaxing her arms and straightening up to her full height, blinking to clear the spots from her eyes. She was ready to follow Dylan anywhere he wanted to go. The image of his blood-drenched shirt . . . of her mother crouching on the narrow corridor floor, with Dylan's blood staining her dressing gown . . .

No. I'm going to stop that from happening.

Somehow she seemed to have made her way around an inexplicable cosmic circle, and here she was—back at the end of the day she died. (The *beginning* of the end, she corrected: the moment when she'd slid off the edge of the spinning record and descended into madness and death.)

"Mary?" Dylan, still whispering, right in front of her. "Will you come back inside? Don't worry about dropping that glass—I don't care about that."

Mary lunged forward and grabbed Dylan's coat lapels, hard. The sensation of returning to her own body was overwhelming; she felt like she had the balance and coordination of an Olympic athlete. *"Joon's out there,"* she whispered in his ear, gripping the thick padded shoulders of his winter coat. "Out on the fire escape."

Dylan's eyes widened. He looked down at her, pointing over his shoulder with his thumb. He had turned white. He didn't look remotely interested in disbelieving her. *Joon?* he mouthed.

Mary nodded, tugging on his coat and beckoning him down the building's ancient stairwell. Dylan vaulted ahead, footsteps echoing harshly against the dirty cast-iron steps as he led Mary past a row of trash pails toward a thick metal door. She waited while he fumbled with a key chain.

Good thing you got your keys, Dylan.

Dylan got the door open and shoved Mary through. (*Don't trust him,* Joon had warned . . . long hours ago, yet moments ago . . . Mary put it out of her head.)

Stop thinking and run, Mary told herself. Dylan snapped on an overhead light and she got her bearings—a narrow, plaster-walled corridor that led past a washer and dryer—and followed him around a corner to another locked metal door. The door's bottom edge rode at least an inch over the sill, and Mary felt cool night air billowing in, caressing her bare ankles below the hems of the borrowed jeans she wore.

My own ankles—my own body, Mary thought luxuriously. She'd told herself not to think, but how did *that* fit in? Why was she back in the middle of the evening? Why was she herself again?

Mary thought she knew.

She realized she'd missed something—that there was an important idea she hadn't quite considered carefully enough. Now it was time to get it straight—to think it through.

"Come on—fast," Dylan whispered as he pushed on the filthy back door. "We can get around to where we parked."

"Joon could be waiting out there—waiting for us," Mary whispered, hurrying to catch up, and following him past the reeking trash cans into the narrow alley behind the building. Even with the sweater, Mary was shivering—the night had gotten colder and the wet wind stung her skin, passing right through the sweater like water through a sieve. Dylan hooked a left and Mary followed. "She's had enough time, right?"

"She'll think we went out the front," Dylan explained as he grunted with the effort of pulling back the edge of a broken chain-link fence. "We've got like a one-minute head start to the car. Here," he added, pulling off his overcoat and shoving it toward her. "You're still freezing from before—put this on."

"But why is she here?" Mary whispered, gratefully pulling the soft overcoat around herself, shivering convulsively as she pushed her arms into its long sleeves. Her feet splashed loudly in the puddles of rainwater that filled all the spaces in the cement around them. The coat was thick and warm—she felt better already. "Why did she tell me not to trust you? I don't—"

"Later, we'll talk later. Get in fast." Dylan was gesturing up the block at his Taurus, about fifteen feet away, and at the stone archway and staircase further down the block; the one Joon was about to emerge out of. "And buckle your seat belt. We've got to get as far away as we can."

"DYLAN, LISTEN," MARY SAID again. "You're smart, right? You can help me figure this—figure this out."

Dylan was leaning forward, pressed against the steering wheel, his dark eyes flicking back and forth as he waited for the traffic signals to change. A light rain was falling again. They were just a few blocks away from Dylan's apartment.

"What?" Dylan's eyes grazed across hers and then he was looking back at the street. She saw his Adam's apple go up and down—he was obviously tense, on edge. "Figure it out—right. That's what we've got to do."

Mary was convinced she'd *already* figured something out—something important.

I've come back as Scott, and then Joon, and then Amy, she thought. *I was each of them for a little while—one small excerpt of each of their lives, on the day I died.*

And they can't remember it.

But the same thing happened to me, Mary realized.

There was a piece missing from *her* day too. After speaking with Joon through the window and then trying to flee from Dylan's apartment, she'd just . . . stopped . . . and when she'd come to, it was much later on. The intervening time was just *gone*.

Now I'm getting it back, she concluded. *I'm "possessing" myself right now, just like I did the others.*

Mary still had no idea *why*—why *any* of it had happened, including this game of cosmic musical chairs she seemed to be playing—but at least it was starting to make some kind of sense.

Maybe there was more she could figure out.

The lights had changed and Dylan sped south, through the deep shadows of the trees that lined Riverside Drive.

"Where are we going?" Mary asked.

"Away." Dylan still sounded strange. "We have to get away. We're in danger." Mary saw his hair toss as he shook his head, trying to clear it. "We're in danger because—"

"*You all ganged up on me,*" Mary interrupted. "Right? You, Scott, Amy, Joon. For my *birthday*, right?"

Dylan wasn't answering. He was staring at the road. She could tell that he was thinking hard.

"You ganged up on me to ruin my day, sending me upstate, and then faking me out, making me think my friends were dead and then—"

"*How do you know that?*" Dylan was glaring at her, his teeth clenched. She could feel the Taurus listing, pulling to one side. "*How do you know—*"

"Wait a minute." Mary had just realized something else. "You were driving me back to town, and Scott's car was *behind* us, Scott and Joon and me—I mean, Amy—chasing you—and then something happened. You changed your mind about something; we nearly had an accident, because you got this funny look in your eyes—"

"*Yes!*"

"—and in the car behind us, Joon said you, um, that you chickened out—"

(*He changed his fucking mind!* Joon had raged. *Goddamned Dylan what's-his-name, he changed his mind! Just like every goddamned man who gets anywhere near that bitch! She batted her eyes at him and he melted and now he's going to save her!*)

"I don't understand how you know that." They had hit another red light. Dylan was rubbing his temples wearily. "I don't understand how you could possibly know that when I *can't fucking remember*—"

"Dylan"—Mary awkwardly reached for his shoulder—"Dylan, calm down and try to help me think. We can figure it out together."

(*Don't trust him!*)

Joon's hands clasping hers through the narrow crack of Dylan's kitchen window. Joon hanging from the rope—her own arms burning with the pain of the ropes in the freezing rain. Joon telling her to run, chasing them, calling her a bitch . . .

"The date," Mary said suddenly. "Patrick breaking up with me . . . you asking me out . . . it was all part of the plan, wasn't it?"

"I think so," Dylan muttered, tapping his fingers on the steering wheel. "You understand I can't *remember* any of it—it's driving me insane. But you're right." He looked straight at her. "Something happened and I woke up; it's like I suddenly woke up driving, and I realized what I was doing. I realized I was leading you . . ."

"*Where?*" Mary squeezed Dylan's shoulder. The light had changed, but it was all right—there was nobody around for miles in either direction. "*Where* were you taking me?"

"The hotel," Dylan whispered, nodding. "Get you out of the hole in the ground; bring you to the hotel. That was the plan. But—"

"The Peninsula? *Patrick's suite?*"

"Yeah." He shot her a frightened, confused glance. "We were *there* tonight, right? You and me?"

"*Yes.* After our date."

"We went on a *date?*"

Jesus Christ, Mary thought. *He really doesn't remember. How is that possible?*

How is any of this possible?

Her own head was beginning to ache from trying to understand what was happening. *And this is* my *head,* she realized in dismay—the one full of wine and vodka and tequila and champagne from five hours ago. The hangover effects had receded, but she still felt a dull ache behind her temples that refused to go away.

"There was something else . . . ," Dylan said quietly. They had stopped for another traffic light, somewhere in the mid-eighties, and he was tapping his fingertips impatiently on the steering wheel. Even here, inside the car, Mary's chill hadn't gone away—she shoved her hands down into her—Dylan's—overcoat pockets to keep them warm. "There was something else that I was supposed to do that only I understood."

"What?"

"I had to—" Dylan squinted his eyes, his jaw muscles clenching as he struggled to remember. "Something about the hotel; something about a gun. I was being told what to do. . . ."

"Being told . . . by whom?"

Joon called in, Mary remembered. *Scott told her to call for instructions, and she did. But I never found out whom she called.*

There was something in her pocket. Mary's fingers, pushed down into the soft recesses of Dylan's right overcoat pocket, brushed against something stiff and brittle—a thick piece of paper.

"By *somebody,*" Dylan responded. The light had changed, reflecting in the shining rain on the wide avenue, but he didn't move the car. "Somebody important . . . somebody I *had* to listen to."

Mary pulled the paper out of Dylan's overcoat pocket. It caught on the fabric, and she had to wiggle it to get it out. There was something familiar about the feel of the paper, something that was making her apprehensive. She held the single page up to the ghostly light from the high, pale streetlights, opened its single fold—and felt the chill return to her spine and the back of her neck as she stared at it.

At the top of the page was an asymmetrical red eye,

almond shaped, simple, yet stylized like a corporate logo. And below that, three lines of text in block letters, neatly handwritten, in a style she recognized instantly.

WHOM DO YOU HATE THE MOST?
WHAT WOULD YOU DO ABOUT IT IF YOU COULD?
TODAY IS THE DAY.

"Dylan—" Mary could barely speak. Ahead of them, the traffic light changed, but Dylan didn't respond; the car didn't move. "Dylan, what—what is this? Where did you get it?"

Dylan didn't answer, and Mary looked over and realized with a sick sort of fascination that Dylan was nearly in a trance; he was staring at the note in Mary's hand the way a cat stares at a motionless bird, unblinking, eyes wide, totally alert.

"Dylan? What's—"

Dylan blinked rapidly, suddenly shaking his head back and forth violently, as if to clear it. "That's it! That's—that's it." His voice was strangely weak, like the awestruck tones of someone witnessing a car crash or a spectacular sunset. "That's the whole thing. Oh my God—"

"*What* whole thing?" Mary's heart was racing. "What whole thing, Dylan?"

"Put that away," Dylan said quietly. His eyes were squeezed shut. "Get that thing away so I can't see it."

Mary folded the note in half, ready to return it to Dylan's overcoat pocket, when she suddenly noticed something else. A weak, fragrant aroma, barely noticeable—nearly recognizable—coming from the parchment in her hand.

Wrinkling her nose, Mary brought the paper close to her face and closed her eyes, breathing in its smell and realizing, with slow, inevitable dismay, that she *did* recognize it; there was absolutely no mistaking it.

The shock, surprise, and dread that shot through her wasn't a flood of adrenaline or fear—it was something else. A deeper, more unsettling sensation, a growing awareness that she was on the edge of real understanding—and that everything that had happened up to this point was just the beginning, just the outer walls of a dark labyrinth she would have to enter.

"What *is* it?" Dylan asked. "Why are you—"

"Turn the car around."

"What? *Why?* I don't—"

"We have to go back uptown. Come on—turn the car around."

Dylan was craning his neck, looking for traffic as he obediently flicked the turn signal. "But where are we going?" he demanded. "What are we doing?"

"We're going to jog your memory."

DYLAN HAD FOUND A parking spot—miraculously—just around the corner on Ninety-fifth Street off Amsterdam, and had quickly locked the car. Mary looked around uneasily at the familiar shadows of her own neighborhood. Now, with the two of them crammed into the tiny elevator on their way to the fifth-floor landing, she found herself wondering just how safe they were.

"Do you have your keys?" Dylan asked. Mary nodded as the elevator door rumbled open (in its usual maddeningly slow way). She led him out, past the dim bulbs and the other apartments and over to the familiar, hateful front door with SHAYNE M still printed on the small card beneath the doorbell (although it had been ten years since her father died).

This isn't a good idea, Mary thought as she snapped the locks open, returning her keys to her—Dylan's—jeans pocket. *This isn't a good idea at all.*

But it couldn't be helped. She *had* to bring Dylan here.

"Your mom's probably home," Dylan whispered in the silence. Mary flicked on the overhead light, leading him over the warped wooden floorboards. *He's been here before*, Mary remembered. *Many, many times—when he was just Scruffy Dylan and I wasn't paying any attention.*

As Dylan walked directly over the spot on the floor where he would end up lying in a spreading pool of his own blood, Mary felt a wave of fear and anxiety pass over her. *We shouldn't be here—this is a big mistake*, she told herself again. *We need to run.*

But there was something else she needed to do too.

"Come on," Mary whispered, pulling him by the wrist, down the apartment's narrow corridor, past the kitchen and bathroom—to the third bedroom door.

Dad's study.

This was the room Morton Shayne had used as an office. His actual place of work, where he saw patients, had been across town, in a shared office that he'd split with a couple of other psychotherapists, but this was where he always did his real work, studying cases and writing articles for journals. Nobody went in except Dad—and since he'd died, nobody ever went in there at all.

But that's not true, Mary reminded herself as she took a deep breath and turned the old glass doorknob and pushed the door open. It creaked against the warped floor and dust cascaded down through the overhead corridor light. *Ellen comes in here. Ellen comes in here all the time.*

The moment the door was open, the stale corridor air was flooded with *that smell*—the most familiar and most melancholy aroma in the world; one that Mary had known her entire life, that permeated her oldest, deepest memories of life as a little girl, of the strange, bright world of early childhood that was gone forever.

The smell of her father's tobacco—his beloved Borkum Riff pipe tobacco.

The tobacco aroma was all over the note she'd found in Dylan's pocket—it was so pungent, so unmistakable that she'd picked up the scent even before she brought the paper to her nose. Now, stepping forward into the pitch black of her father's study, that same aroma, blended with the smells of old books, mildew and stale air, was flooding her nostrils, filling her with nostalgia and sadness and dread.

"Here's the light," Dylan whispered, finding a switch and snapping on the overhead bulb.

The room was tiny, with a narrow window that looked out on the same air shaft Mary's window did. The room was nearly filled by a gigantic oak desk, which was covered in stacks of papers and books and an old, brass gooseneck lamp. The computer was gone. (*Mom sold it,* Mary remembered. *The only time she dealt with this room at all.*) The walls held rows of pictures: of Dad's college days at Swarthmore, of himself and Mom when they were a young couple, of the baby girls in strollers being pushed down Riverside Drive. Morton Shayne's Columbia PhD and his therapist's license were proudly framed on the other wall. Mary remembered everything about the room, even though she hadn't set foot in here for ten years.

But Ellen had. The floor was littered with what were obviously Ellen's belongings; there was a David Bowie CD that could not possibly have belonged to Morton Shayne, who had only liked classical music. There were several of Ellen's schoolbooks on the desk, Mary saw now, along with a worn paperback of *The Fellowship of the Ring* and two or three empty Diet Coke cans in the rusted wire wastebasket.

"Mary?" Dylan said quietly, making her jump. "Why are we here?"

"Have you ever been in here?"

"No. I mean—" Dylan still sounded dazed. "I don't think so. No. Probably not."

Make up your mind, Mary thought, still so intoxicated with the overwhelming pipe-tobacco aroma that she almost imagined she could smell her father. The sorrow and grief that she had avoided so carefully was threatening to drown her. *Make up your mind, because we've got to go.* Again Mary remembered the blood on the floor. *This isn't a safe place to be.*

"Look at this," Dylan said, picking up a book from a shelf on the desk.

The book was old, threadbare: a jacketless hardcover that must have been published decades ago. It was bound in what must at one time have been a luxurious purple cloth binding but had deteriorated over the years to a fuzzy-edged, pale remnant of itself. The spine and cover were bare, except for a partially worn away inlaid gold symbol. The symbol was a stylized, asymmetrical almond-shaped eye.

Dylan carefully swung the book's cover open.

The frontispiece was blank. No publisher's mark, no copyright date—nothing.

"What is it?" Mary couldn't decipher Dylan's expression. He kept turning the yellowed pages, which were ornamented with vertical columns of small drawn figures, ghostly shapes printed in fading ink. The book was so old that the frail, smooth pages were coming loose from the binding. Mary leaned closer as Dylan traced his finger along the drawings.

"*Khetti Satha Shemsu*," Dylan murmured, pointing at the symbols. "I actually recognize that."

"What do you mean, you *recognize* it? How can you possibly—"

"It's what I do," Dylan explained. "Languages, and linguistic history—it's going to be my major."

"So what kind of symbols are those?"

"Hieroglyphics," Dylan told her, flicking on the desk lamp and moving the book under its weak glow. Mary stared at the strange sideways figures—men or women (it was impossible to tell which) with odd clothes and headgear, surrounded by inexplicable, precisely drawn icons. "Egyptian hieroglyphics—from ancient Egypt. From, like, three thousand years ago."

"Is the whole book—"

"There's stuff in English, too." Dylan showed her, flipping ahead in the book. Most of its pages were murky gray illustrations of sheets of hieroglyphics, interspersed with dense passages of English text. "It's some kind of facsimile edition of . . . Look." He showed her the thin, reedy typography on the book's title page:

MAGICKS & INCANTATIONS
OF HORUS THE SON OF TNAHSIT.
Being a Full and Complete REPRODUCTION
of Papyrus Rolls of 2600 B.C., the Tomb of Senneferi
Notes & Translations by
the Hon. Sir Frederick Hollead,
LONDON, 1858.

"What the hell?" Mary flinched as a yellowed corner of the book's title page flaked off in her hand. "What is this?"

"A book of spells," Dylan marveled, his scruffy hair hanging in his eyes. "An ancient book of spells. It must have been, like, a roll of papyrus that got mummified, preserved, from, um, from some kind of archaeological dig somewhere . . . and, like, restored and copied in the nineteenth century, when all those tombs got opened."

"I don't understand—"

"There's a marked page," Dylan murmured, frowning in concentration. "Look."

A yellow and white plastic New York City Transit Authority MetroCard was jammed between the book's pages. Dylan flipped the fragile pages forward and opened the book wide.

THE CURSE OF 7 SOULS

The Highest Servants of the Ancient Magick believed that Man contains seven souls. In mockery of their foolish beliefs, Horus the Son of Tnahsit perfected a vengeful curse to smite enemies with the terrible power of this mystical Number. The Ritual must be obeyed exactly: The Spell-Caster utters the Incantation before an Unclothed Victim Slumbering beneath an open Southern sky, who upon awakening is given an Amulet of Tnahsit as a Keepsake. The Spell-Caster chooses seven Minions, the seven Men and Women who most despise the Victim, and summons them with a written Invocation Marked with a Token of Tnahsit's eye. [*Translated Incantation and Invocation Reproduced below.—F.H.*] The Spell-Caster commands the Minions to bring forth their own Hatred and Wrathful Anger in the torture and punishment of the Victim. If, by the time of one Passing of the Sun, the Curse of 7 Souls reaches its full fruition and the Victim lies Dead, then the Victim's suffering will continue in the afterlife as he revisits the Ba of all 7 Minions, experiencing both the Pain he has caused them, and all of their vengeful Ire. The Soul of the Victim then scatters to Oblivion, unless the Victim has achieved Enlightenment and is reborn as an Akh, or new Soul, so finding a new vessel, or Ka, on Earth. Whatever the fate of the Victim's Soul, when the day is done, the Minions will forget all that they have done in Service of the Curse: their Vengeance shall be complete, and so their memories shall be clean, and no trace of Horus's Magick will remain upon the Earth. Horus ends the Curse with a warning: The Spell-Caster has only one day to fulfill his murderous desires, for if the Victim still lives after a day has passed, then the Spell Expires, and all shall be forgotten.

Mary realized she'd collapsed into her father's leather-covered desk chair while she was reading. She was staring at the page of the book like it was the only thing she could see, the only thing anyone could see, in the entire world.

The Curse of 7 Souls, she thought weakly. *I've been cursed.*

Of course she believed it all, without the slightest hesitation. All her doubt was gone—left behind somewhere around the time she'd come back from the dead and *watched* her friends plot against her—*participated* in the master plan that Horus's ancient spell had somehow actually conjured out of the air. She didn't have any doubt left.

I'm not hallucinating; I'm not dreaming; I'm not crazy, she reminded herself again. *And this all makes sense.*

"Ellen cast the spell," Mary whispered. She was crying, but she couldn't feel it—she only knew because the tears were blurring and stinging her eyes. She didn't feel anything at all. "Ellen cast the spell on me. She"—Mary looked up at Dylan, but she couldn't see anything through the tears— "she hates me. Hated me, like you all hate me—and she did something about it. She did this."

"Are you sure? What about the amulet?" Dylan objected. "Did you ever get anything like an amulet from Ellen? It says she had to give you some—"

"*It was Ellen!*" Mary sobbed, wiping her eyes. Dylan's hand was on her shoulder and she wanted to grab it and clutch at him, wailing in self-pity and sadness and remorse, but she was too numb to move. "Didn't you read what it says? The note with the eye on it! Your amnesia! My own sister wanted me dead because she hates me so much!"

"Wait," Dylan murmured. He leaned his shaggy head closer to the book, peering intently at the murky hieroglyphics. He tapped his finger against a group of symbols so faded and small that Mary could barely make them out. "Wait—this is wrong. Jesus, this is wrong. Ellen needs to see this—"

Boom! Boom! There was a loud banging on the apartment's front door.

Dylan jumped—his whole body tensed. His finger stabbed against the fragile book, and the illustrated page he'd been examining tore free of the binding. He grabbed Mary's hand. She grabbed back, pressing against him.

"Stay here," Dylan told her. "I'll deal with it."

No, no, no—

There was no way she was going to let him do that. It was beginning to occur to Mary that she'd made another mistake, that she'd messed up again and that the consequences were going to be very bad. *Too much time in this room*, she scolded herself as the banging on the front door repeated. *Too much curiosity when Dylan was right all along, we should be RUNNING—*

"Don't go out there," she told Dylan, clinging to him. "Please don't go out there."

"Just stay right here," he told her. "I'll be right back."

Dylan was gently prying her hands away. His attention was still on the torn-out page of Horus's book, and whatever strong impression its tiny symbols had made on him; he brought the page with him as he circled the desk and moved toward the study door. Mary watched him leave the room that she'd avoided entering for ten years, on his way to do the heroic male thing and answer the door.

"*No!*" Mary called out as she sprinted after him, tripping over one of Dad's stacks of old books and nearly toppling to the floor, correcting her balance and stumbling out into the corridor just as Dylan opened the front door. A deafening explosion filled Mary's head like a grenade going off. Dylan was propelled backward, flipping in the air like a drop-kicked action figure and landing on his back on the floor. The gunshot had been deafeningly loud—Mary heard a distant scream from *another* apartment. Bright scarlet blood was spreading out of Dylan. Released from his hand, the page of Horus's book drifted gently to the floor like a falling leaf.

Dylan screamed. The agony in his voice was terrifying.

Mary spun on her heel and ran down the corridor in a blind panic. Dylan was still screaming behind her as she slammed against her own bedroom door, propelled herself inside and then slammed and locked the door.

She could hear footsteps, entering the apartment, walking closer.

"Oh, Jesus—oh, God, it fucking *hurts*—"

Dylan, screaming.

Standing at her bedroom door, trembling with panic like an animal on a busy highway, Mary suddenly noticed something—an object on the floor.

A package wrapped in purple paper.

Ellen's gift.

Stooping, Mary picked it up, tore off the paper and uncovered a small tarnished gold necklace. The pendant was a crude carving of an almond-shaped eye.

The eye of Tnahsit.

My amulet.

It was all true, then. She'd known it already, but this confirmed it. *She made sure I received the eye as a gift,* Mary thought. *To complete the curse.*

Mary leaned against the door and listened as the footsteps approached—slow, measured steps on the creaking floorboards, getting closer and closer.

What do I do now? Mary looked around the small bedroom, panicking. *What the hell do I do now?*

A fist was banging on her bedroom door.

Then she heard a familiar voice—a weak soprano.

"I've called the cops!"

What?

Mary recognized the voice—her own mother's.

She woke up, Mary realized. She'd forgotten all about her mother, but of course Mom was *here,* in her bedroom, probably having locked the door herself.

"Whoever you are, the cops are coming! I called nine-one-one!"

Good for you, Mom, Mary thought, impressed. Outside the bedroom door, the creaking floorboards made their noises again: whoever was out there was leaving. Mary could hear the footsteps hurrying away. Then the front door slammed.

Well done, Mom, Mary thought. She hadn't realized how overcome with sheer terror she'd been until the door closed and she felt safer. Having an assailant with a gun *right* on the other side of her door had been so terrifying that Mary wasn't sure she could deal with anything more.

But you don't have much to deal with now, she told herself weakly, as Dylan continued to scream and sob and Mary stumbled back against her own bed and fell down along it, overcome with weakness and fear. *It's almost over.*

So I have to get it right.

She was sure of that—it was the one thing she was sure of as a familiar haze began to flood her senses and her eyes fixed on the blinding glare of the room's overhead lights.

I've got a chance to make this right—just barely.

She was trying to concentrate as the world filled again with pale whiteness, and the bedroom and Dylan's moans and the glare expanded into a silent inferno of blinding light.

5

PATRICK

SHE COULDN'T SEE—THE air was white and thick. The smell hit her, immediately—cigarettes and pot smoke and booze and sugar, all mixed together into a swill that conjured up every party she'd ever been to or thrown up at or had to clean up. A hissing sound, like a punctured tire, was coming from her right hand, and when she cleared her eyes and looked down, she saw that she was holding an aerosol can and spraying something wet and black onto the wall in front of her.

It happened again, Mary thought, noting the rasping,

boozy taste in her mouth and the itching of her stylish clothes against her tall male body. Her dead spirit (or whatever you wanted to call it) had moved somewhere else, occupying another of the seven souls by means of whom Mary had been cursed.

I'm Trick.

It was obvious even as Mary's surroundings came into focus: she was in the living room of Patrick's suite at the Peninsula Hotel, after the end of the party. The room was quiet—that particular, eerie hotel silence that Mary recognized well from the many afternoons and evenings she'd spent here.

The suite looked totally empty. The smoke was clearing, though it lingered near the wall, where she was standing. The party was over; the guests were long gone. Glancing at Trick's left wrist, Mary saw that his steel TAG Heuer read a few minutes to two (and the blackness outside the window confirmed that that meant two A.M.).

Her hand—Patrick's hand—was holding a spray can that said KRYLON; Mary realized that she—Patrick—was spray-painting the wall. She was adding a large black spot to the end of the word *GOODBYE*.

I saw this before, Mary realized, shuddering slightly at the memory of her final moments on earth. *I came in here and saw the room like this*—looking around now, gazing through Patrick's eyes, Mary could see the floor's entire expanse covered in party trash—*and this word was spray-painted on the wall.*

But it had never occurred to her that *Patrick* had painted it.

Why? Why would Patrick trash his own hotel room? It was such a *sweet* room, as he always said; the arrangement with the hotel meant he could basically stay there forever without—

(*such a sweet room*)

—worrying about the consequences. Mary just couldn't imagine Trick vandalizing his own room. It didn't make any sense, but something about that phrase was stirring a memory in a way she'd come to recognize.

(*such a sweet room*)

SUCH A SWEET ROOM; such a beautiful room. Everyone who came in here, no matter how jaded, always took an involuntary deep breath as they looked around. A decorator had done it all, back in the early nineties; like the rest of the Dawes apartment, it had ended up as a glossy spread in a magazine. The red walls, the enormous handmade child's bed, the bay window facing the park—all of it was perfect, delightful.

And Patrick *hated* it.

Not that he'd *always* hated it. Standing on the soft carpet in his gigantic bedroom in his parents' house on Fifth Avenue, hands in faded jeans pockets, looking around at the cluttered floor and the jaunty red walls, he had to admit that he'd been very happy here. He used to sit for hours on the floor near the huge bay window that overlooked Central Park, playing, coloring and drawing, and if you bent down close to the polished mahogany boards, Patrick knew, you could still see the grooves and scratches he'd made as a five-year-old, pushing toy cars and action figures around. It was, as his mother used to tell visitors, "a perfect environment for a child."

Out in the living room, Mary was talking to his mom. He could barely hear their voices echoing down the corridor, which was the size of a subway tunnel. The Dawes apartment occupied the entire top two floors of an opulently carved white-granite prewar apartment building right across from the ripest edge of Central Park. It was four-thirty in the afternoon, pretty much right after school, and they were here, at Patrick's parents' house, because Patrick needed to get his passport.

Since Dad had kicked him out, Patrick had been putting off coming back here. It wasn't that he *cared*—he was just avoiding running into the old man. Patrick's dad didn't have any sense of time or place, as in "there's a time and place for everything." For Ken Dawes, *any* time and *any* place was appropriate for lashing out at his son (or any other underling who'd displeased him). At restaurants (with patrons turning to watch), driving on the freeway in the Bentley (with the driver eventually putting up the motorized privacy screen), even on a crowded sidewalk, Dad would bellow at Trick at the top of his lungs.

"You've *got* to go there before we leave," Mary had reminded him in the cafeteria that afternoon. "Without your passport there's no *trip*, damn it. Just get it over with." Mary had sucked the last of her milk through her straw, cheeks dimpling prettily around her pouting lips as she did it. They'd been talking about flying to Cabo for spring break, and he needed his passport, as she was reminding him. "I'll come with you and hold your hand."

He'd agreed, and here he was poking through all the old junk on his desk, sifting through printed party invitations and packs of rolling papers and sheets of drawing paper and cocktail napkins and CDs. Just being in the apartment was sucking the life out of him—he felt like he was being smothered—and he sighed impatiently as he pulled drawers open and picked through the contents of shelves, trying to find his passport.

He wanted to be miles away. He wanted to be downtown at the Peninsula, where he felt happy and comfortable and nobody bothered him. If he wanted food, he ordered it. If he wanted company—wanted friends to talk to, even in that random minor way you talk while watching bad TV—he could get on the cell and call his buds, Mason and his crew, or some guys from the Chadwick football team, and they would show up, never too high pressure, never too much or too little energy.

Even Mary could chill in that place, Patrick thought. That was the real miracle. The most high-maintenance, high-strung, high-energy girl in the world, the world's loudest attention magnet, became nearly *subdued* at the Peninsula. It was an incredible thing to see. She collapsed onto one of the white couches and took a few deep breaths and Patrick could see the tension, the constant anxiety she always seemed to be drowning in, flowing out of her.

But here . . . Trick looked over at his old bed, the gigantic custom-made wooden behemoth with the bold blue paint and the full-size FAO Schwarz tin soldiers flanking its headboard. It had cost something like seven thousand dollars. As a kid, he'd *loved* it, but come on—once you've started shaving, how can you sleep in something like that?

It was the whole problem. Patrick couldn't complain about *anything* in his life, because everything he had was such a gift. The world—or, more specifically, his parents—had been overwhelmingly good to him. So anything that went wrong was *his* fault.

Shaking his head to clear it, Patrick looked around at his old bedroom—"old" because, well, he'd been thrown out, hadn't he? Kicked out by the old man—half the people Patrick knew (his relatives, his parents' friends) were appalled and concerned; to the other half (everyone he knew under thirty) it just made him more intriguing—more tortured and romantic and dashing.

Why did Mom have to be here? That was the other thing: the gorgon, the hellion. His mother. Mary was out there right now, discussing God knows what with his adversary, the woman who'd brought him into the world and seemed to regret it more with every passing day.

"*Yes*—" Patrick said involuntarily. There it was—his passport—wedged into a drawer beside a forgotten pair of gold-framed Ray-Bans, a box of Trojans and two metal one-hit pipes. (His mother *never* snooped—it wasn't the WASP way—and he'd always been completely comfortable storing drug paraphernalia in his bedroom.) Stuffing the passport into his back pocket, Trick flicked the light off. He headed out of the bedroom and down the train-tunnel-size corridor, back toward the living room. As always, he could *feel* the weight lifting from his shoulders, just *knowing* that he'd soon be gone from this place.

"—overstep my bounds."

Mary's voice, coming from around a corner, straight ahead—from between the widely spaced Doric columns that framed the oversize entrance to the living room. She was only twenty feet away, but she couldn't see him.

"Oh, not at all, dear!" Patrick's mother's voice. "I'm *so* glad you came to talk."

What the hell?

Patrick stopped in his tracks, not breathing.

"Like I said: what I'm most afraid of is that he'll bottom out," Mary continued. Her voice echoed harshly against the hard surfaces of the apartment—Patrick could hear her perfectly. "I mean, he's been on such a downward slope, with snorting and with booze; without any kind of break, I just don't know how far he'll slip."

How far I'll— What?

Patrick couldn't believe his ears. *She's talking about me,* he realized. *She's talking to Mom about me; she's selling me out.*

"I had no *idea,*" Mom said in her most honeyed voice. Patrick had heard her do this before: she was really good at playing the reasonable, kind saint when she was dealing with anyone outside the family. They never saw the *real* Mrs. Dawes—the one who shrieked or threw plates against the wall. They only saw the sweet-voiced, philanthropic angel whom Mary was talking to now. "I mean, *none*—the poor guy. I just thought he'd gotten, you know, at least somewhat clean."

"Me too," Mary's voice answered. Standing just out of view, not breathing, motionless, Patrick could feel his fingers clenching into fists. His face was heating up. "But in the past few weeks it's just gotten worse and worse. I've been trying to, you know, get him to cut down, to stop at a certain point rather than getting another bottle or whatever, but, you know . . ."

"I appreciate everything you've done," his mom murmured.

"You understand, it's pure concern," Mary went on. The anger and confusion rushing through him was wild, chaotic. The white corridor walls seemed to be closing in on him. Patrick was struggling as hard as he could not to run around the corner and grab Mary by the shoulders and scream in her face, *What the hell are you doing? Are you out of your fucking mind?*

"Thank you, Mary," his mom said solemnly. "Thanks for being so concerned."

Patrick could hear footsteps and fumbling noises, clicking jewelry and the unmistakable sound of a kiss. *Now she's getting thanked for it*, he thought incredulously. *That fucking bitch—she sold me out and she's getting a kiss on the cheek.*

"Found my passport," Patrick said loudly, coming forward into the room.

Patrick's mother (in her standard taupe-colored Chanel suit) and Mary were standing very close to each other in the middle of the living room, near the grand piano—they both turned guiltily and looked at him as he came in, stepping quickly apart.

"Oh, good," Mary said loudly.

"Honey, is there anything else you need, now that you're here?" Mom asked Patrick. He had to give her credit: her face looked completely normal, peaceful and human between her gold Henri Bendel earrings. The beast within was totally hidden. "Do you want to stay for dinner? Your father won't be home until very late."

"No, that's okay—thanks, Mom," Patrick managed to say. He was still trembling with fury. He stared straight at his mother, at the trademark flat expression that made her such a devastating bridge opponent. "We actually have to go. Mary, you want to get the elevator? I just have to say good-bye."

"Sure—bye, Mrs. Dawes," Mary said, heading immediately for the apartment's front door, not lingering for another air kiss. *Not pushing her luck*, he thought. He didn't want to look at her as she moved past, a brunette blur, and headed toward the vestibule to summon the elevator. "Patrick, I'm right outside—"

Patrick and his mother locked eyes across the gigantic living room and it was like one of those old monster movies where the beast slowly emerges—Patrick could see his mother's pupils glinting with fury as Mary's footsteps receded and Mrs. Dawes's genteel public mask fell away.

"Mom," he began helplessly, "I don't know what she told you, but—"

"Don't even start," his mom said tightly, stepping toward him and pointing at his chest with her finger, the way she'd been doing his entire life. "Don't even think about it, you little punk. I *knew* I couldn't trust you. I knew you'd break my heart."

"Mom—" Patrick's thoughts were racing furiously. His behavior in the next ninety seconds was crucial: if he was going to successfully win his way back into his mother's good graces, he had to choose his words carefully. So far, whenever Mom had reprimanded him—and had threatened to take away the golden goose—he'd always been able to talk her down.

"Don't 'Mom' me!" Mrs. Dawes's eyes were now blazing so wildly that she could have been a soap-opera villainess— a realization that would have been funny under any other circumstances. "Damn it, Patrick, I've been *nothing* but kind, *nothing* but understanding of your—of your ugly, *decadent* habits. I know I'm supposed to be trendy and understand your 'disease' or whatever you want me to say, but I just can't do it anymore. No mother could. Thank God for that girlfriend of yours, that's all I can say."

Yeah, let's hear it for Mary, Patrick thought. He felt like he was going to cry, not because he felt so helpless and angry—although he did—but because it just *hurt* to have your mother yell at you like this, call you a "little punk." It didn't matter how little you cared. It didn't matter how old you got. It still hurt, every time, as much as it had when he was a boy. "Again, Mom," he started over, "I don't know what she told you, but Mary's hardly a reliable—"

"Stop it. Just stop this instant!" Patrick's mother spoke through clenched teeth, stepping closer to him and glancing back at the front door through which Mary had exited.

Because we can't be seen fighting, he thought bitterly. *It isn't done. You can call me worthless, as long as nobody overhears, right, Mom?* That painful feeling in his throat—the certainty that he was going to cry—had not gone away, and Patrick swallowed, still staring back at his mom. "I'm all done being manipulated by you! The free ride's over. I want you out of the Peninsula by Saturday."

The words hit him like a smack in the face.

"I'm calling what's-his-name, Grayson, that manager, and cutting you off," she went on. "I'm giving you until Saturday. *Check-out time* Saturday—I'll make it very clear."

"What?"

Patrick realized something right then: she was serious. He really had reached the end of the line.

"You heard me," Mrs. Dawes repeated, quietly, deliberately. "Patrick Kensington Dawes, you are cut off. No more payments. No more credit-card bills."

"But Mom—" Patrick could hear the helpless panic in his voice—the whine of the eight-year-old he used to be, who would argue against being punished; always trying to persuade his parents to take it back. *I'm going to be doing this the rest of my life*, he thought dismally. *There's just no escaping this family.* "Where am I supposed to go? Where am I supposed to live?"

"I don't care!" Mrs. Dawes snapped, and Patrick realized she was close to tears herself. "I don't care where you go, you . . . you junkie!"

"Mom—" He was crying now too, and, more than anything else, he wanted to reach out to her, to touch her. "Mom, please don't—"

Mrs. Dawes flinched. "Get out of here," she whispered. Her lower lip was trembling. "Don't come back until you've straightened yourself out."

Then she turned away and Patrick turned to leave the apartment, his passport shoved pointlessly into his back pocket. He rubbed the tears from his chiseled face, feeling like a child who'd just been sent to his room without any dinner.

"Oh, take a little longer," Mary teased him when he emerged into the vestibule. She was leaning prettily on the open elevator door, holding its heavy brass edge. Her smile faded when she looked at him. "Everything all right?"

Oh, you've got some nerve, Patrick thought dangerously. He stepped past her into the elevator and hoped she didn't notice how his shoulders and arms were shaking with fury. *You've got some nerve, Mary Shayne, I'll give you that.*

"Everything's fine," he lied, still not looking at her. He stabbed the elevator button as the door rolled shut and they began to sink toward the ground floor.

MARY DROPPED THE EMPTY Krylon spray can, staring at the word that was garishly painted across the striped silk wallpaper, feeling a hoarse tightness in her—Patrick's—throat.

The memory, Patrick's memory, was somehow even worse than the others she'd experienced. Scott's hopeless anger at being propelled all over the city with her schoolbooks, Joon's fury at losing Patrick, Amy's rage when her secret, fragile hopes were dashed so coldly—the searing psychological pain of enduring those experiences had been brutal. But this was different, somehow. Milder, yes, but *worse*, harder to face.

I just screwed him over for no reason, Mary told herself, staring at the GOODBYE painted ten feet wide on the wall in front of her. She had assumed, as she'd come through this room, that the word was directed at *her*. But now she realized what Patrick had meant—what bitter message he was leaving on the wall of the Peninsula. *And he's going to be out on the street and it's my fault. No wonder he hates me. No wonder.*

There was somebody else in the hotel suite.

Mary froze, hunching her—Patrick's—shoulders as she flicked her eyes back and forth. She was sure of it: she'd heard something coming from the bedroom. Looking at the base of the closed door, Mary could see shadows moving around—somebody was coming out of there. Mary looked around for a place to hide, but it was impossible; there simply wasn't enough time before the bedroom door swung open.

"Poor Dylan . . . ," Ellen sobbed, entering the room. "Oh my God, poor Dylan . . ."

Mary stared at her, amazed.

Her sister looked exactly as she had hours before, when this same room was packed with screaming, dancing, drinking people. But she also looked completely different. *There you are*, she thought incredulously, gazing across the smoke-filled room at her sister. *The reason this all happened.*

Ellen's eyes were red and raw, her face was deathly pale, and it was obvious she'd been crying. Tears had smeared her inexpertly applied mascara. Her mouth was twisted into an anguished grimace that Mary didn't recognize at all.

"Where *are* they, Patrick?" Ellen demanded—Mary saw fresh tears running down her face. "They called from the *road*. Joon called, like, *three hours* ago, from the road—why aren't they *here* yet?"

"What?" Mary heard Trick's familiar voice croaking the word as she answered. She couldn't believe what she was hearing—even though it made perfect sense.

That's who Joon called, Mary realized, remembering sitting in the backseat of Scott's car, watching Scott and Joon react to Dylan's escape maneuver. *She called Ellen.*

There was a part of Mary's mind that, despite everything, simply couldn't accept Ellen's guilt—couldn't imagine *why* Ellen had done what she'd done. But that part of her mind was losing the argument, and she knew it.

"They'd better get here soon, because Mary's on her way—it's almost showtime," Ellen muttered, pacing back and forth, clenching and unclenching her fists. "How did this all go so wrong?" She raised her glasses to wipe her streaming eyes.

Mary stood against the vandalized wall, staring at Ellen, trying to think of anything she could say—anything she could ask. A glint of reflected light on the edge of her vision made her suddenly remember Patrick's watch—looking down at it, she saw that it was 2:14 A.M.

Ellen just called me, she realized, trying to keep the timing straight in her head. *She called Real Mary, at home, and found out what happened to Dylan. That must have just happened.*

"How did Dylan get *shot*, Patrick?" Ellen's voice had climbed into a register of hysteria that was frightening Mary badly. Her sister was nearly insane with desperate fear and rage. "How the hell did that happen? Can *you* figure it out?"

"No," Mary said, truthfully. She was running out of resolve—running out of reasons to keep struggling, to keep fighting to understand what had happened to her and how to stop it.

(*showtime*)

"I told Joon exactly what to do. I gave her Dylan's address. I told her how to get to the fire escape, and she promised me she'd handle it." Ellen looked at her own watch. "I hope . . . I just hope . . ."

(*showtime*)

Something about that word seemed familiar . . . and, just like that, Mary was recalling another of Patrick Dawes's memories—

THE SKY WAS A vast white dome far above the roof of the Chadwick School, featureless except for a tiny, barely visible flock of gulls high overhead. Patrick stood on the tarpaper with the others, gazing around at the tops of the elegant Upper East Side apartment buildings stretching off in all directions. Looking south, Patrick could just barely see the glittering towers of Midtown—he could even make out the very top of the Peninsula—and, turning his head to one side, he could see the deep emerald bed of Central Park, inlaid into the city like a precious stone in a piece of ornate jewelry.

"Showtime," Ellen was saying. She had to raise her voice

to be heard over the wind. Surrounding her in a circle were Trick, Amy, Joon, and Dylan. Everybody was holding the thick paper notes Ellen had given them—the ones with the three lines of writing below the mesmerizing red symbol that seemed to keep moving, crawling on the page when you weren't looking, like one of those optical illusions you see in kids' books. When he'd first gotten Ellen's text message, summoning him to the roof (the same message they'd all gotten), he'd had no idea what to expect, but once the page was in his hands, any doubts about the oddness of the gathering melted away. *TODAY IS THE DAY*, the note said, and those four words conveyed a wonderful sense of purpose, of *correctness*, that had filled his heart from the moment he'd first read them. He found himself repeating them in his head, over and over, basking in the knowledge that *today* was the glorious day they were going to get Mary Shayne back for everything she'd done to them.

"Mary's on her way," Ellen went on, checking her watch. She'd been talking for a while, explaining her plan, and every word had been music to their ears. "We've still got a few minutes. . . . She's wandering down Madison Avenue, fantasizing that she's Audrey Hepburn." Joon and Amy made faces at this, sneering contemptuously. "No, it's true! She spends an hour each week trying to channel Holly Go-lightly, believe it or not. . . . I've timed her for two months and it's like clockwork. We've still got a few minutes before she gets here. Trick, you know what to do?"

"I sure do." Breaking up with Mary Shayne was such an appetizing prospect that he was bouncing on his toes with impatience—he couldn't *wait* to be face to face with her and do the deed. The fact that it was going to look like a fakeout later in the evening just made it all the sweeter.

"Good. You'd better go straight down to the street and wait for her there," Ellen said, checking her watch. "Next up is Dylan—you're going to ask her out on a date."

"All right," Dylan said readily. "When?"

"It's got to be at the end of the school day," Ellen said firmly. "I want her suffering all afternoon. Joon and Amy, you'll get her ready for the date."

"*That's* our job?" Joon said, sounding disappointed. "That's *all*? That sucks."

"Don't worry," Ellen told her, smiling secretively. "There's going to be more—a *lot* more. I know how mad you are about, well . . ." Ellen trailed off, not looking at Joon, but Joon's and Trick's eyes met, and it was clear to Patrick that they'd both gotten the message.

"What's the coup de grâce?" Dylan asked. His scruffy hair blew in the mild wind. "The big prank at the end," he explained, seeing their puzzled faces.

"She's going to try to off herself," Ellen told them, eyes glittering with excitement. "She's going to put a gun to her head and pull the trigger. The gun won't be loaded, of course, but she'll learn her lesson."

Gun? Amy was mouthing quizzically.

"What gun?" Joon asked.

"Patrick, that's your next job," Ellen went on, shivering slightly in her orange hoodie as she turned toward him. "You know what to do? Are you up for it?"

"Sure," Trick assured her. Ellen had explained that part, moments earlier, while they'd waited for the others to

300

arrive—and now he understood what Mason's nearly brand-new, gray-market Smith & Wesson automatic was for.

"My buddy Mason's coming to the party," he told them all. "He'll have his gun with him. He'll probably hit on Mary—he'll *definitely* hit on Mary," he corrected, making them all laugh. "That's when Joon comes in. Joon, you'll like this guy—he's really ripped."

"Yum, yum," Joon said flatly.

"You're going to have to get the gun away from him," Ellen told Joon in her calm, reasonable, authoritative voice. "Can you do that?"

"Absolutely," Joon said with regal assurance. Trick believed it; Mason loved to show his weapons to girls—he thought it turned them on. Trick was beginning to understand the master plan, and he approved. Ellen was in charge, completely, and it was a good thing, too—it just made so much *sense* to listen to what she was telling them to do. It had made sense since he'd awakened that morning, filled with a strange, calm certainty that *everything was going to be all right*, today—that somebody was going to tell him what to do, and once he'd done it all, the biggest problem in his life would be gone.

"I have a question," Amy said, her red hair billowing around her face as the wind whipped across the roof. "I've got to drive her to that house, right? How will I know where to go?"

"Patrick's job again," Ellen explained. "Patrick, I'll draw you a map; you've got to memorize the directions and repeat them back for Mary and Amy. Your car's ready?"

"Full tank of gas," Trick assured her.

"And I'm supposed to send her a scary text," Joon added. "Right?"

"Right," Ellen affirmed. "Sometime after ten, once Scott signals he's got everything set up at the farmhouse. I'm going to find Mary right then. I'll be with her at the party when she gets Joon's text—I'll make sure she takes it seriously. Once we've got the gun I'll take the bullets out and get ready for the big event while you're giving her the runaround."

"Will she do it?" Amy asked. "Will she actually pull the trigger?"

"Yeah," Ellen said, nodding calmly. "Yeah, you bet she will. You'll all be gone, and she'll think it's all her fault."

"She never thinks *anything's* her fault!" Patrick objected. "She's got the biggest fucking ego on the planet. What makes you think she's even *capable* of blaming herself?"

"That's all bullshit," Ellen said. "She hates herself more than all of us combined. That's why she needs to feel like such a fucking star all the time. That's why she needs to treat everyone else like shit. It's because she can't stand herself. Believe me, she'll do it. She'll pull the trigger."

Patrick found himself picturing that image, and felt a warm rush of excitement. From the looks on their faces, the others seemed to be doing the same thing.

"Okay," Amy said. "I still don't understand what this farmhouse deal is all about, though—it sounds so complicated. *What* do we have to do, exactly?"

"Scott will explain, once he gets to school," Ellen promised, reaching into her pocket and pulling out an enormous, heavy clump of industrial-looking keys. "I prepped him late last night. Once he gets here with all the equipment, he'll fill you in." Ellen tossed the keys across the circle to Amy, who fumbled them and nearly dropped them. "And you can give him these—I forgot to give them back."

Patrick wondered what that was all about—*What are those keys, anyway? What did I miss?*—but as he quickly reminded himself, he didn't need to know. All he needed to worry about was what Ellen had told him to do.

"There's one more thing," Ellen said, pointing to Dylan. "Stick around—I've got to talk to you. Everyone else, it's showtime—let's get moving."

STANDING IN THE WRECKED, deserted living room of the hotel suite, her nostrils—Patrick's nostrils—stinging with the ambient smoke and the acrid stench of the party, Mary reeled from what Patrick's memory had shown her. The efficient, cold-blooded way that her friends had ganged up on her, tricked her, planned the whole thing, was amazing to visualize even though she'd already *known* it had happened—since she'd inferred it from the spell itself, the curse that her own sister had unleashed on her.

(*The Sorcerer chooses 7 Minions, the 7 Men and Women who most despise the Victim*)

Finally, Mary understood her own role . . . the fiendishly clever way Ellen had recruited *her* along with the others.

(*WHOM DO YOU HATE THE MOST?*)

Ellen was right: she hated herself, even more than the rest

of them did (although hearing them laugh at her private *Breakfast at Tiffany's* routine hurt so much that it barely seemed possible). Mary forced herself not to dwell on her self-pity, and to concentrate on the details of Patrick's memory.

What were those keys? Mary thought, picturing the glittering shape that had flown across the rooftop that morning and been caught by Amy. *And what the hell was the "one more thing" with Dylan at the end?*

"Dylan's going to die," Ellen was whimpering. "This is all my fault. It's turned into a nightmare, it's gotten out of control. . . ."

Oh, Ellie, Mary thought. She was nearly trembling with repressed anguish. She wanted to grab Ellen and hug her, try to comfort her—but she didn't move. She could feel her own grief erupting inside of her, and she had to muster all her self-control to suppress it and hide it. She was not herself—literally; she was Patrick Dawes, and she couldn't let her guard down. She had to be as smart as she'd ever been in her life. Scott, Joon, Amy, Mary and now Patrick were five souls.

Five out of seven, she thought grimly. She clearly remembered what she'd read in that antique, threadbare purple book. *7 souls—and then oblivion.*

"Ellen," Mary said, flinching at the familiar bass echoes of Patrick's smoky voice. "Ellen, *why?* Why are you doing this?"

"The same reason you are," Ellen said bitterly. She was crying. "Because I *hate* her. Because I want to get *back* at her."

"*For what?*" Mary yelled, staring at her crying sister in

304

shock and disbelief and sorrow. "Get back at her for *what*? What did I—what did Mary ever do to you?"

"She tried to kill my mom!" Ellen screamed.

What?

Mary was so stunned that she nearly forgot to breathe. *I did what? I tried to kill Mom?*

"What do you mean?" she managed to rasp out. "Tried to kill her . . . when? *How?*"

"Ten years ago," Ellen sobbed. "The day my dad died . . . that's when it happened. The day Mary ruined my mom's life."

I ruined— What?

"I don't—I don't know that story," Mary said.

"Nobody does!" Ellen raged. "Mary acts like it never happened! Mom and I are the only ones who know! Mom never talks about it, but she's got to live with Mary, like, every day, knowing what she did!"

What in the name of God in heaven is she talking about?

"But Mary will know," Ellen whispered. "When this day is over, she'll know."

I will? Mary wasn't sure what to ask next—Ellen's stunning accusations had made it very difficult to think. "What—"

A familiar metallic clatter suddenly filled the room. Mary knew exactly what it was. *Someone's here*, she realized, recognizing the sounds of Patrick's suite door being unlatched and opened—a noise she'd learned to recognize and anticipate after countless room service and valet calls, and all the other Peninsula Hotel benefits she'd shamelessly sponged while dating Patrick.

"*Shit*—is that Mary?" Ellen said frantically, grabbing Mary's—Patrick's—wrist. "Too soon, too soon—we're not ready. . . ."

The door swung wide and bashed into the wall, and Joon, Amy and Scott hurried into the room. Mary stared, wide-eyed. Scott and Amy looked haunted and pale—as pale as Ellen—and their movements betrayed their erratic mental state. Joon was soaking wet, still wearing her sodden party dress, looking almost exactly as she had outside Dylan's fire escape, her hair hanging over her face like black moss. But Mary's eyes fixed on Joon's right hand and what it was holding.

The gun.

That's what's-his-name's gun—Mason's gun, Mary finally realized, remembering Trick's awful dealer friend, the meth head with the ripped body—recalling Patrick's memory of the rooftop meeting. *The gun he brought to the party—the one Joon was supposed to get from him.* It was the entire reason Mason had been at the party—maybe the entire reason there *was* a party. She hadn't recognized it when she'd lifted it to her own head, but now, staring across the wrecked hotel room, she realized it was the same one—the same satin-finish Smith & Wesson automatic.

"Finally!" Ellen shouted. "Where the hell have you *been*? Mary's on her way!"

"Good," Joon said quietly. "Good."

"What do you mean, good? Everything's gone wrong! Dylan's been shot!"

"Yeah," Joon said, smiling with one side of her mouth.

Mary couldn't take her eyes off the gun—the gun that hung from Joon's slim hand like the clapper of a funeral bell. "Serves her right, doesn't it? Now we've *both* lost a guy."

"You fucking *crazy bitch!*" Ellen screamed, grabbing Joon by the throat. *"What the hell did you do?"*

No—no, Mary thought, feeling her breath catching in Patrick's raspy, cigarette-stained throat. *No, please, no—*

"We don't have *time*," Joon shouted back, grabbing Ellen's wrists and easily shaking her hands free. The gun swung around and Ellen and Mary and Amy and Scott all ducked. "Get your hands off me, damn it—and get your shit together. You said she's on her way—we've got to finish this."

"Okay—okay." Ellen was panting, starting to cry again. Mary watched as her sister got control of herself. "Give me the gun," she said, holding out her hand.

Joon met Ellen's eyes and held out the gun, and Mary stared, mesmerized, as her sister reached out and took it, holding it like a trophy, tilting the weapon so the lamplight gleamed on its smooth black surface.

"The rest of you, hide," Ellen ordered. Her voice had changed, Mary realized, powerless to stop herself from walking forward, watching as Ellen carried the gun through the open doorway into Patrick's bedroom, toward the bed . . . and the wooden box that lay on its sheets.

(*Because I hate her.*)

Mary stood there in Patrick's body and clothes with the smell of Krylon spray paint filling her nostrils and stared at her sister as Ellen carefully opened the wooden box, placed the gun inside it and then pulled a folded note from her pocket and put that inside the box next to the gun. The ceiling spotlights flared in Mary's eyes, the white glare filling her vision, expanding like the pain and sorrow in her heart until she had disappeared within a numbing platinum void.

6

DYLAN

BRIGHT WHITE LIGHT WAS shining in Mary's eyes, glittering from the glass spyhole set directly in the center of the white door in front of her. A pounding noise was coming from the other side of the door, shaking it visibly. Mary could feel cold brass in her right hand; she looked down and saw her own hand—a boy's large hand—turning the knob and pulling the door open while the pounding continued. She wanted to stop herself, but she couldn't—there just wasn't time. Dylan's muscles were already moving, turning the knob on the Shayne apartment's front door and pulling it open, and Mary had something like one second to realize where, when, and who she was—and to try to *stop herself*—but it was too late.

The door burst open, practically knocking her backward, and then she was staring out into the fifth-floor landing, where Joon Park stood in her ruined clothes pointing a gun right at her and pulling the trigger.

The muzzle flash and blast were brilliant and loud. The gun jerked, its barrel slamming backward and forward as the cartridge was ejected and a cloud of sweet-smelling smoke filled the air. Mary was blown backward and she felt white-hot agony in her abdomen and then a blast of pain all up and down her body as the wooden floor slammed into her from behind; she was on the floor now, staring up at her apartment's hallway ceiling, with a pool of warmth spreading behind her and her mind nearly comatose with pain and shock.

"*Aaaahh!*" a male voice was screaming—Dylan's voice, echoing inside her skull.

That's me, Mary thought. The pain was so intense that she was convinced she would go insane if it continued.

Joon came forward, into the apartment, still brandishing the smoking gun. The look in her eyes—viewed from floor level—was terrifying. Mary could hear the clatter of footsteps and a slamming door as Real Mary dashed into her bedroom and slammed and locked the door.

"There," Joon whispered. She was looking down at Mary—at Dylan—contemptuously. "Now *you've* lost a guy you cared about, Mary—how does it feel?"

"Oh, Jesus," Mary screamed. She couldn't help it. "Oh, God, it fucking *hurts*—"

Joon had stepped over her and was heading down the corridor toward Mary's bedroom door—Mary could hear her footsteps creaking on the floorboards.

Think, she told herself through the pain. *Think—figure it out.*

Ellen had said that she'd cast Horus's vengeance curse— the Curse of 7 Souls—on Mary because Mary had "tried to kill Mom." Mary couldn't make heads or tails of that remark. She'd come to understand what all the others had against her—why they'd been enlisted in Ellen's curse—but she still couldn't figure out what Ellen, her sister, had against her.

"I've called the cops!"

Mom's voice, coming through her bedroom door. Mary remembered—she'd experienced this same moment already, not that long ago, from within her own bedroom.

"Whoever you are, the cops are coming! I called nine-one-one!"

The next few minutes were hard for Mary to keep track of. She realized that she might be going into shock—she was paralyzed, staring at the ceiling, but she vividly remembered the pool of blood that was spreading on the floor around her. She tried to keep awake, to keep herself rational, but it wasn't easy—she had a strange, hallucinogenic awareness of Joon heeding Mom's warning and running past her, a black and silver blur, waving Mason's gun, and then she realized that her mother was there, crouching over her, a big blur smelling of tobacco smoke and flowers, and she was crying again, staring up at her mother's face from the floor and realizing just how close she was to death—how she'd spent what seemed like an endless amount of time in proximity to death, thanks to an ancient Egyptian sorcerer she'd never even heard of before today.

"Mommy," she was crying. "Mommy, Mommy . . ." She knew that her mother saw Dylan Summer lying on the floor, not her daughter, but it didn't seem to make any difference.

"No, no, no," Mom murmured, stroking Dylan's scruffy hair away from Mary's—Dylan's—eyes. She was still holding the handset of the cordless phone. "No, please, not again, not again . . ."

"Mommy . . . Mommy . . ."

The hallucinatory feeling continued as Mary lay on the floor in the pool of Dylan's blood and heard her own bedroom door bang open, heard Real Mary come out of her bedroom and scream at the top of her lungs.

"Mommy . . . ," Mary moaned in agony. "Mommy, help me. . . ."

"The ambulance is coming," Mom told her in a soothing voice, the one Mary remembered her mother using when she was a little girl. "I've called nine-one-one; I told them gunshot—they're on their way."

Mary was fading in and out of awareness as her mother and Real Mary talked and Mom explained that she'd heard the gunshot and come out of the room. She tried to ignore the pain and focus on their voices. "Ow, ow, ow . . . ," she moaned. "Mommy, I'm dying; I'm really dying. . . ." She wasn't in control of what she was saying; the strange, dreamlike state continued as Real Mary's BlackBerry rang and

Real Mary took the call from Ellen that sent her downtown to her death. Mary tried to interfere—she grabbed her own ankle and said, "No, don't—don't go," but her voice came out in a whisper and Real Mary easily pulled herself away and said something Mary couldn't hear, and then she was gone, on her way to the Peninsula Hotel for the very last time—and Mary was alone with Mom, lying on the floor in Dylan's dying, gut-shot body.

"Please stay awake," Mom begged as she caressed Mary's—Dylan's—forehead. "Don't pass out—stay awake. I can't take it—I can't take this happening again."

That's the second time she's said that, Mary realized. It was hard to think with the pain flowing through her body and her ears ringing and the warm stain spreading beneath her, but she suddenly registered what her mother had said.

"What do you—what do you mean 'again'? Mom—"

"Don't talk," Mom urged in a weak, faint voice, and Mary realized that Dawn Shayne was on the edge of panic—and not just because of the gunshot and the blood. It was something else. "Don't talk, or you'll accelerate going into shock."

"What—"

"Shhh!"

Mary's mother was beside herself—Mary had never seen her in such a panic. She was crouched on the floor with Dylan Summer's blood soaking into her bathrobe like scarlet paint, stroking Dylan's hair and staring with wide eyes like her worst nightmare was coming true. "What do you mean 'again'?" Mary rasped painfully—the effort of speaking each word made her light-headed. "If—if you tell me what you're talking about I'll be quiet."

Her mother gazed down at her, tears in her eyes, her face white, and nodded. "This happened before," she whispered finally. "Just like this. I—I lost somebody I loved. I lost somebody I *really* loved, the same way. He was shot to death."

"You mean Da—you mean Mr. Shayne?"

Is that how Dad died? And nobody ever told me?

But Mom shook her head.

"I did love Mary's father. I did, truly. But"—Mom moved her head then, turning her face to one side as if ashamed or embarrassed—"but I was in love with somebody else. His name was Lawrence—Lawrence Schwartz. And he . . ." Mom's eyes focused back on Mary. "You don't want to hear this, Dylan. It was so long ago; ten whole years ago. Nobody remembers anymore; nobody cares except me and Ellen."

Lawrence?

Mary was stunned. Never in her wildest dreams could she have imagined such a thing. *Mom was in love with a man named Lawrence?*

But the amazing thing was, she *remembered* Lawrence. The name brought an image into her mind: a middle-aged man in a dark green suit with no tie.

Uncle Larry.

All at once, the complete memory was there, as if it had never faded at all. He was always hanging around Mom when the girls were young, and they were supposed to call him "Uncle Larry."

I must have repressed it, Mary thought dazedly. *Sure, I've repressed it, like all those shrinks on television say. Because it made me angry.*

The ten-year-old anger was coming back now; the pain and dizziness were like vodka, poisoning her blood as it drained onto the floorboards, making her drunk with re-membered fury, the kind of deep, unchecked rage that only a neglected child could feel, even if she didn't understand it.

She remembered being forced to spend dismal hours with Mom and Uncle Larry and being told to keep it a secret from Daddy. Mom spent all her precious time with Uncle Larry. That was why she was always running late when she was *supposed* to be picking Mary up from gymnastics. Of course, she managed to pick Ellen up from school every day at three on the dot—all Ellen wanted to do was go home and read books. But once Ellen had been safely delivered back to the apartment, Mom would disappear off to Larry Land. That was where she was every day at five o'clock when Mary would sit waiting for her on the school steps, shivering in the freezing cold, her mittens tucked deep under the arms of her pea coat and her teeth chattering. Mary would convince herself that every passing cab would surely be her mother, but sometimes Mom wouldn't come for hours. And sometimes she never came at all. Dad would show up—after Mom had called him with some lame excuse—and Mary would ride home in a taxi with her fa-ther, pressing against him, warming her hands beneath her arms and gratefully inhaling his Borkum Riff tobacco smell, telling him how much she *hated* Mommy for leaving her out there in the cold so often.

"Dylan?" Mom sounded even more worried. "This is upsetting you—I can tell. Should I—"

"Tell me," Mary gasped. "Tell me what happened. Tell
me who shot him. Please."

"Mort shot him," Mom told her. "Mary's father shot
him—shot him dead."

What?

Mary realized she was probably hallucinating; the
pain and her mother's touch and the glare of the overhead
lights and the accumulated weirdness of the six souls she'd
occupied were affecting her thinking. *Did Mom just say
that she was having an affair with Uncle Larry and Dad shot
him?*

But she wasn't hallucinating, or dreaming, and she knew
it. She'd gotten over that comforting fantasy back when she
was Scott Sanders. This was real, as real as it got.

"Please," Mary whispered painfully. "Please tell me."

"It was so long ago," Dawn Shayne began. "Ten years
ago, but I'll never forget it. The worst day of my life . . . the
day of our anniversary party. We don't talk about that day.
Mary acts like she doesn't remember it."

But I don't! I don't remember it!

"It was supposed to be a good day—our crystal anniversary. We had a big party, right here in this apartment. Mort
and I had invited everyone. But something was wrong. From
the moment I woke up, I felt . . . odd. Like the whole world
was against me. Everything was off-kilter somehow. All of
my friends—even my closest ones—were acting like they
were out to get me."

This is sounding very familiar, Mary realized as Dylan's body began shivering.

"They all did such . . . such mean things to me," Mom was saying. "All of them, all of my friends. I thought it was just in fun; just pranks you'd play on someone. I could have dealt with it if it hadn't been for my family. When your family turns against you, Dylan, well . . . there's no recovering from that. It kills something in your heart, and you just never recover."

"You mean—you mean your husband?"

"I mean Mary."

And here we go, Mary thought, with that same feeling of sick inevitability that she always imagined accompanied capsizing boats as they sank, airplanes that suddenly plummeted, cars that skidded out of control and slid into incoming traffic. *Here we go into the abyss—into the blank spot, the missing memory, the white field of snow.*

"Larry was at the party," Mom said. "I never looked at him—I was sure of that. But Mort *knew* somehow. I could just tell that he knew, and that day"—she shivered, and Mary felt the shiver through Dylan's shoulder—"that day, he was *different*. He had a look in his eyes, a murderous look, that I'd never seen before. I realized he was going to do something violent, something dangerous. I knew we had to get the girls and get away, to escape. Larry had a little place north of Riverdale," Mom continued, still stroking Dylan's sweat-streaked forehead as the hot pool of blood spread beneath him. "A little farmhouse, about twenty minutes out of town."

A farmhouse. A farmhouse in the snow.

Uncle Larry's house.

Mary was listening so avidly, her only real fear was that Dylan would die of blood loss before she got to hear the end of the story. The "visions" she'd been seeing all day weren't visions at all—they were *memories*. Somehow the curse had dislodged the door in her mind that had been shut for ten years, and the memory of that day had spilled out. *I was seven years old*, she remembered. *And we fled through the snow to the farmhouse.*

"We thought we'd be safe there," Mom went on, her voice drenched in the sorrow and dread of her story. "So we got inside and lit a fire and we *were* safe . . . for about ten minutes. Morton had followed us, and he—he drove right there; he got out of the car and banged on the door like he—like a madman. There's no other way to describe it. I *begged* Larry not to let him in, not to open the door, not in front of the girls, but he just went over and reached for the doorknob"—Mom was crying openly now—"and when he'd flipped the latches Mort just *kicked* the door open and sh- shot Larry, point-blank. The worst sound I've ever heard in my life . . . I hoped I'd never hear it again, and I never did. Until just now; until tonight."

"What did you do?" Mary croaked.

"I screamed for the girls to follow me and I *ran*, out of the house, out the back door, into the snow, into the trees. I turned to look behind me and Mary was there, but I'd lost Ellen somehow, and when I turned to go back for her I fell." Mom had lost control of her tears. She was

318

sobbing like a child, trying to find spaces to breathe. "I fell into a ditch, some kind of hole in the ground, and I couldn't get out."

You fell into the ravine, Mary thought. *You fell into that pit and couldn't get out.*

Just like me.

"And she *could* have pulled me out," Mom said firmly, her lip trembling as she stared straight ahead, nodding. "Mary could have saved me; she was strong enough. But she just stood there on the ledge, watching me try to scratch and claw my way out. I *begged* her . . . I pleaded with her. 'Mary, just reach down and help me,' . . . but she *wouldn't*. She wouldn't even *try*—she just stared at me, watching me struggle, and then she turned around and walked off into the snow. I *screamed* for her to come back, that Mommy wasn't joking, that I was *trapped*, but she was gone.

"I was in the hole all night long. There were snakes and worms and freezing water . . . I almost lost both my feet to frostbite, and I got hypothermia. The doctor said I could have died. As it is, the pneumonia ruined my lungs, and"— Mom shook her head, brushing gray hairs from her forehead, the crying apparently over—"and in the morning, when they found me, they found Larry dead from gunshot wounds, and Mort dead too, asphyxiated somehow, like the violence and the cold air had brought on some kind of toxic shock. 'Domestic dispute,' they said at the inquest, like it was some kind of *debate* or something. 'Temporary insanity.' But I lost everything permanently—and I never recovered. Not really. Why would she want to do that, Dylan? Why would Mary want to leave me alone in the cold? Like she *wanted* me to freeze to death?"

(*She tried to kill my mom!* Ellen had screamed.)

"But I know the answer. She didn't love me, Dylan. Not at all. She hated me. And what just breaks my heart is that Mary hates me for being such a useless wreck . . . but she *did* it. She made me what I am, that day. They all did; everybody I loved. Everybody but Ellen."

I ruined her life, Mary thought. *It's totally true—I'm to blame for all of it.*

"You could say it's my fault for cheating on Mort. But you have to understand, that door"—Mom cocked her gray-haloed head backward, indicating Dad's study—"was closed *all* the time. He'd be in there for days, smoking his pipe, with his patient files and his dusty old books. He stopped caring about me, Dylan, but that doesn't mean I stopped caring about him. Look, I still wear the present he gave me—the only nice thing that happened that day." Mom was fumbling at her throat, pulling a gold chain out from beneath the frilled collar of her nightgown. "On the morning of our anniversary, he gave me this necklace. It's Egyptian—isn't it pretty?"

She held the necklace's pendant out, proudly, and Mary stared as it gleamed in the overhead light: an almond-shaped, ornamental Egyptian eye, carved from burnished gold.

Another Eye of Tnahsit. Another amulet.

Mary felt a wave of numb dread flowing over her as she stared at the necklace, its curves glinting as Mom turned it over and over in her hand.

The spell! Mary was thinking furiously. She could barely focus on Mom's voice. *The Curse of 7 Souls! Dad cast it on Mom!*

She put the pieces together. It was easy to understand what had happened, now. Her father, Morton Shayne, had cast the same spell—the Curse of 7 Souls—on his wife, Mary and Ellen's mother, ten years ago. He'd done the same thing Ellen had done: given her an ornament depicting the Eye of Tnahsit. And she'd had the same experience as Mary, the same horrible day (with everyone out to get her) concluding in death and tragedy.

So who were your seven souls, Mom?

But Mary knew part of the answer.

(*A giant figure, limned by moonlight, loomed over her, leaning down like a toppling granite statue—reaching for her. The huge man-shaped silhouette drew closer, its arm reaching forward, and she realized that its huge extended hand was holding something out toward her—a thin rectangle that glowed in the moonlight. A piece of paper—a note. There was writing on the note, which Mary couldn't read in the dark, but it was like all the forces of the universe converged on that single page.*)

The vision wasn't a vision—it was a memory. And as she recalled it all again, it was like a photograph coming into focus; the shadowed figure was suddenly illuminated as he toppled toward her. The dark man was her father, Morton Shayne, standing over her in the snow that covered the Riverside Park playground where he'd brought her, looming over her tiny seven-year-old figure like a giant. And the piece of paper he was giving her was clear; she could read it now.

WHOM DO YOU HATE THE MOST?
WHAT WOULD YOU DO ABOUT IT IF YOU COULD?
TODAY IS THE DAY.

He picked me, Mary realized. *He knew how much I resented her—all that time waiting for Mom out in the cold. I complained to him, so he picked me as one of his seven. And, under the spell, I got my revenge—I left her in the snow to die.*

It wasn't me. It was the spell.

"That's why I can't *remember*," Mary croaked. Her head was spinning like she'd had six shots of vodka—she could barely make her mouth form the words. "That's—that's what the book said."

"Oh my God, Dylan, you're delirious—"

"No! I *understand* it now," Mary insisted, rallying her strength to raise Dylan's scruffy head off of the floorboards. "You forget it when it's all over. That's why Dylan couldn't remember anything, in the car. That's why I've never been able to remember that day! And Ellen doesn't *know* that."

"Dylan—"

"Ellen thinks it was me. She thinks I left you there—and it wasn't me! It was the fucking curse . . . and I can explain it." With a supreme burst of effort, ignoring the agony in her—Dylan's—abdomen, Mary rose on her elbows, getting ready to stand. "If I tell her, she'll forgive me," she panted, her vision doubling with the renewed pain. "She'll forgive me. And she won't go through with it—she'll stop—she'll stop the curse."

322

"Dylan Summer, you lie back down this instant!" Mom cried.

"I can't." As Mary's vision doubled, cleared and doubled again, she saw the page from Horus's book on the floor next to her—the page Dylan had accidentally torn out.

(*the Minions will forget all that they have done in Service of the Curse*)

"What are you doing?" Mom asked, alarmed, as Mary groped on the floor with Dylan's numb, bloodied hands. "Stay right where you are! You can't go anywhere!"

Yes I can, Mary thought grimly, struggling not to pass out as she pressed on the floor and raised Dylan's body to a sitting position. Her fingers were trembling as she reached for the stray page and shoved it into Dylan's pocket. *Yes I can—I have to.*

(*Jesus, this is wrong. Ellen needs to see this—*)

"I have to go," Mary rasped, coughing as bubbles blood of spurted from her lips. Entire new galaxies of pain were sweeping through her as she moved, but she had no choice. She realized she was rambling, deliriously. "I have to show her. . . have to show Ellen what the spell says. Minions can't remember . . . not my fault . . ."

Her mother was staring at her, white-faced. Mary could only imagine what Dylan's blood-soaked, wild-eyed body looked like, but, judging by Mom's facial expression, it must have been pretty bad. She tried to force herself to speak clearly.

"She didn't—Mary didn't do it—on purpose," Mary managed to tell her mother. "She loves you very much—she always did. She's"—Mary could barely speak from the pain of wrenching herself upright and lurching toward the apartment's front door—"she's sorry for what she did. She's very, very sorry."

MARY WAS DRENCHED WITH sweat, leaning on the edge of a No Parking sign in the dark shadows of Columbus Avenue, spitting up blood. There was a spattered, wet-blood trail behind her, leading out of her apartment building.

Incredibly, miraculously, she had made it to the street. Her vision was fading in and out as she slipped against the cold, rain-slicked metal sign and staggered forward, splashing her sneakers in a wide puddle as she reeled from the pain. She turned away from the howling wind, looking up at the dark shadows of the surrounding buildings.

Taxi, she thought desperately. *I've got to get a taxi.*

Mary clutched her bleeding abdomen and stared down the deserted avenue, her vision doubling. She could see the red embers of the traffic lights change to green and she could hear the rumble of approaching, southbound traffic, but she couldn't make out the details—she extended her arm, hoping that one of the oncoming cars was a cab and would see her.

"Taxi!" Mary wailed. *"Taxi!"*

A rumbling, sliding yellow phantom had appeared beside her, its cold steel surfaces still beaded with rain. Mary grappled with the door handle, watching Dylan's fingers smear blood across the door before she managed to wrench it open and tumble inside. Fresh pain lashed out at her from her abdomen, as if someone had just kicked her there, and she clenched her teeth against the agony and leaned over, mustering the herculean strength necessary to heave the cab door shut.

(*heaved the cab door shut*)

"The Peninsula Hotel," Mary shouted. She could only see a blur; she hoped the cabdriver had heard her. He must have heard *something*, because the cab started moving. She stared at the roof of the car, hoping she wouldn't throw up, hoping that Dylan's body wouldn't die before she got where she was going . . . and recalling the memory—Dylan's memory—that had just sprung to mind.

(*heaved the cab door shut*)

SHE'LL COME HOME WITH *you tonight.*

She'll come home with you if you ask.

The thought hit Dylan suddenly as he heaved the cab door shut. He couldn't put his finger on it, but he knew something about Ellen was different tonight. He could feel it in the way she'd stepped into the cab as he held the door for her. Usually, she ducked past him and shuffled herself along the black vinyl seat until she was pressed up against the opposite window, but tonight she grabbed onto the lapels of his gray overcoat, looked him right in the eyes and backed herself in. She planted herself dead center, leaving only a third of the seat for him as he climbed in after her, and she let her entire leg press against his without the slightest hesitation. She even pushed her fragile shoulder against his, as if a third person had piled into the backseat with them, crushing them against the window like lovers.

Like lovers. Finally like lovers, Dylan thought, *even if only for the few seconds it took her to realize she was sitting too close.*

"We'll be making two stops," Dylan told the driver, as he always did after their Saturday-night Chinese dinners at Empire Szechuan Palace. "We're going to drop her home at Ninety-second and Amsterdam, and then I'm going up to One Twenty-fourth and Morningside Drive."

But he secretly prayed for Ellen to correct him. He imagined her telling the driver to forget that first stop and just take her straight to Dylan's apartment. He imagined her falling into his lap and staring up at him for as long as he could resist leaning down to kiss her.

A first kiss. Right here, right now. It didn't have to be in some gondola in Venice, or trapped at the top of some cutesy malfunctioning Ferris wheel on Mott Street; it could just happen in the back of a cramped New York taxicab, surrounded by half-ripped Urban Underground stickers, and the babbling ABC news anchors on Taxi TV, and the overpowering odor of the coconut air freshener dangling from the rearview mirror. They could race up the empty highway, buried so deep in their first kiss that they'd barely notice the Hudson River rolling by, or the George Washington Bridge lit up like a giant prehistoric bird in the black sky. They'd sprint up the dusty stairs of Dylan's third-floor walk-up and crash against the door to his apartment—kissing so passionately after a year of pent-up anticipation that the loose change would be raining from his pockets as he dug blindly for his keys. They'd burst through the door, and he'd scoop her wispy frame up off the floor as she wrapped her legs tightly around his waist, and glide her down the hall to his bedroom, where they'd fall onto his creaky twin mattress with their arms and lips entangled, never even bothering to turn on the lights. . . .

"Dylan?"

"Huh?"

Ellen's voice snapped Dylan back to the quiet reality of the taxicab.

"Where were you just now?"

"I was right here," he said.

"Hmmm." She smiled dubiously out of the corner of her mouth, and then she leaned her head on his shoulder, clasping her hands tightly around his arm. She had never done this before. Maybe they locked arms when they came out of a movie, but this was different; this was more.

He could smell the faint traces of rose water in her short, tousled hair and a hint of Ivory soap on her face. Her black hooded sweatshirt was buried under her black parka, but the hood had gotten caught on his shoulder, stretching her collar out to expose the long, graceful neck that she always tried to hide. The collar was actually stretched far enough to expose a patch of her vanilla skin, running from the base of her neck to the beginning of a beautifully naked clavicle bone. He wanted so badly to follow the entire line of that clavicle, but it disappeared back under her sweatshirt—back under her thick black armor.

That, he supposed, was why he was so in love with Ellen. Because he could never see all of her, no matter how hard he tried. There was always more to uncover, more to figure out, more to learn, just like all those ancient languages that obsessed him. He hated obvious girls with obvious beauty—

girls like Ellen's sister, Mary. Mary was just another one of those porcelain-doll girls who bounced around the Meat-packing District on Friday nights, screaming for love and attention with every skintight outfit, every overbearing splash of designer perfume, every studied feminine pose. Everyone seemed to think that Mary was the Pretty One, but they had no idea what they were talking about. Dylan had the Pretty One right here in the cab with him, resting comfortably on his shoulder, holding his arm just as tightly as she held that beat-up Paddington Bear in all her child-hood pictures. He wanted them to stay this close for the rest of the night, and on through the next day, but he couldn't bring himself to ask. How many more times could he ask? Her answer was always the same and her reason was always the same.

Instead, he asked one of those half-assed leading ques-tions. "Are you tired . . . ?"

"No," she said. "Not at all."

Ellen looked genuinely surprised by her own answer. She began to smile, as if she'd just discovered something truly re-markable. She leaned her head back against the seat, breathed in deeply and let out the longest, most luxuriant sigh. "I am not tired at all," she marveled. "I can't remember the last time I wasn't tired. I feel . . . awake. I think I feel good."

"Something's different with you tonight," Dylan said. "What's going on?"

Ellen turned to him, still reveling in her unexpectedly euphoric moment. "It's Mary," she said simply. "She's taking care of Mom tonight."

"No." Dylan shook his head refusing to believe it. "No, there's absolutely no way."

"I know." Ellen's eyes widened with amazement. "I couldn't believe it either. I ask her every time we go to dinner, Dylan. I ask her to watch Mom for a few hours after eight—just give her the meds and watch a little *Forensic Files* or something. They wouldn't even have to talk. I don't know why I keep asking—she always says no. But tonight, I asked her again . . . and she said yes." Ellen grinned wider than before—wider than Dylan had probably ever seen her smile. "She said yes, Dylan. That means we've got, like, three extra hours to hang out. Maybe even four . . ."

She leaned abruptly onto Dylan's lap and gripped his thighs with her long fingers. His pulse doubled as her face grew closer to his—so close that she became a blur. But he realized she was only leaning over to open the window as far as it would go.

The icy wind rushed into the cab with a deafening rumble, slamming against their faces and blowing back their hair. Keeping her hands anchored on his lap, Ellen stuck her head out the window and breathed in the night air like a German shepherd in the front seat of a pickup.

"God!" she shouted into the wind. "This must be what it feels like when you get out of prison! I'm out! I'm *out!*"

She ducked back into the cab, her jet-black hair blown in all directions and her cheeks flushed a bright and lively pink. Dylan had never seen her look so beautiful. Usually, she looked so much older than her age. He had always assumed that was because of her intelligence, but now he could see . . . it was just the burden. It was the burden of being a mother to her own mother night in and night out. Mary had agreed to babysit their mother for this one Saturday night, and so, for this one Saturday night, Ellen could be what she actually was: a young and adorable sixteen-year-old girl. The strange thing was, with her gorgeous face so flushed and alive and free, she actually looked more like Mary than herself. Dylan hated himself for even thinking it.

Ellen stretched herself to the opposite window and slid it wide open too. Now it was cold enough to see her short, excited breaths puffing from her mouth. Her eyes lit up with inspiration as she grabbed hold of his arm.

"Let's go somewhere," she said.

"Anywhere you want. We could go for coffee or—"

"Morocco. Let's go to Morocco. No, Egypt. Let's go to Egypt. My dad was totally obsessed with Egypt, and I've never been there. You could teach me the language, Dylan—you could teach me everything you know. You should have seen your eyes light up at dinner when you talked about all the uncovered Sanskrit in the Middle East. We could go to Egypt and study Sanskrit! Let's go, Dyl. Let's go tonight."

"I'm not sure we could pull that off in three hours—"

"Well, let's pretend we can." She squeezed the life out of his arm, and when he looked into her eyes, he realized that she meant it. She honestly wanted to pretend they were crossing an ocean tonight. A pretend escape was better than no escape at all. "Please. Can't we just drive to the airport?"

"I'll tell you what," he said. "We probably can't get a flight out tonight, but we could head out to JFK really early in the morning . . . and you could stay over tonight."

Her misty breaths seemed to cease altogether. It was as if the ice-cold wind in the cab had actually frozen her solid. Dylan was holding his breath too, waiting on her next word. But she didn't seem to have one. He instantly regretted asking. He was such a hopelessly impulsive idiot. "I mean, if you wanted to," he added, making it worse. "You could take the whole night off. You could tell your Mom you were sleeping over at a friend's house, and . . ." He wondered how much deeper he could dig this hole.

"Actually, you're kind of my only friend," Ellen said. "I mean, not really, but . . . you know what I mean. I think Mom would figure out where I was staying pretty quick."

"Right," he murmured, feeling his chest deflate under his thick coat. "Good point."

"But . . . I think she'd probably be half-asleep when I told her. . . ."

Dylan studied Ellen's barely blinking eyes, trying to see if she was saying what he thought she was saying. She looked painfully nervous all of a sudden—frightened, even. But she wasn't backing away. She let her face linger next to his, and he could feel her warm breath on his neck, cutting straight through the cold. He let himself lean the slightest bit closer, watching her breaths quicken and become shallow. But she still didn't back away. Finally, in that last fraction of space left between their lips, he felt something give. Something changed in the air between them. If she had wanted to push him back, she would have done it by now. So he leaned forward the rest of the way. She let his lips touch hers so lightly that it was hardly a kiss.

And then her cell phone rang. It screamed out from the

pocket of her black parka. The piercing ring cut through the moment with such laser precision that it carved out a foot of space between them.

"It might be Mom," Ellen mumbled, totally disoriented by the almost-kiss. "No, it's Mary," she said, glimpsing the caller ID. She flipped open her phone and plugged her other ear with her index finger. "Hey, is everything okay? Did you give Mom her—"

She was immediately interrupted by her sister. Dylan could just make out the unbearably singsong sound of Mary's voice on the other end of the line.

"No, wait," Ellen said. "No, you can't just . . . Mary, you can't just leave." Ellen was trying to get a word in, but Mary wasn't giving her a chance. "No, that doesn't matter, Mare, you still have to stay there, or she could . . . I know that, but . . . Oh, come on, doesn't Jamie own the club? He'll have, like, ten more openings before the real opening. . . . Well, he can get them to play another show there—they're like his best friends, they'll do whatever he— Yes, I'm done with dinner, but I was going to sleep over at a fr— No, I know . . . I know . . . ."

Dylan watched Ellen transform with every additional word out of Mary's mouth. He watched her shoulders slump and her neck sink further into her black sweatshirt. He watched a deep, fleeting sadness pass over her eyes, replaced with a heartbreaking sort of dead-eyed numbness. "No, you're right," she said in a near monotone. "You should go. You should definitely go. I'll come back home. Yeah, I'm coming back now. No, it's fine. Really, I promise. It's fine. Right . . . a goddess, I know."

Ellen clapped her phone shut and slid away from Dylan, pressing herself against the opposite door. She rolled the window up and leaned her head against it like a rag doll. She came back to life for just a split second, and pounded her fist so hard against the cab's partition that she actually frightened Dylan.

"Hey!" the driver hollered. "What the hell are you doing to my cab? What the hell's the matter with you?"

"I'm sorry," she called back in a weak voice. "I'm sorry about that, it was an accident." Her face returned to its expressionless state, and she let her head fall back against the window again. "I'm sorry," she said more quietly to Dylan.

"It's all right," Dylan assured her. "It's okay." The streetlights were flashing across her face, but he was sure he caught a glimpse of a tear rolling down her cheek and landing on her waterproof parka.

"Mary's got to go to a club opening tonight." There was no emotion left in Ellen's voice. "She's going to do Mom tomorrow." Dylan wondered how many times he'd heard that before. "I can't come over," Ellen continued. "Not tonight. Mom's going to need her meds and someone's got to keep her company when she . . . It was a bad idea anyway. I don't know what I was thinking. I can't . . . I mean . . ."

"It's okay," Dylan said. "Don't worry about it. Another time."

But he knew there wouldn't be another time. That one half of a kiss was as close as they'd ever come. She wouldn't be coming home with him tonight or any other night. Because Mary made sure of that.

The Pretty One. What a joke. He couldn't imagine anything uglier than Mary Shayne. He pictured her throwing on another one of her obvious party dresses, puckering in the mirror and racing out the door without a care in the world. A cheap imitation of a supermodel in a bad perfume ad. She wouldn't have a second thought about leaving Ellen alone to rock their mother to sleep again; she'd be too busy clinking glasses of free Cristal in the VIP lounge with some spoiled asshole named Jamie whose daddy had bought him a nightclub. She'd sure as hell never think about how she was slowly but surely ruining Dylan's life. He wasn't even sure she knew his name.

Now he wanted to punch something too. Not something—someone. He wanted to punch Mary really, really hard. Maybe that was something she'd actually notice.

IT DOESN'T MATTER WHAT *they did to me,* Mary thought dazedly. Dylan's memory—the strength of his feelings for Ellen and the callous way Mary had kept ruining their romantic ambitions—was no less sickening than any of the other memories, the other grievances she'd experienced since she died. *It doesn't matter how they ganged up on me, because I deserved it.*

I deserved all of their rage; I brought it all on myself.

Did it mean that she deserved to die? Should she stop what she was doing and just expire, right here, in the back of this taxicab, in Dylan Summer's body?

I can't. Mary was pretty sure that there was no way. *It's not over yet.*

"Peninsula Hotel," the driver called out. His voice was

so distant, it was like he was in a different city. "Nine fifty-eight."

"Just a second . . ." Mary was struggling to pull Dylan's wallet from his pants pocket. It was an exercise in pain and blood. She managed to pay the driver and drag herself out of the cab, but she could barely stand. It was like she was falling, even when she was standing still—she was teetering on the edge and she knew it.

(*on the edge*)

She felt like she could almost count the breaths she had left, before she fell.

(*on the edge*)

"THERE'S ONE MORE THING," Ellen said, pointing at Dylan. "Stick around—I've got to talk to you. Everyone else, it's showtime—let's get moving."

Dylan stood on the rooftop of the Chadwick School, hands in pockets, the wind ruffling his hair around his face as he watched the Chadwickites—Patrick and Joon and Amy—move single file through the battered metal door that led back downstairs, into the school. They were following orders, he noted with some satisfaction . . . just like he was. Ellen had told them to go, and had told him to stay, and there was something about *obeying* her that was profoundly satisfying. It was odd, but it was true.

Dylan had felt strange since awakening that morning—but it wasn't anything he could complain about. It wasn't like waking up with a hangover; if anything, it was the *opposite* of a hangover. He felt alert, and refreshed, and exuberant, and *alive*. More than anything else, he felt like he had a purpose, something crucial to do that day.

That great feeling—the one that was filling him with adrenaline and excitement right now, as the door clanged shut and he was alone on the roof with Ellen—had come to a head, had reached a kind of glorious harmonic crescendo less than an hour ago, when Ellen had handed him that wonderful square of paper with the beautiful moving, shifting symbol and the three lines of writing that were, possibly, the most impressive, the most *correct* and succinct thing he'd ever read. WHOM DO YOU HATE THE MOST? The question echoed in his head like a beautiful melody you couldn't get rid of and didn't want to. Of course he knew the answer to *that* question—everybody did. The five of them had stood together on this rooftop beneath the overcast sky and discussed their plan—*Ellen's* plan—for ruining, destroying, humiliating, *punishing* Mary Shayne, and it was like he'd found a new purpose in life; there was just no feeling on earth that could compare to the satisfaction of the day they were about to spend.

"Dyl," Ellen said, coming closer to him, her hands sunk into the pockets of her orange hoodie, in a pose he liked very much, "I've got history class in just a few minutes, but I need to talk to you first."

"Okay," Dylan said, and when the wind blew the scent of her Neutrogena shampoo over him, he felt a tingling up and down his legs that made him want to sing, that made him want to rush forward and grab Ellen and kiss her like he should have done that evening in the taxicab, before her hateful harpy of a sister had ruined it. "What do you want to talk about?"

"I have to tell you something," Ellen said, walking closer across the tar paper. "I mean, I *want* to tell you something. I'm going to tell you a secret."

"Okay," Dylan said. He had no idea what she was going to say. He had some delightful theories, each more enticing than the last, but he really didn't know what came next. If she was going to tell him what to do—give him more of the incredibly clever, incredibly *correct* directions she'd been dispensing—he wouldn't hesitate to do whatever she said.

"You know how sometimes you've got a secret and you just *have* to tell it to somebody else . . . once you've found the right person to tell it to?"

"Sure," Dylan said. He knew exactly what she meant.

"Well, this is one of those times," Ellen said, taking Dylan's hands. The overcast light was glinting off distant windows and Dylan thought he'd never felt so content, so happy. TODAY IS THE DAY, Ellen's note had told him— and he agreed completely. "So I'm going to tell my secret to you."

Dylan was all ears.

"Can you feel it?" Ellen said, moving closer to him. Now she was so close that he could taste her breath, and his head was swimming with the sensation of being so close. "Can you feel . . . today? Can you feel how special today is?"

"Yeah," Dylan said, his breath catching in his throat. "Yeah, I can."

"Tomorrow will be different," Ellen said. Her eyes were

shining, glinting like gems. "I wasn't even sure that . . . that it would work, but it *did*, it *has* worked . . . it *is* working. . . ."

"What?" Dylan asked. "What's working?"

Ellen shook her head impatiently. "It's all about today, Dylan. Today is . . . is everything. It's our one chance."

"Ell, you're not making sense."

"No, I *am* making sense! For the first time, we're *all* making sense. We're finally saying what we really think of her, and we're finally *doing* something. And doesn't it make a difference? Doesn't everything just feel so much better? So much realer?"

"Yeah." He could never, in a million years of studying every language known to humanity, have come up with a more fitting, a more appropriate sentiment. Ellen had hit the nail on the head. "Yeah, you're right. It all feels *realer*."

"So I can do this," Ellen said, tilting her head upward and forward and kissing him, her lips brushing his gently, briefly, before she pulled away, and it was the most exquisite feeling he'd ever felt. It was like being drunk, but, again, it was the *opposite* of drunkenness; it was clarity, purity, truth. "And we can do what we're meant to do today. We can . . . we can take it all the way."

"What do you mean?" Dylan's lips were tingling and he wanted her to kiss him again—the entire lower half of his body felt like it was on fire, about to explode—but more than another kiss, he wanted Ellen to finish speaking. "What are you saying, Ellen?"

"We have to leave it loaded," Ellen murmured, moving her lips to brush his ear. "We have to leave the bullets in the gun."

338

"But—" It was like a shadow had passed over the sun; for the briefest of moments Dylan's euphoria faded, and the cold wind penetrated his clothes like a frozen river. "But wait. You're saying—"

"I'm saying that the prank isn't enough. I'm saying it's enough for *them*, because they don't really know her; they don't know what she's capable of. They don't know what she did to me and my family. But *she* knows, Dylan. Some part of her knows what she did, even if she wants to pretend she can't remember. That's what this whole day is *for*. That's the point. I'm going to make her remember that day—I'm going to dredge up all her memories till she can't deny them anymore, because I *know* some part of her knows what she did, I know it. And she hates herself for it. I'm telling you, if I write her one of the notes and I give her the gun, she will pull the trigger. She'll do it. And then it'll be done. It won't matter how we feel tomorrow. It won't even matter if we remember any of it, because she'll be gone. She'll finally be gone. Don't you want that as much as I do?"

Dylan wasn't sure how to answer that. Of course she was right . . . and he *did* want it as much as she did . . . didn't he?

"So you understand," Ellen said, squeezing his hand, reaching behind his head to tousle his hair. "You understand, when you pick her up at the farmhouse and bring her back, it won't be a prank anymore. You'll be driving her toward a loaded gun. And I need to know you can live with that. Can you do it? Can you do it with me?"

He stared into Ellen's eyes and the bright sky found the specks of silver there, and it was like the sunlight had returned to his heart and he realized he felt nothing but relief.

Mary would be gone and Ellen and Dylan could finally have the life they wanted.

"Yeah," he told her, and meant it. "Yeah. I can do it."

Then their faces drifted together, like opposite poles of a magnet, and they almost kissed again, a second glorious kiss, of many to come—but then they both jumped as the metal door crashed open, and they pulled away from each other in alarm.

"Oh, thank God!" Mary yelled, vaulting onto the roof and bearing down on Ellen. "I can't believe you're up here—" She ran forward and wrapped her arms tightly around her sister, and Dylan stared at her and thought about the loaded gun and realized he was counting the minutes until he could bring her to her dark destiny.

THE TAXICAB WAS PULLING away as Mary staggered to the curb and stared up at the ornate Romanesque facade of the Peninsula Hotel, all lit up with blazing yellow flood-lights like an opera stage.

Her hands and feet—Dylan's hands and feet—were twitching. Mary was graying out, as she walked—the street-lights were like globes of golden mist, amber halos that shimmered in her blurring vision, doubling and fading as she forced herself forward, step by painful step.

Dylan knew, Mary thought. *He was the only one who knew where it was going—who knew I was supposed to die.*

And Mary realized something else, as she stared up at the blurring stonework, Dylan's sneakers splashing water from the sidewalk's wide puddles. *That's what broke the spell,* she realized. *He shook it off, because he couldn't do it.*

He was driving me to the hotel—to my death—and the spell wore off.

Mary wondered if it had made any difference—if Dylan's sudden attack of conscience had gotten him anything but a bullet in the gut. Maybe it had all been for nothing; Dylan's sacrifices and her own had failed to change anything.

No.

Mary stared up at the lights that festooned the hotel, her eyes swimming and blurring with pain and fatigue as the lights seemed to grow into big, gaseous globes, miniature suns casting their rays down on her face.

No, I can't give up. I won't.

Mary's thoughts melted together as the lights got brighter, overexposed lamps burning the film; candles luring moths to their brilliant deaths; the light of the world, growing in its brilliance until nothing was left but light.

7

ELLEN

THE BRIGHT LIGHT WAS the only light—the shining glow of the recessed track lighting in the bedroom of Patrick Dawes's hotel suite (the hotel suite that would be his for just a few more hours, until Saturday's checkout time), where Mary Shayne—Real Mary—was approaching the bed with the wooden box that held the gun.

Mary was standing in the middle of the room, amid the piles of party trash, below the white haze of smoke that still hung in the air. She was Ellen. She knew she was Ellen because she recognized her own scent; she knew it because she could feel Ellen's clothes on her and the cool wind on the back of her neck, exposed by Ellen's practical, shapeless bob. And she knew, because Ellen was the seventh soul.

They were all around her, standing in the shadows: Amy and Joon and Scott and Patrick, flanking her like sentinels. Patrick had just activated the stereo system and Nickelback was blasting; Real Mary, twenty feet ahead of her, in the suite's bedroom, couldn't hear anything from this room.

Mary remembered that distinctly.

This is it, she thought. *This is the end of the line.*

I made it.

Without doing anything to alert the others around her in the darkness, Mary began flexing her feet, getting ready to sprint. When the moment came—and it wasn't far off now, a matter of seconds—she'd have to move very fast.

Staring through the doorway at Real Mary, at her own back, she remembered something. It wasn't her own memory— it was Ellen's—but it came into her head unprompted as she stared through the doorway at herself, clenching and un-clenching the muscles in her—in Ellen's—legs.

IN HER MEMORY, ELLEN was in nearly the same posi-tion as right now, looking at Mary's back—but Mary's back was nude.

They were alone, the two of them, on the second floor of the SoHo Crate and Barrel. In her pocket, Ellen had the keys to the store, which she'd gotten from Scott Sanders, whose father's company owned the building. When she was finished here, she would head to Scott's apartment to give him his note and his special instructions.

The only light came from outside. Mary was completely

unconscious. The Nembutal Ellen had injected into the wine bottle they had brought for Mary's birthday dinner at Eduardo's had done the trick. She'd known that Mom wouldn't touch the stuff, just as she'd known that Mary would have three glasses, no more, no less.

By the time Mom had left, Mary had begun to faint; her head was lolling on her neck and several of the restaurant's patrons had turned to watch. But it was no problem. Ellen assured the maître d' that she'd take care of Mary, and then she'd gotten her outside and into the taxicab she'd had waiting and had brought her sleeping sister down to SoHo, to Crate and Barrel.

A few minutes later, as she pulled Mary's clothes off (accidentally leaving deep scratches in her back that started bleeding almost immediately), Ellen realized she was crying—but she was able to stop herself as she gently lowered Mary's naked, unconscious form onto the bed by the window, glancing though the glass at the wide black sky above Houston Street.

(*The Sorcerer utters the Incantation before an Unclothed Victim, Slumbering beneath an Open Southern sky*)

"Here goes," Ellen said, her hands trembling as she pulled out Horus's book—the one her father had pored over endlessly, leaving reams of notes that she'd studied over the years—and opened it to the marked page.

The wide, dark showroom floor was deserted and quiet as Ellen read the incantation, spreading her arms wide, as the sorcerers did when addressing the pharaohs.

This is for you, Mom, Ellen thought, beginning to cry again. *And for you, Dad—I miss you so much.*

"I Stand in the Center of the Infinite Circle," Ellen recited. She realized she didn't need the book; she had the incantation memorized. "I Stand in the Sign of Blood and Flame. Around Me Billow the Forces of the Air. Around Me Flow the Forces of Water. Around Me Flare the Forces of Fire. Around Me Rage the Forces of the Earth."

Beneath the comforter, Mary was silent and motionless on the wide bed. There was no sign of anything having happened. Outside, a car horn honked; inside, a distant series of clicks and hums indicated that the air circulation system was working.

Are you sure you want to do this?

Yes, Ellen thought. After ten years, she'd never been so sure.

"I Cast Wide My Arms," Ellen said firmly, tears running down her face. "The Powers of Death, the Powers of Life, Are Mine."

IN FRONT OF HER, REAL Mary knelt by the side of Patrick's bed and opened the polished wooden box. She hadn't taken the gun out yet, but she was about to.

Now, Mary thought.

With as little windup as possible, she started running toward herself. She figured it would take something like five seconds to tackle herself and get the gun away—the gun that only she knew was loaded.

She ran two or three paces, the paper plates and plastic cups underneath her trampling feet slowing her down.

Patrick caught her. He wrapped his powerful arms

345

around her, holding her in place. She bucked and twisted, but it was no use.

"Nobody chickens out," Patrick snapped, directly in her ear. "Nobody turns back."

No, Mary yelled—or, she realized, *tried* to yell. With the deafening music pounding, it took her a moment to realize that she hadn't made any sound.

"We're all in this all the way," Patrick said fiercely. "That was the deal."

The gun's loaded, Mary screamed. *Don't you understand? She's actually going to die—*

No sound. There was nothing coming out of her mouth.

In the bedroom, visible through the doorway, Real Mary was pulling the gleaming handgun out of the wooden box. It shone in the overhead lights, a gleaming talisman of death. Real Mary couldn't hear anything—Nickelback was playing too loud.

Mary began bucking in Patrick's grip, trying to catch her breath. She couldn't. She couldn't seem to fill her lungs with air.

Can't breathe, she thought desperately. *I can't breathe—*

Somehow, Patrick sensed that something was wrong; he let go of her, holding her shoulders and staring at her face. "Ellen?" Trick asked, peering at her in concern. "Are you all right?"

I can't breathe! she tried to shout back. But nothing came. Her vision was changing, turning red, getting dimmer. Her ears were singing. She was losing her balance, stumbling backward against Trick's wide shoulders, clawing at the air.

Joon screamed.

The hotel suite's front door had banged open, and Joon had been looking right at it.

Dylan Summer had arrived.

His shirt was crimson with blood; the entire top half of his jeans, down to the knees, was stained dark purple, as if someone had dumped a case of wine on him. He was deathly pale; his face was covered in sweat and his scruffy hair corkscrewed in soaked strands around his skull like seaweed. He was staggering, grimacing with unbelievable pain.

Mary couldn't see behind her, so she didn't know how Patrick reacted to the latest arrival to his suite, but suddenly his hands were gone and nothing was holding her up, and as her ears sang louder and began to sting and pop, and a crimson fog overtook her vision, she weaved and dropped to the floor.

"Ellen?" Dylan shouted, stumbling forward. She could barely hear him—she could barely hear anything. Dylan dropped to the floor and crawled toward her, elbows leaving bloody imprints in the Peninsula's expensive carpeting. "Ellen? What's wrong? What happened?"

Mary had tunnel vision; her brain was losing oxygen. She heaved for breath and failed again—she realized she was about to pass out.

It's me, she mouthed. *It's Mary.*

He understood. Somehow, he understood as he stared down at her. She reached up and pulled the torn page of Horus's book from Dylan's breast pocket. She waved the page in his face, and he took it, confused—obviously, he had no idea how it got there.

Wrong, Mary mouthed. *You said it was wrong.* Dylan was staring at the gray image of hieroglyphics on the page she'd handed him. His eyes widened as he scanned the page.

"The translation's wrong!" Dylan yelled over the music. "The last line of the spell—*he got it wrong!*"

I can't breathe, Mary tried to say. She was beginning to faint. *Help—I can't breathe—*

(breathe)

"He says if the victim lives, the spell 'expires.' " Dylan held up the page and pointed at the picture of Horus's original scroll. "But it's a *different glyph*. It's not the spell that expires—it's the Spell-Caster. If the victim lives, the Spell-Caster expires!"

What—? What does that mean?

But she knew. She knew because Ellen knew—Ellen remembered.

(breathe)

RUN TO AN OPEN *window and breathe.*

That was what Mommy had told Ellen to do when there was smoke and there was fire and she couldn't find a door. Run to an open window and get your breath and then scream for help. Ellen hadn't actually seen the fire, but she had heard the giant explosion at the door, like God had punched a crack in the world, and she had heard Mommy screaming for her to run, so she was running as hard as she could. If she could find an open window, then she could scream for help, and Mommy and Mary would come back for her.

She hated the old wooden house. The little rooms were dark, because Mommy hadn't turned the lights on and so Ellen couldn't see anything. She couldn't see where she was going, but she couldn't stop running, because there were still explosions coming from behind her and the horrible sounds of angry men yelling at each other. She was trying to find her way, but even the walls were a dark black musty wood. In her apartment, there was light everywhere—the duck lamp in her room, and the pretty lamps all over the house that Daddy collected, and the streetlamps on the sidewalk— but she didn't know this place. She didn't even know why she was here.

She finally saw it out of the corner of her eye. A silvery circle of moonlight reflecting off a dusty mirror by the small kitchen.

The sliver of light was coming from a room up the rick- ety wooden stairs. Ellen didn't want to go upstairs.

But there was another ear-splitting boom, and then an- other. Ellen cupped her hands over her ears and screamed a high-pitched squeal, the kind she hadn't made since she was a baby. She knew she would die if she stayed down here. She knew she would burn up.

There was no other choice. If she could get to a window upstairs, then she would be saved. She followed the tiny shaft of moonlight and climbed the tall, narrow stairs with her hands and feet, like she was climbing a ladder on the jungle gym. She scraped her index finger on the scuffed wooden stairs and ripped off a splinter that stung like a shot at the doctor's office, but that didn't matter.

Once she was at the top of the stairs, she realized that the light was coming from a small, cluttered room. The window there was a circle instead of a square.

She walked to the room's warped door, which opened out into the hallway, and grabbed the brass doorknob with both hands—tugging on it with all her strength until the door finally clicked shut. She flipped the lock and then hurried to the circle window. It was too high for her to see out of. She almost started to cry, but she knew there wasn't time. Mommy and Mary would be gone, and then she would be left alone.

I could make stacks from the books.

The window wasn't that far up—just a little too far over her head. If she could stack the books that were on a shelf in the room, then she could climb to it.

Heaving for breath, she pushed the dusty books together and made a stack shaped just like her Paddington Bear stepladder at home, even though her finger with the splinter hurt so bad. She climbed gingerly, step by careful step by careful step . . . and then she could see them! Through the bottom left portion of the window, with her fingers clinging tightly to the frame and her neck stretched high, she could see Mommy and Mary running through the trees, leaving deep tracks in the white snow as they ran.

"Mommy!" Ellen screamed. "Mary!" She rapped her fist against the window as hard as she could, but they were too far away to hear her. She checked the window for a handle, but there was nothing to pull on. There was nowhere to open it.

"Mary!" she squealed again, pounding both her hands on

the window again and again. But she could only watch help-lessly as Mommy took Mary's hand and pulled her through the snow, farther into the trees—farther away from Ellen and the old wooden house.

And then Mommy stumbled. Ellen's eyes widened with terror as she watched Mommy tumble forward into the snow.

Ellen was right about those horrible explosions. God really was punching cracks in the world, and Mommy had fallen into one. She was flailing her hands at the edges of the crack, trying to claw her way back out. But Mary hadn't fallen in: she was standing right at the edge, near Mommy. She could help pull her out. . . .

Only Mary wasn't moving. She was just standing there, stock-still, like a frozen little doll in the snow. Ellen tried to pull herself higher to see better—to understand what was wrong with Mary. She smacked her palm against the win-dow till the skin was pink and burning.

Pull her out, Mary! Give her your hand! You can pull Mommy out of the crack!

Mommy was reaching up for Mary's hand—reaching and reaching—and Ellen kept slapping her raw palm on the win-dow because it was all she could do. But Mary didn't reach down for Mommy. She took a step back. She stepped back from the edge, and she watched Mommy struggle and scream. She watched for a few more seconds and then she turned around and began to walk away.

"Mary, what are you doing?" Ellen howled. "Where are you going?"

"Ellen?" A man's shaky voice came from the hall just outside the door. "Ellen, is that you?" The brass knob on the warped door rattled violently. He was trying to come in. "Ellen, it's Uncle Larry—you've got to come with me now. Right now, okay? Unlock the door."

"Mommy's dying!" Ellen cried out, looking back through the window. "She's dying in the snow and Mary's going away. Why is she going away?"

"Ellen, please, sweetheart, just open the door. We don't have any time."

Ellen heard a pair of heavy footsteps bound up the rickety stairs, and then there was another man's voice in the hall. A very angry man.

"Don't talk to my daughter," the deep, angry voice said. Even though it sounded so horribly mean, Ellen thought she recognized it.

Daddy?

"Mort, something's wrong with you, okay?" Larry said, breathing heavily. "Something's wrong. I know you, all right? We made a mistake, but . . . you're not a violent man. This isn't you. Just put down the gun, all right? Let me get your daughter out of here, and then we can talk. We'll talk—just you and me." The doorknob rattled again—so loud and so hard that it looked like it would burst off. "Ellen, sweetheart, open the door now. Open it."

"She's not your sweetheart!" Daddy growled. "Don't talk to my family!"

"Daddy?" Ellen called out. "Daddy, Mommy's dying in the snow and you need to save her."

"Mort," Larry pleaded. "Please don't. Please. Just let me get Ellen out."

On that last word, Larry broke the knob clean off the

door. He pulled the door open partway, when Ellen heard two more deafening cracks. She covered her ears and backed up against the window.

Larry was standing strangely still in the partially open doorway. There were two little, smoking black spots on his chest, and red blood trickling down his arm. Something was wrong with his eyes. They looked dazed and his arms and his legs went limp. He lurched forward, collapsing at the door.

Suddenly, there was the oddest silence. Ellen was so scared that she couldn't get her body to stop shivering. She felt like she was going to pee.

Larry's body was lying in a heap, in front of the partially open door. Ellen could see only a sliver of the dark hall out-side, and she couldn't see her daddy at all.

"Daddy . . . ? Daddy, are you out there . . . ?"

There was no answer, and she began to shiver worse than before.

"Daddy . . . ?"

She craned her neck to try and see around the door, but loud sounds scared her back against the wall. First the sound of metal clattering to the floor, and then something much heavier. Something big. It hit the ground so hard that she felt the vibration in the wood under her feet.

"Ellen . . ." She heard her name in a choked whisper. "El," the voice said again. "Come to the door."

It sounded like her daddy. Stepping off the stack of books, Ellen crept to the door and peered through the crack, over Larry's motionless body.

She saw her daddy sitting on his knees. His square, stub-bly face was drenched with sweat and as white as the sky. His jet-black hair was stuck to his forehead like a wet mop. He was still wearing his suit from the party, but it was rumpled and dirty, and he was tugging desperately at his shirt collar with both hands.

"El," he croaked. "Something's wrong. Something's wrong with me. . . ."

He was making horrible hiccuping noises in his throat like he was choking—like something wouldn't let him breathe. A flush of blue and purple was showing under his pale white skin, as his eyes grew wider.

"Daddy, what's happening? I don't understand what's happening." Ellen was so scared she couldn't move.

"El, don't hate me," he said. "Don't hate . . ."

And then he stopped. Everything in Daddy just stopped. His head fell to his chest, and then the rest of him fell forward. The side of his face slammed flat against the floor. His bulging eyes were wide open, but he wasn't moving.

"Daddy?"

He wouldn't answer her.

"Daddy, what's wrong? Daddy?"

She darted back to the window and climbed her stack of books, peering out into the distant trees, where her mother was still trying to dig her way out.

All Ellen could do was stand there and watch Mommy suffer. She could only watch and slap at the window with her numb, burning hands.

Where are you, Mary? Where are you? Why did you walk away into the snow? You can still come back and save Mommy. You can save all of us.

* * *

354

IF THE SPELL FAILS, *the Spell-Caster expires.*

It's me or Ellen, Mary thought. *So what do I do?*

But she knew. She'd known for a while; she'd observed over and over that she couldn't change what had happened— thinking about it had been too confusing, and her faith that she could save herself was too strong to let her face it. But she'd always known.

With her final, desperately weak store of willpower, fighting the agony of not being able to breathe, she began crawling toward the suite's bedroom, mustering a hidden reserve of adrenaline that got her to her feet and let her stagger forward through her darkening tunnel vision. She was barely staying upright as she stumbled toward Mary Shayne. Mary had dropped the gun, and in her final moment of consciousness before Ellen's body collapsed from suffocation, Mary swung her arm down and swept the gun from the carpet, pulling the slide back as she collapsed forward onto her own back, pushed her own body down onto the bed, pressed the gun to the back of her skull and pulled the trigger.

III

THE AKH

HE HAD DREAMED OF pain, and golden eyes; rooftops chilled by wind. He almost woke more than once, first in the ambulance, rocking in the traffic, cold metal against his wounded chest, shrill sirens piercing his ears as they roared forward through the night. Then he faded and woke again with a flashlight in his eyes; he had to say his name and he did that, barely, his throat scratching and burning; he smelled pungent antiseptic and breathed cold, dry air. Then he slept without dreams, outside of time, as if the ancient world and the present day were one and the same, merged together as they always had been in his deepest imagination. Awakening for a fleeting moment in cold darkness, hearing the dull, repeated beeping tones of the machines and the ghostly, distant footsteps of a night nurse, he had been afraid, and he must have called out, because somebody came and checked on him, a black silhouette against the emerald green light of the machines, and then he had fallen back asleep again.

Now sunlight flooded through his eyelashes; a warm red glow that made him feel safe. The sheets itched his legs, and he felt a painful tug and a cold numbness across his chest. He tried to open his eyes as slowly as he could, but the brilliant sunlight pierced his eyes and made them stream with tears.

Someone held his right hand and squeezed it. He turned his head, weakly, and the dark blur sharpened until he saw a girl's lovely face, framed by short dark hair and obscured by eyeglasses.

"Hey," Ellen said. She squeezed his hand again, and smiled. She was wearing her burnt-orange Gap hoodie—the same as the last time he'd seen her.

"Hey," he whispered. "Hey."

"How do you feel?" A tear ran down Ellen's nose and she sniffed and awkwardly brushed it away and then brought her hand back to his. "Do you—do you feel all right?"

"Hurts," Dylan whispered. "Not so bad."

His eyes were clearing—he could see the Styrofoam-paneled ceiling and the ancient television that hung above his bed from a black steel post and the wide window that filled the room with sunlight. Between the comblike slats of the blinds, the sky was a rich, bright blue.

"You can breathe," Dylan told Ellen. His voice was coming back.

He heard the unmistakable sound of a man clearing his throat and realized that he and Ellen weren't alone. Someone else was there, on the left side of the room, silhouetted against the window; as his eyes adjusted, Dylan saw a small, well-built man with dark, mottled skin and close-cropped black hair flecked with gray. Under a dark suit jacket and a beige overcoat he wore a white checked oxford shirt that looked like it had been made from graph paper. His bright blue eyes stared right back at Dylan's.

"Dylan, are you all right?" the man asked flatly as he approached the bed. "Do you feel like talking?"

"Who—" Dylan coughed, which hurt his chest, and Ellen squeezed his hand again.

"Dylan, I'm Detective Mateo," the man went on in the same even, quiet voice. "I'm from the fifteenth precinct's detective squad; I'd like to ask you a few questions."

"Questions—"

"It won't take long." Mateo pulled a notebook from his back pocket; he was clicking the button on a ballpoint pen with his other hand. "I promise; I'll be out of here before you know it."

"I've already talked to him," Ellen said. She still had Dylan's hand in hers, and he didn't mind one bit. "I've told him everything I know."

"Who shot you, Dylan?" Mateo raised his eyebrows.

"I don't—I don't know."

Truer words were never spoken. He had absolutely no idea. As his head cleared, he remembered bits and pieces of what had happened; he remembered waking up driving a car, and the frantic nightmare hour he'd spent with Mary Shayne, racing to his own apartment and then ending up at hers, and finding the book of spells in the Shaynes' foul-smelling study—it was coming back to him in more detail—and then going to answer the door . . .

And then, nothing.

"I'm sorry," he told the man with the tanned, pock-marked face and the bright blue eyes. "I'm sorry, I can't—I can't remember."

"That's actually fairly common," Mateo said, sucking in his cheeks as he wrote in his notebook. The ballpoint's scratching was very loud in the quiet, air-conditioned room. "Trauma can cloud a victim's memory, particularly with a violent trauma like gunshot. It generally passes. Here's another question: before you lost consciousness, did you see who shot Mary Shayne?"

Shot Mary— This didn't make any sense to Dylan, at first. As he thought about it, he realized he had no idea how to answer. *This is a homicide detective*, he told himself. *Speak very carefully—he won't miss much.*

"At the Peninsula Hotel," Detective Mateo went on. "You passed out from"—Mateo flipped back a page in his notebook—"blood loss and shock, at approximately three this morning, which is very close to where the coroner puts the time of death for Ms. Shayne. So I'm wondering if you have any memory of her getting shot, Dylan."

"No," Dylan said, a bit too quickly. He was afraid to glance at Ellen, because of course he remembered completely; he remembered Ellen gasping for breath and staggering across the ruined carpet and through the bedroom door, hefting the gun and firing it at Mary's head. He thought he'd never forget it.

It wasn't really Ellen, though. It was Mary. It was Mary, after she died—revisiting the Ka of the seven people who killed her.

"There's a lot of amnesia in this case," Mateo said, frowning at his notebook and flipping pages. Outside the window, a car horn honked—it sounded fairly distant, and Dylan realized he had to be on a fairly high floor. "I've interviewed all five eyewitnesses," Mateo continued, "and I can't get a thing out of them—they literally have no memory of most of the day, if you can believe it."

That's the spell, Dylan thought. *They can't remember.*

"But you know what's funny?" Mateo didn't sound amused at all; he sounded resigned. "I actually *can* believe it. I mean there must have been at least three bottles of vodka for each of them. It was party time, that's for sure." He shook his head. "No wonder nobody knows what happened. They're not even sure how they ended up at the hotel."

"Everyone's out there," Ellen told Dylan, tipping her head toward the room's wood-paneled door. "Joon and Trick and Amy and Scott. They've been up all night—since Mary died. The cops have talked to all of them."

"Not that it's done any good," Mateo said, sighing heavily as he reached into his breast pocket and pulled out a small photograph. "Do you know who this is?"

Dylan peered at the photograph. It was a blurry, black-and-white mug shot of somebody he recognized, but just barely. "He was at the party," Dylan said, remembering a young, chiseled guy dancing with his shirt off. "But I didn't talk to him. Who is he?"

"He's Mason Pike, twenty-one years of age, resident of the Bronx, and he's DOA as of five-twenty-five this morning, Dylan. The reason I'm wondering if you know him—and I've asked all your friends the same question—is that the gun that killed Mary Shayne is registered to him. Exact ballistic match to her, and to you. And not only that"—Detective Mateo flipped another page in his notebook—"the gun's covered in Mason's fingerprints, and Mary Shayne's fingerprints, and a few others we're still working on—two distinct sets of latents."

"And he's dead?" Dylan repeated. The bright blue sky outside the window behind Detective Mateo was nearly blinding him; he was having trouble thinking his way through what he was hearing. "I don't understand. How—"

"Shot point-blank by one Armando Delgato at approximately four A.M.; we've got Delgato in custody. Apparently it was a long time coming: several witnesses from the party confirm that Delgato and Pike had an altercation there earlier in the evening, and according to the hotel staff, a gun was fired." Mateo shrugged. "These white boys trying to be gangsta, thinking they're Bloods and Crips . . . anyway they had some kind of beef and he showed up dead this A.M. The part I don't get"—the detective returned his level gaze to Dylan—"is why bullets from his gun ended up in your chest and Mary Shayne's head. You're absolutely sure you don't remember getting shot? It's not coming back to you?"

"No," Dylan said truthfully.

"I explained it to the detective," Ellen said, and something about her tone made Dylan turn his head—painfully—and look at her. Ellen's eyes looked unusually alert and bright. "Mason was at the party. He's a friend—he *was* a friend—of Trick's. He got out the gun and showed it to a couple of people; Joon Park touched it, and so did my—so did my sister. And so did I."

"And he liked her," Mateo asked. He glanced up from his notebook, where he'd been writing. "He had a real thing for Mary, isn't that what you said?"

"That's right," Ellen went on, and Dylan felt her grip tighten on his hand. "So when Mary brought Dylan home, I figure Mason must have followed them to Mary's house. My house. He must have shot Dylan, and then . . ."

"The emergency call," Mateo said, nodding. "Your mother called nine-one-one at two-oh-four A.M., reporting a gunshot. Which frightened the assailant away—"

"—and he must have followed Mary back to the hotel and shot her there," Dylan said. Ellen squeezed his hand, and he avoided looking at her. It hadn't been difficult to pick up the logic of the story Ellen was telling.

"But you followed him." Mateo was frowning at his notebook. "You got up off the floor with a gunshot wound to the abdomen and made your way down to the hotel to save Ms. Shayne, but you were too late."

"I don't remember," Dylan said again.

Detective Mateo stood motionless, staring at his notebook. After a moment he raised his eyebrows and closed the notebook, audibly exhaling as he reached to return it to his back pocket.

"All right," Mateo said, raising his eyebrows. "I guess I buy it. I mean"—he grimaced—"it's a weird one, make no mistake. But we've got the gun, we've got the prints, we've got ballistics, we've got motives . . . when the lab work comes back, if the prints on the gun are Ms. Shayne's"—he indicated Ellen—"and Joon Park's and Mary Shayne's, then I guess that's all she wrote."

Dylan could hear Ellen exhaling with relief.

Then the door was swinging open and Dylan sat up straighter in the bed as Dawn Shayne came into the room, wearing a black overcoat, her face pale, her eyes red and wounded. Detective Mateo stepped toward her. Ellen reached for her mother and hugged her tightly. "Dylan," Mrs. Shayne said in a husky, tired voice. "I'm so glad you're all right."

"Hi, Mrs. Shayne," Dylan said, trying to smile.

"After what we've been through together," Mrs. Shayne told him, leaning to kiss his cheek and flooding his nostrils with the aroma of cigarettes, "I think you can call me Dawn. You had me talking forever last night, just trying to keep you conscious."

What? Dylan had no idea what she was talking about.

"He doesn't remember, Mom," Ellen said quickly.

"I'll leave you alone," Mateo said briskly. "Dylan, I may

have some more questions for you later, when you're feeling better."

"Are you going to catch the killer?" Dawn Shayne demanded. "Are you going to find the—the monster who killed my daughter? He's got to be caught. I want him *punished* for what he did to her."

"We have a suspect," Mateo told her, "but he's gone—he's deceased, ma'am. That's all the punishment he's going to get, in this life, anyway. Besides"—Mateo was making his way out of the room—"you really shouldn't be thinking in terms of revenge, Mrs. Shayne. It's not a good idea. It's never a good idea."

"Amen to that," Ellen said quietly.

"I'm sorry for your loss," the detective said, nodding at all of them and leaving the room. He pulled the door shut behind him.

Mrs. Shayne stood at Dylan's bedside with her shoulders slumped forward. She struggled through a fit of wet coughs. "It's not fair," she whispered, peering down at the sterile white floor. "I had to stand there and identify my daughter's body and that boy is not even going to face retribution."

"Mom—"

"That boy is already dead—that's not justice." Mrs. Shayne lifted her head and locked eyes with her daughter. "He should have to *pay* for what he did—he should have to *suffer*. He should feel the way I feel right now, every day, for the rest of his life."

"Mom, stop." Ellen wrapped her arms tightly around her mother's stiff body. "We can't do this anymore."

Mrs. Shayne stared back at Ellen. "Do what?"

"I know what it feels like," Ellen told her. "I know that feeling like there's knives and needles in your stomach—like they're just going to keep cutting away at you until someone pays for what they did—but you have to let it go, Mom. Mason's gone. If you let all that anger keep slicing away at you, then you're just going to end up . . . empty."

"I know that." Tears were running down Mrs. Shayne's cheeks. "I know that. I should have let it go. I should have forgiven her."

"Wait, who?"

Mrs. Shayne reached out awkwardly, groping toward Ellen and falling into her daughter's arms. She nestled her head beneath Ellen's chin.

"*I'm* the mother," Mrs. Shayne said, her voice muffled by Ellen's shirt front. "Mary was just a child, Ellie. I should have forgiven her *then*, and we could have had all this time together like a real mother and daughter."

"It's okay," Ellen said weakly. Her face was contorted, Dylan saw—she was beginning to cry. "It's okay, Mom."

"No it's not. I never said it to her. I never told her I forgave her. I thought we'd have more time. Now she's gone."

"But that's just her *body*," Ellen argued. "Her body's gone, but her soul is still here with . . ." Ellen flashed Dylan a glance that he couldn't understand. "I mean, I *think* her soul will stay with us in a way. I think I can feel her with us . . . watching over us . . . hearing us sometimes. Don't you believe that, Mom?"

"I want to believe that." Mrs. Shayne tried to smile.

"I think"—Ellen dug her finger awkwardly under her

glasses and swiped at a runaway tear—"I think she heard you forgive her. And I think she forgives you, too. She forgives you, Mom. She does."

"Is that true?" Mrs. Shayne looked at Dylan. "You told me Mary was sorry . . . you said that she was sorry, and that she loved me. Was that true?"

Dylan had no idea what to say—he didn't understand what Mrs. Shayne was referring to.

"Yes, it's true," Ellen said. "She was sorry, and she does love you. Did."

"Maybe," Mrs. Shayne said. "Maybe."

Dylan watched as mother and daughter hugged each other more tightly, rocking in place, eyes closed, and then Mrs. Shayne pulled away and began to rise to her feet.

"Mom—wait."

Ellen reached her fingers under the collar of her mother's navy blouse and fiddled with something Dylan couldn't see, until she'd pulled it free from her neck—a slim gold chain with a golden amulet hanging from its center. He recognized the symbol immediately—the Eye of Tnahsit—as Ellen flung the necklace across the bed, onto the chair the detective had vacated. It slid to the floor in a tangled, ugly heap.

"But your father gave—"

"I know he gave it to you that day. And that's why you're never going to wear it again. Because we're done with that day, Mom. We're done. Okay?"

Mrs. Shayne took a long deep breath. "Okay," she said quietly.

As she took another breath, Dylan noticed something

strange: Mrs. Shayne's coughs had suddenly begun to subside. Her first deep breath led to another, and then another. For as long as he'd known her, he'd never seen her breathe so deep and easy.

"You sounded like Mary just then," Mrs. Shayne said quietly, rising to her feet. The sunlight caught Dawn's halo of graying hair, making it look oddly beautiful. "I have to rest now. Honey—are you coming?"

"You go ahead," Ellen said. "I'll be along in a minute."

"All right." Mrs. Shayne gave Dylan a watery smile and then disappeared through the door, taking her menthol cigarette aroma with her.

Dylan was starting to feel sleepy again. Ellen sat back down beside him and took his hand. The sunlight shone against the venetian blinds, which shifted quietly in the air-conditioned breeze.

"I miss her," Dylan said.

"You don't have to miss her," she told him. "Remember what you said on our date? What you told me in the restaurant? 'The true mystery of the world is the visible, not the invisible.'"

He squinted at her.

"Ellen?"

"Yes."

Dylan tilted his head on the pillow, gazing quizzically at her.

"Mary?"

"Yes," she said, nodding.

Dylan smiled. His eyes were drifting shut—he needed

to go back to sleep. "Enlightenment is a good thing," he told her. "They say the soul becomes wise at the end of its journey."

"That's what they say."

Dylan took her hand and squeezed it and they smiled at each other in the bright morning sunlight that filled the room.

About the Authors

BARNABAS MILLER has written many books for children and young adults. He also composes and produces music for film and network television. He lives in New York City with his wife, Heidi; their cat, Ted; and their dog, Zooey.

JORDAN ORLANDO sold his first novel before his twenty-first birthday. Besides writing, he creates Web sites and works in graphic design and digital cinema. He lives in New York City. You can visit him at www.jordanorlando.com.